SWEET
SOLITUDE

SAV R. MILLER

For anyone who has ever felt invisible.
I see you.

I am a forest, and a night of dark trees; but he who is not afraid of my darkness, will find banks full of roses under my cypresses.

— FRIEDRICH NIETZCHE, THUS SPOKE
ZARATHUSTRA

NOTE FROM THE AUTHOR

Sweet Solitude is a dark mafia romance and contains graphic violence, sexual assault, sexually explicit scenes, and heavy discussions of certain topics that some may find triggering. Content may not be suitable for all audiences.

Reader discretion is advised.
For a more detailed content warning list, visit savrmiller.com

Though not required, it is recommended to read the King's Trace Antiheroes series in order of publication for the best reading experience.

This is the republished edition with minor changes from the original version. ©2020, 2023

PLAYLIST

"when the party's over" – Billie Eilish
"Closer" – Nine Inch Nails
"Back From the Edge" – James Arthur
"Iris" – DIAMANTE, Breaking Benjamin
"Here With Me" – Susie Suh, Robot Koch
"River" – Bishop Briggs
"Love Somebody" – Lauv
"Ghosts" – Mayday Parade
"My Heart I Surrender" – I Prevail
"Weakness" – Jeremy Zucker
"Animals" – Maroon 5
"bad guy" – Billie Eilish, Justin Bieber

PROLOGUE
KIERAN

Lusty moans spill out into the night air for the third time this week.

I don't know why she keeps coming back. At first, I thought it was to look for the necklace she lost the first night she was here, but when the telltale slapping of skin against skin assaulted my ears, it became obvious her only plight was to get fucked.

Pulling my knees up so I'm hidden behind my brother's headstone, I glance over my shoulder, trying to make out their silhouettes in the moonlight. It's hard, but I'd recognize the throaty, feminine sounds rattling from her body anywhere.

A man ruts into her backside, gripping the pants wrapped around her knees; she's bent completely in half, hands holding on to a tombstone to keep her in place. "Harder," she groans, frustration lacing her tone.

A jolt of electricity shoots through me, hitting me right in the dick.

My cock comes to life as it always does during these

escapades, and I deftly slip it from the confines of my jeans, stroking in short, quick bursts to catch up to where they're at. At this time of night, the King's Trace Memorial Gardens are dreary at best; pine branches wilt above sprawling acres of tombstones, as if bowing in reverence—though the people buried here don't deserve it.

Still, it's quiet. One of the last places I can come and sit in solitude and pretend my ghosts only visit while I'm here.

I almost don't mind that the girl is here disturbing the peace. At least I get something out of it.

The spirits might have other ideas, but that's not a haunting *I* have to take home. Her demons leave when she does.

A groan of frustration laces the cool air, and I frown at the sound in disapproval. I don't know why she insists on frolicking with men who are incapable of satisfying her.

Fisting my cock, I imagine how it'd feel to walk over and stab this guy in the gut for not giving her what she desires. How she'd look up at me with fearful eyes, not yet totally aware of what she should be afraid of.

Or of who stands in her midst.

I'd reach out with a bloody hand and tilt her chin up, smearing red across her porcelain skin. Painting her like a fresh canvas. A brand from the King of Darkness.

Without preamble, I'd grip my rock-hard shaft in the opposite hand, trailing the tip along her stained chin, and then push into her tight little mouth. Her eyes would widen, maybe even tear up, but she'd take it like a champ. Because it'd be exactly what she wants.

I don't know *how* I know that she's looking for a particular kind of fuck. Something raw and dark and dirty that makes her body spasm long after I've finished inside her. But

I do. And God help me, imagining shoving my cock down her pretty throat makes me so hard, I start to see stars.

She'd swallow every single drop, turning onto her hands and knees before I even had to ask, offering her ass without a single word. No protest, no qualms, no qualifications. Complete and total submission, just the way I fucking like it.

The way I can tell—feel in my bones—she needs.

And I'd take her the way I like, hard and fast and *mean*, whether she ended up enjoying it or not. At the moment, she might let fear rule her, let it permeate her orgasm in a way that makes her hate me. Afterward, though, when she's sore in the shower, she'd remember how goddamn good it felt.

Pumping my cock in real time to the tune of her soft cries, wondering how loud she could get if someone were doing it right, I come all over my hand, narrowly missing my jeans and avoiding my brother's plot. This time.

Wrenching a tissue from my hoodie pocket, I clean up, my chest heaving with the aftershocks.

Jesus Christ, I've never wanted a woman this much. Not to the point where I'm content with just watching, listening, night after night like some sick fucker.

I'm addicted, and I don't even know who she is.

Yet as I hear them pack up and tell each other goodbye, I find myself staring at the trees surrounding the cemetery, hoping once again that she'll come back.

My hand slides into my pants pocket, fingering the gold chain inside. The heart-shaped locket at one end. It feels expensive and important, so I can't imagine she's unaware that it's missing.

If nothing else, I suspect she'll eventually come back to look for it. Maybe then I'll come forward and take what I want from her.

In truth, I'm not sure why I haven't.

Maybe I just enjoy watching.

But I know that if she doesn't return, I'll find her.

Juliet

A sinister force lives in King's Trace, breathing life into its poorly paved streets and tainting its water supply.

Something evil.

I used to think it was my asshole father's existence soiling our little town, but the cloak of darkness has yet to let up since we had him cremated.

According to the tabloids who have nothing better to do than run stories on the affluent figures in town, it's because King's Trace exists primarily under the thumb of organized crime. They say with criminals running everything from small businesses to legislation, it's impossible for any of us to exist outside the shadows.

They aren't really wrong; death permeates our air quality, making it hard to inhale without simultaneously getting the blood of your neighbors on your skin.

The Montaltos, an Italian American crime unit originally from New York, bankroll our police, judges, and lawyers; they pay them to create a facade of order, undercut only by their protection racket and drug trade. They cater to the wealthy tourists that vacation in our town, gentrifying it to the point of being nearly uninhabitable for the majority of King's Trace residents—a massive percentage of whom live below the poverty line.

Two years ago, my older sister, Caroline, married their terrifying and downright delicious *capo*, Elia Montalto, and nothing for us has ever been quite the same. Months after they married, my father, a once-highly respected senator, allegedly committed suicide—after being exposed for corruption and the abuse of my sister that he spent so long denying. After that, my mother skipped town, forcing me to move in with Caroline, and I now have a brother-in-law, a niece, and a nephew on the way.

An actual family. One that cares about me and wants the best for my life.

It's what I've always craved, but what the one I was born into wasn't capable of giving.

Yet something feels... off. There's an emptiness within me, a tumultuous pit of despair inside my soul that refuses to close or be filled.

A sadness I simply cannot shake.

And for the first time in my life, I actually *want* to.

Or I should, anyway. Should want to better myself and erase the misery that threatens to suffocate my lungs every second of every day.

Since I moved in, Caroline and I are closer than ever—on the surface, at least. Three years my senior and forced to grow up at a young age to keep our father satisfied, she's always been my fiercest protector and greatest ally. But the attention she's been giving me lately as I try to navigate this new reality feels smothering. Like I might collapse if she doesn't stop pressing in, trying to reach me as my mind floats on.

Her worry forces me to keep secrets and harbor ill-will.

Logically, I know it's selfish of me to feel that way. But I can't make myself stop. Guilt and resentment have built a wall of impenetrable stubbornness inside me, and I've not yet determined how to break it down.

I'm not sure I want to. Right now, it's the only thing keeping my stupid heart safe.

I know it could be worse. I could be stuck living with the Ivers, who Caroline almost married into instead. They're a very private Irish-American family with a Maine lineage dating back to its foundation, and they run a massive cyber-security firm with varying degrees of criminal clientele. Stonemore, a town just slightly bigger and wealthier than King's Trace, is where their biggest client exists, an organization rivaling the ferocity and business of the Montaltos.

No one really knows much about the family outside of their shady affiliations, and that the mother is sick, the oldest son is dead, and the youngest—the only daughter—purportedly normal. Their sweet little princess.

Rumors abound about the middle child, Kieran. His reputation reaches far and wide—tales about the sharpness of his alluring appearance and the delight he takes in misfortune.

They call him the King of Darkness, a moniker whispered and carried by the wind, polluting the air with its villainy.

He's a murderer, an unhinged hermit that feeds on the souls of the innocent and the guilty. He is their reckoning.

But I don't know if I believe them—he's not sought me out, despite the guilt clogging my arteries; a weight so large and encumbering that it's getting impossible to carry around without breaking down.

Every piece of online advice I've found says we carry our shame in different ways; some let it root physically so it takes a toll on our bodies, while others let it fester in their minds like a slow-acting poison hell-bent on utter destruction.

I exist in a mixture of the two, torn between missing my

father—the father I thought he was and wanted him to be—and being glad he's dead. Torn between hating how he paid attention to Caroline and being disgusted with the truth behind that recognition.

For the past year and a half, I've found myself at his grave on a regular basis, sometimes dragging along some unsuspecting guy looking to get his dick wet in the ultimate form of disrespect. Other times I'm by myself, wishing I could vandalize the damn headstone the way I let alcohol violate my liver or boring men leave me unsatisfied.

Tonight, though, as the stranger from Crimson—Elia's nightclub, a place I'm not allowed inside of, but that I still poach from as patrons wait to be let in, illuminated beneath the building's giant red neon sign—pushes to his feet and leaves me before my father's grave, I just feel empty.

My hand absently reaches for the heart-shaped locket that normally rests against my collarbone—a muscle reflex, since I've been missing the necklace for several weeks now.

It's a purely sentimental object, not worth mourning except that it solidifies the guilt swarming inside me, making me ache with misery. I can't help viewing its loss as a sign from the universe that I'm doing everything wrong.

That I shouldn't be here.

The stranger tucks his dick into his jeans and excuses himself, leaving the eerie graveyard with its myriad of headstones and monuments and ghosts. I dig my heels into the dirt as I yank my pants up and flip onto my ass, sending a curse to my father in the afterlife as I glare at his plot.

Dominic Harrison.

An entire life lived, and only that epitaph left in his wake. Nothing about being a husband, father, senator, or associate to the mob. Just his name.

It was Caroline's decision; I wanted to leave him unmarked and make it harder for anyone to find him.

Easier to forget.

Letting my face drop into my hands, I feel tears sting my eyes at the same time that familiar sensation washes over me; the one I get every time I come here, that keeps me coming back even though the walk home is a pain in the ass.

It's a tingle that starts at the base of my spine, slithering upward and spreading out to my extremities, and that only accompanies complete darkness. Silence. An awareness only felt when you're completely and totally alone.

The realization that, no matter what, you never actually are.

1

KIERAN

BOYD'S SHOULDER brushes against mine as he leans in to inspect my handiwork, and irritation at his micromanagement makes me grip the circular saw tighter. Shifting my weight into the task, I hover over the bloodless corpse, ignoring the way his dead eyes stare up at the ceiling.

The Montaltos just *had* to remove his eyelids, as if they knew ahead of time that I'm haunted by the stony, defunct gaze of my older brother Murphy. Now, I'm adding this man to my arsenal of nightmares.

So much for the semi-truce I concocted with their boss, Elia, back when we put aside our rivalry—a rivalry built on little more than a pissing contest between powerful men. I'm sure he did this to get under my skin, and as I cast a quick glance around the room, I'm torn between irritation and reluctant admiration.

It's quiet here, almost eerie; the one-bedroom cottage sits on the desolate side of Lake Koselomal, tucked away in the woods across from the elite housing strip where Elia Montalto and his perfect little family live. Just far enough away from my family's wretched mansion that I can come here to escape the oppressive grounds.

And to work.

No one else visits besides Boyd and me. Kal Anderson stops by on occasion, but only because the mafia doctor has a rap sheet filthier than mine. He's not afraid of the darkness lurking here and inside me because his past is muddier, something he can't outrun—though it's clear he tries.

Boyd takes a step back, scrubbing a gloved, tattooed hand through his dirty blond, medium-length hair. I glare at him as he clears his throat, pulling at the smock draped around his neck, and blows out a long breath. I can barely hear him over the buzz of the tool in my hands.

The brown skin on the corpse's ankle splits, a canyon sinking open with each turn of the blade, and soon skin breaks away to reveal muscle and bone; if he hadn't already been drained of his blood, I know my living room would be a fucking disaster.

Luckily, the Montaltos had already taken care of that part; I can only imagine how badly he tried to fuck over the leading organized crime family in King's Trace to deserve such a fate, especially given Elia's reputation for being merciful. But it's not my job to care or feel sympathy.

I don't think I could, even if they paid me to.

I'm here to clean up since Kal isn't around to do anything. Normally he'd be the one they called in to take care of their messes, but the already-elusive man's been MIA as of late.

It helps that the Montaltos pay an exorbitant amount of money for corpse disposal, but honestly, I'd probably do it for free.

For fun.

The skeleton collection in my bedroom closet is proof of that.

Boyd scratches behind his ear, looking impatient. As usual. How we've remained friends in the years since meeting in college is beyond me; my tolerance for bullshit is unnaturally low, and his propensity for being an arrogant, pushy asshole is unparalleled.

But he's about the only one who can stomach me for long periods, so I keep his ass around, despite how he dethroned me at my family's own cybersecurity company.

Water under the bridge. Kind of.

It's not like I couldn't have taken the job at Ivers International if I'd wanted it. My father's made that abundantly clear.

I would just rather spend my time doing this.

The corpse's foot falls to the hardwood floor, a dull thud barely audible above the saw motor. I flip the switch, turning it off while I move to the other foot, and Boyd shoves his hands in his pockets. When I've severed the opposite limb, he bends and scoops the feet into a black plastic bag along with the man's previously removed hands.

Evidence. The Montaltos like proof of a finished job, especially considering I'm not actually one of them.

Hauling the body up by the armpits, I'm surprised by its density despite the complete lack of blood and the organs sitting on my dining table. I move toward the heated metal tub at the other end of the room. Boyd walks out for this part, never willing to stick around until the end.

Which is odd, considering it never takes much convincing of me to get him to come along for these jobs. I ask, and he's there, almost as if whatever we do within the confines of these walls is preferable to what he faces at home.

Perhaps he's just holding on to the remnants of his conscience, and leaving at this point is his way of staying grounded.

Lucky for me, my conscience is long gone. Sold with my soul, lost and never to be found again.

Pushing the corpse up and over the edge of the tub, I watch as it bobs in the water and lye mixture, sinking and returning to the surface. Pushing his head beneath the water with a gloved hand, I wait; bubbles pop against the liquid, and I shove him deeper, wanting to speed up the process.

As the bubbles slow, I feel his body sag with the weight of taking on water, like a capsized boat in the middle of the ocean.

It'll be a few hours before he's completely dissolved, and even then, I'll still have to dispose of the coffee-colored milkshake of flesh and muscle. Not to mention clean the bones and add them to the others.

But I won't be back until the early hours of the morning, since I agreed to go to this fundraising gala tonight; my parents think it'll be a good chance for me to get out of the house and show support for whatever charity they've adopted this year.

No part of me wants to go and leave Murphy's ghost alone to roam our mansion, but I also don't want to be left there by myself. At least when everyone else is home, he has extra targets.

Doesn't necessarily concentrate all his afterlife energy on taunting his murderer.

Boyd comes back in, phone pressed to his ear, speaking in hushed tones.

I don't bother trying to hear what he's saying.

Turning my back to him, I begin stripping off my protective gear, revealing the crisp, black suit my younger sister, Fiona, insisted I wear tonight. "You ready to go?"

He pulls his phone away, tapping at the screen before slipping it into his jacket pocket. "Just gonna leave the body out in the open?"

"Is he out in the open? I think, if someone walked by for whatever reason and peeked into the windows, you'd just see a tub filled with a questionable liquid."

"And a myriad of power tools. In Kieran Ivers's house." He cocks an eyebrow. "Totally normal circumstances."

Shrugging, I round the tub and head for the front door. "Anyone that wants to come poking around is not gonna live to tell the tale." Yanking my Armani winter coat off the wooden rack in the corner, I tug it on and smooth down the collar, pulling the door open to brace against the chilly March air.

"What a totally normal thing for someone to say," Boyd mutters, removing his equipment and slinging his jacket over his shoulder.

My fingers brush against the cold metal of the locket I picked up at the cemetery, my mind flashing to the moans of the girl who's periodically graced my dreams ever since. I've been wearing the gold, heart-shaped pendant since I discovered who it belongs to while scrolling through Fiona's social media one day, now strangely unable to part with it.

I thought by now she'd have come looking for it, but it seems I'll need to seek her out instead.

Which is why she's partially responsible for me going tonight; something tells me Elia Montalto's sister-in-law might make an appearance, considering the *capo* himself owns the venue.

I swallow over a knot in my throat, thinking back to the last time I stepped inside the colonial-style art center. The blood I cleaned off the walls, the groans of agony drowned out by the erratic beat of my heart, the skin beneath my grip as I sliced Senator Harrison open, making him pay for crimes against his family.

A reckoning he was not at all prepared for, if the darkness surrounding his dead body in the aftermath was any indication.

Of course, that could've been mine. It's hard to differentiate, and I stopped cleansing myself long ago. When these contracts became more frequent, and I put on the biggest hit of all.

Against my own flesh and blood.

Boyd catches up to me as I get to Fiona's Jeep; she'll probably throw a fit over me taking it, but I needed the large, leather back seat to transport the circuit judge's body. "Let's go."

MY MOTHER'S hands shake as she tightens the bow tie around my neck, a tremor wracking her body that she pretends not to notice.

But I see it. My eyes glue to the wobbly movements, unease settling in the pit of my stomach like a concrete brick being hurled at me by the universe. She fumbles with the collar of my shirt, a single, harsh breath the only indication of her irritation.

We've been here three hours at this point, mingling and

networking with the entire goddamn town. My father announced a prize raffle early on and kicked off the starting bid at a cool million, citing the charity's importance to the family in light of my mother's diagnosis.

Lewy Body Dementia. Never would've imagined my beautiful, vibrant mother suffering from such an illness at this stage in her life, yet as her hands tremble so hard that she can't finish dressing me, there's no denying it.

I can tell she's tired from basking in all the attention tonight even though she was the one who insisted on coming. It's why I swept her into this alcove, away from the crowd for a moment, allowing us a beat to recharge.

Gently removing her hands, I reach up and grip the tie myself, finishing the job. She takes a step back, admiring the handiwork with a crooked smile. Her dark red hair is twisted in a tight, elegant updo with a pearl brooch pinned to the back, holding it all together.

"How do I look?" I ask even though I don't actually care.

She beams as much as she can when portions of her body refuse to cooperate with the signals from her brain. Her smile opens, lopsided and toothy beneath the simple gold mask covering half her face, while an almost imperceptible twitch sparks beneath one of her green eyes. Still, she pretends she looks normal for our family.

For me.

"Like a handsome prince ready to rescue his princess."

I roll my eyes. "I'm pretty sure you're the only one on this planet who thinks of me as a hero."

She reaches out, squeezing my bicep. I don't miss the way she clings to me as she steps forward, as if she doesn't trust herself to walk on her own. Turning so we face the large, floor-length mirror bolted to the art center wall, she leans into me, studying our masked reflections.

Compared to anyone else, Mona Ivers is frail. Fragile. Especially in her current state, flitting around public venues like her body isn't constantly on the verge of shutting down.

Next to me, she looks like a small, withered woman—like someone who wore out her rosary beads early on in life. As if she had birthed two sons who gave her an endless supply of prayer content, and then wasted her better years trying to redeem us.

Now, Murphy's dead, and his blood stains my hands, no matter how many times I've tried to rid myself of him.

How she can see anything redeemable here is beyond me.

"You're *my* hero," she says in a low voice, our gazes connecting in the reflection. Offering me another half smile, she turns and pulls me from the alcove to the ballroom lined with oval-shaped tables decorated with expensive linens and china.

We weave through the crowd, settling in at our family's spot near the stage. My father stands to the side, chatting animatedly with Orlando Montalto, the former patriarch of the Montalto family. The latter reaches up and scratches at his graying beard beneath his dark Pulcinella mask, regarding my father with a blank stare.

Melanie Smith drapes herself over my best friend, shooting fuck-me eyes my way; her mostly fake tits bulge from the tight red minidress she has on, her black hair falling over her shoulder and between the valley of her cleavage. Unlike the Ivers clan, Mel's the only one not wearing an ornate gold Colombina mask, a staple of our charity events; hers is scarlet and bedazzled, setting her apart from us. Thank fucking God.

My dead brother's clingy ex needs to be as disassociated from us as possible.

She winks as if I might be inclined to ditch my family and drag her to an empty bathroom. As if I'd betray Boyd, who she's officially here with, or leave my mother out here to fend for herself.

I mean, I would. Probably will. But not just yet. Mel's got a sweet fucking mouth, even if the teeth inside are resin and her tongue sometimes feels like sandpaper when she's high.

Judging by the way she gazes at me, pupils slightly dilated and unfocused, she is right now. Practically has been since my brother's death.

At my side, Fiona twirls a strand of dark red hair around her finger, popping a pink bubble of gum against her mouth. "I knew you'd try to sneak off before the night was over."

Straightening the lapels of my suit jacket, I bring a wineglass to my mouth and take a long drink of the merlot inside. "You smell like smoke. Seems all the Ivers kids are prone to breaking promises."

Her eyes widen, stealing a glance at our mother, who sits swaying to the jazz music coming from the band onstage. "I'm sorry we can't all exercise the utmost control over our addictions."

"You just lack adequate willpower."

"Okay, dick. Maybe I have reason to be stressed. Ever think about that?"

Sliding my gaze to her, I feel my heart pound against my rib cage. My palm slips against my glass, and I return it to the table before it falls from my grasp. *What the fuck could she be stressed about?*

Instead of asking, I shrug. "Maybe you shouldn't have picked up smoking in the first place."

She scoffs, flipping me the bird with one long, mani-cured middle finger. "Hindsight is twenty-twenty, you know. If all of us could go back and *not* make mistakes, we'd be in much better shape. But we don't exactly get that option."

Ignoring her, I scan the room for the billionth time, looking for the golden-blonde hair that seems to be exclu-sive to the Harrison sisters. Since seeing her on social media and noticing the necklace she wore in a picture she'd taken at Christmas, I've spent countless hours researching the Harrisons until I knew with certainty that I needed to make myself known to the beautiful, depraved siren.

I've already spotted the older, pregnant one attached to her husband's side, but the younger spitfire has yet to be seen.

I know she's here, though. Her darkness permeates this room, the stain of what she does in the cemetery—with complete disregard for how she might not be alone during it —is a beacon to my lost soul. It's a light trying to call me home and find a way to make the evil surrounding me worse.

As if she's a magnet I'm drawn to, I find Juliet Harrison tucked between the doorway to the bathrooms. The silky black gown she has on clings to each and every supple curve, her smooth, ivory skin glowing against the material, making my mouth water with a desire I haven't allowed myself to feel in a long time.

Her blue eyes, the only identifying asset through her sequined black mask, coast over the crowd, searching for something. A hollowness is present in those cerulean irises that cuts to my bone. Such raw, unencumbered sadness, but when our eyes meet, something in her snaps.

She blinks, and it's like an ocean dries up, emotion washing down the drain. It knocks the breath from my lungs like a kick to my chest I don't see coming.

And can't defend against.

Instead of looking away like any decent person would, I watch her spine straighten, her breasts straining against the thin fabric of her dress, and her chin tilt up in defiance. As if she doesn't like knowing what I saw a moment ago.

Like she thinks she can hide from the devil.

But the thing about the fallen angel of light is that he's connected to the whims of the people; he sees our deepest desires, our secrets, our sins. And right now, I see a million different ones flashing across her vision, all worthy of repentance.

I want to know why she goes to the cemetery; if the ghost of her father follows her around the way Murphy's does me, as if he has some kind of claim on my life since I took his.

I want to know why she has sex on her father's grave. Want to know if it's the same reason I visit my brother so often, as if it's possible to absolve myself of the guilt. To curse him, even in the afterlife.

I want to know if she knows I'm the one who killed Dominic Harrison, damning him to a fiery eternity in her sister's name.

Swallowing, I watch, a hunger awakening in me that would terrify even the most deviant mind, as she finally tears her gaze away, slipping dutifully into the seat beside a beefy man I assume to be a bodyguard. She speaks to him, but he doesn't even seem to register her presence; he stares straight ahead, on high alert, as if there are dangers here.

He's right. But he's not looking in the right places for it.

Juliet's aura seems to flatten, her body sagging against her table as she picks up her wineglass and downs the entire drink in one swig. She doesn't look up again and instead focuses on the dinner plate in front of her, and my dick hardens at the blatant agony ebbing off her in waves.

Boyd leans into me, jutting his chin in Juliet's direction. "Christ, if you stare at her any harder, she's gonna wind up pregnant."

Flattening my mouth, I reach for my drink and bring it to my lips for a quick sip. Trying to sate the fire in my blood brought on by this magnificent specimen. And to distract from the enticing image of burying my cock inside what I suspect is a glorious, tight little cunt and pumping myself dry.

Emptying my seed and soul into her body, like she might be able to carry the weight of it all better than me.

Desire pools in my gut, making my dick throb in my slacks. I need release, need some fucking reprieve from being out in public for the first time in months. For agreeing to pretend for one night that my family isn't completely bonkers, and my mom isn't losing her memory and ability to function with each passing day.

That I'm not a complete monster.

"Tell me you're not about to slink off and fuck her." Boyd frowns, tossing his napkin on the table and sitting back, looking at me. The tattoos I know line every inch of his skin peek out from the collar of his shirt and his cuff links, flickers of bold linework and color against his tan skin seeming to move when he does.

"I'm not." My eyes flicker to Mel, who's watching the two of us intently. A smile curves over my lips; she practically purrs, and Boyd shakes his head. Like he wasn't expecting this.

Excusing myself from the table at the exact moment Melanie stands to go to the ladies' room, I walk briskly to the back of the ballroom and slip through the open doorway. There's no line for either restroom, and Mel presses her back into the door, gripping one side of my suit jacket and pulling me in with her.

She's not exactly who I'm aching for tonight, but it's better than nothing.

2

JULIET

ASIDE FROM THE Montalto Arts Center, a large, white colonial-style building with massive double-paned windows and crystal chandeliers in every room, not many venues in King's Trace are worthy of a fundraising reception. Most of the town is Mafia-owned and off-limits, or residential zones and forestry, and there's a barely breathing downtown peppered with various local businesses and decrepit cobblestone streets lined by pine trees.

The most elite members of our city live on a strip of land overlooking Lake Koselomal, or in the gated cookie-cutter Locust Grove neighborhood my family used to live in. Now, Caroline and I live on the strip with her husband, and it makes sense that a man as rich as God would own one of the only elegant buildings in town.

The only place we ever seem to hold any kind of event, as if Elia has a monopoly on gatherings.

Caroline turns in Elia's arms for the millionth time tonight, staring at me over his bicep. Her blue eyes glitter through her white rhinestone mask, tickled at my venture into the real public for the first time in weeks. She doesn't know about my nighttime adventures, though. And although I should be excited about getting out of the house after moping around for months, I can't seem to muster anything other than absolute dread.

Maybe it's because I still haven't found my locket, despite spending the majority of my time scouring the cemetery for it during the day.

Because her own life is so hectic lately, being a wife, mother, and bakery owner, Caroline has yet to notice my naked neck. And while I'm relieved, because she's an insane person who would only worry or be hurt that I misplaced the gift she got me years ago, it also reinforces the invisibility I've come to wear as a second skin.

Right now, I'd give anything to be wholly transparent. For people to look through me. But all eyes seem glued to us tonight; my sister, pregnant with her second child, glowing against the backdrop of the arts center, and her entirely too attractive husband, a known criminal and altogether terrifying man.

They've been the talk of the town since their elopement, and while Caroline in a previous life seemed to always disdain the attention she received when our father dragged her to events, she eats it up now, comfortable in the spotlight in a way I've never been.

Caroline leans away from Elia and clasps her hand around mine, pulling me from the wall I've been clinging to and into her side. I sink into her warmth, trying to extract some of the happiness from her, wondering if a sliver would be enough to light up any part of me. "You doing okay?"

I shrug. "Peachy."

"You're quiet tonight. I'm a little worried we brought you out too fast."

"Jesus, I'm not a feral animal. I don't need to be eased back into the outside world. And while I definitely would've preferred to stay behind with Phoebe and Poppy tonight, I'm still *fine* here. Stop worrying so much."

"That's kind of my job, Jules."

"No, it really isn't. You're not my mother, despite whatever the crazy hormones surging through you are saying." I blink, frowning. "I'm an adult. I don't need you constantly looking out for me."

"I'm just afraid you're repressing—"

"So what if I am?" I put my free hand on my hip, raising my eyebrows. "As the former Queen of Repression, you should be used to dealing with it."

Offering me a sad little smile, she squeezes my hand and releases it, dropping the subject. This is how most of our conversations go nowadays, obliterating all the closeness we've garnered as she worries more and more about my mental well-being, and I can't help but push her away.

As soon as she lets go of me, Elia's arm circles her waist again, pulling her into his body as if he can't stand not to touch her. Even for a second.

Jealousy prickles in my belly, a low boil threatening to overheat, as I move my gaze from her in his arms to dart around the room and meet a stare more jaded than my own. A man in a fancy gold mask covering only his eyes regards me from his table near the stage, recognition flickering in his bright emerald irises.

It unnerves me, as if he's looking right into my soul.

My spine straightens of its own accord, my chin tilting in

defiance, and I sever our connection before it can go any deeper.

Benito, one of Elia's bodyguards, gives me a short nod as I plop into the seat beside him, glaring out at my sister and her husband as they entwine mid conversation. I don't begrudge Caroline her happiness—after spending her whole life as our father's dirty little puppet, she's certainly earned it—but it's hard to look at them together.

Elia's love for her bleeds out of him like ink on a white piece of paper, staining everything in its path. He stares down at her like she's the entire fucking universe, and everyone else in the room is merely stardust.

No one looks at *me* like I bring the sun up every morning; they just look through me, seeing my body but nothing else. Like I'm completely hollow inside. Useless and stupid, like my father always said.

From the corner of my eye, I see Elia kiss the crown of Caroline's hair—golden waves, just like mine—and fold her into his body, as if he's trying to shield her from the crowd. My stomach churns, violent and angry; I reach for my wineglass, sucking down the liquid like a porn star swallowing a big fat load.

I scowl at nothing in particular, slamming the glass back on the table, and my gaze again land on that same pair of mesmerizing eyes. They're bright against his mask, a contrast I'm not prepared for.

Gazing into them feels like being hit by a bolt of lightning. I'm paralyzed as he stares back, unblinking and tilting his head slightly as he tries to figure me out.

He's attractive. I can tell even with the mask. So I let myself lean into the attention for a moment. Let his interest wash over me, heating my wretched bones.

A slow, devastating smirk curls at the corners of his luscious mouth, and a pulse kicks up between my thighs as I imagine those lips dragging along my skin, goose bumps popping up in their wake. Dark brown hair curves up over his head, just long enough to drag my fingers through and yank if he were to bury his head between my thighs, and his sharp, stubbly jawline leaves me breathless.

I'm a sucker for symmetry. Art. And this man is nothing short of the work of Michelangelo. A masterpiece in a black suit and white bow tie.

He tears his gaze away, leaving me hot and needy. I rub my thighs together beneath my tight dress, wishing I could provide better relief.

After a few moments, Elia leaves Caroline dancing with his second-in-command. He plops into the seat across from me with a broad smile plastered on his perfect face. Honestly, having these two men in the same room should be a fire hazard.

Carding a powerful hand through his inky black locks, my brother-in-law raises his thick eyebrows at me. "Tired of mingling already?"

"I was tired of it before I got here."

The smile fades and turns down. His gray eyes peer at me, looking for truths I'm not willing to give. It's bad enough that I moved in with them, but if he thinks having me under his roof means I'm suddenly going to crack open my chest and show him the bruises on my soul, he has another think coming.

At another time in life, I would've spread my legs for a single night with this dangerous man. But that would've been it, and it would've been a disaster.

It's just hard to reconcile the low simmer of attraction I

have for him with his obvious, overbearing love for my sister and their children. Not that I'm *jealous*, per se, but I wouldn't exactly mind if they kept their PDA in the bedroom.

"Why'd you insist on coming, then?"

I glare at Elia, hating how parenthood has convinced him and Caroline that they need to be my surrogates. Their constant concern and worry grate on my nerves, like nails on the chalkboard of my soul. I want to declaw them, cut their fingers off so they can't scrape their way in.

"I don't know," I say. "Sometimes people do stupid shit."

Cocking an eyebrow, he leans back in his seat. Neither of us acknowledges Benito's presence, but the bodyguard doesn't care; he just sits, staring ahead, silent. Watching, working.

Elia squints at me. "Speaking from experience?"

I shrug. "I am known around King's Trace as the fuckup Harrison. Do the math."

"No one thinks of you as a fuckup." His voice softens, relaxing the creases at the corners of his eyes. "Just a little... lost."

Snorting, I pick at my napkin, hating how the assessment hits the target right on the fucking head. Not that anyone seems to be searching for me. "How is that better?"

"Lost people can still be found. They have the chance to return home."

"And those who don't want to be found? Those who set off on journeys by themselves, looking for adventure and *life*? What about them?"

His head tips to one side, stormy eyes narrowing as he studies me. He's the only man in the building not wearing a mask, as if his mere presence negates the dress code. As if we need to be aware of who he is at all times. "Is that what you're doing? Looking for an adventure?"

I don't know what I'm doing anymore. My life has veered far from its original track, and I forgot to leave breadcrumbs. "I'm just looking."

"Nothing wrong with that, I suppose. So long as you know what it is you're looking for." I just look at him, watching him reach a hand up and smooth it over his five o'clock shadow. "Do you, Juliet? Have you got it all figured out?"

"I'm working on it."

He taps the table twice, his jaw dropping as if he wants to say more; instead, he nods at Benito once, smacking the table more forcefully with his palm as he stands. "Don't wander off. I don't want to have to send Gia after you again."

"Why don't you and Caroline just get me a leash?"

"Watch it, smart-ass. In case you were unaware, our daughter has a leash, and I'm sure your sister is one crazed hormone away from buying an adult-sized one for you."

He stands, tossing me a wink; as he maneuvers through the ballroom, the crowd parts in his wake, like they're afraid of getting the stain of murder on them. Or perhaps afraid of getting in his crosshairs.

Glancing around, I realize the guy with the golden mask has disappeared. Desire flees my body, and I slump lower in my seat, reaching for the wine chilling in an ice bucket at the center of the table.

Benito adjusts his collar as I wrench off the cork and pour the rest of the bottle into my glass, but he stays silent. Of course. No one ever wants to halt my self-destruction.

No one ever looks at me long enough to see it.

I sip the wine, loving the bitter taste it leaves on my

tongue, and watch Elia now spin Caroline around the dance floor. He whips her out in a controlled sweep, careful not to harm her, and then winds her back into his arms. She smiles up at him, and he tilts her chin with one hand, bending to capture her lips in a tender, passionate kiss.

His free hand settles on her rounded belly, evidence of their perfect little life that I'm only encroaching on. Staining. Breaking just by being in their presence.

My stomach flips, nausea rising like a high tide; I spit my drink back into the glass, tear off my own mask, and let it drop to the table, excusing myself in a rush to the bathroom. Clutching my abdomen with one hand, I shove the door to the ladies' room open with the other, pausing for the briefest moment as my gaze connects with the piercing green eyes from before.

I don't have time to really register the scene before me because the nausea can't wait; it bubbles up into my throat, pushing its way through, and I spew on the floor as the door swings closed.

Swiping across my mouth with the back of my hand, I take a step away from the beige puddle at my feet and drag my eyes up to his, still encased by his mask, the breath catching in my chest.

The girl from his table, the one in the short red dress with the massive tits, is on her knees in front of him, sucking his dick like her life depends on it.

Although, I suppose she's not really doing the work; his long fingers are twisted into her hair, propelling her back and forth on his cock while his hips piston with each movement.

Soft gags fill the room, neither of them appearing disturbed by the vomit on the floor, and his gaze remains on mine. He's staring a hole through me as if he sees everything I keep hidden from the rest of the world.

Instead of finding some kind of peace in that, instead of it sending another bout of arousal shooting through me, I double over, cupping my hands on my knees, and vomit again.

3

JULIET

THE BRUNETTE PULLS AWAY JUST LONG ENOUGH to wrinkle her nose at the mess on the floor. "Are you kidding me? Can't you puke somewhere else, alky?"

"It's a public bathroom," I mutter, my eyes glued to the man's dick, red and hard and angry. She starts to respond, but he turns her head and feeds himself back into her mouth, picking up where he left off.

"I usually charge for an audience." His rich and smooth voice, like melted chocolate, sends a shiver through my body. "But seeing as how you're already here, I guess I'll give you a show."

I should get the fuck out of here, but it feels like my body weighs three thousand pounds and I've not adjusted to carrying around the weight. My feet root in place, a tree standing its ground even though it has no business doing so, and confusing arousal flares in my core as I watch him.

Watch *them*.

He fucks her mouth harder, his eyes darkening as they

rake over my form, and her sounds get louder. Sloppier. I can feel myself getting wet, despite the clear taboo of the situation, and my tongue darts out to swipe along my bottom lip. A growl emits from his throat, and the veins in his hands seem to bulge against his beige skin as he picks up the pace, his strokes longer and deeper.

And fuck, if I don't wish that were me. On my knees, getting used by this glorious stranger.

Jesus. What is wrong with me?

He never once looks away from me. It's like our gazes have interlocked, tied together in a singular knot, and we're unable to break free unless someone cuts it.

Grunting, as if close to an orgasm, he tilts the woman's face up and shunts his cock deeper into her throat, holding her still. Several silent beats pass, and I'm still standing here watching like a fucking sicko.

When he doesn't pull back, dread creeps into my bones; she smacks his thighs, squirming and squealing around his shaft, but he ignores her.

He just keeps staring at me with a glint in his eyes I can't quite interpret.

His face twists, a low moan pulling from his chest just as her hands go limp at her sides. Thrusting a few more times, he freezes, and at that moment, I *know* he's just come down her throat.

While she passed out.

Nausea threatens again, but something else ebbs through me. Something wicked and depraved. Butterflies take flight in my stomach and electricity zings down my spine, making my thighs tingle.

I'm frozen, confused—feeling like a voyeur and like I've betrayed all of womanhood by watching this happen.

He pulls her off him, her lips somehow managing a popping sound as he yanks his cock from her body; she falls to the floor as soon as his hands leave her hair, and he steps over her unconscious form to inspect himself in the mirror.

"I..." Blinking, I take a step back, my ass connecting with the door. "I need to go get someone to clean this up."

"You don't want to join?" His fingers fumble with his bow tie, adjusting and pulling even though it looks straight to me. He meets my gaze in the mirror, and a slow grin slices his face in half; it's devilish and crude, and my body heats with desire.

Fear douses me like an ice bath; glancing at the girl passed out on the floor, I contemplate my next move. If I make a run for it, he's sure to catch up before I get back to the visibility of the ballroom.

He's over a foot taller than me and probably has a good hundred pounds on me, making me a perfect target to over-power. I don't want to join the girl on the floor.

Swallowing over the knot forming in my throat, I shake my head. "No, I really don't."

Turning on his heel, the man smooths his hands over the lapels of his dark, expensive suit and stalks toward me. I shrink as far into the metal door as I can, the handle digging into the base of my spine as I try to remain out of reach. He stops when he's just a breath away, twirling a lock of my hair around his middle finger.

The scent of alcohol and mint assault my nostrils, and I inhale a deep breath, trying to keep them and his sudden proximity from affecting me.

He just fucked a girl's mouth in public until she passed out. You absolutely should not be attracted to him right now.

Still, I can't stop the quiver in my thighs as his chest

brushes against mine. Dropping the strand of hair, he brings the same hand to my throat, his thumb pressing against my chin and angling it upward. His green eyes scrutinize mine, searching. For what, I can't be sure, but I don't like what it does to me.

Longing crops up low in my belly, knotting my insides and making me sweat.

"Are you okay?"

I blink, not expecting that.

He gestures with his free hand to the pile of vomit on the floor. *Oh. Duh.*

"Peachy. Just some... bad wine."

His lips purse as if he doesn't quite believe me. "Why are your pupils dilated and unfocused, then? And you're clammy. Shaky." A grin spreads across his face, lighting his features despite the mask he wears. I itch to reach up and brush it off to reveal his identity, but he has me pinned. "Do I make you nervous?"

"I mean, I just puked. I think those are pretty normal post-vomit bodily functions."

"Maybe." A teasing glint dances in his gaze, and I notice a busted blood vessel in the corner of his left eye. I can't help wondering if that's a result of the orgasm or something else, but then he continues talking, drawing my attention to his plush mouth. "Or maybe you liked what I was doing to her. Maybe you don't know what to do with your gut reaction."

"You're joking, right? What would I find exciting about you fucking some other girl's mouth? I don't even know you."

"Do you always need to know someone in order to find them attractive? To find their actions enticing?" Tilting his head, he studies me through narrowed lids. "Or are you embarrassed by the things that turn you on? Think you're too good for a little depravity?"

My brow furrows. *Is he serious?* "She's *passed out*. You sexually assaulted her, and you're probably planning what you can do to me as we speak. Who would be turned on right now?"

Fire flickers in his eyes, and his nostrils flare as if the very idea of hurting me excites him. "First, that was consensual. Ever heard of erotic asphyxiation?"

I shake my head, and he shrugs.

"She gets off on that shit. I do too, but I feel it's important I point out that I did *not* force her to do that. Mel got on her knees willingly, knowing exactly what I like."

He drops his chin, scanning the length of my body, gripping my jaw in his long, powerful fingers. My cheeks heat as he steps closer, pressing his length into me. "And for what it's worth, I *am* thinking about all the things I could do to you. But they wouldn't be things I'd force you into. You'd love every second of it."

Pulling myself from his grip, feeling defiant, I glare at him. "If you think I'd let you do anything like that to me, you're insane. I don't even *know* you."

"But I know you, *Juliet*. And believe me, there's a sexual beast inside you, waiting for someone to discover it. Tame it. I might be that man."

I snort, ignoring the fact that he knows my name. After spending the night glued to my sister's side, a Mafia queen in her own right, I'd be more surprised if he didn't recognize me. "Has that line ever worked for you?"

"A lot of things work for me, kitten." He yanks back, disconnecting our bodies, and I can't stop the wave of disappointment that floods through me at the loss.

Stupid.

Trailing his index finger down the column of my throat, he continues his descent between the valley of my breasts, over my silky dress.

He swirls around my belly button, the outline clear through the fabric, and stops at my pubic bone. "I could drag you to the sinks by your hair and lick you till you're raw. That'd work, for sure."

My thighs clench, my pussy throbbing. I don't know why, but I want him to keep going. Even though he's a psycho, even though I don't know him, even though I just watched him face-fuck another woman. I want him to cup me, to shove my dress up over my hips and fuck me bloody against the door, until my skin blooms red with his handprints and my throat is sore from screaming his name.

Whatever that may be.

"Would you like that, Juliet?" He bends, his nose brushing against my hairline. "Would you like a stranger to take you in public? Fuck the spoiled brat out of you?"

One large fist tangles in my hair, yanking at the roots and forcing my head back so I'm glaring up at him.

My stomach flutters, confused emotions swirling around as my brain tries to fight off the lust I have for this stranger with logic. On a gasp, my lips part, the slightest breath of air slipping out and brushing across his skin. His eyes light up, his grip on me tightening, and I find myself wishing he'd release me so that I could drop to my knees.

Make him forget about the girl from before.

He seems to read my thoughts, a dark chuckle rumbling in his chest. It sends a tremble down my spine, divine yet dangerous, and my mind swims with possibilities. "You *are* a spoiled little brat, aren't you? Can't stop thinking about how you might get me to ditch Melanie and keep me for yourself. I can fucking *smell* the jealousy on you." Inhaling, he shoves his cheek against mine, breath hot against my ear. "I'm not sure you'd be able to keep me invested, kitten. I have quite the appetite."

His words give me pause, and after a moment, I'm no longer stripping for him in fantasy land; instead, I'm back in a dirty public restroom, this stranger accosting me with his large body after making another girl pass out. *Right in front of me.*

"This is verging on sexual harassment." Shoving him away, I scowl, not missing the way his gaze seems to dull as we disconnect. "Who are you, and how do you know who I am?"

"I'm quite versed in the happenings around town. Especially those supposedly fascinating." Gripping my shoulders, he shoves me aside, reaching for the door handle. "Pity that you don't actually seem to be that interesting, after all."

"I'm interesting. Maybe you should try picking girls up in a way that doesn't involve groping them in a bathroom."

"Ah, but then you wouldn't fear me. And where would the fun be in that?" He takes a wide step back, increasing the space between us, and stuffs his hands in his pockets. I should turn and run, go find my sister and her husband, but there's no telling how far I'd even get.

Or if this man would kill me, given a chance.

The sad, miserable part of me wants to test him. Give him a reason to hurt me. Make him drown out the sorrow finding safe harbor inside my heart.

End this suffering.

But I don't move, even as he allows me the chance to leave the restroom first. I stare past him for what feels like hours, unseeing and barely hearing, and only turn my head as he pulls open the door and slips outside.

A glimmer catches my eye as he moves, a gold, heart-shaped pendant drawing my attention to his neck. It peeks out just above his collar, caught on an undone button, and I blink in disbelief. *No fucking way.*

"Hey, wait. Is that—"

But he doesn't wait for the rest of my question, slipping out of the bathroom and into the throng of people crowding the hallway before I can finish my sentence.

CHASING the man out into the street isn't my best idea, but it's the only thing flashing through my mind at the moment. I leave the bathroom, the unconscious girl, and my vomit behind, my feet protesting as I sprint in my heels through the hall and out the front doors to the wraparound driveway.

My head swings left and right, frantic in my search for the mystery man. I reach up and scratch at my throat, the absence of my necklace suddenly raw and suffocating.

The cool night air is sharp on my skin as I stand outside the art center, my dress providing almost no extra warmth. Rubbing my arms, I scan the front lawn, studying the figures spread out in social clusters, some drinking from champagne flutes and giggling, others engaged in hushed conversation or leaving the party entirely.

No one looks at me, though. I may as well not even be standing here, shivering.

Holding my chin up, I approach a middle-aged couple; the woman has a pink stole wrapped around her biceps, a bright elephant brooch pinned to one side while the man dangles an unlit cigar from one corner of his mouth.

Tapping on his shoulder, I give him my best Juliet Harrison smile. "Long shot, but is there any chance you saw a man in a gold mask come outside? He has something that belongs to me, and I'd love to get it back."

The man squints, as if trying to place my face in the dim lighting provided by the party inside. "No, ma'am, I can't say I did."

Nodding, I start to turn away when the woman clears her throat, reaching out and gripping my forearm. Her French manicure bites into my skin, urgent and unyielding. "A *gold* mask?"

"Yeah."

"You're absolutely sure that's the color?"

"*Yes.*" *Jesus, what is with this lady?* Her eyes grow wide, and she yanks her hand away as if I've burned her. I rub at the marks she left; the pair takes a collective step back, and I'm starting to feel like a leper. "Okay, well. Thanks for the information."

"Young lady," the woman says, drawing me away from my retreat, "the Ivers are the only family in there with gold masks tonight."

"*The* Ivers? Ivers International, Ivers?" She nods, and I pinch my eyes closed, an unsettling feeling taking root in the pit of my stomach.

"If your masked man is that Kieran, you're much better off without whatever he has, dear." She gives me a sympathetic smile, looping her arm through her companion's and tugging him away, like they're setting themselves in Kieran's sights just by talking to me.

Grumbling to myself, I drift toward the side of the building, away from the bustling crowd and the intruding light.

Darkness feels so much better on my skin, like a shroud I don't have to pretend in.

I pull my phone from my bra, unlocking the screen and scrolling through messages. They're mostly an unread conversation in a group chat between my three best friends and me. Selma, Carter, and Avery were having an argument hours ago about what bar they should celebrate at since Selma officially passed her CPA license exam, despite her parents' disapproval in her career choice and refusal to fund her schooling.

They wanted her to follow in her father's footsteps and become an anthropology professor, but she'd refused, only interested in shaping her own path.

I'm still not convinced that a career doing taxes is the best way to do that, but she's happy, so I'm happy for her. And though she doesn't drink or really dance in public, she always comes out with us anyway, pretending not to drool over random women and trying to keep us out of trouble.

Swiping out of the message thread, I clear the screen and tuck the phone back inside my dress, leaning against the side of the building and dropping onto my ass. The ground is cold even through the fabric of my dress, and the air keeps a steady crop of goose bumps on my skin, but I don't make a move to go inside.

Propping my head against the wall, I let out a soft exhale, watching my breath puff above my face. A part of me wants to text the group chat to see if the girls found somewhere to go, but the other part knows Caroline will send a search party out for my ass if she catches wind that I even sniffed in the direction of a bar.

Like I don't have a handle on my drinking.

Please. It's been days since I stole a swig of scotch from Elia's home office. Even longer since I smuggled vodka upstairs to the spare bedroom I've been occupying, hiding it in my backpack to avoid my sister's watchful gaze.

Right now, I wish I'd at least downed some Russian liquid confidence before coming tonight. The two glasses of wine I had inside were not nearly enough.

I stare up at the moon, contemplating the likelihood of ever getting my locket back, and a thick fog of misery begins to settle in my bones, pulling at the haphazard thread holding my soul together.

Kieran Ivers has it, and I don't really want to consider why or how. Just the fact that it's in the deranged murderer's possession is enough to turn me off to the idea of securing its return.

The memory of being so close to him just moments ago resurfaces, and I ignore the way my body responds, as if he's a normal guy and not someone the entire town fears.

My chest tightens and my legs shake as a sharp pang lances through me, and I push those thoughts aside as the events of the past two years begin a marathon in my head.

Caroline's whirlwind wedding to a man with others' blood on his hands, our father being outed on accounts of corruption and abuse toward her, his supposed suicide, my mother's subsequent disappearance, and the birth of my niece, Poppy. It's all been so much, I'm not surprised Caroline just recently got around to changing her surname.

Now, she's officially a Montalto, and the only Harrison left in King's Trace is me.

It's fitting since I've felt alone my entire life, anyway.

Tears prick the backs of my eyes, and I dig the heels of my hands into them, trying to tamp down the emotions surfacing in my stomach. I don't want to break down here, where reporters from *The Gazette* are probably mulling the grounds, waiting for me to do something newsworthy.

Or, rather, some*one*.

I stopped doing that, too, though—well, for the most part. I've come across my own vagina way too many times while browsing low-budget porn sites, and it was starting to make me feel vile.

Used. Cheap. Just like Daddy always said I was.

It's not actually been that long since I lost my locket in the graveyard, but I still can't help the sadness that worms its way inside my chest at the realization that I've lost, possibly forever, the only gift anyone ever gave me. And the gifter doesn't even seem to notice its absence.

I wonder if she'd notice *mine*, or if the glow of her perfect life would blind her to that, as well.

Laughter filters around the building, a few voices rising above the general din of the crowd, and I kick my ankles together, waiting for someone to come looking for me. At this point, that Benito or Gia, Elia's right-hand man, haven't erected a full-on search party is slightly alarming.

A soft sob wracks through my chest, breaking the barrier of emotion within me; it pushes through like a flood obliterating a poorly made levee, and I welcome the release it brings. Like a torrential downpour following a month-long drought, tears stream down my cheeks, unbidden.

Uninhibited.

I struggle to catch my breath, panic seizing my insides, but I don't pull myself from the onslaught; it shoots through me like a star falling to the earth, bringing with it a great, unexplainable explosion of despair.

So I sit away from the partygoers, folded into myself, and let the tears fall freely. Here, tucked in the dark, where no one can pretend they care about me.

4

KIERAN

My father crosses his arms over his broad chest, yanking the gold mask from his face and leaning against the side of his silver Aston Martin.

A midlife crisis car if I ever saw one.

"Where ya been, boy?" Scraping a hand through his dark hair, he tosses Melanie a quick, unimpressed glance; she's got her arm hooked around my neck, her body like jelly against my side as she tries to remain upright.

I stuff my hands into my pockets, wishing she'd let go of me. If he wasn't standing here, and if I didn't feel like tying her to my bed tonight, she'd still be sprawled out on the bathroom floor, dress hiked to her hips, bare pussy on full display. "Had to grab this one from the restroom. Didn't want to leave her behind."

"Wasn't she Boyd's date?"

"Yeah, so?" Cocking my head to one side, I pin him with a pointed look. "We're used to sharing things."

Clearing his throat, he pushes off the side of the car and

opens the back of the SUV. "You don't think she'll puke back there, do you?"

Glancing down at her slumped form, her droopy eyelids and smudged makeup, I can't be sure. "If she gets sick, just stick her head out the window."

"Jesus, Kieran. She's not a goddamn dog."

"No? She sure licks my dick like one."

"Fucking hell." He shoves past me, but I don't miss his lips fighting a grin. "I'm gonna go find your mother. Maybe keep the dick talk to a minimum when she gets here?"

"Sure, Dad, but we can't hide the fact that I have one from her forever."

He guffaws, trying to cover it in his sleeve, and stalks off. I wait until he's disappeared back inside the art center before I jerk away from Melanie. She stumbles, catching herself on the car door at the last second.

"You're... being... rude," she slurs, leaning to brace her arms on the leather back seat.

My gaze travels down over her ass, and thoughts of yanking it up and fucking her in public flash through my mind. But I hesitate, and instead push her inside the vehicle, folding her limbs so she fits. "Sober the fuck up, or the only bed you'll be sleeping in tonight is one made of dirt."

"Are... you threatening... me?" She hiccups, pushing the hair from her face without looking at me.

"If you have to ask, then no. I'm just not gonna entertain a drunk bitch tonight. Or any night, for that matter. Not my cup of tea."

She slumps, her head tilting back to rest against the seat, and within seconds, a light snore fills the air. Sighing, I reach into my pocket and pull my phone from my suit, scrolling through Juliet Harrison's social media. I don't have any accounts myself, but fuck if hers haven't been entertaining.

Pictures and videos of her floating in an in-ground pool, clad in a bikini so small it should be fucking illegal; of her and her sister and some blonde toddler; her and two other girls at a nightclub in Stonemore, shaking their asses and acting belligerent.

It's a profile that likely looks a lot like something Melanie would have, yet I find it supremely less irritating. Something about the sad little brat intrigues me, calling to me like a beacon in the night.

I want to know more about her. *Need* to.

Harassing her in the bathroom hadn't been part of my plan, but when the opportunity presented itself, I found her too tempting to turn away. To let go without harm—without the knowledge that I possess something she misses.

She's lucky she got out of there in one piece, if the ideas pumping to my cock were any indication; when I do get her beneath me, *fuck*. It'll be the most gloriously disgusting act she's ever committed.

The blood heats in my veins, pulsing and humming with intense desire.

Checking to make sure Mel's limbs are safely inside the car, I slam the door shut and turn on my heel, scanning the area as people trickle out the front of the building. The Montaltos haven't come out just yet, but they can't hide in there forever.

Fiona shoves open the front doors, ripping her mask from her face and letting it fall to the ground. Behind her, Boyd trails close, a strained expression on his bare face; he reaches out to grip her shoulder, and she shakes him off, smacking him away.

I cock an eyebrow as she pushes me aside, pulling open the SUV's back door and climbing in over Melanie's sleeping form. She holds up a pale palm, cutting me off before I've even opened my mouth. "No, I don't want to talk about it. But you'd better tell your friend he needs to respect that he's not *my brother* and back the hell off."

At my side, Boyd rolls his eyes. "Those theater lessons are really paying off, Fi. Dramatic as ever."

"What happened?"

Fiona whips her head from side to side, clamming up the way she always does when someone brings up something she doesn't want to talk about. The stubborn gene hit her hard when she was born.

I glance at Boyd expectantly. He chews on the corner of his bottom lip, casting my sister a sideways look with his cryptic, hazel gaze. Not liking the secrecy pumping between them, I push the door closed and face him. "What's going on?"

"Nothing. Your sister was about three seconds from getting into a car with some random guy. He looked shady, so I stopped her."

"Who was it?"

"I don't know, some frat boy from Stonemore." He shrugs, scrubbing a hand through his hair.

Stonemore sits about forty-five minutes from King's Trace, has a slightly bigger population, and acts as a hotbed for the worst of Maine. The Stonemore Gang, an Irish organized crime unit the Ivers have been tentatively allied with for decades, runs that town the way the Montaltos run ours, except they sprinkle in human trafficking.

I've been trying to cut my ties with them for years, but since Murphy's death, it's become nearly impossible. I'm more tightly wound up in their dealings now than ever before.

My nose scrunches in disgust. "A frat boy?"

"He was wearing a goddamn letterman jacket, for fuck's sake. Would you have let her go off with him?"

I shrug, because I tend to trust my sister's judgment, and return my attention to the building just as Elia leads his family out; one arm is slung over his pregnant wife's shoulders, holding her as close to him as possible, and the other is cocked as he examines his watch.

Juliet lags behind, eyes downcast, face sullen. It makes my heart stutter.

They pause at the curb, and I watch this made man cup Caroline's cheeks and press a soft kiss to her lips. He smooths his hands over the blue fabric stretched tight around her rounded belly, then says something to his guard and slinks back inside.

Caroline turns, gripping her sister's biceps and giving her a little shake, making her laugh. But the humor doesn't reach Juliet's eyes; I can tell even from yards away. It's forced, a mask she dons when a physical barrier isn't available.

I want to tear it off. Find out what monster lurks beneath.

My hand goes to my neck as Boyd rambles on beside me; I grip the gold locket between my fingers, keeping my gaze trained on the little bird. Finally, her sister moves to the side and Juliet glances around, meeting my eyes.

A smirk tugs at one corner of my mouth, and I pull the chain out, quirking an eyebrow. I know she wants this, and now she knows I have it.

I just don't know if she realized exactly *who* I am until this moment.

Her forehead creases, a glare turning her facial features

downward. She taps her sister's shoulder and points in my direction. Caroline squints at me, then at Boyd, her jaw dropping open slightly.

Two years ago, their father tried auctioning the elder sister off to me in an attempt to pay off his debts to me and Stonemore. I'd never admit it publicly, but his offer wasn't one I'd ever consider. Not only does the idea of an arranged marriage make my dick perma-soft, but Miss Priss would never have been able to satisfy me.

Juliet, though, is a different story. She's haunted *just* enough that I'm beginning to think I could do whatever I wanted, and she'd just lie there and take it.

Like a good little slut.

A sharpness in her gaze, though, suggests she might resist at first and put up that bratty defense, but I don't mind. I'll relish in breaking her and have her eating from the palm of my hand like she can't fucking live without me.

Dragging myself from her frosty blue eyes before I bust a nut from imagination alone, I turn on Boyd, dropping the chain back beneath my shirt collar and stuffing my hands in my pants pockets.

"What are you doing?" he asks, nodding over my shoulder. "Why are you harassing Juliet Harrison?"

"I'm not harassing her."

"Then why does she look like she wants to murder you?"

Turning my head slightly, I slide a quick glance from the corner of my eye. Sure enough, she's still watching me, staring daggers into my back. They'd hurt if I had any conscience at all.

"She walked in on Mel and me earlier this evening. Thought I was raping her."

He clips out a laugh. "*Raping* Mel? I don't think she ever learned the word no when it comes to sex."

The comment sends an uneasy ripple through me, but I swallow over it, acting unaffected. "In any case, it was a mere misunderstanding. She doesn't seem to have taken it well. I guess she thinks of herself as the savior of womankind or something."

"Not a savior, but not a silent bystander, either." Her lilted voice floats around me, a chirping that sets my skin on fire. It's hard to decide if the flames are pleasurable, even as I move around to face her.

The soft contours of her high cheekbones and heart-shaped face are highlighted in the rays of light pouring from the night sky. I find it difficult to catch my breath for a moment.

Fuck, she's even more beautiful than I realized inside.

Her stare hardens. "I doubt I can save all women from you, but at least I stopped you tonight before you did anything worse."

A grin spreads across my lips, pulling them back over my teeth before I can stop the reaction. "And I told you, I wasn't doing anything to her that she didn't ask me to."

"I find it hard to believe anyone would want to pass out with a dick in their mouth."

"Well, kitten," I choke out, a knot rising in my throat as I rake my gaze over her tight little body, a hunger igniting within that I've never felt before, "maybe you're not sucking the right dicks."

"Jesus Christ." Boyd shifts, eyes darting back and forth between us. Heat radiates off her body, drawing me in, and mine sways, trying to press closer to her. I fist my hands in my pockets, restraining myself, and he takes a step forward, offering her one of his. "Sorry, my friend here has no manners. I'm Boyd Kelly."

"I know who you are. Cyber Engineer at Ivers International, right?" Cracking a smile, she levels me with a pointed look. "Wasn't that your job at some point?"

Gritting my teeth, I force my smile wider. "I resigned. You're gonna have to try harder if you want to rile me up."

"I don't want to do anything to you."

"No?" I slide closer, edging my friend out of the picture. She tilts her chin up, not looking away even as I tower over her. *Jesus, she's small.* Malleable. I'd give anything to take her home tonight, strap her to my bed, and lick the skin clean off her body. Fuck her until she offers her soul on a silver platter. "What're you doing over here, then?"

"You have something that belongs to me."

"Mm, you'll have to be more specific."

Her jaw clenches, the muscles in her cheek jumping as she struggles not to lash out. Violence practically vibrates from her body, the desire to accost me making her tremble.

Hit me, baby. Make me bleed.

Boyd clears his throat, shoving me back with his shoulder. He stares down at Juliet the way *I'm* staring at her—like the Big Bad Wolf who's three seconds away from devouring her—and I fucking hate it. Want to slit his throat and watch the desire drain from his body along with his blood.

"If this guy has something of yours, I can almost guarantee you don't want it back." He hooks his thumb in my direction, and I resist the urge to reach out and bend it until it breaks. My parents are due back any minute, and that won't look well. "There's no telling where he's had it."

She blinks at him, pursing her lips. "Maybe, but this is important."

"Why?" he asks.

Crossing her arms over her tits, she shrugs. "It just is, okay? We aren't friends, so I don't need to give you my life story."

Cocking my head to the side, I study her tiny form, the way her plump bottom lip quivers, and she refuses to look me in the eye. Fear? Shame? I can't quite tell what emotion it is keeping her demure, but it's a flint, sparking a fire deep in my stomach that I'm afraid only she can extinguish.

A plan pops into my head, and I push Boyd entirely out of the way, gripping her chin between my index finger and thumb. I yank her face toward mine, admiring how her skin glitters under the night sky, and bend so only she can hear me.

Distantly, I can hear my parents approach, can hear Elia Montalto asking where the fuck his sister-in-law went, can feel Boyd move away from us. But I don't care.

Our gazes connect, green and blue stars mixing with one another. They burn bright yellow, and I breathe out a soft gasp, trying to ignore how my body hums at our proximity.

There's a mixture of emotions flashing in her irises; her eyebrows draw inward, and she tries to retreat, but I pinch tighter, keeping her in place. "What would you do to get this locket back?"

Her lips part, eyes drifting to mine as the words fall from my mouth. "W-What?"

"What would you *do*?" I ask.

My mother's voice reaches my ears, inquiring about the girl in front of me, but I don't respond. I'm lost at sea, drowning in her, and I don't think I want to be rescued.

"Anything," she breathes, her pink tongue darting out to taste the corner of her mouth, and the muscles in my shoulders relax, tension I wasn't even aware of dissipating at her answer.

For some reason, I believe her. Believe that this locket means more to her than her own life, that she'd do whatever it takes to get it back. I just don't understand *why*—what event or person got in her head and devalued her?

Who hurt you?

The question flares inside my brain, unwarranted, but it doesn't stop me from wondering how I might do the same.

"Oh, kitten." Releasing her chin, I shake my head, feeling my darkness spread through my body like poison ivy and coating every nerve ending. "You're gonna regret that."

Juliet

Elia's burning holes into my head with his glare as I make my way back over to him and Caroline, my dress swishing pleasantly against my legs with each step I take. The threat in Kieran's words should give me pause and make me uncomfortable, but I can't stop thinking about the way he stared into my eyes, held me captive to the muted desire swirling in those striking emeralds.

Like he saw something worth looking at.

"What the hell was that about?" my brother-in-law snaps, jaw set in a hard line. "Why were you talking to Kieran Ivers?"

"Obviously, I was asking when he'd be free to murder me." I lift a shoulder, plastering on my most saccharine smile and loving the twitch that thumps beneath Elia's left eye. "Jeez, it was just a conversation. We ran into each other in the bathroom, is all."

"*Gesù Cristo.* You've been alone with him twice tonight?"

Again, I shrug, casting a sideways glance at my sister. She swallows, fidgeting beside him, and I'm starting to wonder what the fuck they know that I don't. "*What*? Am I supposed to ignore the only person here to give me the time of day tonight?"

Even if it was only to taunt and terrify me.

Not like I can't handle that.

"*Yes!* Especially when that man is a fucking murderer."

Something cold seizes my veins, like ice exploding inside me. I know, of course, the rumors about Kieran. But hearing it come from someone in his world makes it real. And it's extremely hard to reconcile the deal I just made with the devil.

Still, it's not like the *capo* of the Montalto crime outfit has any room to talk. "Takes one to know one, right?"

Caroline wraps a hand around his bicep, tugging him toward the limo that Leo, another of Elia's men, pulls up in. "Elia, we can talk about this tomorrow. Not here—too many eavesdroppers."

I frown. "What's there to talk about?"

He shakes his head, his features softening a fraction as he considers me. "You like that he looks at you, Juliet? That he makes your insides all warm and fuzzy? Tequila has the same effect, and it won't leave you dead in a ditch somewhere."

My nostrils flare, anger bubbling up inside me. "Maybe not the way you do it."

He scoffs, disgust flooding his features, and pulls himself

from Caroline's grasp. The disappointment lacing the firm downward curve of his lips hits me in the gut as he turns, but I steel myself against it.

That doesn't stop the lump from forming in my throat, like a rock I can't swallow.

Leo throws open the back door of the limo as Elia stalks toward the limo. He climbs inside, angrily jerking his limbs as he folds himself into the back seat, and then he reaches out to pull the door shut, cutting off the rest of the world.

A few reporters appear on the front lawn as if conjured by Montalto family drama.

Except it's not Montalto *family* drama because I'm not one of them. And on this night, the sudden and decisive write-off by the *capo* himself proves it.

Caroline exhales, linking her fingers through mine. "I warned you, Jules. Elia and Kieran are rivals."

"I thought you said they worked together."

She nods with a strange, distant look in her eyes. Her free hand falls to her belly, rubbing back and forth over the swell. "They did—do, I guess—but I don't think they spend very much time in the same room. Kieran just helps out whenever Kal can't."

"What does Kal do, again?"

Chewing on her lip, she hesitates. "Honestly, I'm not a hundred percent sure. But... he didn't earn the nickname Doctor Death around town for nothing."

The lump in my throat expands, cutting off my airway as I think about Kieran's nickname and the rumors about him. King of darkness. Hermit. Satan.

Murderer.

Something tells me the death he deals in is less honorable than what Elia does, and as we make our way to the limo, I toss one last look at where the Ivers still stand beside their own vehicle, speaking to one another.

He's watching me, and it sends a shiver down my spine, because I don't think he ever looked away.

5

JULIET

AS SHE PASSES BY ME, digging into her apron pockets for a pen, Caroline knocks my feet off the counter; they fall to the floor with a thick thud, nearly startling me off the barstool I'm propped up on, trying to force myself back to sleep.

It's proving impossible, though, especially with my niece babbling to herself on one side of the little bakery, traveling the beige ceramic tile with a wooden spoon in one hand and a metal bowl in the other. Every few steps thirteen-month-old Poppy takes, a prop drops to the floor, the sound echoing in the mostly empty storefront.

I'm nursing a slight hangover after last night's gala and family drama. When we got home, Elia went straight for his room. Caroline followed right after, shooting me an apologetic smile as she ascended the wrought-iron staircase.

When Phoebe, Elia's bartender-turned-babysitter-and-bakery-moonlighter, left moments after our return, I'd slipped into the home office, stole a bottle of forty-year-old Highland Park scotch, and ducked into my bedroom with it tucked under my arm. I'd crawled into bed and FaceTimed

Carter and Avery to lament my woes and have their eyewitness account of my backpedal into hell.

My phone died, and I passed out before my fifth sip. Still, it was enough that I'm feeling the effects today.

Cursed with an inability to turn off my biological clock, I found myself waking with the sun and heading to the cemetery. It's become something of a routine at this point, although now I suppose I have to consider Kieran's apparent whereabouts when I go. I'm still not sure how he came into possession of my necklace, but I spent the morning hoping he'd be merciful and just return the damn thing to the grave I likely lost it on.

He hadn't as of this morning, and I shudder to think of what he plans on making me do to win it back. It chills me to wonder about him watching me when I've been there.

Each time I leave the King's Trace Memorial Gardens, swearing curses on my bastard father's soul—one for being a bastard, and another for making me miss him still—I end up *here*, seeking absolution. *Care's Crazy Cupcakes*, the dream that her husband made come true.

It's a quaint little building with pretty paisley wallpaper and a small dining area on one side. The windows are long and rectangular, propped open despite the cool temperature outside, as if my sister is trying to entice customers.

Caroline doesn't even know I visit the gravesite, yet I tiptoe around her as if the evidence of my betrayal might bleed through my skin.

Guilt claws at the corners of my soul, searching for a way to tear it from my body. A part of me wishes it'd find out how and rid me of the crippling shame knotting my insides.

Unfortunately, when you grow up as the family disappointment, you learn to hide the embarrassment. How to ignore the sharp-edged frowns hurled at you by your frosty mother and the complete lack of interest from your father.

You bottle it up and bury it so far beneath the ocean of cataclysmic emotion washing around inside you, because focusing on the lack of reaction would be detrimental.

Eventually, you lose track of its placement, unable to find where the absence ends and you begin.

Caroline comes back around the pristine white granite countertop and drops her clipboard in front of me. "Okay, let's talk about last night."

I groan, her voice splitting the hair on the back of my neck. "I sincerely don't want to."

She frowns, maneuvering herself onto the stool next to me. It's no easy feat, considering the ever-increasing size of her belly, but she makes it work. Propping her elbows up, she swivels and faces me. "How much did you drink?"

"At the party? Almost nothing." Her blue eyes narrow, studying me, and I let out a huff of air, pressing my forehead onto the cool countertop. "At home, I don't even remember. Too much, probably."

It's a lie, but she doesn't notice.

She nods, unsurprised. *Of course, she's always worried about me backsliding.* "I thought we were done with this, Jules. You said when you wanted to avoid any more videos getting leaked online that you'd be more careful."

"I am being more careful. I drank *at home*. Under the watchful gaze of you and my crazy, overprotective brother-in-law."

"We weren't watching you, and he's not crazy."

"Caroline." I slide my hands over hers, giving her a pointed look. "He's a *little* crazy. But it's fine. I always knew whoever you ended up with would be."

She rolls her eyes, pushing me away with a soft laugh. "We're just worried about you, you know. It feels like you closed up after... well, everything with Mom and Dad, and we're just trying to make sure you're okay."

"I'm fine." I bite the inside of my cheek, steeling myself against the pang in my chest. "Peachy, even."

"That's what everyone always says." She glances over her shoulder, checking on her daughter, and then leans in closer to me. "So you and Kieran?"

My face pinches like I've just sucked on a lemon. "We had a *conversation*. Seriously, that's all."

"He was touching your face. Guys don't do that to girls they aren't interested in."

The memory of his breath, peppermint and hard liquor mixed, coasting over my skin sends a wave of hunger through me, twisting my stomach until it feels like a tornado within. I recall how he peered into my eyes as if trying to figure me out, find what makes me tick; how badly I wanted him to.

Maybe it's stupid, but even the rumors aren't enough to keep me from wanting him.

If I'm destined to carry this heavy soul, burdened with the weight of my convictions, I can at least have a little fun first. And when he slipped a dated business card into my palm last night before we parted, I knew instantly that was what I wanted to do.

Necklace or not.

But Caroline doesn't need to know that. She doesn't need to know how I plan on letting this evil, rotten creature devour me, stake me through the heart, and leave me in a bloody, bruised, *satisfied* heap of quivering flesh.

That'll be our little secret.

I clear my throat, redirecting my thoughts and the conversation. "So... is Elia *really* mad?"

She heaves a sigh, and I swear I feel it settle heavily between us. "He's not mad. Just confused, I guess. I mean, neither of us thought you *knew* Kieran Ivers, and the next thing we know, you're ditching me to go speak to him."

"I don't know him," I mutter, thinking about the mystery hidden in those electrifying eyes, the demon he keeps as a soul.

"Right." She gives me some serious side-eye but doesn't press further. "In any case, just make sure you're safe around him. He's... not like the Montaltos. Or even Kal. Kieran's a different breed entirely."

Nodding, I don't mention how I already know this, don't say I can see it in the ghost clinging to his back. In his haunted gaze and the sunken shape of his cheeks when he isn't paying enough attention to puff them up. How I can practically taste the danger when he's close.

A different breed, indeed. Something terribly dark and sinister. The beautiful face of evil.

LATER THAT WEEK, I meet up with Avery, Selma, and Carter at The Bar in Stonemore, the town bordering ours. It's just far enough away that I can drink to my heart's content and not feel guilty for being unable to control my every urge.

I've curbed the *problem*—excessive drinking—and I'm of age now, so where's the real danger?

Sitting in a dimly lit corner of the venue, pacing myself and listening to my friends bicker, I can't shake the feeling of being watched. But that's the thing about going out in public after holing yourself up for months—paranoia strikes, lacing your every thought, until you can't even enjoy a group outing.

Most likely, I'm just feeling Jace Allen's hot gaze from across the room and allowing my ill will toward him to muddy my good time. It's been a while since I dragged the firefighter to the cemetery for a mediocre midnight romp, and I wish he'd stop staring like he wants a repeat.

"It still feels so weird to me that one of us has a legitimate grown-up job," Carter says, sucking on a lime wedge after downing a tequila shot. She spits out the rind, pinching her blue eyes closed and popping them back open.

My official best friend since grade school, she's the only one to ever be able to keep up with my drunken episodes, often joining me in my stupors.

Selma, the responsible daughter of Egyptian immigrants, sips on a club soda, vigilant about her surroundings. She never relinquishes complete control, afraid her parents might find out that she's clubbing with us and cut her off financially. It's a wonder she agreed to come out tonight at all.

She runs light brown fingers over the gray headscarf that covers her hair and neck, somehow avoiding getting her many rings caught in the fabric. "Are any of us surprised I was the first, though?"

Carter snorts, reaching for another shot off the table we're seated at. "Were we surprised Ms. Stick-up-her-ass graduated with a boring degree? Definitely not."

Avery and I share a look, shifting in our side of the wrap-around booth. If nothing else during these outings, we can always count on these two to argue. Sometimes, to the point of us being asked to leave a venue.

I adjust the front of my strapless minidress, a sparkly sequined number I dug out of Carter's closet, and down the remainder of my amaretto sour. We've been here an hour, and they've been fighting nonstop.

"It's not my fault you guys aren't striving for success." Selma shrugs. "If not moving up in the world is fine with you, then you've already achieved everything you set out to do, right?"

"You're gonna be an *accountant*," Carter snaps, rolling her eyes. She tugs on one of the loose brown curls springing from her updo. "You didn't discover the cure for cancer or anything, bitch. Besides, college isn't for everyone."

College was never even on the horizon for Carter; the Mackenzies are as esteemed as the Harrisons once were, with her father being a renowned pediatric surgeon in Portland and her older brother Caden attending law school in New York. Her mother died when she was an infant, and while the others in her family focused on careers and education as a way to combat the grief, she dove into art.

She sells her abstract paintings at galleries throughout the state of Maine, making a decent living, but her father—and Selma, for that matter—refuses to acknowledge it as a profession.

Avery, on the other hand, developed a pain pill addiction her sophomore year at Bates, left for a stint in rehab, and is playing catch-up at Stonemore Community.

"We have to admit that Jules was pretty close." Avery bumps my shoulder with hers, hazel eyes gleaming under the poor bar lighting. Her deeply tanned skin sticks to mine as she makes contact, and the humidity of the packed floor starting to take its toll on our presence, and it makes me squirm. "Why'd you drop out again?"

"I didn't *drop* out of Farmington," I say into my empty glass, glaring at the maraschino cherry I've left behind. *I flunked.* "I went on a hiatus. Big difference."

"When are you going back?" Selma lifts a sharp brow.

"Whenever I feel like it." I stab the cherry with my straw, watching its insides turn out, and glare at my friends. "Did we come here to celebrate or talk about my mediocrity?"

"For some reason, it always seems to come up." Avery shrugs, pushing her dark brown hair from a bronzed shoulder.

"Because you're always bringing it up," I mutter, scanning the crowd pulsing around us, looking for a distraction. I find it in the burly blond across the room, a Stonemore Fire Marshall shirt clinging to his defined torso, throwing darts with a couple of his buddies. Reaching into my dress, I fix my cleavage and smack my lips together.

"Are you about to ditch us to go have club sex?" Carter frowns, twisting in her seat to glare at Jace across the room. "You do this every time, Jules."

"You're starting to sound a lot like my sister."

"I don't know if I should be insulted or not."

Grinning as they collectively roll their eyes, I push out of the sticky booth. After giving my phone a quick once-over, ensuring I've not gotten any worried messages from Caroline or Elia, I stuff the device into the built-in bra of my slinky dress and give my friends the finger, ditching them to shove my way through the crowd.

I love them, but holy shit, I'm starting to remember why we don't all hang out together anymore. As adults, we've begun succumbing to societal demands of how we should be spending our time, either rejecting the standards or embracing it, and it's making the whole of us aggressive.

As if we're each other's competition and not there for moral support.

In any case, I don't feel like rehashing the details of why I went on a leave of absence at school—especially considering my sister thinks I've started back up again, two classes at a time.

She doesn't know that I withdrew midway through my last semester—overwhelmed by the atrocity my life had become and the failing grades I'd accumulated—and have yet to return.

Not that I don't *want* to go back, I just haven't decided where I want to go or if I really want to commit to marine biology. It intrigued me as a kid, still does, but the desire to pursue it is lacking lately.

And therein lies my problem. The desire to do anything, really, is nowhere to be found.

Making my way over to Jace, I sidle up to him as he cocks his arm, sliding my fingers just above the waistband of his light-wash jeans. I shouldn't be indulging him right now when I know he wants more than I'm capable of giving, but I need to get out of my head for a bit.

"Juliet." A wide grin splits his puffy lips, and he turns his chin down, throwing a dart without even looking at the board.

His blue-green eyes sparkle as he stares at me, and a low simmer starts somewhere in my abdomen, burning and churning like an unwatched pot.

"Jace," I purr, stroking his bicep and fluttering my eyelashes. "Fancy meeting you here. No fires to put out tonight?"

"I'm off duty." The flames dancing in his gaze tell me that while he might not be putting any out, he's not opposed to starting some. "This is the only place near my house that serves on Sundays and isn't ensconced in criminal activity."

Like Crimson, Elia's bar. Jace is too nice to point it out to me, but the unspoken implication hangs in the air between us.

It's an active venue, but it also acts as a front for the Montaltos drug business, prostitution, and is rumored to harbor the many souls of those who've died there.

I shudder to imagine my father's ghost stuck in those walls since I'm sure my brother-in-law had a hand in his alleged suicide. That's why I refuse to give them my patronage.

More importantly, Elia would probably drag me out by my hair if he caught me inside again. The one and only time I went, he busted me for using a fake ID with Caroline's name and picture, and I ended up spilling my guts due to the alcohol ruminating in my stomach.

We haven't spoken about that night ever since, but I know it softened him toward me, which is never what I wanted.

I didn't want him to pity me after I pointed out my troubles. Even then, I was searching for the love he'd already promised to my sister. Hardly anything's changed in the years after.

But I don't want to talk about any of that; don't want to think about the people waiting for me in King's Trace.

"Speaking of being near your house," I say, dropping my voice and pressing my breasts into his side, "what're the chances you'd be willing to take me back there tonight? Ditch your friends, see who can make who orgasm faster?"

Choking out a cough, he tugs a broad hand through his

short locks, his smile stretching Joker-style. "Not interested in any public adventures tonight?"

Internally, I cringe, remembering our last hookup. "We should probably give that particular place a rest. It doesn't exactly see a lot of action, so we might catch it on fire."

Jace laughs, raising one arm and calling for another round to his friends chatting at the dartboard. He slides the opposite arm around my shoulders, pulling me against him, and I shiver with the force of his gesture. The possession of it.

Unfortunately, my mind replays a different type of possession; how it felt to have Kieran Ivers's hands on my skin, gripping my chin, forcing me to look into his explosive eyes. How it felt like a claiming all on its own, like he was letting me know he wasn't done.

Still, I haven't heard from him since that night at the gala, and I'm starting to come to terms with the fact that I likely won't be getting my locket back.

Or I'm trying to, anyway. Hard to let go of the only sentimental gift anyone ever gave me.

Desperate to stifle the sadness threatening to flood my body like a volcano on the precipice of an eruption, I step up on my tiptoes and graze Jace's ear with my lips. "Let's get out of here."

His eyebrows shoot up, his free arm moving to encircle my waist. He's firm against me, his muscles hard and well-maintained, but there's hardly any heat between us. Not the kind that scorches you where you stand.

Which is the kind I want.

Fires can be made, though; all it takes is a little effort and the right equipment.

And Jace Allen definitely has that.

I slip out of his hold and take his hand in mine, tossing a wink over my shoulder at both our groups of friends. Selma and Avery shake their heads, whispering conspiratorially, while Carter shrugs and gives me a thumbs-up. Jace's friends heckle as I lead him through the crowd to the back of the building. Bypassing the dingy, packed restrooms on one side of the hallway, I keep pulling until we reach the door with the big red exit sign above it.

Shoving it open with my shoulder, I whirl around and push him against the brick wall; the alley behind The Bar is almost always deserted because of the amount of trash that accumulates in their dumpster, but it works as a hidden space for a quick fuck.

Jace threads his fingers in my hair, bringing my face to his to connect our lips; I can barely see him in the flickering streetlight, but he doesn't seem to mind. He pulls back, stroking my cheek with his thumb, and turns so I'm against the wall, grinding his pelvis into mine. "Are you sure you wanna do this? We *are* in public."

"I don't care."

He smirks, gliding his lips along my jaw. "Shit, Juliet, I didn't know you were such an exhibitionist."

Sliding my arms up and around his neck, I push off the ground. Linking my legs around his waist, I drag his face back to mine, shutting him up. I don't want to talk about my kinks, or how he thinks he might be able to handle them. I can already tell he can't, can feel it in the hesitation when he touches me—his uncertainty with being rough and domineering like he's afraid I can't handle it. But I don't want his niceties, like the way his hands stay respectfully above my belly button and his lips feel like butterfly kisses.

I need a distraction, something to drown out the noise in my mind.

A hard, dirty fuck. One that sucks the will to live from my being and thrusts it back in with a new sense of purpose.

No one ever gives me that.

The pads of Jace's thumbs are rough against the skin of my thighs as he pushes my dress up, slipping his hand beneath my thong's thin, lacy black fabric. I buck against him as he sweeps through my sensitive flesh, dropping one hand to palm the bulge in his jeans. I've just started to yank down his zipper when his index finger pushes inside, making me gasp.

"That okay?" he asks, pulling his head back to look at me and pumping slowly.

Refraining from rolling my eyes at his need for permission, I nod furiously, shoving my hand inside his pants and pulling him out. "Perfect."

I stroke up and down his shaft as he thrusts in and out of me. While Jace isn't exactly satiating in every context, he's got a big enough dick and usually gets the job done with his fingers after. So even though we lack the kind of heat that makes it feel like your skin is melting off your body, my pussy still drips at the sight of him.

He knows the drill. When I'm wet enough to his liking, he withdraws and lines his dick up with my entrance, gliding it through my arousal. My juices coat his tip, and my core clenches wantonly. I watch as he presses in, parting me—but then he freezes, fear lacing the frown on his face.

"I don't have a condom on," he breathes, and I can almost hear the strain in his voice. Can feel the sweat as individual beads pop up on his forehead.

Chewing on my bottom lip, I shift, trying to pull him

closer. I'm not thinking straight—buzzed or high on the prospect of sex, I can't tell. "It's okay."

A shocked wave of air smacks me in the face, and he shakes his head, pulling away and setting me on the ground. "I'm not gonna put your safety at risk, Juliet." Stuffing his hand in his pocket, he pulls out a foil packet, giving himself a few pumps before tearing it open with his teeth and rolling the condom down over his dick.

As I stand there, cold seeping into my flesh, dress still hiked up, my desire begins to fade. But I'm already deep in this; what would the point of backing out now be?

If I don't do this, I'll look like a tease, even though Jace Allen isn't who I want to fuck tonight.

The reality of *that* internal confession, that I'm honestly offended that a psychopath didn't contact me this week for sexual favors, is too much to bear, so as Jace steps back in and drops his hands to my hips, I turn and face the wall.

Unwilling to share the shame overtaking me.

His grip is soft, ghostlike, and he pushes in gently, afraid of breaking me. Unaware that I'm beyond repair. That something broken can only be shattered so many times before it barely exists anymore, like dust incapable of further damage.

My forehead falls to the brick wall as he presses in and out of me for several minutes, boredom edging out any remaining sexual ache; he comes on a soft moan after a few solid thrusts, sliding out of me without even noticing that I didn't finish. Brushing a hand over my shoulder, he kisses the bare skin there. "You okay?"

"Peachy." Forehead still flush with the wall, I reach down and adjust my dress, disappointment rattling through my body.

Disappointment with him, myself, my life. The world in general.

"That was great," he says, and I hear the zip of his jeans as he tucks himself back inside. "Want to come back in and play a round of pool, or grab some pretzel bites?"

Smothering the hysterical laugh bubbling up inside my throat, I shake my head, pulling off the building and turning to look at him. "No thanks. I'm gonna call my sister and ask her to come pick me up."

He hesitates, confusion knitting his brows. "Did I do something wrong?"

"No, Jace. You were exactly what I was expecting." He opens his mouth to respond, but I offer him a smile and pat his chest. "Don't read too much into that. Go—go back inside and hang out with your friends. I'll be alright."

"I'm not sure I should leave you in this alley by yourself."

"Christ, Jace, it's *Stonemore,* and I'm practically a Montalto. What's the worst that can happen? Besides, Caroline will be here soon."

Pressing his lips together, he finally relents, slipping inside without further complaint. I sag against the wall, a ball of misery wedging itself deep in my throat, and try to focus on the night sky.

The stars are more plentiful out here, but it's not because this town is any less corrupt than mine. Maybe just slightly more removed from the evil lying in wait in King's Trace.

A tremor fights through me, threatening to remove the sutures barely holding my battered heart together. I choke on a sob, unable to ward off the unmistakable wave and unsure of the cause. An eerie feeling settles over me and amplifies my emotions.

I cast a glance down the alley as a few tears spill over, sure now in my convictions that I'm being watched.

And as a tall figure steps out from the shadows, I begin to regret asking Jace to leave me out here.

Before he even speaks a single word, I know exactly who the body belongs to, like we're two finely tuned magnets connected on an axis. Like our souls speak to each other on another level.

I just don't know yet what he wants with mine.

6

KIERAN

She doesn't know I'm watching her. Doesn't know that seeing this stranger's hands on her flesh lights my skin on fire and pumps venomous rage through my veins. Control sweeps through me, keeping me from stalking over to where he holds her against the bar wall and tearing her from his arms.

But I'm barely hanging on to my sanity; as their mouths connect and he lifts her into his arms, I feel it slipping away, possessiveness clawing its way up my spine. An unwelcome tsunami of red-hot jealousy I have no business allowing but can't seem to extinguish.

He has his hands on something precious and fragile, something that doesn't belong to him. Greedy little shit that I am, I can't stop myself from wanting to peel him off her, snap his veiny neck, and fuck her on top of his corpse. To thrust into her from behind while she holds herself up and away from his lifeless body, trying not to mix fear and ultimate pleasure.

Until I'm the only man she ever wants inside her again.

Boyd brings a half-burned joint to his lips, inhaling deeply, silent as we observe this tryst. "Remind me why we're here?" he asks after a few minutes.

"She owes me." *Sort of.* Semantics, really.

"And you want to collect now? She looks busy." He chuckles out a plume of smoke, leaning against the shrub at his side. We're situated just outside The Bar's back alley, having been on our way out of a meeting with Finn Hanson, boss of the Stonemore gang and club owner, when I spotted my kitten inside.

With her friends, she'd been laughing, carefree, and reckless. I'd slunk off to the side, observing her the way a wildcat eyes its prey, noting the exact second her undeniable sadness washed over her. A great reminder, one that propelled her out of her seat and into this meathead's arms.

I hadn't been planning on following her all the way outside, but as if an invisible tether tied me to her, my legs carried me out here before I had the chance to miss the coupling.

The firefighter's hand caresses her thigh, making a slow ascent up and beneath the hem of her short dress. They're breathing heavily, but even I can tell something's off. There's no spark, even as her head tilts back on a satisfied sigh and his wrist pistons into her.

My hand balls into a fist at my side as she pulls his dick out, allowing him to feed himself into her. The contents of my stomach threaten to spew if I don't distract myself, so as he sets her back down and rolls on a condom, I turn to my best friend.

"Unclench." He laughs, sucking on his joint again, hazel eyes glittering in the streetlights. "You're the most tightly wound guy I know, and you don't have a claim on this girl. Regardless of what she owes you."

Shaking my head, I don't concede or deny. "I just wasn't expecting her to go off and fuck some guy before I've even had my turn."

He stares over my shoulder, eyes darkening as he exhales. Pointing his joint toward the muffled grunts, he shrugs. "I don't think she'll even remember this dude after tonight."

For her sake, I certainly hope not.

We wait a few more minutes, hidden in the darkness, preying on this most depraved act of sin; when a final, guttural groan elicits from the man's throat, I turn, eyes boring into her as she turns around to face him. She's unhappy, sullen, her soul sinking into a pit of her own making.

They have a short conversation, and when he returns inside, the muscles of his back are straight. Rigid. Guess his orgasm wasn't strong enough.

My sweet, naïve little brat slumps against the wall, a strangled cry shaking her body as she stares up at the stars. Searching for something she won't find in the universe, something that doesn't exist. A resolution or purpose; the desire for it all lines the slope of her delicate shoulders, the soft curve of her neck, the tenderness with which she allows herself to break when she thinks she's alone.

Boyd flicks ashes to the ground, positioning his joint between his teeth. "Need me to leave?"

Pursing my lips, I stroke my chin, debating approaching her at all. On the one hand, she did agree to do anything to get her locket back. I finger the jewelry around my neck, considering her vulnerable state, and that now might be as good a time as any to initiate payments.

Boyd holds up his hands, taking a step back off the curb into the street. His forest-green Harley sits a block away, and he nods at me once before spinning and heading toward it. I don't know if he'll wait for me or leave me to call a cab, but either way, I'm glad he's gone.

I don't want to share this beauty with anyone else. Don't want them to see how good it feels when she breaks.

I've not taken three steps before she stiffens, swiping beneath her eyes and cutting them toward me; as I become visible beneath the streetlight, a soft breath of air whooshes out of her—in relief or surprise, I can't quite tell.

Either way, it doesn't faze me.

"How did I know you were the one watching me?" Her voice shakes slightly, and she clears her throat, tilting her chin and straightening her spine.

A grin slices across my face, stretching painfully. "How did *I* know there's a sexual beast inside you, waiting to be awakened?" I stop several feet away, sweeping my gaze over her form. The sparkly, strapless dress she wears is wrinkled in a few spots, evidence of her unholy tryst, and her golden hair is tousled, her makeup smudged at the corners of her ocean eyes. "Exhibitionism, Juliet? Very classy."

"So is voyeurism," she spits, disgust lacing her tone.

Fuck, her attitude sends a shock of electricity down my spine to my balls; they spasm as my cock jerks, imagining the ways I can screw the brat out of her.

"I didn't deny being a sexual deviant, kitten." Taking a step closer, I widen my smile as she presses into the brick behind her, crossing her arms over her breasts as if shielding herself from me.

As if that's even necessary at this point.

"What are you doing here?"

My tongue clicks against the roof of my mouth, my legs bringing me even closer. So close, I'm assaulted by the myriad of scents clinging to her exposed skin; luscious lavender and vanilla, natural musk mixed with latex, and—worst of all—another man's cologne.

I swallow down the urge to haul her to me, bend her over, and fuck her till she sweats off his residue. To stuff her tight little holes with my dick until I explode inside every single one, filling her to the brim so she's overflowing with my cum.

Hatred rears up inside me, a punch to my gut, searing open my intestines. *I want to slit the throats of every man who's ever had her before me.*

"What are *you* doing here? A dark, lonesome alleyway is no place for a girl like you."

She snorts, the gesture softening the glare crinkling her eyes. "A girl like me. Tell me, stranger, where does a girl like me belong?"

"On her knees, preferably. But I could deal with tied to my bedposts, naked and afraid." There's a sharp intake of breath as I loom even closer, towering above her tiny body with a maliciousness she's likely only seen from one other man in her life.

The man I murdered for her sister.

For her.

"Very funny."

Thick black blood runs rampant under my skin, taunting me. Pushing me, drawing me under its darkness. A beast within, quickly unraveling at the sight of her, pure and innocent and so fucking *spoiled*.

"Am I laughing, sweetheart?" She gulps and turns her gaze down toward the ground. I edge in closer, wishing I could bottle her fear. "Do I scare you?"

"No." *Defiant to the end.*

I smirk, raising my hand and scraping the tips of my fingernails down over her bare shoulder. Collecting DNA, an implication I usually avoid. But there's... something about her. Something begging to be hurt.

And I want to be the one who brings her harm.

"You should be terrified."

"Am I some kind of game to you?" Her head pulls back as she glances up with steely eyes, the strength within her bleeding through. A broken, confused spirit trying to find its footing. "I'm a human being, you know. As unfamiliar as you might be with the concept, I have feelings."

"Does it hurt them to know I find you attractive?"

"Well, no—"

"Then what's the problem, kitten?" We're so close now, the fabric of our clothing can almost touch; if I reached out and slid an arm around her rounded hips, it would take the smallest yank to bring her flush against me, for our body heat to coagulate in the air and our skin to burn at the contact.

But I don't. Not yet.

"You *know* what the problem is." Her chest heaves, breath mingling with mine.

Dipping my index finger beneath her chin, I tip it up farther, exposing the smooth column of her neck. Unable to resist temptation at its finest, I bend against my will. Gliding my nose along the sensitive flesh beneath her ear, I inhale her alluring perfume, wishing I could tattoo it into my nostrils.

"I can assure you, I have no idea."

Her throat bobs, working over a swallow, and my eyes glue to the movement. I move forward, pressing myself into her, for a moment wishing it was enough to absorb the pain seeping from her pores. Wishing I could offer her more than a broken soul and a disturbing fuck.

My teeth itch, dying to sink into her. To draw blood and mark her as mine.

Still, I withhold, noting the goose bumps popping up along her skin and the hitch in her breathing. She's afraid now, terror mixing with arousal, and I don't want to push her over the edge too soon.

She needs to be eased into this world of depravity, not thrown in without a life preserver.

As she glares up at me, the stars dance in her irises, knocking the wind from my lungs like being hit by a two-by-four. She's so fucking beautiful, I can feel myself getting lost, straying from my path of resistance and darkness. Wishing I was light, something worthy of tainting her.

"You said you'd give me my locket back if I did whatever you asked."

"That sounds like me."

"But then you didn't contact me all week."

"To be honest, kitten, I was waiting for you to call me. *I* gave *you* my card, remember?"

She rolls her eyes, scoffing. "Please. Like the former cybersecurity engineer of a tech company couldn't figure out how to contact me if he really wanted to."

"Oh, I wanted to. Badly." My thumb strokes over her cheekbone, rough against her perfection. "But I have a reputation to protect. I can't very well come off as some desperate beta male."

Blinking, she shakes her head, pulling away from me. "Can we just...?" Trailing off, she sighs, nibbling on her plump bottom lip. "Can you tell me what you want me to do so we can get it all over with?"

"Are you tired of me already?"

She makes a face, her mouth twisting into a mangled frown. "I barely know you."

"But you *want* to *get* to know me." My free hand falls to her hip, gripping the fabric of her dress between my fingertips. *Goddamn, she's so fucking soft.* Clay I'm going to enjoy molding.

"I didn't say that," she mutters.

I tsk, cocking my head. "Kitten, I need you to stop lying to me. You think I can't smell the truth on you? It's *sweet*. Saccharine. Your lies are bitter and off-putting."

"Oh, jeez, I'm sorry. I forgot I was here to cater to your fucking needs."

There's my little hellcat. Her fire sends a live wire straight to my dick, and I grind my pelvis into her, loving the gasp that escapes her as she tries to fight the attraction boiling between us. "I'm going to have the best time fucking the insolence out of you."

"Yeah?" She grins, her misery dissipating, replaced with burning desire. It catapults her forward into me; her hands flatten against my chest, claws digging into my black dress shirt, and her tongue darts out, swiping at the corner of her fuckable mouth.

Stepping up on her tiptoes, she links a hand around my neck, dragging me to her; her lips graze the shell of my ear, making my throat constrict. "Good fucking luck, Ivers. I won't make it easy."

If I don't disconnect right now, I'm going to bust a nut in

my fucking slacks without any kind of stimulation. Like a thirteen-year-old virgin. A shiver skates along my shoulders as I wrench myself away, ignoring the burn searing my balls at the denied release.

Soon.

"I'm gonna hold you to that." Flicking the end of her nose, I step back until there's a safe, respectable distance between us. "And believe you me, I fully intend to collect."

She grumbles something unintelligible, and I start to walk away, leaving her alone.

Pausing, I turn, piercing her with my gaze as she stands, trying to collect herself. "Juliet?"

"What?"

Narrowing my eyes, I drink her in one last time. "Don't fuck anyone else in the meantime. I'd hate to have to murder someone for touching you."

When I get home, Fiona's sitting on the front steps of the ivory tower we live in—an incorrect moniker dubbed by the King's Trace papers. Really, it's more of a Gothic mansion, inhabited by the Ivers bloodline since we first crossed over from Ireland in the late eighteenth century. With its sprawling gardens, the tall, ivy-covered stone walls, and stained glass windows, it looks more like a church than anything else, though no deities exist inside.

They can't when a family of unholiness lurks in its depths.

"Where the hell have you been?" Fiona asks, popping a pink bubble against her lips as I approach. "Out prowling the cemetery again for our dear brother's ghost?"

"Nope. Caught a cab from Stonemore since Boyd left me up there." It's well past midnight, and she's sitting in a pair of pale-yellow pajamas, her dark-red hair wrapped in a towel.

"What were you doing in Stonemore?"

Sighing, I flop down on the stone steps beside her. "Working."

An elegant eyebrow raises in suspicion. "You don't have a job."

"Not officially." Pressing my lips together, I turn my face up to the full moon, basking in its fluorescent glow. Hoping she doesn't push further.

While Murphy and I spent our childhoods making our parents turn gray prematurely, Fiona was always the more responsible one. The *good* child, a princess necessitated by two hellions before her. It's certainly made our mother's life easier, especially since her diagnosis, but it's forged a wedge between us I've been trying to hack away at for years.

Since Murph's death, particularly. As if my soul had fragmented when it left my body, leaving behind a part desperate for some kind of emotional attachment. For someone to get me.

Still, I can't tell Fiona exactly what it is I do for a living; she knows about Ivers International's ties to organized crime, knows that our father pulls more weight with the Irish Mafia than he cares to let on, but she doesn't know the gory details.

Doesn't need to. She's as innocent as someone like us can get. Cursed to share blood with evil.

"Well, Mom's been worried sick about you. Says she can't rest unless she knows you're safe in the house."

"Does she not remember that I technically don't live here?"

I regret the words before the sentence has even finished falling from my lips; of fucking *course* she doesn't remember. That's part of the disease.

God, I'm an asshole.

Fiona senses my shame, offering a soft frown, but doesn't let me off the hook. "She barely remembers to eat, Kieran. You expect her to keep up with your living arrangements?" She pops another bubble, turning to study me with her doe eyes. "Besides, you *kinda* live here. I mean, you never sleep at your cottage. Too much fuel for nightmares there?"

I cast a sharp glance at her, clenching my jaw. *There's no way she could know, right?* My father and Boyd are the only people who really know what I do, what I've done, that she would have interacted with. And other than rumors that fill the tiny streets of our small town, no other claims hold any merit.

Swallowing down the fear racing inside me, I aim for nonchalance. "What do you mean?"

"Well, you know, it's easier to forget your demons when you're not all by your lonesome."

Nodding, I accept her answer, relief washing through me at her ignorance. She must just think I'm torn up over Murphy. "Yeah, I guess." Knocking her knee with mine, I redirect the conversation. "How come you're still up? Don't you have an early class?"

Her face pinches together. "Don't remind me. Seriously, who let me enroll in *psychology*? I have about a thousand assigned readings. I thought freshman year was supposed to be primarily partying and gaining weight."

"You'll be glad for the education in a few years. Trust me."

She nods, wiping her mouth. "Do you ever regret not going?"

Yes. "No. I stopped having regrets a long time ago, Fi. All they do is weigh down your progress." With that, I get to my feet, push the towel off her head, and make my way inside.

The grand foyer is empty, along with the kitchen and living room, so I pad farther into the belly of the mansion. The ceilings are tall and vaulted, the walls dark, and miniature chandeliers hang throughout, providing sporadic lighting. When I reach the back, I find my mother crouched on the floor in the greenhouse, an extension built right off the screened-in back porch. She's scooping pieces of orange ceramic and dirt into a dustpan, even as a nasty tremor works through her body.

Her hair falls around her face, loosened out of the perennial bun she keeps it in, and I watch silently as she sets the brush down, clasping her left hand with her right as if trying to force the shake from her body.

But like an earthquake splitting tectonic plates, it can't be reversed or soothed. Just ridden out.

I slide open the glass door, the humidity from the multitude of tropical plants smacking me in the face, and clear my throat. "Need some help?"

Glancing over her shoulder, she sits back on her knees and tries to smile. "There's my boy. Where've you been?"

Shaking my head, I go inside and ease the door shut behind me, taking over the cleanup. I sweep the remaining dirt and ceramic pieces into the pan and dump it into the little plastic bag at her side. "Just conducting some business for Dad in Stonemore."

"Stonemore?" Her green eyes narrow, a knowing look passing over her face. "What's he got you doing there?"

84

"Just some stuff that Murphy left unfinished." Namely, a body count he didn't live up to. So here I am, on the hook for his mistakes like I am for his murder.

Because having his ghost paint the walls in his blood and fill my ears with his agony wasn't quite enough. No, Murphy Ivers was an overachiever in every sense of the word, except when it came to owning up to his mistakes.

Fuck, I need to visit his grave.

I haven't gone since seeing Juliet at the gala, as if I can find atonement in her proximity. As if her innocence, her naivete, can provide me some relief from the guilt threatening to swallow me whole, or the nightmare living in my bones.

"Well, I wish your father wouldn't involve you in that stuff. Like he doesn't know your soul is fragile." She reaches up and grips my shoulder, pushing herself into a standing position, and pats my cheek with one cold hand.

It's not fragile, Mom. Just missing. Absent.

Sold.

"It's not a big deal, Mom. Really. You don't need to worry about me."

She scoffs, swatting at me. "That's like telling a goldfish it doesn't need water to survive. As long as I'm around, I'm gonna worry about my kids. That's the mark of a good mother."

Swallowing through the swelling of my throat, I stand to my full height and offer her my arm. Her white terrycloth robe brushes against the floor; every day, it sweeps lower as it becomes more difficult for her to straighten her spine.

Assisting her out of the greenhouse and up the back staircase, I drop her off in the master suite she shares with my father—he's slumped over in their sleigh bed, a newspaper crumpled on his chest, black reading glasses perched haphazardly on his nose. I turn to her as she walks inside, cocking an eyebrow.

"Do you need help getting in bed?"

She clucks her tongue at me, pausing her staggered steps. "No, baby. If I do, I'll call your sister. Go on and get some sleep; you look like a zombie."

Still, I hesitate.

Leaning against her cherry wardrobe, she folds her arms over her chest. "Kieran, is there something else you need?"

I shake my head, running my tongue over my teeth. "You say a prayer for Murphy lately?"

"Oh, sweetheart." She sighs, her whole body seeming to sag with the movement. "You know these days, I only pray for the living. It's up to you to keep his spirit at bay. The rituals I've taught you are good for that."

Nodding, I acquiesce, letting any further comments die on the tip of my tongue, not wanting to worry her. I pull the door closed and turn on my heel, making my way down the hall to my own bedroom. Once inside, I shuck off my clothes and slip into the shower, washing tonight's blood off my body. It's invisible at this point, having already been rinsed once, but you kill enough people, and it seems to never really disappear.

When I finish, I towel off and slink under the comforter on my bed, whipping my phone out and scrolling through Juliet's social media. Gripping my dick in hand as I drool over a picture of her tanning topless, her slender back to the camera, I can almost imagine I was the one fucking her tonight.

And even though I wasn't, I know I *will* be. So goddamn soon.

7

JULIET

SWIPING the message from my screen before I'm tempted to reply, I lean between the two front seats of the car and peer into the dark at the swamp dungeon ahead. The little cottage is sheltered by a plethora of forest, so deeply entrenched I'd never have thought to come here on my own.

It's like something out of a fairy tale, with pale yellow siding and tall, single-paned windows perfect for admiring Lake Koselomal. A stone walkway overgrown with weeds is barely visible in the light provided by the porch lamp, and two shadows move fluidly behind the sheer curtains, their actions inside a complete mystery.

I look at my stepcousin Luca from the corner of my eye. "How did you find this place?"

He shrugs a shoulder, dragging a hand through his blond hair. "Wild guess. It's still in his brother Murphy's name, and

I don't think anyone is insane enough to step foot here after what went down when he died."

Swallowing, I try to process this information. Kieran's older brother was murdered a couple of years ago, and the details were kept under wraps. All anyone in King's Trace could figure out was that it was likely gang-related and some sort of brutal home invasion.

But no one ever knew where Murphy lived; the Ivers are notoriously secretive, and after this happened, the whole family folded inward, clamming up, and became virtual hermits. It's only been in the past few months that they started attending things again, like the fundraiser from the other night.

"Kinda weird that this is right across the lake from Elia and Caroline."

Luca's jaw clenches, his fingers flexing on the steering wheel. "Knowing Murphy, it was probably on purpose. I'm sure he was spying on us Montaltos at some point."

Ah, yes, the world of the Mafia. Luca serves as one of Elia's soldiers, but since some kind of infidelity mistake in the early days of the latter's marriage to my sister, he's only been allowed guard duty at Crimson.

My phone buzzes again, and my internal organs groan in protest. Unlocking the screen, I grit my teeth at the message waiting there.

> Unknown: I don't appreciate the silent treatment.

Unable to stop myself, I pull up the touch keyboard and let my thumbs fly.

Me: And I don't appreciate the orders. I'm not your girlfriend or your little plaything. You can't tell me what to do.

A few minutes pass with radio silence; Luca shifts in his seat, shoving his door open and climbing out of the car to make a phone call. I glare at the shadow dancing behind the curtain, hating the way I can tell exactly who it belongs to, as if we have some unspoken connection tethering our hidden selves to one another.

He's doing something laborious, that much I can tell; his form is continuously doubling over and straightening again, and he's using various tools, their identities obscured by the light and sway of the curtains.

As if sensing something amiss, the shadow freezes in its spot, turning—though I can't tell if it's toward me or away.

Or maybe I don't want to think about what it means if he's looking out here.

What he'll do if he realizes I'm technically on his property, scoping out the place so I can return later and take back my locket. Technically, I suppose I could have gone to his family's mansion on the other side of town, but I can't imagine trying to get past those walls.

At the cottage, a hand goes to the figure's head, working in quick jerks, and then it disappears for a few minutes, leaving me staring at nothing. I glance out the rear window, searching for my cousin in the dark; he's standing off toward the lake, phone pressed to his ear, gesturing animatedly at the sky with his free hand.

I go to open the car door, but it's locked, and the child-proof button's only accessible through the doorframe. *Well, shit.* Even though Luca's standing right there, Kieran's disappearance from my line of sight sends an eerie shiver up my spine.

Because despite the blatant flirting and the allure of his innate darkness, there's still something very off about that man. Something sinister lurking in his soul, if he even has one. Something I'm afraid of.

Something that can hurt me.

Without the fog of lust clouding my judgment, making me agree to anything he says, panic seizes my chest instead, fear scraping its nails against the chambers of my heart.

Several minutes pass with Luca still not paying me any attention, and finally the shadow is back, something large and oblong-shaped over his shoulder. My fingers shake as I reach up to adjust the zipper of my jacket, pulling it down to allow my lungs room to breathe.

He releases the object, and it falls to an invisible surface with a lifeless thud; I can't hear the drop from here, but I can tell that whatever's in there with him is no longer animate.

This was a very bad idea.

I wasn't planning on striking tonight, but Luca had initially agreed on account of not having enough to do outside of being a glorified bouncer—incidentally, I also had nothing to do. My friends went back to their normal, adult lives and I've just been chilling at Elia and Caroline's, watching nature documentaries and eating far too much takeout.

Not to mention, I just want my fucking necklace back. And at this point, I'm willing to try anything—especially if it means potentially avoiding contact with someone I suspect may be Satan himself.

Inside the house, the shadow's arm crooks, elbow jutting out by their head, and suddenly my phone vibrates long and slow, indicating an incoming call. That unknown number flashes on my screen, making my fingers shake as I decline.

I swallow down the bile in my throat, wishing Luca would hurry the hell up, or at least turn and keep an eye on me.

My phone rings again, the same number popping up. Again, I hit the little red button, glaring out at the shadow hidden inside the cottage. *Stop calling, psycho.*

I'm just about to send him a text saying as much when his number pops up a third time; anger pulsates through my veins, the demand for my attention pissing me off too much to keep from answering this time.

Accepting the call, I hold the phone up to my ear and open my mouth to speak, but he beats me to it. "Who else are you fucking?"

I blink at his harsh tone, and my mouth dries up, making a response difficult. The figure behind the curtain stands impossibly still, and now I'm positive he's looking out here—I just don't know if he can see me.

I scratch at my neck, feeling a flood of hives break out along its base. "I don't know what you mean."

"Yes, you do." Kieran's voice is low, almost a growl, and the sound alone makes my thighs clench despite my reservations. It's the kind of sound you want spoken into your skin. The kind that raises goose bumps the way Jesus raised the dead—that says this dangerous man is in control of everything and I'm merely a pawn in his weird game of chess.

Dominant. Commanding. Strong.

Everything I'm not.

A curse comes over the line at my silence. "I asked you a question."

"I heard you. I'm choosing not to respond."

"I see." A few more beats of quiet settle between us; I glance back at Luca, who is still heavily engrossed in his own conversation, and then back to the house. The figure is gone again, and a chilly air cloaks around me in the car, making my pulse jump. "Am I to assume you don't want this necklace back, then?"

"I didn't say that."

"Then tell me who's been inside you. Tell me whose throat I need to slit for touching something that belongs to me."

Against my better judgment, my heartbeat stutters, though I try to convince my brain it's just because I'm cold. The swelling in my chest knows better, though. "I don't *belong* to you."

"But you do, kitten. And until you've repaid me for keeping your precious necklace safe, you're all fucking mine, and I don't share. So tell me; who you've spread your little whore legs for since I saw you last?"

"First, I'm not a whore, and second, fuck you. Why do you think you can talk to me like that?" And why does it make my core throb with excitement, like a thousand little butterflies taking flight inside my womb?

Why does it make me want to keep goading him and see how far I can push his buttons?

"You may not be *a* whore, but you're bound to become *mine*. A dirty little slut just for me." I choke on my spit at his crassness, at how far this conversation dove off the cliff of rationale, and he chuckles. "Does that intrigue you, baby girl? Are you interested to know what I'd do with you?"

My tongue weighs heavily in my mouth, absorbing all the moisture within and making my voice come out tight and small. "No."

He tsks, and I can just imagine him pacing inside the faceless cottage with a wicked smirk on his face. Enjoying how he riles me up, maybe even palming himself as he considers his fantasies.

Between my thighs, an ache flares, dull and pulsing. Needy. I shift in the seat, checking to see if Luca is anywhere near done yet—he's not, although he does at least spare me a single glance, turning his head just as quickly, making me wonder who the hell he's talking to.

"Lying is a terrible disease." Kieran's voice drops, dipping into a smooth caress, making me tremble. My fingers grip the phone tightly, keeping it from falling from my hand. "Am I going to have to cure you, kitten? Fuck the denial straight from your body? Break you open with my cock and steal your tired little soul?"

I can't speak—my breath hitches, my chest heaves, and my stomach warms at his words. And even though it's not actually been *that* long since I've been fucked, something tells me the experience would be entirely different with Kieran.

Satisfying in a way it's never been with anyone else.

Which makes me positively sick, because he's essentially threatening me with violence. But Christ on a cracker, no one's ever said anything hotter. No one's ever been able to turn me into a quivering puddle just with the sound of their voice.

"I hear you breathing. Quick, labored breaths that tell me everything I need to know. So, are you ready to tell me who's had you this week?"

"No one," I say on an exhale, hating the way I cave. Hating how it makes me feel simultaneously aroused and weak.

"You're sure? No one else?"

"No."

He hisses, but I can't tell exactly why. "Good girl. In that case, I'll forgive your little outburst tonight if you agree to do one thing for me."

"I'm already on the hook with you, so I'm not sure I should be adding to the list."

The shadow reappears in the window, and this time it pulls the left corner of the curtain aside, and I can almost make out his bright, gemstone eyes in the dark, which is crazy since I'm over a hundred feet away and tucked between the trees, but still. I know he's there, looking.

What do you see?

"Go out with me."

My eyebrows shoot into my hairline, anxiety rising in my throat and clogging my windpipe. I catch a glimpse of Luca from the corner of my eye as he switches his phone off, stuffs it in his pocket, and makes his way back to the car. "What?"

"Honestly, Juliet, I don't make a habit of repeating myself."

"I don't think I can—"

"I'm not requesting your presence. I'm demanding it. Go out with me, or I'll give your necklace to my terminally ill mother. Ever asked a dying person to return a gift? It's like getting sucked into a black hole and never being able to find your way out."

Luca's at the side of the vehicle, yanking open his door and climbing back into his seat. He glances at me as I shrink into the opposite door, dropping my voice to a whisper. "What's wrong with your mom?"

"Go out with me and maybe you'll find out."

I bite my lip, aware of the way Luca's head tilts, straining to hear my conversation. I tuck myself even further into the door, trying to shield it from him and carefully considering my response.

I want the necklace back; every day that passes without it fills me with unending dread, making me feel like an asshole for losing the only gift anyone ever gave me.

But is it worth selling my soul?

"Juliet," Kieran continues before I've spoken again. "If you don't agree in three seconds, I'm coming outside."

Everything inside me freezes, and my gaze darts to the curtains; he's pulled them back entirely, so I can see the faint outline of his hard, lean body and nothing else. Like an angel of death lying in wait.

Luca's watching now, too, his hand reaching for the .22 strapped into his belt.

"What are you—"

"Don't play dumb, and don't fucking lie again."

That sharpness is back, the dominant, unwavering edge making me dizzy with unbidden desire. Making me feel like the only thing I can do is agree. "Okay."

He curses under his breath, frustration lacing his tone. "Okay, *what*?"

"Okay, I'll go out with you."

A soft crinkle sounds on the line, and I picture his sinister, incinerating grin. "Good girl." The term of endearment should bug me, should make my skin crawl, but there's a perverse sense of accomplishment that washes over me when he says it that I can't quite tamp down. "Now get the hell off my property, before I gut the person in the car with you and trap you inside here with me."

He clicks off the call, and I let the phone fall from my

fingers into my lap, stunned by the direction that interaction went.

Luca shifts, twisting around to look at me, and furrows his brow. "Who was that?"

"No one," I say, the lie harsh to my ears. But I can't very well tell him I've just agreed to a date with a monster—what would Elia do if he found out? "Who were you talking to?"

Looking at me for a long moment, he finally sighs and turns back around, inserting his key into the ignition. "Gia asking about Crimson business. Nothing exciting." He starts the car, flipping on the headlights, and takes one last glance at me. "You get a good enough feel for the lay of the land? I mean, we didn't get out and scope tonight, but I think he was watching, anyway."

"Yeah." Nodding, he backs out of the little alcove of trees we're parked beneath and starts down the gravel driveway. Out the rear window, I watch the little cottage grow smaller as we approach the main road, becoming obscured by woods, and wondering what the hell I've just agreed to.

Kieran

My heart pounds against my rib cage as the Town Car disappears between the trees, elated that she agreed with only a little coercion. Not that I'd expected anything less— my sweet kitten isn't used to being told what to do. Her instinct is to fight it, fight *me*, and act out.

Too bad she doesn't know how fucking hard her defiance makes me. Doesn't know how I dream of coaxing the brat out of her, turning her over my knee and giving her the discipline she clearly never received from another. How badly I want to tie her down, tease her until she's crying with denied release, and fuck her so hard that she leaves a hole in my mattress.

Obviously, her showing up here tonight was unexpected; I have no clue how she knew where to find me. Murphy's house isn't listed anywhere that I know of, and I have no neighbors on the lake.

I suspect a Montalto accompanied her since they'd be the first to access such sealed information. Probably that idiot cousin of hers, the blond one who's always sticking his nose into the Harrison sisters' business.

Still, I can't very well worry about that at the moment.

Walking to my kitchen sink, I turn the faucet on with my elbow and let the water steam, pulling the gloves I donned for my phone call off and dunking my bloodied hands beneath the spray. I scrub my nails into the stained skin, pumping soap into one palm and lathering it, washing the red off me.

This wasn't a normal job; in fact, it wasn't a *job* at all. It was justice.

Scooping the pile of clothing off my table and into my arms, I grab a flashlight from my tool bench by the door and make my way to the backyard. Flipping on the light, I scan the fresh square of dirt just off the property line, making sure the body's fully covered.

Buried upright, a few inches beneath the soil, in case any cadaver dogs ever come looking. They get confused if it's only a small patch of dirt.

My brother's words of wisdom flash in my mind, and I shake them off, trying to burn the memory of his ghost as I toss the Stonemore County Fire Department T-shirt into the fire raging within the stone pit Murphy built years ago.

Reaching into my jacket pocket as I dump the man's boots into the flames, I dig out the tiny USB flash drive I found on him, clenching my jaw. For a moment, I consider holding it for ransom as a way to drive out the other assholes who dared record someone against their will, but at the last second, I flick it in, watching it melt slowly on top of the disintegrating fabric.

The last of the incriminating evidence.

8

KIERAN

My father adjusts his glasses just as they slip off the edge of his nose, pushing them up with one finger. Leaning back in his oversized leather desk chair, he regards me with an unreadable expression, brown eyes burning a hole into my forehead.

"I think we need to talk about Murphy." His expensive, custom-tailored gray suit almost shines under the fluorescent lighting in his office, the whiteness of Ivers International's tile floor and walls damn near blinding.

A place rife with sin and corruption hiding under a guise of purity.

Shifting in the plastic chair he keeps for guests—one of those blue school seats designed to be as uncomfortable as possible—I cross one leg over the other, fiddling with my sleeves. I've known for days now that this subject was brewing in the back of his head, could see it in every glance he threw at me when I came home late at night, drenched in the scent of fresh death instead of its stale presence.

He knows I haven't been going to the graveyard, knows

99

I'm not atoning for my sins. Of course, my brain knows it as well, and itches every day I force myself away, my nerves eating at the veins threading my insides together.

"*Dia thar gach rud.*"

God over everything.

The mantra, paired with a sage and salt sprinkling over the grave in question, is the main ritual my mother taught me. A prayer she imparted to us as kids, so we'd never question how to seek forgiveness or how to ask for it on another's behalf, though I think God knows better.

Knows I don't mean it.

For a superstitious, traditionally Catholic family, refusing to plead with our demons for forgiveness is on par with blasphemy, but I've been a bit too preoccupied with a certain enticing little creature to really give a shit whether Murphy rests well in the afterlife or not.

It's not like he deserves my groveling.

Not like us Ivers men can ever truly be forgiven.

"I'd rather talk about Mom."

My father rolls his eyes. "I know you would; you love deflection. But we need to hash this out already."

"Fine. What about him?" I ask, forcing nonchalance into my tone and knowing my father can see right through it. You don't get to be the CEO of a tech empire and an associate for the mob without learning a few tricks along the way.

"When's the last time you visited him?"

"Earlier this week, maybe? I don't know, Dad, I do a lot of different things. It's hard to keep up."

His mouth works into a thin, firm line, and he leans forward, clasping his hands together. They're meatless, striped with the blood pumping beneath his almost translucent skin, but they hold the weight of his deepest trans-gressions.

Mine live in the slump of my shoulders and the shadows in my mind.

"Jesus, Kieran, you know you're supposed to be going there daily. What if something happens to him?"

Even though I know he means Murphy's *grave*, some-thing pinches in my chest at how protective he seems over his dead son. The actually evil one, the real monster; it's as if he forgot I only pulled on the wolf's costume in light of his death and that I wasn't born this way.

And how I'm being raked over the coals for not visiting his empty resting place. For not keeping it safe from the people who still have issues with my dead brother.

Good thing he doesn't know how I've desecrated the site myself.

"About that—when and how did that become my responsibility?"

"Who else would you propose to do it? Do you honestly trust any of the fuckers around here to keep watch?"

I shrug. "You could do it."

His dark eyebrows rise, wrinkling his forehead. "I'm almost sixty years old, Kieran. What am I supposed to do if there's an ambush?"

"You're right." I match his expression with an exasper-ated one of my own, eyes widening and mouth scrunching together. "If only there was something you could use, some kind of *weapon*, that'd make defending yourself easier."

A knock sounds at the office door, and his assistant Valerie's voice comes in over the intercom. "Sir, Mr. Kelly's here for your two o'clock."

"Send him in." There's a loud click behind me, the sound

of several locks unlatching at once, and then Boyd enters the room with a manila envelope tucked under his arm. He takes a seat in the chair beside me, giving me a curt nod, and I raise an eyebrow back in acknowledgment.

Out of principle, we don't interact much in the municipal Ivers International building because doing so draws attention to the shift in our friendship dynamic. Highlights how Boyd Kelly, son of a groundskeeper and a third-grade teacher, leveraged his friendship with me to steal my position at my family company.

Of course, that's just how the town tabloids phrase it; Boyd didn't—wouldn't—willingly take anything from me. He's a different breed of asshole than the rest of the men in our circles; secretive for seemingly no reason, as though the skeletons in his closet are any dirtier than the literal ones in mine.

Still, to keep the peace, we rarely discuss Ivers International, so sitting next to him in the CEO's office in the middle of a workday is slightly daunting.

My fingers grip the plastic chair between my legs, and I'm a bit envious at how much he looks like he belongs here —in his navy suit, black suspenders beneath the jacket, and his moussed hair. It makes me itch.

"What've you got?" my father grunts, shooting me a look that says our conversation is far from over.

"Just the Stonemore financial audit you asked for." He pulls the envelope from under his arm and slides it across the desk. "It looks like you're right. They're funneling money in from somewhere, and it doesn't appear to be coming in through the more common illegal routes in this part of the state."

"So they're not trafficking drugs." My father pulls the

files out, spreading them across his desk and scanning them, eyes darting along each page in time with his pointer finger. "At least, not anymore. The Montaltos are the last ones they skimmed?"

"Yes, and it looks like it stopped right around the time Dominic Harrison... committed suicide."

Swallowing over the sudden dryness in my throat, I shift in my seat, aware of their eyes on me as I lean forward, pulling the sheet closer. "They got caught stealing from Elia and switched tactics. So what? That kind of shit happens all the time."

"Not with organized crime, especially a unit so widespread and established." Boyd pulls out another envelope, fishing a handful of tickets from it. He slams them on the desk, shoving them in my direction. "This is a pile of women who were either sold or in line waiting to be sold to various prominent businessmen and politicians in the state. You remember when Harrison was trying to sell you Caroline?"

I roll my eyes. "Of course. First time I ever considered paying for pussy." My father glares at me, and I shrug. "What? I didn't do it, did I?"

"You don't have to be so damn crass," he mutters, gesturing for Boyd to go on.

Boyd slides me an uneasy glance, and I nod my assent. "Well, in any case, obviously Caroline was just one of many paid-for brides, but she was the only one within the last few years who didn't go missing before her official purchase date."

"So what? Stonemore's picking girls up and selling them? What's that got to do with us—flesh sales aren't anything new, and they're older than even me, son." My father folds his hands over his stomach, tapping his thumbs. "I'm not getting involved in that shit."

"No, of course not." Boyd's cheeks hollow out with the breath he draws in, mouth poised to keep talking, but he seems to think better of it and nods instead. The skull tattooed on his throat dances as he swallows. "Anyway, I just thought you should be aware of where the majority of their money's coming from and going to. Probably seventy-five percent of their revenue in the past year is from these sales alone."

"Are they drawing attention to the organization?"

"Not yet."

"Okay. Keep an eye on their official expense reports, and see that they're using the shell corporations correctly, so we don't somehow get dragged into that business. I have a hard enough time convincing people Ivers International is legitimate when there are rumors about what my son likes to do in his free time."

Smirking, I get to my feet, taking that as my cue to leave. "You know what they say about rumors, Dad—most are based on some kind of truth."

He opens his mouth to say more, but I don't hear anything as I draw my hoodie up over my head and pull the strings tight, unwilling to let anyone know I stepped foot back in this place. Unwilling to give in to the temptation to stop and peek over people's shoulders, make sure they're taking the security and coding aspects of this place seriously.

Boyd catches up in the decrepit elevator, following three stories down and out into the heart of downtown King's Trace, keeping pace beside me.

"Well?" I ask after a stretch of complete silence, reaching my black Volvo parked on the curb at the end of the sidewalk. "Did you follow me out here to ask for a ride somewhere?"

"Everywhere in King's Trace is within walking distance." He reaches into his suit jacket, pulling out a USB that looks an awful lot like the one I destroyed the other night. "Recognize this?"

I tear the plastic from his hand, closing it in my fist and glancing around to make sure no one's watching. Although, who the fuck am I kidding? *Someone* is *always* watching.

They made that clear two years ago.

Frowning at the device, I give a small shake of my head. "Where the hell did you get this?"

He squints at me, hazel eyes searching my face. "You know what's on there?"

My gaze narrows in turn, suspicion flooding my chest, gnawing at the frayed edges of my brain. I take a step forward, my hands flying to his lapels and gripping hard, yanking him off the curb.

Holding him in place, I breathe harshly into his face, rage simmering like a watched pot itching to boil over. "Do *you*?"

We stare at each other in silence, neither of us blinking, and finally he lets out a sharp curse, exhaling. He sags against my hold, and even though we're evenly matched in build, the anger infused in my blood gives me an advantage, adrenaline pumping through me, keeping him upright.

"What the fuck is going on, man?" he asks. "What aren't you telling me?"

Fisting his suit jacket tighter at the base of his throat, I whirl around and shove him up against my car. Violent fury beats in time with the pulse in my neck, blurring my vision and making me light-headed with need.

A desire to kill that runs deep, the single legacy of Ivers men past.

Bloodlust we've never been able to curb or sate. A curse that cost my brother his life and will probably cost me mine.

Jerking Boyd toward me just to push him back into the car door, I relish in the wheeze that puffs out of him. I release one lapel and crush my forearm to his throat instead. The car isn't tall enough to offer any kind of support, so he just hangs there, restrained, glaring at me.

My hood falls off in the struggle, and some people give us funny looks as they pass by, but no one dares cross Kieran Ivers.

"Who gave you this?"

"Christ, man, no one. It got dropped off with the mail while I was at lunch. Now, get the fuck off me." He moves, shoving me away and slipping out of my hold; I let him, trying to grapple with the information he's given me.

Dread creeps up my spine, a silent demon intent on disaster, and I glance around to make sure no one's paying us any attention; everyone seems to purposely avoid our alter-cation, knowing no good would come of getting involved.

Dragging my palm across my mouth, wiping away some of the sweat that's collected at the corner of my lips, I droop against the Volvo and face my friend.

He rubs at his neck, adjusting the collar of his dress shirt and watching me. When he cocks an eyebrow, I sigh, finally pocketing the USB drive. "I thought I burned the last of the evidence."

"What evidence?"

"Of... stuff Murphy did for Stonemore. Stuff they paid him to do, but he died before he finished. I've been trying to keep up with it, tying up his loose ends and destroying anything that ties him to it all, but I thought I was done. Thought I'd tracked down the last associate with proof of his crimes."

Boyd frowns. "So you're... what? Filling in for him?"

"No, I'm erasing the trail he left behind. That's what Finn's paying me for." My voice drops to a whisper, the faces of many nameless girls flashing behind my vision, making my heart stutter in my chest. One girl in particular stands out, and my spine aches at the memory of Mel's broken, beaten form, and how she begged me to put her out of her misery after what they'd done.

How I couldn't grant her even that.

A part of me wonders if the girls on the list Boyd showed us upstairs have any crossover with the girls my brother corralled. If Stonemore is secretly re-involving themselves in the trade that Finn said they were done with.

"Then what's the problem, if you're doing what they asked?"

I'm not surprised he doesn't quite get it, considering his involvement with the Irish mob is secondhand and only through me. And further still, no one knows the exact circumstances of Murphy's death. They don't know the secrets he took to his grave, the ones that eat me alive at night like worms feasting on dead flesh.

Don't know how they changed me.

Stained me.

Made me irredeemable.

"I'm not doing *exactly* what they're paying me to." I lean more of my body weight into the vehicle, pulling the flash drive out and staring at its tiny plastic shell, dwarfed by my large palm. "And this says my time is running out."

I MAKE it to Murphy's grave in record time, speeding through downtown to reach the outskirts of King's Trace. His is a monument, an upright, oblong-shaped marble statue with his name and death dates inscribed on a plaque at the bottom.

Inconspicuous. Scoffing as I inspect the site, I notice a note taped to one end of the stone; it's folded into a small square and plastered to the grave with silver duct tape, and when I rip it off, a wave of impending doom settles over me, like the rain clouds up above crashing down to earth.

As if they've finally gotten their fill and can no longer hold themselves up.

Our family crest is drawn on the sheet of paper right below *"Diar thar gach rud,"* the words crossed out with dark red ink. Stapled beneath the drawing is a picture of a stack of playing cards burning on top of a wooden table.

My chest tightens, my heart shriveling inside the cavity. It's a message, although backward and based on a silly superstition, and impossible to ignore. Pocketing the sheet of paper and shoving down the ball of dread that's risen in my chest, I move around to the back of the headstone.

A giant cross streaks the rear of the monument, the same dark red from the sheet of paper. Stepping closer, I squint my eyes, inspecting more closely, and note the brown hues, the unkempt way the lines of the cross drip onto other parts of the stone.

This isn't spray-paint or ink.

It's blood.

And it isn't your run-of-the-mill vandalism; in fact, most

King's Trace residents know better than to step within six feet of an Ivers tombstone, aware that darkness is contagious. Alluring. An aphrodisiac even the strongest can't resist.

Panic grips my heart, squeezing it in its fist, and my vision blurs around the edges as I try to remain upright. I reach out, clutching the sharp edge of stone, and stagger forward as a harsh, ear-piercing ringing echoes in my eardrums.

White noise tunnels through me, making itself at home, and I fall to my knees, my palm splitting against the statue. Blood beads in the wound, decorating it the way stars pop up in the night sky, and the ringing continues, increasing in volume until all I can do is crumple.

It's a reminder of the souls in purgatory waiting for my prayers.

One soul, in particular.

Instead of going home and spending my evening playing Scrabble with my mother, I leave the cemetery and haul ass back to the cottage. I park behind the house, my hands shaking as I toss the sheet of paper on top of the pile of incinerated items left haphazardly in the firepit.

Because I've been distracted by Juliet, enticed by her bratty attitude and defiant beauty the way ancient Greek sailors found destruction at the hands of sirens.

She's a disturbance, one I need to fuck out of my system so I can refocus on my greater purpose. Unlocking the back door and pushing it into the wall, the knickknacks on the bookshelf across the room clatter. I reach up and tug on her locket, still secure around my neck, and imagine the ways I might use it to mark her.

Brand her with my violent love.

Destroy her, steal her soul for myself, as if the light in hers might drive out the darkness in mine.

I move to the kitchen sink, fumbling for the hot water knob, and watch as it fills the stainless steel tub. Steam rises in the air in front of me, and I plunge my hands inside, wincing against the sharp burn and scrubbing my fingernails against the veiny flesh of each palm. Wishing I could forget the memory of her soft, porcelain skin, and how good it felt to touch her.

Trying to erase my sins from where they've embedded themselves in me. A ritual that never seems to work correctly.

The cut on my palm screams in protest, but I don't stop. I scrub the scorched skin as it blooms bright red, scouring every inch until my hands begin to crack, peeling and splitting like rotting fruit, and pain courses through every fiber of my being. Blinding, excruciating agony that has less to do with the physical hurt I've wrought on myself than the torture my mind keeps up.

Less to do with my bleeding hands and more to do with my bleeding heart.

A creak somewhere in the back of the cottage catches my attention, pulling me from my hand washing; I freeze, flicking the water off, and hold my hands out of the sink. They air-dry while I listen for more, suspicion worming its way down to my core and drawing the muscles in my stomach taut with vexation.

Drying my hands off the rest of the way on my pants, I dig into a drawer and fish out a syringe and insulin bottle, though that's not what's inside. I fit the tip of the needle into the soft top, turning it over and withdrawing the drug, then toss the bottle into the sink and position the needle in my fist. My thumb sweeps over the plunger as I move toward my bedroom in the back, my jaw clenched tight.

All of the white doors are shut, and I know there isn't enough hallway closet space for someone to hide in. Kicking open the bathroom door as I pass it, I stick my head in, scanning the room, and find it empty.

My eyes lock on the bedroom, the last door at the end of the hall, and a sinking feeling settles in my gut, constricting my throat and making it hard to breathe. My nostrils flare, and I shove the door open with my boot, coming face-to-face with the last person I ever expected to be in here.

9

JULIET

My palms feel slick against my bare thighs as I press them
in deeper, trying to make myself as invisible as I normally
feel. I focus on regulating my breathing to a long, slow
inhale and exhale, timing it to calm my racing heart and
push out the tremor in my arms.

Moving my head down a fraction, I peer out through the
slat in the closet door at the petite redhead seated on Kieran's bed. Her long, pale legs are crossed, her hands clasped
over her knees, and she sits there, unmoving, staring at the
door as someone moves around in another part of the
cottage.

This was a bad idea.

I hadn't been expecting anyone to be home when I
finally broke into this house, thinking the security here is
probably less intensive than what they have at their
mansion, since technically this place is off grid. My plan was
to get in, see if he'd discarded my locket, and get out without
having to interact with Kieran ever again.

Partway through my search through his ancient chest of

drawers, though, Fiona Ivers had come in and situated herself in the room, forcing me to take cover in the first available hiding spot: the closet.

It smells like mothballs, a hint of masculine cologne, and death, and I've been trying to keep myself from dry-heaving for over an hour.

If he hadn't taken his sweet time contacting me again after forcing me to agree to a date, I probably would've already fucked him and been on my way by now, but with every day that passes with no word from him, unease bears down on my chest like an unstoppable avalanche, threatening to pull me under if I don't get the necklace back.

Caroline still hasn't even noticed that it's missing, and I'm starting to wonder if I've put more meaning into the gift than was ever necessary. But I'm too far in this now to lose face and give up; if nothing else, I want Kieran to lose this game we're caught in, for him to be the one that relinquishes his power.

For once in my life, I want to *win*.

Being trapped in his closet is not the easiest path to victory, but if I'm quiet enough, I'm hoping I can at least sneak back out unscathed. I don't want to imagine what he might do to me if he sees me here.

The bedroom door flies open, slamming into the wall to the left of my head, and the force of it makes my teeth rattle. My lungs seize up, stalling my breaths—a reflex I learned as a kid when my father would get drunk and go looking for Caroline.

A scratchy knot lodges in my throat as I think about the nights I spent listening to her sob herself to sleep in her room across from mine, and how many times I'd wake up in the mornings and let my father convince me she was just being dramatic. That he hadn't hurt her. My stomach churns, bile burning the base of my esophagus, as I think about what he was actually doing to her.

Pressing the back of my hand to my mouth as Kieran comes into view, I will the vomit away and shove my secret guilt to the recesses of my brain where only my demons can access it.

I step back into the coats hanging around me, trying to immerse myself in the laundry as Kieran regards his sister with an expression of pure rage. The hollowness in his cheeks is highlighted by the heat staining them, while his dark brown hair is slick with sweat, eyes red-rimmed and crazed, as if he's recovering from a month of no sleep and starting to hallucinate.

"What the fuck, Fi? How—what are you *doing* here?" There's an instrument wrapped in his palm, but I can't quite make out what it is before he shoves it into his hoodie pocket, carding a large hand through his hair.

"I think the better question is, what are *you* doing here, Kieran? Spending half your time in this... mausoleum." His sister's voice is calm, collected, and slightly terrifying. *Is that a family trait?*

"Actually, no." He flops on the bed beside her, dropping his back to the mattress and pulling his arms up above his head. *Christ.* His hoodie rides up with the movement, revealing rippling stomach muscles just above the waistband of his jeans, and my mouth practically salivates at the sight. "In the history of every question that's ever been asked, *that particular one* has never been the better question. Try again."

"Well, brother, you're not an easy guy to get a hold of. You haven't been home much lately, so I figured I'd ambush you in your house of horrors. I've still got my old key from

Murphy." She folds her arms across her chest and moves to look down at him. "What the hell is this place? Some kind of shrine?"

"It's my house."

"It looks *exactly* the way it did when Murphy lived in it."

"Him dying didn't suddenly make everything unusable. Besides, aren't you and Mom really into recycling and shit? You should be praising me for my conservation efforts." There's a twinge of something that flashes across my vision, some kind of sick excitement at the notion of Kieran Ivers caring about the planet.

Of a monster caring about something other than himself.

The abandoned marine biologist in me soars, inappropriate in its timing and subject. Especially considering he doesn't *actually* care about the planet—his tone says that much. He just wants Fiona to stop worrying.

And that makes my heart lurch in my chest, a violent jump that startles me in the small space, because I've never related to anyone more.

His sister glances around the room, raising a perfectly sculpted eyebrow. "Doesn't it creep you out that he died here?"

Kieran doesn't say anything for a long time. The silence stretches so thin between them, a film of omission floating in the surrounding air. His fingers stroke the spindles on the pale wooden headboard, and I track the movement with my eyes, my pulse kicking up between my thighs.

I squeeze them together, reminding myself that I'm not welcome here. That I'm an intruder trying not to be discovered, and that he'd most certainly kill me if he found me.

After what feels like a lifetime, Kieran exhales, working his jaw. "Ghosts don't haunt places, you know. There's nothing here in this house that knows something I don't, or has seen something I haven't. Every ghost exists within the living."

"That makes your being here alone even worse."

He shrugs. "Do you have a reason for breaking in, Fi? Because I have to say, after the day I've had, I'm not in the mood to entertain."

Gulping, I take another step back, the clothes rustling slightly. My elbow knocks into the wire shelf behind me, the items placed there making a dull, hollow clink as I make contact. Fiona starts talking about some acting classes she's been taking at some theater with her friends, and how their parents are hopeful he'll attend some production she's helping put on in the summer. But I can't focus on any of that, because when I turn my head to make sure I didn't knock anything over, I'm met with a plastic bag, stuffed to the brim with bones.

They're different shapes and sizes and a myriad of colors ranging from dark, dirty brown to a crisp, clean white, indicating both their length of time in this closet and the level of care taken to cleaning them.

My mouth drops open on a silent scream, and I clamp my hand over my lips to stifle the vomit rising like a river rapid, on the very cusp of spewing over. Hysteria clouds over me; even though I have no way of knowing whether these are real human remains or not, something tells me there's no way Kieran fucking Ivers would have *fake* bones in his home.

Body shaking, I bury myself even farther into the clothes, struggling to keep my breathing at a reasonable rate. Sweat drips down my forehead, and my stomach twists around nothing, trying to ground itself in my mounting anxiety.

I can barely see them through the door now, but I notice

that Kieran's body seems stiff. He sits up slightly, narrowed eyes dancing around the room, even as his sister drones on about college. They finally land on the closet, and my heart fucking stops beating while he stares, cocking his head to the left.

He can see me. He knows I'm in here.

And I've never been so close to pissing myself in my entire life. Not during one of my formerly frequent blackout benders, not when I was a kid and had to sleep in Caroline's room when the monsters under my bed kept me awake at night.

After a moment, he seems to shake himself out of whatever hold the door has on him, turning his head to engage with his sister some more. He nods and "Mm-hmms" in all the right places, offering an air of attentiveness, but something still feels off.

His posture is too rigid, his body not turned enough to be completely unfazed by the noise in the closet. And I'm pretty sure he's going to kill me when he finds me here.

"...so Dad dropped me off to make sure you're still coming to his birthday thing this weekend. At Opulence?" Fiona snaps her fingers in front of his face, evidence that he's been as zoned out this whole time as me. "Hello, Earth to devil? Are you going or not? Mom said she needs to finalize the reservations."

"Did you really come all the way out here just to ask if I'm attending a birthday party?"

"You weren't answering my texts."

"It's... been a rough day."

"Yeah, so? That doesn't give you an excuse to blow me off. You don't have enough siblings to do that anymore." Huffing, she gets to her feet, sweeping her dark red hair off the shoulder of her cashmere sweater. "And for the record, I came by to check on you. But as usual, you're too much of a dick to appreciate that anyone gives a shit about you."

"I'm not worth it."

"Worth what?"

"Your concern. The shits you give. Any of it. Give them to someone who matters."

She scoops a black leather purse from the floor beside the bed and slings it over her shoulder, pausing only to stop and cut him one last glance. "When are you gonna stop punishing yourself for the stuff he did?"

"When there's nothing left to be punished for."

She frowns, her delicate features sloping downward. "He's gone, Kier. Isn't that punishment enough?"

"Death is an escape, Fiona. Not a sentence."

Nodding, she moves toward the door. "I wasn't talking about Murphy." And with that, she leaves the room, pulling the door shut with a soft click behind her.

My eyes and ears feel like they've been set on fire, guilt for intruding on this intimate moment punching me in my already distressed gut.

Another door in the house opens and closes, jostling the bedroom door with it. Kieran lays back on the bed, resituating himself so his head is propped up by the headboard, and stares at the wall for a long time, blinking only on occasion.

Shifting forward, I press my nose into the slat on the door, watching as he breaks from his trance and lifts his hips, unbuckling his jeans and shoving them down his thighs. He kicks his legs free, revealing tight black briefs that hide absolutely nothing, and then he reaches up over his head and shakes out of his hoodie.

It comes off in one pull, and he settles it by his side as he climbs back into position, back against his pillows. My breath comes in sharp puffs as I drink him in; though he's incredibly tall and lean-looking with clothes on, the defined ridges of his chest and stomach make my core throb, the corded muscles of his biceps making me drool.

He looks powerful, so comfortable in his glorious body, and fuck if I don't want him, even with the literal skeleton in his closet.

What the fuck is wrong with me?

Chalking it up to a momentary lapse in sanity brought on by my prolonged stay in this tight, enclosed space, I relax slightly when his one arm slips beneath his head. He wiggles around, getting comfortable, and my hands curl into fists at my sides with the effort it takes not to go out there and mount him.

Because that would be completely insane, right?

A harsh shiver skates down my spine when he shifts again, his hand sliding over his abs and drifting beneath the waistband of his briefs. A lead weight drops in my stomach and my thighs clench, moisture pooling between them as I realize where this is heading.

Somehow, now I'm the voyeur, our roles completely reversed and making me dizzy. I flatten my palms against the sides of my thighs as he pushes his underwear down, just low enough to hook them beneath his swollen balls.

Jesus Christ.

Even from where I'm standing, I can tell he's fucking huge—I didn't get a great look at it at the fundraiser, but it's on full display now. The angry, reddish shaft dwarfs his palm as he wraps his fingers around it, pumping a few times to get started. He pulls his hand away, cupping it around his lips and spitting, and then brings his fingers back, pinching the head of his cock in a way that makes me squirm.

Squeezing my eyes shut, I try to block out the soft grunts falling from his lips and the slick sounds of him fucking his hand, hating how badly I wish it were me out there. Dropping to my knees, sucking him into my throat, letting him dominate me the way I can tell he wants to.

My lips part of their own accord as the mattress springs creak under his weight, and even though I can only see the black of the back of my eyelids, my skin feels like it's on fire, wanton desire coursing through me and filling me with immense confusion.

Is it a genetic thing, wanting to fuck guys driven by violence? Is Caroline aware of the moral dilemma she faces as a woman who allows herself to be dominated by a man with more blood on his hands than we have in our bodies?

Or is the darkness just *that* enticing? Something that draws you in because you can't fathom how anything can exist without even a hint of light, and then traps you with its succulent beauty.

My eyes pop open, taking in this vile man as he brings himself to the brink of pleasure, and I know I've never seen anything more captivating. His eyebrows pull together, his hips pistoning in an effort to meet the thrusts of his hand, and his chest rises and falls like he's just gone for a long run.

Heart pounding and head swimming with lust, I fiddle with the waist of my leggings, the pulse between my thighs intensifying as he draws closer to release. Pressing my lips together to keep a moan from falling out, I deftly slip my right hand beneath my bottoms, pushing past the thin elastic of my underwear, and swipe over my clit.

A full-body shudder wracks over me as I shift, widening

my legs for better access and keeping my gaze trained on Kieran. He groans, the sound low and primal as it sets my soul aflame; I graze my clit again with the pad of my index finger, jolting at the sensation. It's been far too long since I've come this way, much less with a man around.

That he doesn't even know I'm in the room makes me feel naughty, heightening the arousal in my veins. Pushing firmly on the side of my clit in a way that makes me come quickly, I slowly massage myself, growing wetter as I approach my climax.

My skin is silken, damp, and smooth, and my legs feel like liquid as I swirl my finger around in tight circles. Ecstasy pulses through me and beneath my fingerprint, drawing the muscles in my abdomen tight. Short breaths escape me as his become louder, harsher, and his face twists up as if in pain at the same moment I move lower and shove a finger inside myself.

Pumping in half-strokes, all that's afforded me by the awkward position in this closet, I watch him come undone, coming on a hiss and fucking his fist like he's churning butter.

He growls at the ceiling as thick, sticky ropes of release decorate his stomach, and I stroke forward against my G-spot, coming at the same time his mouth drops open and my name falls from his lips.

Trying not to think about *that*, I swipe my free hand across my forehead, pushing sweat from my skin.

His head falls back against the pillows, and he stays like that, completely unmoving for so long, I think he's fallen asleep. I inhale slowly, exhaling through my mouth, as my pussy throbs from my orgasm, electric shocks making my clit vibrate even as I pull my hand out and collect myself.

I don't know exactly how long I stay like that, fear and exhaustion keeping me from moving, but after a while, his breathing seems to even itself out, and I decide to make a break for it.

Now or never, Juliet. Get out of here while you still have a chance.

Opening the closet door slowly, careful not to jostle anything in the process, I tiptoe from the little space and make a beeline for the door.

Something stops me from leaving, though; the entire reason I came here in the first place. And since it wasn't anywhere to be found in the house, at least where I searched before his sister showed up, I'm inclined to believe it's on him instead.

Thinking back to the night we met, how he wore my necklace, I straighten my shoulders and turn on my heel, determination clouding my judgment. At this moment, whether it's confidence brought on by an unexpected orgasm or just plain stupidity, my legs carry me back over to the bed.

And there it is—my gold, heart-shaped locket clasped around his neck, begging for its rightful owner to reclaim it. I study him for a few moments, ensuring he's at least left the REM stage—his eyeballs don't flutter behind his lids, and his breathing is long and deep. I don't know how light of a sleeper he is, but this might be the only chance I ever get.

Leaning over his disgustingly sculpted body, I reach for the clasp with shaking fingers, unhooking the chain and sliding it from around his neck, careful not to so much as breathe in his direction.

My heart rate skyrockets, my knees wobble, and it takes every ounce of energy in my body to keep my core upright and away from him; I remove the chain from his body, but as I move to get down off the bed, a hand whips out and locks around my wrist.

I'm met by blazing green eyes, and my fist curls around my necklace, protecting it, as he drags me into his chest, his free hand digging beneath his hoodie on the bed. I open my mouth to speak, to apologize, to say *anything*, but then there's a sharp pinch at the base of my neck; my hand flies up to cradle the site of pain, and I watch as a large syringe falls onto the mattress with the plunger pushed all the way down.

10

JULIET

EXISTING inside a vacuum is an experience I've dealt with my whole life—at first, it was just a side effect of being the forgotten child, and then it became a coping mechanism.

Something I strove toward on my weekends, a way to fill the parental neglect etched into the fiber of my being. A way to alleviate the miserable hurricane constantly raging in my soul, a distraction from the overwhelming, all-consuming sadness.

But *this* is new.

Blinking my eyes open, I stare up at a blindingly white popcorn ceiling; it's vaulted, meeting in a sharp peak at the middle, with a brass fan dangling from it that blows cool air down on my flushed skin. My mouth feels parched and sticky, like I've just sucked on a wad of cotton balls that absorbed every ounce of saliva on my tongue.

I try to swallow over the dryness, but there's no traction, nothing to move down my throat, and my muscles refuse to cooperate. A dull ache flares in my shoulder, spreading along my collarbone, and I try to reach an arm up to press on the point of pain, but nothing moves.

Like I'm submerged in Jell-O and my limbs are suspended separately from the rest of my body.

For once, I feel nothing—and that includes the cracks in my wretched heart. I'm unable to feel exactly where it's split, or to feel where it bleeds out slowly with each passing day.

And even though I know it's not real, that something bad is happening, I latch on to it.

Embrace it.

Who knew this was what not hurting felt like?

Voices play at the edge of my eardrums, muffled and indecipherable, and I flick my eyes downward, aiming them at my body. My vision blurs like bright city lights reflected in a rain puddle, harsh as a thick throbbing sensation shoots through my forehead. I wince—or at least, I try to. But still, my body doesn't react.

Under normal circumstances, panic would've settled in by now, seizing my ribs and squeezing until they break, but there's an eerie, misplaced calmness settling in my gut.

Misplaced because I know something isn't right. I don't recognize the room I'm in, can't place the smell of cleanser and smoky pine, and can't muster up any fear at being completely incapable of moving, no matter how bad I will it.

Caroline's going to kill me.

The thought floats on repeat in my head, bouncing off the walls like a rubber ball in perpetual motion and making me dizzy. A man's voice pushes closer, and if I could *just turn my head*, I know I'd be able to see its owner. Be able to remember how the hell I got here.

He sounds far away and too close all at once, his words

somehow smooth and coarse at the same time, like crushed velvet.

"Oh, kitten, what have you done?"

My hip dips outward, and a dark, shadowy figure leans into the corner of my sight—a handsome face I know I've seen before hovering above mine.

His dark brown hair sweeps slightly over his forehead, and I take in his sharp, high cheekbones and the stubble lining his jaw as he watches me, his eyes searing a hole in my soul—green eyes with deep purple bags beneath them and soft crow's feet at the corners, showing how a malicious life ages you. How your demons take years from you, even when you offer them your soul.

A pair of eyes that have haunted me from the first day they landed on mine.

Somehow, being this close and unable to focus on a single other sensory detail highlights his imperfections, and my gaze zeros in on each one, trying to commit them to memory despite the metaphoric tar spewing into my heart. Tainting the emotionless void I've slipped into.

Whatever's going on here, he's behind it.

And being at his mercy doesn't terrify me like it should.

I try to open my mouth and ask what the hell happened, what I'm doing here, but he tsks, covering my lips with his large palm. Alarm scrapes across my brain like a sharp blade slicing into my flesh, jarring in how quickly it surges through me.

Why can't I feel his hand on me? I can *see* the shadow of him holding me down, but there's no sensation. No heaviness from his weight, no prickle of fear that heightens my arousal when he's close to me.

Is this what being dead feels like? Am I finally burning?

"Shh, sweetheart. Don't waste your energy. You're gonna need it later."

Another voice pierces my ears from the opposite side of the bed. A tall man—too tall, taller than the other—with sun-kissed skin and hair darker than the blackest abyss in the ocean, crosses his arms as he stares down at me, a disapproving frown on his chiseled face. He looks older than Kieran—though his brown eyes lack that ghastly sheen, they sport a bit more wear and tear.

"Goddamn it, Kieran." Though visibly stressed, the tall stranger maintains a certain calmness about him as he scrubs a hand over his face, digging into his jaw with the heel of one palm. "Why doesn't anyone ever call me for normal shit?"

Kieran shifts, not removing his eyes from my line of sight. They warp under my perusal, his irises stretching and vibrating like an endless vortex. I feel myself being sucked in like a moth to an open flame and can't do anything to stop it.

My heart pounds against my ribs, the sound ricocheting off the walls and echoing in my eardrums. He watches with an anger that I can't quite comprehend.

"You're scaring her," the other man snaps.

But Kieran doesn't mind. It's exactly what he wants.

A sinister smile stretches across his mouth, his lips curling back over his teeth as he looms closer—but when I blink, he's back in place, stoic and still, as if he never moved in the first place.

"I'm *supposed* to scare her." He glances at the man, finally, allowing me some reprieve from the paralysis his presence puts me under. "Fear keeps her safe."

Maybe that's it—maybe my dissociative state has to do

with the mere presence of this demon, like he's sucking my soul straight from my body. Maybe that's why he's so close.

Maybe he just can't stand to be away.

The thought slips from me, a message stuck in a bottle and tossed to a tumultuous sea, as the room around me ebbs in waves, waxing and waning against my strained consciousness. It melts, the beige walls splintering into little pieces and the men above me glitching out like a television with a bad connection.

"Is she okay?" Kieran's voice floats closer even as his form gets farther away, and I try to squirm on the bed, try to grab his attention and pull him back in. I don't know why, but I don't want him to leave.

Still, my body doesn't cooperate.

"She looks pale." A cool weight presses on my forehead, but I can't quite pinpoint its origin. "Could she be having some kind of reaction?"

"That's a risk with all drugs, yes." The older man's voice is hard. Angry. It warms my insides that someone feels something on my behalf. "What the fuck were you thinking?"

"I wasn't. Not really." A pause, then a deep, labored breath. My vision starts to gray, color exploding like fireworks and then leaching from sight. The room gets smaller and brighter until all I see is nothing. "She *broke in*, Kal. What was I supposed to do?"

"The answer is never drug the woman you're attracted to. Trust me on that one."

My jaw slackens while they banter, and as I draw in a soft breath, I'm able to produce a modicum of saliva on my tongue. I swallow, letting it lubricate my throat, and try to concentrate on fixing my vision. My body feels simultaneously hot and cold as I struggle, wishing I hadn't ever come to Kieran's in the first place.

Shit. That's what I was doing. I broke into his cottage, watched him get his rocks off, and tried to take back my necklace.

What the hell happened after that?

Blinking, spots of the room I'm in start to reveal themselves again, the light above me splitting into a prism of textures—each one more intricate than the next.

"Will she be okay?"

"Did you give her more than the recommended dosage?"

"I don't..." Kieran trails off, and I feel a soft pressure near the outside of my right thigh, as if he's touching me. But I can't see it, can't know for sure. I lean into it, loving how it scorches my skin, spreading its warmth along my sweaty, tender flesh.

"I don't know," Kieran admits. "I wasn't thinking."

"How much did you give her?"

"Less than I gave Murphy."

Silence. An eerie feeling inches along my chest, making the cavity feel impossibly tight. Like a thousand little critters infesting my body, trying to force me to share the warmth with their parasitic bodies.

I writhe on the inside, attempting to drive them out, but they're cold-blooded and need the heat. Need to feed on my sad, black heart and gnaw on my bones until I'm unrecognizable.

Maybe that was Kieran's plan all along. His way of getting me out of his head.

A small memory floods my mind as I try to reason my way out of the itchiness, filling me with immense dread as the man of my nightmares materializes in front of me. He leans in, and I can feel his minty breath wash over my face, can feel his grip on my hips, pinning me into the mattress.

"Bones," I rasp, a word finally escaping me. Lifting a weak hand, I point my index finger toward the closet across the room.

The corner of Kieran's mouth turns up, his expression morphing from concern to something evil. Vile. Terrifying. If I were in my right mind—if I could move—I'd be getting the hell out of here.

"Look, Kal, the bad little kitten wants to play." Kieran hauls himself up on the surface I'm on—a bed, presumably, if this is still the room I passed out in—and straddles my thighs; a blast of cool air hits my flushed skin as he peels my leggings over my hips and down to my knees. And all I can do is watch, once again robbed of the ability to speak.

A flash of white-hot electricity zings through my abdomen, but still I have no clue where it's coming from.

Pressure builds between my legs, knotting my stomach muscles, and I watch as his hand disappears between my thighs. The likely culprit. "You like games, right, Juliet? Let's play, shall we?"

Despite my incapacitation, my body hums with excitement, blood rushing between my ears and heading south.

"Kieran—"

He holds his hand up to the other man—Kal, apparently, and I can't help but wonder if this is the same one on Elia's payroll with—shushing him. "She's a big girl, Kal. She can answer a few questions."

"You're just gonna sexually assault her until she tells you what you want to hear?"

Scoffing, Kieran smirks down at me, reaching behind his

neck to pull his black hoodie off in one fluid movement. "It's not sexual assault. She wants this. Wants me."

"She's not—"

"She's lucid *enough*. Christ, Kal, if you're gonna be a pussy about it, get the fuck out. I don't want you seeing this shit, anyway."

"Oh, suddenly you're not into sharing?"

My eyes widen—I think—and something shifts against me, a crushing weight on the flat of my stomach as Kieran moves up my body. His face falls dangerously close to mine, his nose almost brushing against my forehead as he breathes, "Not her. Never her."

Against my better judgment, and since I don't seem to have control over my body, a flutter ripples through me, culminating at my core and making me wish I wasn't in this catatonic state so I could actually enjoy what's happening.

Moving back down, Kieran settles beside my calves and spreads my legs as far apart as they can get with my pants stuck at my knees, and I watch his fingers draw light circles on the inside of one thigh, feeling my pulse at my throat and in my pussy, beating in time with the stuttered breaths rushing from my nostrils.

He watches me, amusement dancing in his eyes, and I want to wriggle out from beneath him and his lust. Away from his sins, the skeletons hidden in his closet, and the stolen innocence on his hands.

Hands. Focusing on his right as it pinches my skin between two fingers, I notice the cracked flesh; it's rubbed red and completely raw, lined with bloody cuts and rough against me.

Catching sight of where my gaze has settled, he continues his ascent, bringing the tip of one finger to the edge of my pussy, stroking lightly at the bottom of my lips. I can't see his hand anymore, but it doesn't erase the image of his broken flesh from my mind.

Even with my brain in its current state.

Because those hands look familiar—like the hands of a guilty conscience.

A tormented soul.

When he cocks an eyebrow, a silent question, my mouth falls open again. "*Bones*. In your closet."

"Ah, yes, tell me what you think you saw, kitten." He swipes up my seam, his fingernail ghosting against my most sensitive flesh, and my insides curl into the gesture, twitching and twisting into the pleasure it brings.

It should hurt, should make me uncomfortable, but there's a power in his movement. A hunger in his eyes, something I've been desperate for my whole life.

And all I ever wanted was for someone to give it freely, without me having to beg for it first.

"Why do you have that stuff in your closet?" I whisper, unable to project my voice any louder. I'm still floating, one foot in the room and the other somewhere in space, searching for a way back. The question repeats in my mind over and over, all I can concentrate on other than the feeling of his hands on me.

"Why were *you* in my closet?"

I open my mouth, shaking my head, and feel a sharp prick at my entrance as he swirls around, dipping the tip of his finger inside. Clenching at nothing, a wave of darkness floods my mind, trying to pull me under, and I'm struggling to stay afloat.

"Ah, ah. Don't lie to me."

"I'm not—"

He shifts, shoving inside me in a single, harsh thrust; I can almost feel him in my throat. "Who sent you here?"

"No one." My chest heaves, my brain on the verge of blacking out entirely, as a pang of desire builds where he strokes. "I came on my own."

Bringing his other hand between my thighs, I watch as he strums over my clit with his free thumb, making my hips buck off the bed as sensation returns to my extremities. But it's not a controllable sensation—in fact, I'm pretty sure the only one in control of my body is Kieran.

Swallowing, he adds three more fingers, eyes glued to the movement. The stretch is oddly glorious—painful but exciting. And even though we're going from zero to a hundred without even so much as a kiss, I can't stifle the moan that rips from my throat as he stuffs his fist as far inside me as it'll go, the thumb on his opposite hand still moving in lazy circles.

I feel full, a fuzziness throbbing in my belly, and stars twinkle across my vision like I'm staring at the naked night sky.

Kal, still standing off to the side but turned away from the bed, is completely forgotten. I toss my head into the pillow beneath me as Kieran increases the speed of his pumps; they turn angry, punishing, and the look in his eyes sets me off.

The way those green irises flare, pupils dilating as he works me, scraping against my inner walls and pressing into that sweet spot with his knuckles, tells me he's on the edge of control. That he's slipping, losing the civilized part of him that keeps him from hurting me.

From taking me.

My lips part, my pussy fluttering around his hand as

lightning zips through my body, setting every nerve ending on fire. Pain mixes with pleasure as a blinding hunger powers through me, tunneling from my toes to the top of my spine.

I undulate completely when he pinches my clit, making my entire body convulse with the euphoric force. My heart spasms with the come-down, and I lie there, still unable to do anything but *feel* as he continues thrusting into me.

"Fuck, you're beautiful when you come." He pistons his wrist, slowing his speed but upping the vigor, almost like he's trying to hurt me. My core clenches around him, and he groans, shifting his weight so he's on top of me again. "Christ, kitten, you're tight. Keep doing that and I might have to fuck you before you've recovered."

"You can't—"

"I could," he interrupts, yanking his hand from me just as I'm nearing the edge of another release, leaving me empty and aching. I whimper as he brings his fingers to his lips, his tongue darting out and gliding along each one, licking my obvious arousal off him. "If Kal weren't here. I don't want him seeing me fill you with my cum, though. Don't want him to see how my dirty girl gets off on that shit."

Kal scoffs, the sound soft and almost inaudible.

My heart swells, my stomach lurching into my throat at the image of him taking me raw and spilling inside me. It's such a primal, animalistic fantasy, and it makes my head swim and toes flex with renewed desire.

"And I would, you know. Stuff that tight little cunt so full that when I finished, I'd leak out of your fucking mouth." He grins, releasing his index finger with a loud, succulent pop, and extends his arm down to me, brushing against my own lips with the same hand. "Open, baby. Taste how bittersweet those lies make you."

The figure in front of me morphs again as I try to press my lips together, the edges of his skin zigzagging against the pulsating walls behind him. I fight him—fight the thick darkness towering over me, threatening to drag me by my ankles to hell—and then everything's blurring, webbing together in an impossible gradient of color, exploding behind my eyelids just as he breaches my mouth.

I'm relaunched into the stratosphere, staring down at my body—alone in the cottage bedroom, leggings up and untouched around my waist, eyes hazy and unfocused, body numb and vacant.

As if he never burned me in the first place.

11

KIERAN

KAL SLAMS THE FRONT DOOR, dragging a hand through his obsidian hair, tugging on the ends as he paces the porch. Relaxing into my chair, a green portable folding contraption I dug out from the crawlspace, I take a swig of my beer, watching him.

He stops after a pregnant silence, turning and placing his hands on his hips. The trench coat he has on makes him look an entire foot taller than me rather than two inches, and it seems to glow against his golden skin. "You know she thinks you're in there, right?"

"What?"

"She's having a goddamn hallucination. Eyes constantly flickering back and forth, completely unfocused, trying her best to move her body around. I'm hearing half of an entire conversation she thinks she's having, but she has no idea that she's in there alone and unable to move a muscle other than her mouth." He frowns, his stare hard. Livid. "This is fucked, even for you."

Regret pulls the tendons in my chest tight, pain coursing

through them, but I ignore it. Stamp it down and shove it in with the weight of my other mistakes. Digging the heels of my boots into the soft dirt beneath me, I shrug, feigning nonchalance. "How an intruder reacts to a drug, my *defense*, is not my problem."

"She's half your size, kid. All you had to do was open the closet and show her you knew she was there. Hell, you could've easily overpowered her and just tied her to the bed." Crossing his arms over his chest, he glares at me. "As a medical professional, I can't—and don't—condone this kind of shit."

I almost snort. Some professional. "But you condone standard torture and murder. Good to know where you draw the line, I guess."

"That's *work*, Kieran. Where do *you* draw the line?"

I swallow, the knot in my throat smarting as saliva glides over it. In all the years I've known Kal Anderson—which, admittedly, aren't actually *that* many—I've never seen him get this worked up over anything.

He's a stoic, unfeeling man—the man who taught me which ribs to drive a knife between to achieve the quickest hemorrhage, and how to gradually remove pieces of flesh from a person, interspersing each cut by pouring salt in the open, bloody wound before severing the head from their body.

This is the man they call Doctor Death—who some avoid even glancing at, afraid that a fraction of his attention might doom them for eternity.

My brother, though active in organized crime much longer than me, taught me next to nothing. Kal was the mentor guiding me through every hit, every disposal, every new demon acquired.

The man does this for a living—the real living, not the clinical doctor front he puts up. I know he keeps his medical license so he can volunteer his time around the country, but he's a part of Ricci Inc., the criminal organization leading the Montaltos from Boston. Kal's sudden moral compass gives me whiplash.

I grip my beer bottle and point it at him. "You're the one who gave me the Ketamine."

His dark brown eyes narrow. "And you know exactly why I did that. Try again."

Holding the bottle between my thighs, I hold up my hands, palms out. "Look, I don't know what you want me to say. I wasn't thinking. Juliet Harrison gets under my fucking skin, and it's impossible for me to be rational around her."

"Let her go, then."

I blink, gripping the neck of my bottle until my knuckles whiten in protest. "What? Why?"

"If she messes with your head, you need to stay away from her." He glances away, his throat bobbing as he stares out over the horizon; the sun sets slowly over Lake Koselomal, a watercolor of pinks, oranges, and blues, stealing his attention for several beats.

Kal isn't the kind of guy to stop and admire the sunset. I can't help wondering what North Carolina did to him. If that's even where he was.

It's not like anyone really knows anything about him or tries to verify anything he says or does. We just know he's a fantastic killer, and somehow an even better healer... but only when he wants to be. That's why the people around town pretend they don't know the rumors about his body count, or only whisper when he's not around.

He's broken glass, all cut edges and a smooth top

surface; a man born without a soul, unbothered by the fact that I sold mine. The only non-relative that doesn't fear me.

Except Juliet.

After Murphy's death, Kal took me under his wing but seems to have forgotten to impart the most important lesson of all—how to deal with our actions. The weight of my sins is a constant burden, changing me physically and deteriorating my mind, but Kal seems to be in perfect condition despite being some years older than me.

A pang of jealousy bubbles up inside me, but I tamp it down, scaling back. Just because I can't see his demons doesn't mean they aren't there waiting for him to slip up, so they can take over.

Just like mine.

"I'm not letting her leave here," I say finally.

There's no way I can just forget her.

"You're gonna kidnap a *capo's* sister-in-law? This isn't New York; we're in King's Trace, Maine, and you're gonna reignite some petty rivalry because she broke into a house *you* didn't bother decking out with your own security system?"

"I'll just let Elia know what I'm doing."

Kal pinches the bridge of his nose, turning to give me an incredulous look. "Do that, and everything you've done over the past few years is for nothing. Your brother's death is in vain, all because you insist on a pissing match. News flash, Kieran. She's already fucking terrified of you."

His words shouldn't warm my chest, shouldn't send a perverse shock of satisfaction down my spine, but they do.

Because I want her afraid.

Need her to be.

Fear mixed with anger makes for a volatile emotional cocktail, driving people to do things they normally wouldn't.

That'll be the only way I get to have her. A temporary fix for the obsession taking over me, but maybe it'll be enough to satiate my thirst for her blood.

Kal shoves his hands in his coat pockets, the collar straining tight against his neck. "You'll want to check on her in half an hour. She's probably starting to crash, depending on how much you actually gave her."

"Are you leaving?"

"I have shit to do, shit I was *doing* when you demanded I come here. Which, by the way, I don't know when you started giving me orders, but I don't fucking like it."

Scrambling to my feet, I let the beer bottle drop to the ground; its warm, brown liquid spills out, spraying my shoes, but I ignore it. "I needed help."

"I told you what I think you should do."

"And you're gonna leave, thinking I'll listen?"

He grins out of one corner of his mouth, taking a step away from me. "Denial is common with made men."

"I'm not a made man."

"No?" He continues backing away, refusing to take his gaze off me as he approaches where his Ferrari sits at the edge of the lot beneath a roof of tree limbs. The red paint glistens, entirely out of place here in the woods.

Hell, everything about Kal's out of place for the entirety of King's Trace. No one really knows how he got here, or why he stuck around—we don't dare ask, either.

The man is an enigma, mysterious and elusive. Dangerous—probably more so than me.

Our only difference is his moral compass, apparently.

"You think you can work for the Mafia without becoming

one of them?" he asks. "Without succumbing to the depraved, luxurious lifestyle? Lay in bed long enough with dogs, you wake up with fleas, kid. Might want to check yourself for bite marks."

~

AFTER KAL LEAVES to go do whatever shit he needs to, I find myself back in the cottage bedroom, studying her. She's less catatonic than before, but now there's a rigidity in her limbs that makes me uneasy.

Like a caged animal, as I click the door shut and make my way to the nightstand, she watches me, waiting to strike. I set a bottled water and the anti-nausea pills that Kal gave me beside the pillow and perch on the edge of the mattress.

Gulping down a breath of air, she licks her lips, staring at me wearily. "What're you gonna do to me?"

Stroking my jaw with the tips of my fingers, I shake my head. "I haven't decided yet."

"I should be home by now. My sister's probably worried sick."

"You're not going anywhere."

She starts to sit up and pushes her weight into her palms, but I move closer, glaring, and she drops back until she's flat on the mattress. Fear laces her features for the briefest moment, causing a short-lived tremor to ravage her tight little body, but when she blinks, it evaporates. Wrath takes its place, basking in the quiet glow as it soaks up the sweet solitude in her heart.

I need to ask her what the hell she's doing, who brought her here, and what all she knows, but I can't stop thinking about how beautiful she looks all helpless and fragile on my bed. Too weak to move, yet aware enough at this point to know she's made a grave mistake.

She's sweaty, strands of golden hair plastered to her forehead, sapphire eyes hard as she tries to glare a hole through my body. I reach out to brush her skin clean, and she jerks her head to the side, pulling just beyond my grasp.

Agitation licks through me like an uncontained wildfire, and I shift forward, clutching her chin in my palm, forcing her neck straight so she has no choice but to look at me. "Juliet," I grind out through clenched teeth, hating and loving the heat in her icy gaze. It makes my dick twitch, even as fury swirls around my insides, spurred on by her being here and the events from earlier. "You're not in a position to fight me. Cooperate, or—"

"Or what?" she spits, trying to tear herself from my grip. Though she's likely still feeling the after-effects of the drug, it doesn't put out the storm in her gaze. "You'll kill me? Do it, see if anyone gives a shit. I certainly won't stop you."

My hand falters, cramping beneath the conviction in her words. "What the fuck?"

"What? Never had anyone beg you to end their life before? That seems unlikely, given your supposed profession."

Squinting down at her, I study the deep circles under her eyes; she blinks, her lashes fluttering against the purpled skin, and it makes my throat tight. She looks *too* haunted, too much like me.

I clear my throat, pinching her chin tighter between my thumb and forefinger. "What do you know about my profession?"

"Wouldn't you like to know."

There's a dangerous glint in her eyes, a blade she's

discovered and latched on to as her only weapon of defense against me. Unfortunately for her, it's that goddamn attitude that draws me to her in the first place.

How can someone burn so brightly, so frequently, and still strive to keep their flames hidden? To blanket them with undeserved sadness and smother them with her guilt, as if she doesn't have every right to smolder.

And how can I simultaneously want to extinguish her and keep the inferno raging?

I frown at her, trying to dislodge my wandering thoughts. "Why are you here?"

"None of your business."

"Kitten, I don't think it's anyone's business *but* mine."

"Fuck. You," she snarls, the venom in her voice still not matching the limpness of her limbs. She folds her lips together and pushes them back open with a thick *pop!* that has my dick hardening of its own accord.

The defiance is threaded into her bones, and she doesn't even realize it. Or maybe she does, and she likes riling me up as much as I like her doing it.

Shifting closer on the bed so my knee presses between her ribs and the mattress, I release her chin and ghost my middle finger over her lips; she clamps them together, as if she thinks she can keep me out. "You should be careful how you talk to murderers."

Her eyes narrow, breaths increasing in frequency as she struggles to maintain sanity. I shouldn't be teasing her like this when she's still got drugs in her system, but for some reason, I can't seem to stop.

Even though I'm angry at her presence, angry that she's here of all fucking places to accost me, I can't refrain from touching her. Can't stop the live wire of desire coursing through my veins and pumping life into my bloodstream.

Mouth dropping open, the tip of my finger grazes the inside curve of her plump bottom lip, and she speaks over it. "You should be careful, threatening people with very little will to live. That's not a war you'll win."

"Christ, so fucking dramatic, kitten. You'd get along swimmingly with my sister." My fingernail taps against a tooth as my finger slips deeper.

"I'm *not* dramatic."

"All spoiled brats are."

"I'm also not a spoiled brat."

My finger pushes in farther, hooking inside her bottom row of teeth and keeping her focused on me even as she tries to drop my gaze. "Then what are you?"

"About to bite your fucking finger off if you don't take it out of my mouth."

Heat pools at the base of my spine, climbing its way toward my brain, and I suppress the shudder trying to ripple through my body at the malice in her tone. She could cut me with her words if I gave two shits about them.

"You'd like that, wouldn't you, you sick fuck?" She grins up at me around my finger, and I can't help imagining how perfect she'd look trying to speak with my cock in her throat.

A punishment befitting her numerous crimes.

Ignoring her, I twist, retracting my index finger and shoving my thumb into the knuckle. I press the rough pad against the flat of her tongue, enjoying the thunder that flashes in her eyes as she bites down around me.

"Fuck." Her teeth hook into my skin, making me see stars for the briefest moment. Swinging my leg onto the bed, I move to straddle her waist, breaching her lips with the top of my fist. She clenches, her jaw fastened and immobile, but I stuff my knuckles in anyway. "Open, or I'll break your jaw."

She thrashes, slackening her jaw and inadvertently allowing me access. It's too tight of a fit, probably impossible, but fuck if I don't want to test her now. See how far she'll go before she breaks—see if something already broken is even capable of further destruction.

Leaning over her head, I let my mouth fall open, a thick string of spit dripping out and onto where her lips try to keep me out. It lands just below her nose, and I bend down, using the tip of my tongue to spread it lower. She growls, the sound sending a shiver across my skin.

"Careful, kitten, or I might flip you over and stuff both my fists in that tight little ass instead."

She whimpers as I try to maneuver myself inside her mouth, now aided by my saliva; her eyes widen, hips bucking and making me hard as a fucking rock. Her struggle is fuel to my own personal fire, throwing all thoughts of caution and getting answers right out the window.

My fist is huge, and her jaw only relaxes so much, even with me forcing it open. If I don't stop now, I'm actually going to hurt her.

But that's the entire point—discipline. She didn't ask for it, but that doesn't mean she doesn't want it. I can see in the way her irises flare like stormy ocean waters that she needs someone to make her submit. Break her spirit in a way that isn't meant to hurt, but to *heal.*

Like no one else has ever cared to before me.

Tears well up in her eyes as she squeals something unintelligible, and the whole situation pisses me off—the forbidden aspect presented by her brother-in-law and my general existence, plus the fact that I'm certain she's untrust-worthy now.

Pressing once more, harder than before, I roll my hips into hers, loving how her cries morph into a low moan.

Her eyebrows raise as if she's confused by the hot-and-cold act I'm giving her, so I rock into her again, ensuring my enraged cock shifts right against her core.

Yanking my fist from her mouth, I give her one single second to work her jaw back into commission before I'm moving off her, settling my ass onto the mattress, and pulling her on top of me.

Spreading her legs so they bracket my hips, I reach up and tangle my fingers in the roots of her hair, tilting her head back. She braces her hands on my shoulders, blinking hard like she can't keep up. Frozen, we stare at each other in silence for several beats.

She watches my throat work over a swallow, hunger burning in her gaze and making my stomach tighten with anticipation. Of what's coming and the danger of this woman. The uncertainty heightens my arousal, and my dick swells to a point of pain inside my jeans.

Our breaths mingle, and her chest heaves. Flattening my palm against the small of her back, I pull her closer, as if trying to erase the space between us. Her cunt lines up with my throbbing erection, and she grinds down in a slow circle, drawing a guttural sound from deep within me.

It's possessive. Animalistic and otherworldly.

And it feels so goddamn good. A way to sate the beast inside me.

Her gaze falls to my lips as she continues dry-humping me, hesitation clear among the chaotic clash of emotions in her perfect irises. "What are we doing?"

"Whatever the fuck I want, kitten." Not *we*, lest she believe she holds any power here. "Think you can keep up?"

A soft gasp escapes her as I wrap my free arm around her waist, her breasts grinding against my chest, and I use the brief loss of reality to dip my mouth to her throat. She smells so fucking delicious—like vanilla and lavender. It's alluring and hypnotic.

Gliding my nose along the smooth skin of her neck, I follow the trail with my lips, reveling in the way she shudders in my grasp.

This is exactly what I've wanted since that first day in the cemetery.

Everything else can wait.

"You *drugged* me," she whispers, her fingers reaching up to curl into my hair. She pulls at the roots like she's trying to weed a garden, and I grunt at the pressure.

"You broke into my house." *For reasons I've yet to understand.* But there's still time to find answers. To have her open up to me. For now, I want nothing more than to bury myself so deep inside her and embed myself in her soul that she's never able to sever the tie between us.

"This is insane."

Yes, yes, I am. I grin against her skin, nipping lightly and rearing my head back. Fisting her hair tighter, I slant her head and lick the tip of her nose. "All the best things are."

And when I fuse my mouth to hers, a kaleidoscope of colors bursts behind my eyelids. It's been years since I've kissed anyone, and suddenly I'm propelling off a proverbial cliff with no parachute or landing pad in sight.

12

KIERAN

JULIET SOFTENS AGAINST ME, melting like chocolate left in the sun. Her lips sear into mine, blazing a path straight through my body; a firestorm ignites on my tongue, ecstasy electrifying my nerve endings and tearing a gasp from my lungs at the contact.

My hands fly to the back of her head, fingers tunneling into her golden tresses and holding her to me. The sensual assault dizzies me, and I squeeze my eyes tight in an attempt to ward off the shock of it all.

Our flesh sizzles where we connect, sparks shooting down my spine, and she moves her head beneath my grip, deepening the kiss. She breathes a soft moan into me as her tongue slips teasingly past my lips—just the tip darting out to lash against my teeth.

A siren beckoning a sailor to chase.

To capture.

Ruin.

I growl low in my throat as my mouth pursues hers; she

tries to pull away and disentangle herself from me, but there's no chance I'm letting her go now. Not when I've finally gotten a taste of heaven.

If this is as close to paradise as a man like me gets, I'm drawing out my stay.

Cupping the back of her skull and tilting her head back even farther, I shove my tongue into her mouth, sweeping inside the wet warmth and seeking hers out. It wars with mine, a battle of wills we're both on the verge of losing.

Her hands slip from my shoulders and claw into the back of my neck, dragging me even closer. The slight bite of pain from her fingernails sends a wave of fiery arousal over me, and one of my hands drops to her waist in an attempt to steady myself.

She shifts, pushing her hips closer to mine. The delicate curve of her ass is entirely too prominent through the thin material of her leggings. I release her head, letting my palms skate down her slender back. My fingers press into the ridges of her spine on the descent, making her shiver and arch into me; she moans, the sound impossibly soft and feminine, everything a woman like Mel can never be.

Genuine and sensual. Naturally pornographic without even trying.

My hands pause at the top of the swell of her ass, and I can't stop myself from manhandling her. Hooking my thumbs in the waistband of her leggings, I don't pull away from her mouth as I begin working them down over her waist.

After a moment, when I've bared the smallest fraction of her smooth, creamy flesh, she tenses, dropping so her ass is flush with my thighs and halting me. There's a sheen of something unfamiliar—fear, lust, and confusion, the stuff she keeps hidden—reflecting in her eyes. They're wide, vulnerable, and the way she stares makes something deep within me shift, like a tectonic plate moving at the start of an earthquake.

Clearing her throat, she begins climbing off my lap, trying to readjust her pants—but I don't release the fabric, balling it in my fists and yanking her even closer.

"Don't fucking run from me," I whisper, my voice harsh even with the softened speech.

I don't miss the way she flinches or the tension that knots in her muscles beneath my touch. "I *have* to."

"Why?"

Blinking at me, she gives the slightest shake of her head, sadness overtaking her features. Her baby blues turn down, and the flushed heat of our rushed encounter drains from her delicate cheeks. "I can't be with someone like you."

Be with me? I refrain from commenting about how we're not about to ride off into the sunset and aim for the other part of her sentence. "Like me?"

"I'm not stupid, Kieran. I know all the rumors can't be false. You proved today that there's probably more truth in them than not, anyway."

"By drugging you?"

"Drugging me, leaving me here to deal with it by myself. I dreamed—" Her voice breaks, a sob catching in her throat. She coughs through it, trying to gloss over the emotion, but it tugs at something in my stomach, making me nauseous. "It doesn't matter. I don't know what I was thinking coming here. Getting involved with you. I'm really sorry I bothered you, but I don't think I can go through with this. I-I won't tell anyone about today, I swear. If you have to keep my locket as some sort of souvenir or trophy, that's... fine. My dad was fond of his prizes, too."

I put the locket away while she was unconscious, noting that she had it in her hand but somehow not admitting to myself that it was what brought her here. I'm still not convinced it was the *only* thing.

Or maybe I just don't want to believe it.

Still. The fact that she just compared me to a man I murdered—a goddamn pedophile, no less—causes an ache to flare up in my chest. It's a rapid pounding I can't shake, amplified by the disappointment she flashes at me.

But there's something else there, too—something that still looks a lot like desire. A flame she can't put out, no matter how she tries to justify letting me go.

Something begging me to fight for her.

To prove her wrong.

My fingers curl into fists, allowing her to disengage while I try to collect my thoughts.

As she slides off my lap, a possessiveness like I've never known rears up inside me, burning the edges of my already-charred heart. Instead of being normal and letting her leave, especially considering she's only just coming down off an impromptu trip, I move with her.

She isn't paying me attention when I push off the bed and move behind her; as she plants her palms on the mattress, steadying herself, I grip her shoulders and shove her belly-down onto the bed.

Her head comes up, mouth sputtering as she tries to free her hair from where it's trapped against her lips, and she thrashes as I dig my knee into her back. "What are you—"

"I feel like there's been some sort of miscommunication, sweetheart." As she squirms beneath me, I plant my other knee beside her thigh and grip her leggings in my hands again. "I don't care what you think of me, and I'm not asking for permission to fuck you. That's not the kind of guy I am. I'm *taking* your body because you already promised it to me."

Instead of pulling her pants down, I claw at the seam lining the crack of her ass and give a sharp tug in opposing directions, tearing a wide hole that has her crying out in pained, shameful pleasure. Her plump flesh comes into view, the red lace thong she has on doing nothing to hide her from me.

"Oh my *God*, asshole! These are Lululemon. You can't just—"

She cuts off on a startled gasp as I slip my index finger beneath the scrap of material covering her beautiful cunt, coating the tip in the wetness that's collected on her swollen pink lips. I stroke her center, loving how her hips buck up against me in both an attempt to get me off her and get herself off.

I can tell she wants more—can feel it as she strains into my touch.

She just doesn't want to admit that she wants it, in true brat form.

So she'll make excuses, poor comparisons, to try to turn me off. Because no one else has ever cared enough to call her on her shit. To make her *own* the attitude she tosses around like a weapon.

"What happened to taking me out on a date? Treating me like a person?"

"Bad girls don't get dates, kitten. They get fucked."

Dropping my knee to the side of her other thigh, I lean down and wrap my free hand in her hair, nails biting into her scalp as I tilt until she meets my gaze. Never pausing my strokes against her most sensitive flesh, my lips curl against the shell of her ear. "Don't even try to deny that you want this. You're *drenched*."

The flat of my index finger smooths over her clit, drawing a moan from her that moves through me like spun silk; my muscles tighten, nostrils flaring as wicked heat pools at the base of my spine, and I struggle to maintain control.

Still, she's not done fighting. "*Fear* is an aphrodisiac."

"Are you afraid, baby girl?"

Her throat works over a swallow, and I fist her hair harder; pain laces her features, but she pretends I can't see it in the strain of her gaze. "That's what you wanted, wasn't it?"

My eyes narrow, and I let her loose from my grasp with a harsh shove. Her face bounces off the bed, and before I can worry if I've given her whiplash, I push off her and drop to my knees on the floor.

She recognizes the loss and tries to scramble up, but I wrap my hands around her calves and drag her down to the edge of the mattress, pushing her thighs apart and tearing her leggings so her entire ass hangs out.

Christ, she's the most beautiful thing I've ever seen.

Leaning in, I glide my nose along the soft skin where the under curve of her cheeks meet the tops of her thighs, inhaling the enticing sweet scent that lives in her skin. Her ass arches up, trying to push me away, but my grip on her legs tightens, pressing her back in place.

"You smell like a liar," I murmur on an inhale, lining my face up with the crescent-shape of her cunt. "Keep pretending you're only turned on as a by-product of your fear, sweetheart, and I'll give you something to be afraid of."

My tongue swipes at the corner of my mouth, my dick straining painfully against the zipper of my jeans, and I edge closer, letting the tip of my nose nudge between her lips. The sweet muskiness of her arousal sends a dizzying spark through me, zapping every nerve ending in a body-wide power outage.

An image of the men before me, on their knees like this before *her*, flashes uninvited in my mind, reminding me of the things she needs to be punished for. With one hand, I sweep through her slick flesh, collecting her arousal on my skin, and the other wraps around the lace between her cheeks. A rough yank causes the fabric to tear, and she squeals as the elastic bites into her skin, dropping her face into my comforter with a grunt.

"Ready to admit anything yet? Or are you gonna continue being a fucking brat?"

Silence. I grin, knowing she isn't going to answer, anyway. The heat of her thighs scorches my forearm as I continue stroking her center, proving that she's as worked up by all of this as I am. Maybe even more so, if my girl's looking for a fight. A distraction.

My girl.

Jesus, get it the fuck together, Kieran.

"Juliet," I warn, warding off the inappropriate thoughts. "I'll give you to the count of three. One."

She rocks from side to side, stretching her hands out and gripping the edge of the bed even as she tries to free herself from my hold. But she doesn't deny me. Doesn't verbalize her resistance.

"*Two.*" Adding my middle finger to the ministrations, I swirl around her clit, feeling it pulse beneath my touch. Her body quivers, a hurricane of refused desire building up inside and readying itself for release.

"Fuck you," she grits out, fingers flexing into the bed as she tries to hold herself up.

One of my fingers breaches her tight cunt at the same time as I bring my palm down across the meat of her ass cheek, a deep-red print popping up. A strangled howl tears from her throat.

"What the fuck?" she pants, trying once again to twist away from me until I push farther inside and deliver another round of smacks, the need to brand her skin overtaking the rest of my senses. My dick jumps in my jeans, swollen to the point that it actually hurts to be crouched down like I am, but I ignore it as I lave my tongue over the ruby-colored, inflamed topography I've created.

"*Three*," I finish, shifting from one cheek to between the two, burying my face between her thighs before she even has time to suck in another garbled breath. Lapping against her velvet lips the way I imagine Adam bit into the forbidden fruit in the Garden of Eden, I can't stop the moan that escapes me as I finally taste her on my tongue.

She's sweet, like honey and sin combined, coating me as I press in deeper. My hands grasp her hips to keep her from moving up the bed. Her mewls spur me on, driving me absolutely mad, and the tightening of her thighs against my jaw has me finger-fucking her even faster; I stroke forward against her inner walls, hitting that spot that this position gives perfect access to.

"Oh, *fuck*—"

Pulling back just enough to add another finger, chin dripping, I pinch the ass cheek I haven't pinkened and blow on her skin. She flinches, her breathing becoming even more labored, and I smile despite the fact that she can't see me.

"I warned you," I note, licking her from top to bottom,

massaging in and out of her tight ring of muscle and loving how it makes her flutter around my fingers.

"You spanked me!"

"You needed it." My hand stings as I do it again, harder this time because her back talk is starting to piss me the fuck off. People don't talk to me like she does—not virtual strangers, anyway, and the fact that she does it and thinks there won't be consequences is proof that I'm being too soft.

Withdrawing my hand from her and standing at the foot of the bed, I use her calves to flip her onto her back so she's facing me. She's flushed, confusion drawing her eyebrows together, sweat slicking her skin and bringing me to the precipice of release.

"Are you serious? You're not even gonna let me finish?"

I run my palm down the front of my jeans, trying to relieve myself, but the sight of her chest heaving does little to calm my situation. "Strip." My voice is harsh, but she doesn't even bat an eye as she sits up, reaching under the hem of her shirt, and yanks it off over her head.

My perfect little slut, ripe and ready for me.

She's left in a red bralette, lacy just like the thong I tore from her body, and I gulp as my gaze rakes over her tight, petite figure. Her stomach is flat, toned, meeting the flare of her hips and rising to the gentle swell of her breasts.

I step forward, squinting as I study her; her nipples are puckered, but that's not what draws my attention at first. Pulling down the flimsy cup so it sits beneath her tit, I rub my thumb over the silver bar piercing the dusky pink peak. My dick twitches as her breath catches at my touch, and I cock my head as hers drops back, face pointing toward the ceiling.

"No one knows I have them."

That's right, give me every first you have left. Swallowing down my need as my control threatens to unravel, I yank the other cup down in a similar fashion and gently tweak the hardened buds. "Fuck, sweetheart. These are the hottest things I've ever seen."

"Don't call me that."

I pause. "Call you what?"

"Sweetheart. Baby girl. They're condescending. A way for you to distance yourself from me." Something shifts as she speaks, a heat overtaking her that makes my body feel like it's melting; she sits up straighter, sliding her ass down the bed so she can slip her thighs on either side of my legs, and her hands come up to cover mine, squeezing her tits with a force I wouldn't have thought nipple piercings would allow. "I'm not some fragile little princess, and I don't want your distance."

My throat feels tight as I stare down at where our bodies meet, my brain struggling to keep up with what's going on. I'm supposed to be punishing her, but for some reason, I'm the one who feels like he's dying.

"What should I call you?" Slipping my hands from her, I push her down by her shoulders until her back is flat against the mattress and plant my hands beside her head. Caging her in. Reminding her who's in charge.

Tugging her bottom lip between her teeth, she slides one hand down the front of my chest, fingers toying with the waistband of my pants. "Kitten. I like kitten." She pops open the button on my jeans, reaching until she feels the rock-hard skin beneath. There's a vulnerability here, something she's giving me in allowing any of this.

In playing along—I don't suspect she's ever given in before. Too used to pleasure being handed to her on a silver platter, she's never had to stop and consider that maybe what works for everyone else isn't what works for her.

I knew it that day in the alley, that something in her encounter with the firefighter was missing.

Me.

"Have you ever called anyone else that?" Her tiny palm curls around my shaft, giving me a solid pump that has my elbows buckling and my hips jerking into her.

"I've never wanted to," I admit, unable to keep the truth at bay. Unable to think about anything except getting inside her. My hands fall to her thighs as she pulls me from the confines of my jeans, her thumb swirling around the bead of precum that's collected at my tip.

It throbs in her grip, my pulse so present there that I can't feel it anywhere else.

Shifting back just long enough to discard my hoodie and wriggle from my jeans and boxers, I climb back on top of her and settle between her legs. She tilts her head as I pepper kisses along her jaw, allowing me better access, and I swear at this moment, I've never wanted anything more than to crawl inside someone, sew our souls together, and never fucking let them go.

She's so fucking pliant, and all I want is to bury myself in her, fuck her until she's one with my mattress and unable to erase my fingerprints from her skin. I slide down her chest, running my tongue over the metal adorning each nipple, and she bucks against me, fingers diving into my hair. Yanking tightly, she forces me closer; I fit as much of her tit in my mouth as I can, sucking with a vehemence that'd make a vacuum jealous.

A whimper draws my attention, and when I glance up to

see her head thrown back in pure bliss, I freeze, releasing her. "You don't come until I say you come."

Her eyes widen and then narrow, little slits of defiance that send a perverse shiver down my spine, pooling at the base. "You can't tell me what to do."

"I can, and I am."

I fist my cock, giving it a few strokes, and run it through her slit, lubricating it and making her moan. Goddamn, she looks like an angel spread out beneath me, even in her odd state of half-undress. Something about her still being partially clothed makes me even harder, and I'm nudging her wet hole before I realize it.

Pausing for a second, I raise an eyebrow. "Birth control?"

She licks her lips, reaching up to play with her piercings; I swear, I almost come on the spot. "Does it matter? You're going to do what you want, anyway."

I don't appreciate how she's making this out to be a burden I've placed on her, but whatever. We'll deal with that later.

She's not wrong, either way. Birth control or not, I know exactly where I'm coming, and I don't have any condoms here, anyway.

Lining up with her entrance, I push inside in one swift thrust, reveling in her shriek as it echoes against the walls.

Fuck.

She's incredibly tight, especially since I left her on the edge, vying for a quick release. I'm barely hanging on as it is, liquid hot hunger aching in my balls as they threaten to spill early.

Holding my breath and posture rigid for several moments, I wait for the thirst to subside slightly before pumping again, bringing my hips flush with hers. She gasps as I bottom out, bumping against her cervix. Her hands fly to my shoulders and dig in for the ride.

"Holy shit," I groan, unable to keep my feelings at bay. "This is... fuck, kitten, your cunt is divine." I pick up my pace, loving how her tits bounce in time with each thrust.

She whimpers, raising her hips to meet mine, sending jolts of pleasure through my veins the way ecstasy delivers blinding euphoria—slowly, tantalizingly, and with purpose. I struggle to swallow over the knot in my throat, brought on by her utter perfection; reaching down to where we're connected, knowing I'm not about to last and that she needs to finish first, I circle my thumb in tight little motions around her clit, paying close attention to which maneuvers have her choking in rapture.

"Harder," she moans, pulling my free hand from its position on the bed and bringing it up to her throat. On instinct, my fingers wrap around the delicate column, pressing at the sides just enough to scatter her breathing. She tightens around me, eyes glazing over, and I know she's close.

I fuck her hard, as if I'm trying to split her body in two, and she knows it. Loves it. Her cunt clamps down so tight around my cock that it almost pushes me out entirely, but I shove myself in to the hilt, nearly passing out from the grip of her inner muscles.

"I'm—oh, fuck, Kieran—"

"Come, kitten. Come so goddamn hard around my cock that both of us see stars."

"I don't know—I've never..."

My thrusts falter, and I peer down at her. "No one's ever made you come before?"

A rosy tinge paints her cheeks, and she wiggles her hips to get me to move again. "Not like this." Her fingers flex against mine on her neck, and she flutters around me. "I guess they didn't know what I needed."

An animalistic noise rips out of my chest, startling her as I begin pistoning into her again—so sudden and hard that my dick starts to feel raw. "You're goddamn right they didn't know. And no one else gets the fucking chance. This filthy little cunt is *mine*."

Tears stream down her cheeks as the headboard smacks into the wall, and I increase the pressure on her throat. "*Say it.* Give yourself to me."

Shaking her head, I watch her mouth part as her orgasm crests, but I withdraw immediately, reveling in the frustrated sound that gurgles in the back of her throat. "Say it right now."

"Fuck, okay. Yes. It's yours, Kieran. This pussy belongs to you. *Please* let me come."

Mounting her again, I bend her legs and grip beneath her knees, taking her even rougher. This angle lets me go deeper than before, and I can almost feel the air being shoved from her lungs with each brutal stroke. The bedsprings groan in protest.

"I want to make you come until you bleed and black out from the pleasure I'm giving you." My voice is barely more than a growl of desperation as sweat pours down the sides of my face and my entire body coils tight.

Nodding enthusiastically, Juliet takes everything I give her, absorbing my vile sexuality like a sponge. A wicked smile bares her teeth to me, her blue eyes glinting deviously. "Yes, *daddy*."

Even though she says it to spite me, it's that one word that, although I've never allowed anyone to call me it before, sends us both into a cataclysmic vortex of release, our bodies undulating together like we were made for each other.

She comes violently, milking me and writhing, her body like a wave controlled by the pull of the moon; pleasure ebbs through her in effortless, hedonistic spasms, crashing onto the shore and pulling me over the edge along with it.

13

JULIET

I *JUST HAD sex with a murderer.*

Kieran yanks his dick from me and drops to his forearms. His face falls into the crook of my neck as he struggles to regulate his breathing. The warmth of his skin on mine shouldn't affect me the way it does, shouldn't make my abused pussy clench as it tries to cement his cum into its walls, but *fuck me*, it does.

Pinching my eyes closed, I steel myself against the butterflies in my abdomen and block him out. Block out the guilt threatening to drag me beneath its murky waters.

I blame the fact that I've never experienced anything this intense, and certainly not with any of the numerous men I've been fucked by, but still. I should know better.

If my father could see me now, he'd make sure the shame embedded itself into my skin. Make sure I felt his disappointment like a kick to the gut, a paralyzing injury only he was ever capable of inflicting.

That familiar ache, the guilt and nostalgia coming together to weigh down on my chest, settles deep in my bones; misery clutches at my rib cage, threatening to saw it apart, and I bury my face into Kieran's shoulder without thinking as I try to push it away.

Luckily, he doesn't seem to mind the contact. One large hand comes up to cradle my head to him, and he smooths his palm over my hair—gentle strokes I wouldn't have expected from a man like him.

It soothes the saddest bits of my soul, like sunshine breaking through the cracks and lighting me up inside.

But that sunshine turns to thunder as it threads into my shoulder muscles, like a wrench tightening the tension in my stomach. There shouldn't be comfort here in this evil man's arms. I should be afraid, disgusted, yet it feels like he *gets* me.

I don't even have to open my mouth, and he hears what I'm saying.

It's a powerful feeling, being seen after a lifetime of invisibility. And it knots my body in confusing, opposing sensations.

My mind wanders to my sister, wondering how she found herself able to accept the bad in Elia. How she came to terms with his penchant for violence and the men who've suffered at his hands. Some who've suffered because of her.

Caroline. I can't even begin to imagine how worried she is. I have no idea how much time has passed since I broke into the cabin, and I'm sure that when I leave here, my face will be plastered all over town offering a reward for my swift return.

As if anyone would keep me.

An ache spreads across my forehead as Kieran plants an open-mouthed kiss on the side of my neck, causing goose bumps to spring up in his wake. He smells like sex and mint —sinfully delicious, with the slightest hint of soap.

"Turn it off." His voice is muffled, and the vibrations from its deep cadence tickle my skin.

I blink at the ceiling, my brows knitting together. "What?"

"Your brain. The intruding thoughts ruining your after-glow. I just felt your body lock up like you've realized what just happened and have started overthinking it." He pulls his head back, emerald eyes staring deep into mine like he wants to dive inside and drown in my depths. "Just enjoy the moment, kitten."

"I can't," I whisper, hating the defeat lacing my words. My throat clogs, emotion getting caught in the passage. "This was a mistake."

"No, this was a conscious decision between two sexually compatible adults. Don't let fleeting regret taint the best orgasm of your life."

His head dips to my collarbone, tongue darting out and gliding across the expanse. I suck in a deep breath as one of his hands comes up, cupping my left breast; he thrums a thumb over the silver bar in my nipple, and my back bows as electricity ebbs through me, spreading from the puckered peak to the tips of my toes.

My bralette is still in one piece, but I don't expect it to be for long.

"I really love these," he says, almost reverently, as his mouth travels lower, sucking the opposite nipple into his mouth.

Hot, liquid fire rages deep in my belly as his teeth scrape against my skin. The clink of metal against bone coupled with his wet suckling has my vision blurring, toes curling into the comforter.

He grins around me, biting harder and coaxing a low moan from my lips. "I bet you can come from this alone."

I shake my head, breathless, and he tsks, pursing his lips and sucking until it feels like my skin is being torn from my body. The pain spirals with the pleasure, a furious cyclone of conflict and lust that makes my body go numb.

I'm weightless, lost in a sea of floating ecstasy, as he pinches my other nipple, tweaking it roughly. "Come for me, kitten. Show me you can be a good girl."

So I do—as if there's nothing else in the world I've ever wanted than to be stuck under this man's command. As if I have no other choice.

My pussy clenches around nothing, my thighs straining so hard it causes a painful throb to ignite at the base of my spine, and I see stars as he continues, working me until I dissolve into a useless pile of jelly.

He flops down on the mattress beside me, breathing heavily, and I take stock of the room, unable to do anything else. The furniture is a pale oak, worn and dated, with no personal effects decorating anything. A single window on one wall is boarded up, barring most of the light from outside, though a faint warm glow peaks through the wooden slats.

The room is a blank slate—a fresh canvas whose artist is too paranoid to mark with any indications of his life.

At least, that was Luca's assessment of the rumored homicidal hermit. That Kieran holed up in his family's mansion after his brother's murder because he believed the killer would come after him, and it drove him to resign his position at Ivers International and take up a life of crime.

If his reaction to an intruder is any indication, Luca was spot-on, and I'm an idiot for coming here. For *sleeping* with him.

And we didn't even use protection.

"So. Nipple piercings." He turns his head, raking his gaze down my face. "Wouldn't have pegged you as the type."

"Shows how little you know me."

"What were they—some thinly veiled attempt at pissing off Mommy and Daddy?"

My throat burns. I've barely let myself even think about the bitch who left town right after my father's death. Haven't let myself deal with that rejection—although it was hardly shocking. After Caroline moved out, my father was the only thing keeping my mother from entering an early grave herself, and without either of them in the house to serve as a buffer between her and the child she always hated, well.

I'm only surprised she didn't leave sooner.

"Have you ever just wanted to do something for you?" I ask after a few beats of thick silence. I'm not sure where the question comes from exactly, but it slips through my fingers like water, and I can't stop it once it's out.

The piercings may have been some miniscule act of rebellion, but I mostly just did them because I wanted to. Because after my father's death, I realized that all the time I spent desperately trying to gain his attention and approval ended up being useless.

If I'd spent even half that time trying to get my own approval, maybe I wouldn't be so fucked up now. Maybe I'd like myself and not hate how guilty I feel about everything.

Kieran looks at me for several long minutes, like he's seeing inside my head. Noting where my brain has run off to.

He doesn't soften his gaze; if anything, it becomes more intense. Electrifying.

Finally, he gives a small nod. "I just did."

My stomach flips, rejecting the vulnerability in those words from this virtual stranger. This bad, terrible, handsomely terrifying stranger.

This stranger who's looking at me like he wants to kiss me again. Who I'd let kiss me again if he leaned in.

My entire body cries out in protest as I break our connection. Biting my lip, I roll to my side and sit up, pulling my knees to my chest and wrapping my arms around them as I change the subject. "So do I need to worry?"

He seems to sense the shift in tone and launches into an easy retort. "That I'm addicted to your glorious cunt? Absolutely." He chuckles, the sound rich and smooth and entirely too mesmerizing for the person it rumbles out of. A smile lights his entire face, revealing disgustingly perfect teeth, and the sight of him so relaxed and carefree pricks at something in my chest.

"No, not that." I pick at a frayed piece of the gray down comforter by my foot, pulling the strings tight between my fingers. "About diseases or something."

He blinks, and the ease from before deflates. "Excuse me?"

Gulping down over the bile that's risen in my throat, I dig my fingernails into the curve of my heel, refusing to lose my nerve. "You didn't use a condom, and I don't know where you've been."

He sits up so fast it nearly gives me whiplash, the happiness draining from his face like an unplugged bathtub. Leaning close, he sneers, a quiet fury making his eyes vibrate as they glare down at me. Like gemstones, they glitter in the overhead light, a stark contrast to their hardened nature—to the beast sitting here versus the man who just fucked me like he wanted to keep me.

"You think I'd endanger you like that?"

I don't want to tell him the truth, don't think he deserves it, but the lie dies on my tongue as he reaches up and tangles his fingers in the ends of my hair. Withering under his hard gaze, I swallow. "Yes."

He yanks, jerking me into him, and I shift backward to try to keep away. One large hand palms my jaw, and I glance down as he smooths his thumb over my bottom lip, noticing his raw, red flesh with clarity for the first time. His hands are cracked, fissures of distress lining them, bloodied in some spots and scabbed over in others.

My mouth drops while silent rage simmers in his green eyes, dangerous embers looking for something to spark on. I don't get the chance to question him. And he doesn't get the chance to lay into me because in the next second, his bedroom door flings open, banging into the wall so hard that the doorknob gets caught in the plaster.

Boyd Kelly stands in the frame, arms crossed over his broad chest, and levels his friend with a steely look. I know of him mostly due to his association with the Ivers family, but I've never really gotten a good look at him in person. He's tall—about Kieran's height—and though the two men reportedly share their stoic, private nature, Boyd's hazel eyes have an edge to them that Kieran's don't. Not even when he's actually mad.

There's something in Boyd's gaze that almost unnerves me. Something cold and angry looming permanently within that would send a shiver down my spine if my embarrassment meter wasn't already maxed out.

Kieran swears under his breath, shoving me back on the bed and covering my body with his, angling his ass toward the door even though I'm more clothed than him.

This cottage gets more action than Grand Central Station.

"Jesus, Boyd, don't you fucking knock?"

The polished man sweeps a hand down the front of his navy suit, the ghost of something I don't quite understand pulling his features taut. My gaze snags on the expanse of ink on his neck and fingers, harsh line work disappearing beneath his suit jacket.

"Get dressed," he clips, unbothered by the situation. I can't help wondering how often he's stumbled upon his best friend in a similar state. "We've got to go."

"I'm fucking busy—"

"Your father was shot."

Kieran swears again, scrambling off me and searching the room for his discarded clothing. Boyd glances at me with complete disinterest, but I cover my breasts with my forearms, anyway.

"What happened?"

"We suspect Stonemore rogues, but I don't have all the details yet. Someone shot out one of his tires when he was driving home, and then got him when he pulled over."

"Someone *shot* a prominent member of King's Trace society, and no one was around to witness it?" Kieran huffs, angrily shaking his boxers and stepping into them. "Sounds about right."

"That's why we're thinking it's mob-related." Boyd shrugs, running a hand through his curly hair. His eyes slide to me again, narrowing slightly, and I feel myself shrink back reflexively.

For some reason, the accusation settles on my shoulders.

Maybe because of my relation to Elia, or maybe because no one in this town is trustworthy.

We speak at the same time, Boyd's voice even, mine frantic.

"You don't think *she*—"

"I didn't have anything to do with—"

"Look at her again, and I'll break your fucking spine." Kieran's vicious snarl cuts us off as he zips up his jeans. "Actually, get the fuck out. Go wait in the car; I'll be there in a second."

Cocking an eyebrow and still defying his friend, Boyd glares at me as Kieran pulls on a dark green jacket. Finally, he turns on his heels and exits the doorway, leaving me alone with my monster.

Walking back to where I'm still seated on the bed, Kieran stares at me for a long beat of silence, an unreadable expression on his face. He reaches out after a moment, roving his eyes down the length of my body—it sends a sharp vibration up my thighs, making my pussy quiver in anticipation.

His fingers glide over my nipple, tugging at the piercing, and I bite back a moan at the sensation that ripples beneath his touch. "Don't you need to go?"

"Unfortunately." Closing his eyes, he cups the bottom of my tit and tips his head back toward the ceiling. "Fuck, what I wouldn't give to spend the night inside you."

My mouth dries up, my heart drumming loud in my ears. It shouldn't warm my insides so much to hear that. But I can't help it—can't help how I'm drawn to his odd warmth. The kind that burns ice cold when you touch it but smothers you with its heat somehow just by being near.

Neither hurts bad enough to keep me away.

It seems odd, especially given the circumstances. Kieran

no longer seems interested in the why behind my presence in his cottage, and I can't find myself to question what he did with my necklace.

Almost as if neither of those things matters anymore.

"Do you want me to come?"

Pun intended.

"No, sweetheart. If I take you with me, I'm gonna be tempted to fuck you in every unlocked supply closet at the hospital."

I lean into his touch, the blood humming in my body. "We could check on your father first, then slip away." I don't know why I'm arguing, but clearly, the idea of getting another mind-numbing orgasm turns my brain to mush.

"As tempting as that sounds, I'm afraid I need to limit my distractions."

"Are you gonna let me go?" I figured he'd tie me to the bed and make me wait for him to return.

"I don't have much of a choice, do I?" He sighs, releasing me and taking several steps back. Dragging his hands through his dark brown locks on a sigh, he bends and scoops a T-shirt off the floor, tossing it toward me. "Wear that home. It's not much, but it should cover your ass from wandering eyes."

Yanking it down over my head, I try not to inhale too deeply as it settles over my body, the thin white cotton soft against my heated skin. "Thanks."

Clenching his jaw, he nods once. "I'm serious, Juliet. That cunt of yours is *mine*. If I hear anyone else has had a taste or copped a feel or even *looked*, I'll burn the entirety of King's Trace to the goddamn ground."

I don't think he means it—maybe his emotions are just raw because his father's been shot, and he's channeling it into me. Still, I can't deny that his possession makes my thighs clench deliciously. "Okay."

"I'll send someone later to make sure you've vacated this place properly. And then I'll come by to collect."

"Collect what?"

"The rest of your payment." His eyes glitter, a wicked smile stretching over his face, making him look like the Big Bad Wolf. Like he'd give anything to devour me.

And because I'm the Little Red Riding Hood in this story, I just know this isn't going to end well.

I DON'T HEAR from Kieran for the rest of the week; after returning to the house and sleeping off my weird drug-and-sex hangover, I mostly mope around while Caroline complains about pregnancy, Elia ignores me, and my friends continually try to get me to go clubbing with them.

My bedroom is one of several spares Elia had, though I don't understand why he was living in the large, Victorian-style mansion before he even had a family. Still, I'm grateful the large, oblong space allows me some reprieve from the prying eyes of my surrogate parents—instead of dealing with them, I bury myself in the plush red and white sheets on the king-size upholstered bed and spend my time scrolling online marine life forums, my heart yearning for the schooling I cheated myself out of.

When I'm not doing that, I'm staring at the white walls or out one of the three large windows overlooking backyard and dreaming of Kieran's dick. Which inevitably sends me into a shame spiral where I wonder how I could've let all that happen and *still* not get my locket back.

Weak and spineless. My father's mantra, the words he branded into my skin, repeat in my head and keep me awake at night.

Selma sits on my bed a few days after my cottage encounter, propping up on her elbows, studying me with her russet eyes. I refused to go out, so they all came here. "You look weird."

Raising an eyebrow, I jerk my chin in her direction, not removing my focus from my laptop screen. "*You* look weird."

"You're not even looking at me."

Pulling myself from the UNE Marine Biology program page, I swivel in my desk chair and face her.

She blinks up at me from over her phone, silent for several beats. Then, "You had *sex!*"

My cheeks heat; Avery and I share a look, and she mutters, "Here we go," under her breath. Selma flips her off, tossing a red throw pillow in her direction, and Avery laughs.

"You're not a fucking psychic, Selma. You always think everyone's having sex just because you aren't."

She looks like she wants to respond, something poised on the tip of her tongue, but then she clamps her lips together and shifts, swinging her head in my direction. "Okay, well, if it's not sex, then why do you look so flushed?"

Groaning, I turn back to my computer and resist the urge to check my phone. I shouldn't be salivating for Kieran's call, but he did say he'd be collecting on his payment, and I'm itching to get my locket back.

Yeah, just the locket. That's it.

Exhaling, I lift a shoulder, settling on the easier topic to explain. "I think I'm gonna try to re-enroll in a marine biology program, but I'm still weighing my options."

"Have you even told your sister yet that you stopped going?" Avery asks, picking at her chipped purple fingernail polish.

"Nope. She knows I got a scholarship when I first applied, so she thinks that's taking care of expenses."

Avery snorts. "Does she know how long a bachelor's program lasts? Because I hate to break it to you, but most people have graduation plans by the time they turn twenty-two, and you're not a good enough schemer to pull *that* off."

I stick my tongue out at her. "Caroline thinks I'm doing a dual program that combines the bachelor's and master's. Some schools offer them, and they sometimes take an extra couple of semesters."

Selma purses her lips. "And why can't you just tell her you dropped out?"

A shadow passes beneath the doorframe, pausing in the hall for a moment before continuing along. I lower my voice and scoot away from my white desk near the door, angling myself closer to the bed. "I just don't want her to worry. You know how she is; it's only gotten a thousand times worse since our dad died, Mom left, and Poppy was born. She shouldn't be spending her time agonizing over my mental well-being when I'm doing just fine."

"But... you're *not* fine." Avery points a finger at my chest.

Of course I'm not. But what does telling Caroline accomplish? She's not my personal savior.

An ache flares in my chest, making my heart shrivel as I think about how I wasn't her savior, either. How, when she needed me all our lives, I didn't even know. Didn't help her once.

Some sister I am.

The external observation raises my defenses, like iron

walls shackling themselves around my heart. "And it's my prerogative not to be, isn't it?"

Avery opens her mouth to say more, but then Carter's busting through the en suite bathroom door, her hair wrapped in a towel and her blue eyes lined with thick, smudged makeup. "Okay, bitches, the air in here is extremely pessimistic. Time to stop being fucking party poopers and get dressed. We're going out."

14

JULIET

Spicy, woodsy cologne hits my nostrils before anything else, and I don't have to open my aching eyes to know Elia's standing close, probably judging me. "So. Marine Biology?"

Lifting my head from the back of the white suede couch, I glance at my brother-in-law as he flops beside me, the movement shuffling my body weight. It's the first time he's initiated a conversation since the fundraiser, and the topic makes me uneasy.

The hangover pounding between my ears doesn't help. Carter's dragged us out clubbing every night this week, making the four of us sample the hottest bars from here to Augusta, and I've never been more exhausted in my life. Last night, Selma swore off going out with us ever again.

I've only heard from Kieran twice in this time. Once, after I swallowed my pride and asked about his father—a question he redirected to the healing of my pussy. The other time, it was a picture of him, shirtless from the waist up with his fingers wrapped around the chain of my necklace, abs on delicious display. I didn't respond to that one, instead saving it in a private, hidden folder on my phone for late-night use.

Because try as I might, I can't stifle my attraction to that man. Which is why I stopped replying to him; I don't need his complications. Don't *want* them, regardless of how he makes me feel.

He's probably not the only man out there who'll see me. Maybe the others haven't been looking hard enough.

I'm sure they'll still want me after our town's most notorious psychopath put his dick in me.

Not that I would volunteer that information, but something tells me Kieran would.

"What about it?" I ask my brother-in-law.

Elia taps his dimpled chin with his index finger. "Can you tell me how many major groups of animals live in the ocean?"

Blinking, I sit up straighter, my spine stiffening. "What are—"

"Or what percent of our planet's water supply comes from the ocean?"

I groan and collapse to my side, covering my face with my hands, peeking out at him through the spaces between my fingers. He looks dapper in his typical all-black suit, the style mandatory among the Montaltos and a stark contrast to the casual attire Kieran usually wears. In fact, the only time I've seen him in a suit was the night of the fundraiser, and it's becoming harder to imagine him that dressed up again.

"Jules." Elia frowns, flicking my knee, drawing me from my thoughts. "What are you doing?"

My head throbs. "Dying. Is it not obvious?"

Rolling his eyes, he settles against the couch and

stretches an arm over the back, studying me. His gray eyes rove over my face, searching for something—what, I have no idea. They probe, unwelcome, making me squirm. "You know I get donor emails from Farmington, right? Emails that keep me updated on the ways the school likes to spend my money."

My throat tightens, closing around any words I try to muster. Apprehension swims in my veins, making everything in my body lock up as our gazes connect. I swallow, my voice hoarse when I'm finally able to speak. "I... didn't know you were a donor."

"I wasn't." He crosses one leg over his knee, resting his thick wrist on top. His suit jacket sleeve rides up, revealing a ridiculously gaudy watch that I think he only wears when he needs to intimidate someone. Because money is the greatest bit of leverage a person can have. "Until your father passed, and your mother skipped town. Caroline and I took over dependency roles, mainly for tax purposes, but that also had to do with your financial aid for school."

Fire rains down my esophagus, landing in my gut and incinerating everything in sight.

"I'm on scholarship."

"Even scholarship students fill out financial aid paperwork in case your award money doesn't cover everything." Cocking an eyebrow, he gives me a pointed look. "I don't recall helping you fill anything like that out."

"Maybe you forgot?"

A smile tugs at his lips, making him look slightly younger than his thirty-two years. For a moment, he looks more like the brother I've come to know, relaxed and at ease in his living room—closer to the man he lets himself be around my sister and his daughter—but then he blinks and it ends. His stormy eyes bore into mine, an accusation on his tongue, and I brace myself for the verbal assault.

But it doesn't come. Instead, he relaxes into the couch cushions, props his feet—clad in ridiculously expensive Italian leather—on the coffee table, and closes his eyes. Mimicking my stance.

"What're you doing?"

One eye pops open just long enough to peek at me and shuts again. "Nursing a hangover, same as you."

"I'm not—"

"Juliet. Let's limit the lies for one afternoon, shall we? If you don't deny anything, I don't have to pretend later to your sister that you're fine."

"But I *am* fine."

He's quiet for a long, long time, the only sound in the spacious living room our deep, level breathing. I tuck my head into the cushion behind me, staring up at the ceiling fan as it spins, taking my gaze around and around with it.

"It doesn't help, does it?" he says finally, his voice low. Upstairs, a door opens at the end of the hallway—Caroline checking on Poppy after her nap—and he glances back as if to make sure we're still alone. "The drinking. Our demons always come back when we recover."

Pinching my eyes closed, I let out a soft breath, trying to ignore the sadness pumping through me. The weight of his words feels like a burden on my chest, heavy and suffocating, even though I know he doesn't know exactly what he's talking about. Doesn't know how deep my darkness and misery run.

I heave a sigh as the couch shifts. His palm grips my knee, giving it a tight squeeze. "If you really want to enroll at

UNE and make it look like a seamless transfer to your sister, I'm gonna need you to do something for me."

My throat constricts as my eyes pop open. "How did you—"

"Mailers." Pulling a folded, colorful flyer from his pocket, he smooths the admissions paper on his leg and holds it out. "I can get you in for late summer if you want."

I stare at the paper, my heart thudding against my rib cage. Anxiety washes through me, my father's belief that I'd never finish my degree looping in my head and making me hesitate.

After a moment, I exhale, letting the flyer fall to the couch. "I can't. I already missed the application deadline, and I—"

Elia holds up his hand, cutting me off. "King of King's Trace, sweetheart. Not to mention married to a high-profile alumna. If you really want to go there, and you *really* want to continue majoring in marine biology, I can pull strings and have it done. Universities bend over backward for the right amount of money."

"Are you gonna tell Caroline I'm not currently a student?"

His jaw flexes as he looks me over, considering. I know that regardless of what he says, he'll still likely end up manipulating the situation so my sister finds out. It's just how he works.

But still, a wave of relief washes over me when he shakes his head, the movement so slight I almost miss it. "I won't tell her if it's that big of a deal. But there's one condition for all of this."

"Name it."

"Therapy."

My eyes bulge, and I startle. "What? You want me to see a shrink?"

"Yes." He tilts his head, his eyes growing glassy and distant. "There's nothing wrong with it, you know. Needing help. Your sister sees one twice a month. I attend with her on occasion."

"Yeah, but you guys have things only a therapist could help with." Even as I cross my arms over my chest, I know the sentiment extends to me. Can feel it in the hollowness behind my wrists, the dull, sad thump of a heart that seems to beat only when I don't want it to.

He shrugs. "We all have our ghosts, Juliet. But *you* choose to let them haunt you."

I part my lips to say that I'm not sure the black hole in my chest can be exorcised, but I press them together a moment later instead. He doesn't need to know the details. Doesn't need to know that I tried therapy before, when my mother didn't know what else to do with me and needed a place to stick me when she'd get her Botox injections.

He doesn't need to know that even paid professionals don't want to hear about me. Don't understand me. That the only person I've ever felt could see inside my soul is the greatest monster I've ever known.

So I nod, holding my hand out. "Deal. On a trial basis."

He grins, his hand enveloping mine, secrets swimming between us like all the unknown creatures in the sea— patiently waiting to be discovered, but completely at peace with the realization that they may never be.

∾

CARTER'S GRIP on my hips slips as we grind on The Bar's dance floor, our sweaty bodies trapped between dozens of others in a myriad of shapes and sizes and colors. Her leather mini skirt is slick beneath my fingertips, and the tiny sequined halter top she has on scrapes against my bare skin.

Selma sits at the chrome bar in a pair of wide plaid pants and a baggy sweater. Her long legs dangle off the stool as she watches us with a resigned expression. Avery didn't come out tonight, saying she has a shift at the diner in Stonemore she works at in the morning, so it's just us three tonight.

I don't tell Elia or Caroline that, of course, because if they knew I went with less than our agreed upon group number, they'd make me take security detail. And I'd die before letting Leo or Benito accompany me to Stonemore, where I go to forget.

A tall blonde approaches Selma, leaning against the counter and striking up a conversation; I don't miss the way her eyes seem to light up at the interaction, but there's no time to decipher the twinkle because Carter spins me around and pulls my back into her stomach, lips curling over my ear.

Music reverberates in my skeleton, alcohol driving the fluidity of my movements. When she dips a hip, I dip the opposite, and we're gliding against one another, the outside world completely forgotten.

Carter's the closest thing I have to a sister besides my actual sister, and distraction's always been her best talent outside of painting. She knows I need to get out of my head, even if she doesn't know exactly what's going on in it.

My hands come up above us, tangling in her dark hair as our bodies twist and sway to the bass bleeding from the speakers. The tight, light pink, crushed velvet minidress I have on feels silken against my flushed skin, drawing the attention of some wandering eyes around us.

An excited buzz works over my skin, part arousal from the dancing and part thrill from being watched. My stomach clenches as she slides a palm over it, then down my hip and the outside of my bare thigh.

In high school, we blurred the line between friendship and more several times. We haven't since, but right now I'm certain we're both remembering the soft slide of our skin pressing together, and the heat from every shared kiss and deviant caress.

"I think we have an audience," Carter rasps, her lips brushing the shell of my ear. Her hand comes up and grips my chin, forcing it in the direction of the back hallway.

It's dim, lit by a singular light fixture, but I'd recognize those emerald eyes anywhere. They burn bright against the strobe lights on the dance floor, envy pulsing in the air between us. My lips curl into a sickly sweet smile as I bring Carter's hand away from my chin and guide it down the length of my curves, reveling in the murderous scowl that transforms Kieran's shadowy face.

He said he didn't want to share me, but then he practically ignored me all this time, too. And I'm getting tired of letting everyone have me however they please.

We don't get to have life both ways—we either *have* cake *or* eat it, but we can't have them both. The universe doesn't work that way.

Or, at least, mine never has. I'm used to begging for even a scrap of someone else's cake.

"So let's give him a show." I wink at Carter, pressing into her.

Dressed in a suit that makes him look somehow more

devilish than usual, Kieran leans against the back wall by the office, never removing his gaze from me. Not even when Carter takes over, high on the music, and cups my breasts through my dress, or when I tilt my head back and rest it on her shoulder as we continue grinding our hips.

A part of me wonders what he's doing here, especially dressed so impeccably, but I shove the thoughts away before it can take root.

Pressure erupts in my lower belly, both at the naughty dance I'm entangled in with my best friend, and at being watched by the only man to ever turn my insides to jelly. My lips part of their own accord as he reaches up and loosens his black tie, his knuckles pulling it away from his neck, and then the office door beside him opens and he straightens, blinking out of the lusty haze he'd fallen into.

A tall, muscular man with a tattooed face frames the doorway, ushering Kieran inside, and as the door slams closed, I snap out of the daze I'm in and yank myself away from Carter.

She's so drunk, she barely even notices my absence. Shouldering my way to the bar, I reach for Selma's club soda and down what remains in her glass, trying to calm my racing nerves.

Selma cocks an eyebrow, the blonde from before long gone, and gives me a contemplative look. "What was *that*?"

"Beats the hell out of me." I slam her glass down on the counter, catching the attention of the stocky, bald bartender, and jerk my thumb over my shoulder. "Can you keep an eye on her? I'm gonna run to the bathroom."

Selma shrugs, pinching the fabric of her headscarf between two fingers. "Yeah, I guess. Although, I have to tell you, if she gets into a fight tonight, I'm leaving her ass here."

Nodding, I give her a salute and turn on my heel, pushing through the crowd to get to the back of the building. The line for the restrooms disappears down a narrow hallway, bending at the corner and ending at the bottom of a decrepit staircase.

"Oh my God, Taylor, did you *see* Kieran Ivers here tonight? Have you ever seen someone more fuckable?" A girl in leather pants leans into her friend's side at the back of the line, swaying on her feet even with the assistance.

Her friend nods, face giddy, her sparkly bronzer glittering in the shadows. "Girl, yes. And his reputation around here doesn't even matter. I'd ride his big dick and let him kill me afterward. I don't even care. I have needs too, you know."

My face scrunches at their backs, my stomach churning with misplaced jealousy. I don't have a claim on him any more than he does me, so I force myself to relax. To breathe.

"You really think his dick is big?" Leather Pants asks, eyes widening.

"For sure. You know he used to sleep with one of the reporters at *The Gazette.* The one who died? I heard him and his friend used to share her, and that—"

Removing myself from the line, I decide to find a different restroom, unwilling to subject myself to any more rumors. *You're not supposed to care, remember?*

Curse my heart and vagina for being wholly incapable of doing anything my brain asks.

Navigating slowly through the packed hall, I brace myself against the stench of body sweat and booze. My gaze snags on the stairs—years ago, during our first encounter at The Bar, a cousin of Avery's told us about a private family-style bathroom on the second floor, though that level's always been off-limits to the general public. Right now, I'm just buzzed enough to be curious.

Tiptoeing up the steps, I'm careful not to put too much weight on my heels so as not to draw attention to myself. I grip the banister when I get to the top, stopping in my tracks. Two hooded silhouettes stand at the far end of the hallway, bodies angled toward one another as they speak in a hushed foreign language.

The only words I can make out are *Kieran Ivers*, because apparently he's incredibly popular at this bar. But then they switch to English, mentioning something about the culprit behind the shooting of Craig Ivers. I still have no clue what condition the patriarch of the Ivers family is in, and something angry ignites in my chest at the realization, followed quickly by white-hot rage over the fact that I even *care* that I don't know.

It's not like I have any right. Kieran doesn't owe me anything, really. We barely even know each other, and sex certainly doesn't make a relationship.

I wouldn't let him in if the situation were reversed.

The two figures at the end of the hall repeat the Ivers surname over and over, their tone hostile, and it makes the hair stand on the back of my neck—I have no idea what exactly Kieran's involved in, but if this is Mafia stuff, I *know* I can't be spotted.

I might not technically be a Montalto, but I'm still potential collateral. That's why I'm not supposed to go out alone.

I don't want to put Caroline in that position—one where she'd have to choose and sacrifice to secure my safety. Don't want her to worry about me.

Besides, what the fuck do I care about Kieran or his family for?

These people are nothing to me except a stain on the town I live in and a pain in my ass.

Moving my foot back down onto the step just behind me, I start my descent back into the crowd below, but then a hand is snaking around my waist at the same time another clamps down over my mouth, shoving me all the way upstairs. The two men whirl in my direction, cursing in their native tongue as fingers dig into my hip, bruising me.

My legs flail as my assailant pushes me closer toward the men, and for a split second, sick hope blooms in my chest that maybe Kieran came for me after all, that he's about to save me from this disaster I've thrown myself into.

As I'm rammed into the wall at the end of the hall, my lip connecting with the plaster and splitting, I realize what a pipe dream that is.

There are no saviors in reality.

Just monsters with different masks.

They pry my arms behind my back, securing my wrists together above my ass as my assailant fits his entire body into mine. I will tears away as pressure builds behind my eyes, unwilling to make things worse for myself, remembering how Caroline said her despair only seemed to egg our father on when he beat her.

"Montalto," one guy spits, his saliva spraying my cheek.

I almost retch.

A shiver skates along my spine as I struggle, realizing how deeply fucked I am if we're as secluded from the rest of the club as I think we are. I could maybe fight off one of them, have gotten used to kneeing guys in the balls for getting too handsy with me, but *three* of them is probably not going to happen.

"Please," I slur, the alcohol in my blood trying to catch

up with my situation, slowing my movements. Delaying them. I think one of the men mutters something about a "spy," and I latch on to the word, trying to appeal to their logic. "No, no! I'm not a spy. I was just looking for a bathroom. Please, let me go—my friends are waiting for me."

The man at my back barks something to his cohorts, and I hate that I can't even see what any of them look like; I try to turn my head as the other two scurry off, but their hoods are drawn too tight and then there's a fist twisting in my hair, forcing my face into the wall.

Metallic liquid blooms in my mouth as I suck on my lip, trying to add some reprieve between me and the space I'm losing. I swallow over it, hating how it warms my stomach, and try again. "*Please*, I won't tell anyone about this. Just let me go."

I hate that I have to beg for a shred of decency. Hate that even as the words fumble past my lips, I know I won't receive any.

He grunts something unintelligible, and I feel his fingers glide along my spine, to the edge of my dress. They graze the hem, the back of my thigh, and I bite back a scream, trying not to make things worse.

"Beautiful," I hear him say, and dread swells inside me, an expanding canyon of blackness I want to swallow me whole.

Panic takes siege of my insides, like a tornado threatening everything in its path, and instead of it driving the fight within me, instead of using my fear to kick and claw my way out of this mess, it takes over.

Paralyzes me.

Locks my soul inside a tight little cage and tosses the key.

Weak and spineless, indeed.

I shrivel into myself as this vile man reaches around, hiking his hand up my skirt and playing with the band of my thong. He sweeps his fingers over my sensitive flesh, his breath and weight heavy against my back as he strokes and violates me. All I can do is close my eyes as I have so many times before and pray it's over quickly.

With men like this, it always is. Even if it seems to drag on for centuries, leaving you feeling like you've lived a thousand lifetimes, each one of them worse than the last.

I'm supposed to expect it, I think. That's what my parents always said—that one day my lifestyle would catch up with me. I suppose drunken trysts and revenge porn weren't enough for the universe.

Maybe this is my punishment for my encounter with Kieran. A soul for a soul, so to speak.

The stranger's arousal presses into my backside, and I clench my jaw, trying to imagine I'm not here at all. That I'm a kid again, learning to bake a cake alongside my sister, and not being molested in a dirty club.

The man whispers something into my ear, and I lean as far away as I can get with him holding me in place. One hand leaves me, and I hear the faint release of a zipper. My muscles tense, my body going rigid when I feel the head of his dick prod against my skin.

I squeeze my eyes tighter, trying to keep him off, and he cracks my head against the wall, shouting something that sounds like a curse; my skull bounces against the surface, stars dancing in my vision, and I think I black out for the slightest second.

Bile rises in my throat as he pushes his hips forward, smushing me and fitting himself between my legs again. But before he has a chance to assault me further, I hear the faintest popping sound, feel his hands strain for a moment and then go limp around me, and find myself covered in a hot, thick liquid.

His body drops, releasing me, and I spin on my heels to see what the fuck just happened.

Kieran stands less than a foot away with a pistol in hand, blood spatter covering the lower half of his face and decorating the collar of his suit. When I glance down and realize I'm also covered in fluid and brain matter, I can't stomp down the vomit.

It pulses up and through my throat, and I double over, finishing on top of the corpse at my feet.

15

KIERAN

I'VE NEVER WANTED to believe myself an inherently violent man—that's a brand that, no matter how far into the darkness I delve, I've always liked to think passed me by. A curse on the Ivers men that somehow skipped my birth.

Yet, deep down, I know the truth. That there's a very thin barrier between my sanity and the bloodlust. The thirst for another's agony, and the desire to fold their pain into some sort of offering for the evil I sold my soul to.

As Juliet empties the contents of her stomach onto the lifeless body of a man who was dead the second he laid eyes on her, malice spikes inside me and pulls each muscle tight, unrelenting in its hold. My chest heaves as I struggle not to bend and disembowel the fucker right in front of her, figuring she's already seen enough tonight.

Pulling my phone from my suit pocket, I send Finn and Boyd a quick text, letting them know what's going on and that I need a cleanup crew, stat. They're still downstairs in the middle of a meeting, but Boyd replies with a simple thumbs up emoji immediately.

I tuck the dirty gun into the holster around my waist, watching as Juliet straightens, wiping her mouth.

Reaching out, I brush her bare shoulder, fully aware of the tremor in my hand and how I resemble my mother in this instance. It's a startling contrast, the soft woman before me and the one at home, tainted by a background of brutality.

She recoils, fueling my irritation.

"They mentioned you. And your father. I wasn't trying to get involved. I was looking for another bathroom, but when I tried to leave, I guess they saw me." She sniffles, and my entire body stiffens at her words, locking in on the fact that she said they mentioned me.

As if they were predators stalking the club, waiting for someone to accost—as if they knew she would be important to me.

"What'd they say about me?" I ask, eyes narrowing. Fear surges through me, agitating my already on-alert nerves, and I'm more suspicious of her now than ever.

Not necessarily because I think she has anything to do with the person who shot my father, but the fact that we don't have a suspect and I don't particularly trust her family doesn't bode well. The Montaltos are shady, and I wouldn't put it past Elia to send his siren of a sister-in-law to seduce me, just so he could take me out once and for all.

Perhaps this entire thing is a ruse meant to trap me. To get me to lower my guard so they can attack and get rid of me.

The way they tried to get rid of my brother.

It's irrational, I know, but I can't stop the thoughts as they root inside my mind. Can't stop them from barreling out of me, paranoia lighting a fire I've been keeping hidden in the shadows of my heart since Murphy's death. I've always known they'd come looking, demand the flash drives, the evidence. *What if the Montaltos are in on it?*

"Who is this man, Juliet?" I demand, kicking at his lifeless body. "And what were they saying about me?"

She straightens, wiping her mouth with the back of her hand and glaring at me, stepping back out of my reach. "I don't *know*."

Her voice cracks, nearly unraveling my resolve—but instead of going to her and sweeping her into my arms the way my heart wishes, I'm reminded of the danger and it sends a jolt of angry electricity through me, renewing the vibrations rattling my bones.

She glances at the body, then up at me, eyes shimmering with unshed tears. "How could you..."

My cruelty centers on her without another source to funnel it into. I latch onto it, unsure of how else to process the situation. Anger and jealousy boil over, propelling my tongue. "How could I *what*, Juliet? Save you? You're welcome, you ungrateful little brat."

Her mouth falls open, her back connecting with the wall as I advance on her. I stop a few inches away, not quite touching, but still close enough that I can smell the fruity cocktail on her breath.

"Jesus, you're drunk too? Is that what all of this was tonight, then? The show with your little friend earlier and this just now? You're just being your regular little cocktease self?"

The memory of her dancing with her brunette friend makes my dick jerk behind my slacks, but I ignore it, focusing on the issue at hand. Trying to defuse the anger inside me before I explode.

Her big blue eyes stare up at me, temptation given form, but I resist. Something isn't right here—with her. I need to find out what, before the idea of another man's hands touching her—*enjoying* her—drives me insane.

Though it may already be too late.

"Or maybe they hired you to make me jealous, enlisted your help because they know you make me a weak, possessive bastard. Was that it, baby girl? Did they think I'd still want to fuck you even after they'd had their turn?"

"What?" She blinks, swallowing hard. "Why are you... you think I *wanted* what just happened? You think I asked that guy to force me up here and grope me against my will?"

I lift a shoulder, the rest of the club a mere blip on my radar as I absorb the confused sadness pooling in her gaze. More than anything, I want to reach out and erase it from her eyes, to soak it up so she doesn't have to feel it anymore. But I don't. I *can't.* "You liked it when *I* did it."

Something cracks in her features; her face falls, misery marring the curve of her lips and the corners of her eyes. For the first time, I notice a cut on the edge of her lip where blood has dried, and a small scrape at her hairline. It feeds the hole in my heart as my pulse jumps into my throat, my stomach sinking as it capsizes from her overwhelming sadness.

My stomach sinks, and I wish I could eat my words. Swallow them down where they can't hurt her. It's immediately clear that my initial understanding of the situation was incorrect, and I'm tempted to give her my gun and tell her to make me apologize for assuming the worst.

Still, I don't. That's not the role I'm able to play here. Not while so much remains unanswered.

"Right." She shakes her head slightly, then ducks around

me and smooths her hands down over her dress, adjusting the skirt and purposely not looking at the body on the floor. His blood still stains her porcelain skin, and the sight irritates me even more. "That was the same thing, I guess. Congratulations. I'm going home now."

Cursing under my breath, my hand whips out and encircles her wrist, halting her departure. "You're not going anywhere. You really think I'm gonna let you out of my sight after tonight? That I'm letting you go ever again?"

A mix of desire and wrath flashes in her eyes as she yanks against my hold, trying to pull away and ignore the intended double entendre in my words. "I'm not going anywhere with you."

"Oh, kitten, do I really need to remind you that I don't require your cooperation? If I want you to come, you will." I raise my eyebrows, loving the light blush that creeps across her pretty cheeks, wishing I could enjoy it more—but the fucker that assaulted her still needs to be disposed of.

"What are you gonna do, Kieran? What could you possibly do that could be worse than what almost happened tonight?"

Confusion and sorrow take hold as her face crumples with her confession, and I feel torn as I watch her succumb to the fear saturating the air around her. "Oh my *God*. He—he almost—" she breaks off on a hiccup, folding her arms around her torso and withering onto the floor like a wilting flower; beautifully spent. Broken.

Dead.

"Get up," I snap, nudging her with the toe of my shoe. I don't want Boyd or Finn to see her like this. Don't want them to know there's a desolate little soul inside her, begging for someone to relieve it of its lonely, desperate ache.

An ache for love. Life.

Meaning.

Don't want them to know I see it because it's the same thing I feel inside myself.

A sob wracks through her body, shaking her like a catastrophic earthquake—unstoppable in even its smallest form. More cries fall from her lips, raspy and raw, as if they're being torn right from her chest, and she curls into a ball at my feet, struggling to catch her breath.

Her face is taut as she bawls, tears shining in the dim light above us, and it makes my throat clench and my stomach flip. They quickly transform into stuttered, wet breaths, and with every passing second, she seems to gulp in more air more frequently, until she's gasping and clawing at her neck.

I shift on my feet, wondering where the fuck my men are, watching her convulse beside a man I've just shot point-blank. A man who was about to *rape* her. Who didn't care about anything except that she's a hot piece of ass he wanted to sample for himself.

My hands curl into fists at my sides as I imagine how the rest of that scenario would've gone, the realization that a Montalto wouldn't dare touch the sister-in-law of their boss without her express permission. And maybe not even then.

The odds of her involvement with any of this, especially considering the protective nature I know Elia exudes over his family, dwindles, and with it, so does my resolve.

Boyd and Finn appear at the top of the stairs at the same time I crouch down and scoop her tiny body into my arms. Two Stonemore guards trail them, pausing at the beginning of the hall and turning to keep watch.

Jerking my head toward the bloody, almost unrecognizable heap, I set my back against the wall, facing away from the crime scene and settle Juliet in my lap as she soaks my dress shirt with her tears. Her body shakes, and she mumbles something incoherent, her grip on reality gone as she falls into what reminds me of the panic attacks Murphy used to have.

Smoothing my hand down over her hair and pressing her face into my chest, I see the questioning look Boyd gives me. I shake my head, not wanting to discuss anything except the man at our feet. He leaves for a moment and returns with a hand towel, remaining silent as I use it to clean as much of her skin as possible.

I don't even bother with mine, unwilling to disturb her further.

Finn scrubs a hand over his blond hair, tied in a bun at the nape of his neck. He lets out a string of Irish curses as he inspects the body. The shaded clover tattooed on his cheekbone dances as he grits his teeth.

"Shawn O'Connor. One of my men." He glances up, clenching his jaw. "What the fuck is going on, Ivers?"

"He had his hands on her." I speak over Juliet's head and her wails; she fists my shirt in her hands, like she can't get close enough. And despite the anxiety weighing down my bones and the anger simmering just beneath the surface of my skin, despite her trauma and how it's manifesting through her right now, I want to help her get closer. Want to keep her tucked away from the rest of the world, safe in my arms.

Threading my fingers through her hair, I massage her scalp, loving how it doesn't cause her to flinch away. It could be that she's not got a single foot in reality at the moment, but whatever it is, I take it as a small victory. Her body's immediate acquiescence to mine—proof that, defiance be damned, she already knows who owns her.

"I feel like that's your answer for everything," Boyd says, watching me with a curious expression. His gaze drops to the girl in my arms and softens before he turns and snaps on a pair of rubber gloves he pulls from his pants pocket. One of the guards comes over with a zippered black canvas bag, dropping it on the floor beside the corpse, and then returns to his post.

Finn frowns, still waiting for an answer.

"She said they mentioned my name and my father's name. I don't know anything else, but I can't believe someone working for you—or Montalto, for that matter—would try to... take someone in such a public place. Most perverts wait for complete solitude; they won't take their chances with a crowd just at the bottom of the stairs."

Juliet's sobs begin to subside as some tension drains from her body; I feel her slump into me more, the effects of adrenaline and alcohol wearing off.

"So what? These guys were waiting for you, and she wandered into an unlucky situation?"

"Seems like it."

Pinching the bridge of his disfigured nose—because the leader of the local Irish Mafia can't be without a few physical imperfections—Finn exhales a harsh breath. "Fuck. Okay. I'll get my men on it." I cock an eyebrow and he rolls his eyes. "One of my *good* men. Now, take the girl and get the hell out."

Ignoring Boyd's watchful gaze as I climb to my feet, I adjust my hold on Juliet so her knees dangle over the crook of my elbow, propping her neck on the opposite arm. We head downstairs and leave out the back door where she disappeared with that firefighter weeks ago, and I walk out onto the street to where my father's driver, Francis, is parked.

Since my father's been bedridden in the aftermath of his injury, Francis doesn't have anything else to do, so I've been letting him drive me around. Although a part of me suspects it's my father's way of keeping an eye on me, knowing this vehicle is probably bugged by now. He probably thinks I'm scouring the city trying to find the person who shot him, but in truth, I've done little since the incident aside from wonder what my beautiful brat has been up to.

Clearly, my decision to stay away for her safety was within reason. I hadn't known she'd show up here tonight, though, and hadn't planned on coming to meet with Finn until two hours ago, when he said he wanted details on my father's case.

But now I'm glad I was here.

Who knows what would have happened otherwise?

Juliet leans into me, drifting in and out of sleep, somehow relaxed in my arms. I cradle her in the back seat of the Town Car, her staggered breaths wrecking my insides.

"I'm sorry, baby. I'm sorry they hurt you," I whisper into her hair, aware she probably can't even hear me. I don't know that I want her to, anyway. "It won't happen again."

Like paranoia, violence runs in our family, and it exists in the very fiber of our being, sewn into the fabric replacing our souls. It keeps us up at night.

It's what I promise for the futures of the men who assaulted the little bird in my lap.

I don't drop Juliet off at her house, don't want to think of what might happen if she's not being constantly watched. So instead, I bring her back to the mansion and manage to carry her up to my bedroom without disturbing anyone else in the house.

Settling her in the middle of my bed, I strip off my clothes, leaving my boxers on, and climb in behind her, pulling her back flush against my stomach and hating the calm that overtakes me at her being this close.

At her being safe.

16

JULIET

"If you believe I'm leaving her here with your psychotic ass, you have another think coming."

The sound of Elia's voice, dark and curt like he's speaking through his teeth, pulls me from the slumber I've tumbled into. Blinking, my eyes dart around the unfamiliar room, trying to get accustomed to the sleek black furniture and muted earthy decor against the blanket of darkness.

It takes a moment for me to realize I must be in Kieran's room, in his family's infamous mansion—the one no one outside the family has stepped foot in, aside from maybe Boyd Kelly. I glance around, adjusting to my surroundings enough to make out a dresser across from the four-poster bed and the door beside it, where shadows dance in the light spilling beneath.

Is Elia here?

My body is on high alert, searching for the singular source of comfort I had through the night. Even in my state of shock, Kieran kept me close, wrapped in his embrace like he'd rather die than let me go.

I'd never felt safer, not even while living with one of the most protective men on the planet. And even though my brain recognizes the error of my desires, I can't deny it felt good to be cared for by someone who's willing to kill for me.

God, he killed someone right in front of me. Kieran's brazen take-charge nature followed by his domineering attitude had made me weak in the knees even before I caught sight of the blood staining his neck and pooling at our feet.

Most of the night is a blur, but I know he saw my breakdown. Know that's the only reason he brought me here instead of back home, as if he could sense that being left to defend against my sister's incessant prodding wasn't what I needed.

As if he sees more of me than he lets on.

They say the devil knows our deepest hungers, the dirty and depraved inclinations we keep stuffed away out of fear of them being misunderstood.

I'm starting to believe the infamous, anonymous "they" are right.

My arms stretch out, feeling along the satin sheets for the body I know I fell asleep curled into, but I'm alone. More memories of the night before pulse behind my vision, making me nauseous, and I sit up on a gag, trying to will away the need to vomit.

An unknown, unfamiliar man's hands, rough and calloused against my skin as he attempted to violate me; the unnatural angle his lifeless body landed on when he fell to the floor, his head missing large chunks and leaking.

Nausea catches at the base of my esophagus, and I cup my hand over my mouth to catch anything that slips up.

"There's a trash can by the nightstand if you need to puke," a sharp, feminine voice says, hurling through the room like a knife, jarring me. A shadowy figure lounges across the room on a loveseat situated beneath a massive window with thick black curtains, the light from her phone screen barely illuminating her soft features and fiery hair. "Just try to get it in the liner; if the help has to wash out another bin, they'll probably quit, and I refuse to mop the kitchen ever again."

Kieran's sister.

"The help?" I croak, trying to focus on her words and not the way my throat aches and throbs, bile collecting at the base, just waiting to be released. My lip smarts, and I raise one hand, running over a small scab at the corner of my mouth.

"Uh, yeah. That's what some people call maid services." Fiona's head cocks to one side, and I can feel her peering at me in the dark. "I'm surprised you don't know that—I thought you were rich."

Pressing a palm to my stomach in an attempt to ease the violent cramping that flares up, I shake my head. "I'm not rich."

"*Right.* Yet the man standing in the hall arguing with my brother tells me something different."

Rubbing the sleep from my eyes, I wince at the soreness radiating through my biceps at the simple gesture and ignore her comment. Outside the room, someone shouts, but I can't exactly make out what's being said. Either the language is garbled or my brain is.

My nausea subsides, simmering low in the pit of my stomach, and I drop my back to the plush mattress, reveling in the way my body sinks into it. I wish it'd pull a *Nightmare on Elm Street* and drag me inside. Spray my blood on the walls as a permanent reminder of my mundane existence.

Fiona breaks the silence. "Were you really sexually assaulted last night?"

I blink at the ceiling. "What do you mean, was I *really*? Most women don't lie about shit like that, you know."

"No, I-I know that. I just mean, *is* that what happened? Or did my brother make something up to justify making me babysit a hungover stranger he's trying to bed?"

"You say that like he's done that before."

"*Kieran* hasn't."

My mouth drops open, a response poised on the tip of my tongue, but it dies when I realize I don't actually want that statement clarified. Whatever apparitions keep her up at night are not my problem.

I have more than my own fair share.

Sleep pulls at the corners of my eyes, making them droop as Fiona switches her phone off and gets up, coming to perch on the edge of the bed. "Kieran's never brought anyone here before, you know."

My eyes close. "I didn't ask him to bring me here. I had no say in the matter."

"Doesn't change the fact that he did. Here, of all places, as if our father isn't recovering from a bullet wound in his shoulder and our mom isn't decaying in front of our very eyes." She gasps softly, turning her head toward me so I can just barely make out the gentle curve of her pixie nose. "Sorry, too much information. I have a shitty habit of over sharing with strangers. One of many, I'm afraid. Point being, our hands are kinda full here, but that didn't stop my asshole brother from assigning me to his flavor of the month."

Peeling my tongue from where it's wedged to the roof of my mouth, I force down a swallow, ignoring the burn in my chest at her words. I open my eyes again and glare at her, wondering what the hell she's doing here when she clearly doesn't want to be.

"I can see you, you know," she says. "My eyes adjust really well to the dark." The flashlight on the back of her phone shines in the next instant, illuminating the room.

"Sorry, I'm just..." I trail off, taking her in as she twirls a lock of dark red hair around her finger. She lacks the gaunt, haunted look that plagues her brother, but there's an air about her that makes me nervous. Maybe it's the slight tapping of her fingers against her thigh, methodical and practiced, in three lyrical increments. *Tap, tap, tap.*

Zeroing in on the movements, I find myself unable to concentrate on anything else until her hand freezes and slips beneath her thigh. Her knee bounces slightly, jostling me on the bed, and I hear the distinct pop of bubblegum smacking against her lips.

"Are you still feeling nauseous? Do you need a cold compress or Zofran? My mom's medicine cabinet is pretty well stocked. I could grab something from there." She lifts a shoulder, her knee pausing for a beat and then starting back up. After a few minutes, her finger joins in, and annoyance courses through me, radiating outward in waves.

The perfect hostess. Generational wealth and high society wrapped in a neat, pretty package, plagued by a need to fill every pause and silence.

If I didn't know better, I'd never be able to guess any relation to the cold, brazen man occupying most of my thoughts, and I can't help wondering what the hell made him that way.

My mother used to say that people aren't born into darkness; they're thrust *from* it, birthed into a stage of innocence. It's our inability to resist our temptations, to curse the devil instead of give in, that stains our souls with the weight of corruption.

"Humans are weak," she'd say, raising a perfectly arched brow in my direction. As if to emphasize my own vulnerabilities and the fact that she found me the weakest of all. "They think they're invincible, that nothing can touch them, and that's how sin gets in. It slithers through the cracks in our superficial armor and seeks out souls to steal."

"Don't ever think you're immune just because you think you can recognize evil before it hits. The devil is a master of disguise."

Warned me against a life of deception, yet *she left me.*

The biggest liar of all.

A woman more concerned with status and money than the children she brought into this world. Her nose always turned up at us, her judgments reserved for Caroline and me alone, as if we were the worst things about this planet.

They shouldn't, given I haven't heard from her in nearly two years, but her words ring in my ears as I sit, the silk comforter soft beneath my palms, wondering which Kieran is the real one.

The abrasive bully holding my locket hostage, or the man who *killed* for me?

Clearing my throat, I shake my head at Fiona and finally answer her. "No, I'm fine."

"Oh. Okay." Her hands fold and settle in her lap, and we sit in strained silence for several beats, listening to the muffled noises drifting in from the hall. If Elia is *here*, that means Caroline probably is as well—and that she likely knows what happened last night.

Another addition to her long list of reasons to worry about me, one I don't feel like dealing with right now. In fact, the thought of dealing with anyone at this point has me seeing red, shoving back the covers, and pushing off the mattress.

"What're you doing?" Fiona asks as I kneel and feel around on the floor for my belongings.

My fingers brush against one Louis Vuitton heel, haphazardly splayed by a bedpost, and I grope along the slick hardwood flooring for the other. "I need to go."

"But your sister—"

Pausing, I turn and point at her with the bottom of my shoe. "Look, as much as I'd love to get into it with a complete stranger about why I don't really feel like dealing with my completely overbearing sister right now, the more pressing matter to me is getting the fuck out of here. So either help me so I can get out of your hair or *stop talking*. I have a body hangover from hell, and you talk way too much."

"Jesus, fine. Where's your other shoe?"

"How should I know? Turn your flashlight on."

"But my phone's about to die."

I glare at her, blinking rapidly. "We're *in your house.* Charge it when I'm gone."

After a moment's hesitation, she turns the little light on, illuminating the corner of the room I'm crouched in; there's a gray rug on one side of me, halfway beneath the wooden, black wardrobe against the wall, an abstractly shaped marble sculpture sitting on a glass coffee table, and a chessboard turned over on the floor near the love seat, its pieces scattered about.

Fiona drops to her knees at my side, pointing her light beneath the furniture and bending to look under. "Kieran doesn't know how to play chess. Clearly. He's been trying to teach himself for years, but he gets mad when he can't beat someone and ends up throwing the game. Literally."

I smirk at the image. "Who does he play against?"

Her arm disappears below the wardrobe, her cheek meeting the hardwood as she reaches back. "Uh, he used to play with our mom, but she can't really grasp the pawns anymore. Now, I don't really know. His demons, probably."

Frowning, I reach out and run my finger along one of the glass playing pieces closest to me. A king, the most important piece in the game—the only piece without a genuine opponent. "What demons?"

She glances up at me, withdrawing her arm and pulling into an upright position. The flashlight shines under her chin, showcasing her wariness. "You're right, I do talk too much. And I don't think we're gonna find your shoe. Knowing my brother, he probably burned it or something, anyway."

Scrambling to my feet, I drop the heel in my hand. Outside, the voices get louder, more discernible now, telling me they're close. *Too close.* If I don't leave this second, I may never get the chance.

I rush to one of the large windows across the room, pushing the thick black curtains aside and unlocking it. Sliding the frame up, I feel Fiona at my back, watching me. She holds out a hand, offering my phone in her palm. "He made me keep it."

Stuffing it inside the bodice of my dress, I hike a leg over the windowsill and let it dangle; it's been a long time since I've scaled a wall, but nearly every house in King's Trace was built with decorative staccato stonework, giving teenagers endless opportunities to sneak out their windows at night. The Ivers mansion is no different, and I fit the side of my foot on the edge of the first stone, balancing myself.

"Kieran killed someone for you, didn't he?"

Fiona's voice is soft. Knowing. When I glance back at her, she crosses her arms over her chest, and I shrug. "It was self-defense, kind of."

"That doesn't make it less meaningful."

Swallowing down the verbal diarrhea that burns at the base of my throat, I blow out a breath, shifting my weight as I prepare to drop. My toes scrape against the rough surface of the wall, gripping the slight step. "It was nothing."

"Look, I know the rumors about him."

I wait for a beat, then raise my eyebrows, shifting farther out the window. My back bends as I duck beneath the pane, turning to stare at her through the glass.

Her red lips purse—in the faint moonlight, I can see she has a thin layer of makeup on, despite it being nighttime. Or early morning, rather. Her big doe eyes watch me thoughtfully. "Just... don't believe everything you hear."

My mouth parts to question her at the same time the overhead light flips on, and the bedroom door flings open. Kieran's hand on the gold knob keeps it from slamming into the wall. His blazing green eyes meet mine, and even though I recognize the fury there—despite how it turns my insides to mush—I don't waver in my decision to run.

His chiseled jaw ticks, and I notice he's still in the same crisp, bloodied suit from last night, and every bad memory comes rushing back, a dam breaking inside me. The assault, the vigilante justice, my panic attack. Being held and feeling safe in this vile man's arms.

Not hating at all how warm he made me feel.

I watch him take a step forward, and his lips curl around the word *"Don't,"* but I don't give him a chance to convince me to stay.

Taking my mother's advice and ignoring the paralyzing

pang it sends through my heart, I hoist my other leg over the windowsill and run.

THE SOUND of gravel crunching beneath tires makes goose bumps pop up on my skin like bubble wrap; I wrap my hands around my biceps, smoothing them down against the cool, dewy spring air, and stalk forward without paying the vehicle at my side any attention.

Still, I know who's there even without looking. I've been followed by her more times than I care to admit.

Caroline rolls the passenger window down, idling at my side as Benito in the driver's seat keeps pace with me. My feet protest, cramped and raw from the trek down the hill the Ivers's mansion sits on, but I don't stop.

"Juliet." Her tired voice assaults my ears, making my head swim more than it already is. Hangovers and serious conversations do not mix. "Get in the car."

"No thanks. I can walk."

"You're gonna walk all the way across town without any shoes?"

"Looks like it." I can practically hear her frown, but the car doesn't stop creeping alongside me.

There's a soft click, and then the creak of the car door as it's pushed open; Caroline climbs out, one hand pressed to her belly, a coat zipped up to her neck. She unwinds a red fleece scarf and drapes it around my bare shoulders, falling into step with me.

I didn't realize how cold it was until this moment, and instead of instinctually rejecting the garment, I reach up and pull it tighter against me.

Linking her arm through mine, we continue down the desolate street, lit by occasional street lamps and Benito's headlights. "Do you wanna talk about it?"

"No."

She sighs, slipping her hand into mine. "Selma and Carter dropped your purse off at the house, so at least your license and cash didn't get lost."

My eyes burn as I focus straight ahead, my body feeling wobbly and more empty than usual.

"Elia's gonna find the other two men who attacked you."

No part of me even wants to think of them right now. "I don't want anyone getting hurt because of a bad decision I made."

Caroline freezes, her arm strangling mine as her grip tightens impossibly, nails biting into my skin. "The decision to use the bathroom? Jules, you didn't ask to be assaulted. You know that, right?"

I nod because I'm supposed to, but the truth bubbles in the pit of my stomach, a boiling cauldron of shame threatening to scar my soul. Caroline might not believe in karma, but that doesn't mean it doesn't exist. It doesn't mean I didn't deserve what almost happened last night.

Bad things happen to bad people, and with the secrets I harbor, I'm afraid I might be the worst of all. Worse than the men who kill and torture for a living, worse than the man my father turned out to be, worse than the woman my mother is.

Because what kind of person would miss a father like the one I had, or crave the attention of a mother who never wanted her in the first place? Who would find solace in the embrace of a murderer?

So maybe this is my penance. Maybe the demons I'm plagued by manifest physically when ignored for too long.

"No one has a right to just take what they want from you without your permission." Caroline shakes her head, pulling me forward as she begins walking again.

"All right, Care, I get it."

She pauses a second time, pulling her arm from mine and putting her hands on her hips. "I don't think you do, Juliet. I feel like you think I don't pay attention to you and that I don't know you, like I haven't spent my entire life studying everything about you. Protecting you, trying to save you from yourself. *You* are your worst enemy because you don't respect yourself."

My mouth falls open, prepared to ream into her for slut shaming, but she holds her hands up, halting me. "No, I don't mean the meaningless sex. I mean the way you treat yourself as if you don't have the right to feel. You brush your pain off, even when it destroys you, like you..." She cuts off and reaches out, brushing a strand of hair from my face. I hate the tears I see brimming behind her cerulean eyes. Hate the way they claw at my heart, constricting my throat as my soul begs me to open up to her. "Like you think you deserve it."

A burn flares in my lungs as I stifle the ache behind my eyes.

"*Nobody* deserves to be treated like they're not worthy of human decency. I thought I'd done a better job of teaching you that, but it looks like our parents did a worse number on you than I realized." She tilts her head, a single tear slipping down over her cheek. "They really broke you, huh?"

I want to say no, want to lean on her strength and claim it for myself. Because despite the abuse Caroline suffered, breaking was the one thing she never did. And I never could comprehend it because I always seemed to bend to anyone's will if they just asked.

Standing here, with her trying to see into my soul, I start to feel like I'm careening off a cliff as my body dive-bombs through the air toward a fiery pit—a place to land where I'll feel nothing but the flames licking my skin, incinerating my body until I'm a heap of bones.

Bones that may break, but at least I won't have to feel through an atonement.

A reckoning.

But instead of answering, of defending *or* implicating myself, I crumple. The weight of the past twenty-four hours gets too heavy, and I sag silently into my sister's arms, letting her lead me to Benito's car so he can take us home.

Caroline's best friend, Liv Taylor, is there with a sleeping Poppy in her arms. She greets us, raking a hand through her thick black braids and handing my niece to her mother. Gripping my arms with her brown hands, Liv gives me a comforting smile, the marketing mogul more demure than I've ever seen, then excuses herself for date night with her girlfriend.

Shifting her toddler onto her hip and cradling the back of her blonde head, Caroline looks at me from her end of the upstairs hall. "You know where I am if you need me."

I nod, and she says Elia will be home soon, but I'm not really hearing her. The words move through a dense fog, slow like molasses; as she disappears inside her bedroom, I push the door to mine open and make a beeline for the shower in the en suite bathroom, not bothering to flick on the light.

Naked and situated beneath the scalding spray, I lean

against the white tile wall and let the water punish me. Let it remove the feel of a degenerate's hands on my skin at the same time it erases the scrape of a lover's before that. There's no way to separate what it eliminates, no way to only scrub one from my body.

It all goes, and it isn't until my skin starts to blister that I peel myself from the stall and wrap a towel around my body as I walk back to my room. My hand pauses over the light switch, a prickling sensation sweeping up my spine as that familiar anti-loneliness—the kind I usually feel at the cemetery—settles around me in the dark.

"You ran." That smooth, rich voice cuts through the air, making my toes curl involuntarily as it snakes over my body.

I swallow, squeezing a handful of wet hair in my hand. "Apparently, it's what I do."

Kieran's quiet, and it makes my stomach flutter in fear. Of what, I don't really know.

My finger moves to flip on the light, but he speaks before I do. "Stop."

"What?"

"Stop running. It makes it harder to save you."

A hum threads through my veins, unbidden, igniting my soul. *The perfect distraction.* So instead of turning the light on or asking what he's doing in my bed, or how he got in without Elia or my sister knowing, I let my towel drop to the floor and make my way to him.

I can only barely make out his silhouette in the moonlight spilling from the curtains; his back is against the cushioned headboard, legs outstretched, arms by his sides. His green eyes give the slightest glow, just enough for me to feel like I'm being zapped by lightning and left for dead.

It's a bad idea, letting this dangerous man comfort me, but it doesn't stop me from seeking it out, anyway.

He pulls back my down comforter as my knees hit the mattress, and I lay on my side, letting my wet hair soak the pillow beneath me, watching as he mimics my movements; he stands, discarding his own clothing, and slides in next to me.

For a moment, we just stare at each other from our halves of the bed, but then he's reaching out, his strong arms encircling me, and I can't resist the urge to burrow deeper into his skin, wishing I could just hide inside it. Bury myself alive in his body.

It's not until I'm drifting off to sleep that I note the slightest hint of a metallic scent on his collarbone, but I'm too content to care.

17

KIERAN

BLONDE HAIR CASCADES against the white pillowcase in my peripheral vision, tickling my neck as Juliet thrashes in her sleep. A horrible habit that keeps me from ever really leaving REM, but having her next to me makes the slight insomnia worth it.

Two weeks of this weird little arrangement we have; I spend my days tracking the person who shot my father, the ones who assaulted her, and taking jobs for Stonemore and myself, and then haul myself through her window when the moon is in the sky and spend the night in her bed.

I shouldn't allow myself to get this close to her, especially in my former rival's home, but there's something magnetic about her. A pull I'm incapable of resisting that keeps me coming back.

It helps that she sleeps naked.

As she tosses again, rolling to face me and crushing a pillow against the wall, my hand slips beneath the cover and over her smooth, taut porcelain skin. My palm fits perfectly into the curve of her hip, like we're the lost pieces of a jigsaw puzzle someone finally found and put together.

My fingers flex, indenting her flesh as I shift her closer to me, pulling her flush against my chest. It's how I prefer to wake her up when seven o'clock rolls around and I leave her.

Baby blue eyes peer up at me from behind hooded lashes, foggy from a fitful sleep, and she lets out a soft groan. "This is so weird."

One corner of my lips quirks, a tingle working its way over my body at the feel of her warmth pressing into me. Abandoning her hip, I slide my hand down and cup the back of her thigh, hiking it up and over my waist, fitting her pelvis into mine.

What's *weird* is that we've been doing this for weeks, and I've not been inside her even once. She lets me hold her, lets me run my tongue along every inch of her sweet flesh and drive her wild with my fingers, but anything beyond just doesn't happen. My mother would tell me to be patient, that she's been through a traumatic experience and needs to trust me before she can allow herself to be vulnerable again, but it's not *her* that stops us.

It's me.

Paranoia rages through my heart and mind like a white rapid, and I've suddenly forgotten how to swim against the current. I can't stop thinking about that day at my cottage and the night at The Bar together as if they're one singular moment in time and not separate incidents.

Can't stop imagining the grubby hands of a cock-sucking pervert molding themselves to her skin each time I remember how glorious it felt to be inside her, and it kills me. Renews the violent rage stamped on the hole where my soul used to be and reminds me of my lot in life.

Protector. Avenger.

Murderer.

Juliet presses her nose into the dip of my collarbone, and I feel her tongue dart out and swipe up as she shifts her hips, making every nerve ending in my body combust. "You're broody this morning."

"Not broody. Just thinking."

Her wet, warm mouth glides along my skin, making a slow ascent up the column of my throat. "Mm, right. Do you ever get out of your head?"

"I think I remember asking you something similar not too long ago."

She grins, her lips curling against me. The slight scrape of her teeth against my jaw makes me hiss, and my hand lashes out, fisting in her hair. Holding her still. Her smile widens, the flat of her tongue caressing where I've trapped her in short, pointed flicks.

All I can think about is how it'd feel lapping at my cock, how I'd have her lick me from my balls to the tip and then thrust inside her mouth without preamble. How it'd feel to make her choke on me.

I stiffen inside my boxers, the warmth of her pussy scorching where it connects with my hip, her tongue sending pinpricks of euphoria down my spine. She sinks her teeth into the skin just beneath my ear, and my eyes roll back in my head as if possessed.

"Juliet." My voice is higher than usual, tight and strained, as if undergoing torture.

"Hm?" she hums, dragging her teeth down and starting her descent. Shifting, she throws her other leg over me and settles down on my dick, her arousal seeping through the thin material separating us.

Gripping the bedsheets, I let out a soft moan as she rocks over me. Resistance feels futile. "I can fucking smell you, kitten."

Those mesmerizing, glassy eyes shine down at me—a startling contrast to the sad soul I've come to know within these four walls. Something has changed, although I can't really be sure *what,* because she doesn't ever want to talk.

Not that I particularly want to listen, but still. Our dynamic has shifted, turned on its axis, and I find myself struggling to keep up. We still haven't gone on the date she owes me, nor has she gotten back her locket from me.

So far, all I've done is mock, harass, and drug her. I've killed for her. It's the last bit that frightens me.

You can't keep killing for others. My father's words from the night after The Bar incident ring in my ears, and my fingers dig into her fleshy hips involuntarily. *What do you get out of it?*

I couldn't tell him about the secret satisfaction in serving the ultimate piece of justice. As longtime Mafia associates, we're not supposed to feel connected to the evil things we have to do. They're supposed to be a means to an end, a way for us to maintain power and influence in town and uphold generational wealth.

But fuck, if putting a bullet in the man who touched Juliet didn't blind me with pleasure.

"You know," she says, gently dragging her nails down the lines of my chest, over my abdomen, toying with the waist-band of my underwear. She looks so fucking angelic sitting on top of me, breasts perky and pink and proud, unabashed in her truest form. Like she trusts me, trusts that I like what I'm seeing. "I can *feel* you. If you deny me again, I might have to castrate you."

My hands snake up her sides, coming around and moving over each breast. They're delectable handfuls, their weight heavy against my palms, and I brush my thumb over the piercings, loving how it makes her shudder. "Do you think there's a reason I deny you?"

Her chin tilts up, and her eyelids grow heavy. "I'm sure there is, but it's probably a bad one."

"Or maybe it's for your safety." Rolling one nipple in my palm, I sit up slightly and lean forward, sucking the opposite one into my mouth. I lave over it, pulling it between my teeth, and press a hand into her back as it arches into me.

"Maybe you should stop being so concerned about keeping me safe and just do what feels good." On a gasp, her hands fly to my hair and tangle in the dark strands, fitting more of her tit into my mouth. I suck harder until it feels like I could yank the piercing free, and she's writhing, her pussy dripping on me.

Releasing her with a succulent pop, I trail my tongue to the other peak and repeat the process, my dick pulsing with each little whimper that falls from her mouth. *Fuck, I want her badly.*

But the evil inside me refuses to cooperate. Refuses to give in when I know she isn't ready.

Just when I think she might come from the stimulation alone, I pull back, pressing the softest kiss to the silver bar splitting her nipple. "I have to go."

Her eyebrows draw inward as she glares at me, coming down from her high. "Why do you even bother coming here if you aren't going to fuck me?"

"I *told* you why."

Those men are still out there, and I know it bothers her, though she won't admit it. We've been over it several times since I started coming, not that I think she pays any attention to my reasoning. Juliet likes pretending she's fine, and whenever I bring up what happened at The Bar or ask if she's okay, I'm encroaching on her delusions.

So she pretends I come to fuck her, and it angers her when I don't.

"Well, stop." She slides off my lap, yanking the comforter over her exposed figure. Internally, my entire body aches at the loss, at the sight of my briefs damp from her, but I ignore it. "I didn't ask you to be my bodyguard. Elia has plenty of those."

Swiping a hand down my face, I sigh and throw my legs over the side of the bed. "Okay. I'll stop coming by, then. You're right. You probably don't need the extra protection." Or the comfort.

"Whatever." She scoffs, resurrecting her defenses; a wall goes up between us, taller than I'm used to navigating. I get to my feet as she rolls onto her side away from me and pulls the covers to her chin. "I'm sure you have other girls who need your attention, anyway."

This is exactly what you wanted. The fear, the hatred, the strength in her sadness. In her emotions. Whatever shell she's concocted in the past couple of weeks just hides her secrets, and I'm fucking tired of trying to figure out the truths she keeps tucked close to her chest.

Tired of trying to figure out if she's the enemy or just a miserable girl with no one to love her the way she deserves.

Heat flashes behind my eyes, though, at her attitude, and I'm clambering back onto the bed, ripping the comforter from her body, and covering her with my own before she has a chance to suck in a breath of surprise. She opens her mouth to speak as I shove down my boxers, my dick hard as fucking steel as it springs free, but I clamp my hand down over her lips, muffling any potential protests or back talk.

"This what you want, kitten? Is this why you lash out, why you antagonize me? You want me to punish you? Fuck you until you can't breathe?" Stroking myself against her swollen lips, collecting her juices and reveling in her squirming, I line my tip up with her entrance and thrust my hips forward, burying myself to the hilt in one push.

Her answering moan and the way her eyes glaze over have me almost blowing my load, and I stay still for a moment to try to get a grip on the spiral. When it's settled and spread evenly, I shift backward and plunge right back in, pushing her thigh down until it brushes the mattress, opening her up so I can hit even deeper.

She gargles with each drive of my hips, the sound making my balls seize up. "Don't fucking move." I leave her body entirely, leaning over the bed to sweep my hand along the ground. When I feel the lacy fabric of her panties from the night before, I scoop them up and climb back on top of her.

"What are you—"

Balling the underwear in my fist, I shove them between her lips, cutting her off mid-sentence, and then take her wrists in one hand and pin them into the mattress above her head. With my other hand, I feed myself back into her wet pussy, the image of her stretching around me enough to make me dizzy. "I'm giving you exactly what you need, baby. Now shut the fuck up and take your punishment."

Her throaty moans are a fucking symphony, and I ram into her in one fluid motion, my balls slapping against the crack of her perfect little ass.

"Do you ask me shit like that just to piss me off?" I snap,

my grip on her wrists tightening as my hips piston brutally, the skin pinkening where we connect, her sensitive flesh swollen with desire. Christ, I'm the worst kind of man, but there's no turning back now. "There aren't other girls, Juliet. You really think I want pussy that isn't yours?"

There are fresh tears in her eyes as she shakes her head, her back bowing, pelvis rising to meet each thrust. My legs start to feel numb as blood rushes to my cock, but I don't let up even a little.

Her head bounces against the pillows as I fuck her so hard, my dick starts to feel like it might split in half. "Or do you ask because you want me to give you permission to fuck someone else? Huh?"

I shove the panties farther into her mouth with my free hand, fingers keeping the material lodged at the back of her throat. She gags, her breaths harsh against my knuckles, face turning red, but still I keep on. "*No one* touches you and lives. Do you hear me, kitten? Anyone even *looks* at you for too long, I'll slit their throats and bathe in their blood."

I feel the flutter of her orgasm before it wracks through her, but in the next second it's taking over, rippling through her like a tsunami. "Give it to me, baby. Show me who you belong to."

Her nails claw at the surface of my skin, and a muffled wail tears itself from her chest. She waxes and wanes around me, growing impossibly wetter, and I continue my assault all the way through.

The circulation to my dick gets cut off as she detonates, and I feel my own release pooling in my balls, sending fire through my veins as I try to stifle it. Try to prolong this.

Reaching up, I pull the underwear from her mouth, and she lets out a shocked cry at the brute force. I pick up speed, the bed creaking beneath us, just as one of her hands breaks free from my grasp, her palm connecting with the side of my face. My thrusts stutter as we blink at each other, the sting hot against my cheek, sending a sharp spike of lust down my spine.

If it were anyone else, I'd pull out and leave. Maybe even murder them for touching me like that. But the fire blazing in her eyes is so at odds with the detachment I've seen from her over the last couple of weeks that I don't mind.

Clearly, my previous approach wasn't working. This is what she needs.

I'll take whatever she shoves my way if it means she feels something.

Even if it hurts.

I release her other hand and shift so I'm on my knees, pulling her legs over my shoulders and shunting into her even deeper.

"That's fine, kitten. I fucking love your claws."

"Oh my God, Kieran—"

"Shut the fuck up and keep your hands above your head. Brats don't get to speak."

Her teeth sink into her bottom lip, her tits bouncing with the force of how hard I'm fucking her, and my grip on her thighs makes my knuckles bloom white. Sweat slicks down my spine, the scent mixing with our natural muskiness and her sweet perfume, and I start to see stars as my orgasm builds, pressure in my stomach pulling my muscles tight.

"Tell me who you belong to."

"No one."

"No, goddamnit, say it right now." I pinch one nipple hard, loving how it makes her clench around me. "Are you mine?"

She throws her head back, lost in ecstasy. "Y—yes."

"Yes, what?"

Her eyes fly open, blazing with another impending release and all the passion that's been missing this whole time. She knows exactly what I'm holding off for; I can see it in the glint that takes over, the devilish smile that lights her face. "Yes, *daddy*. I'm yours, and only yours."

I explode without another breath, white-hot electricity shooting up from my balls, and pump her full of my cum until I nearly blackout from the bliss zapping every nerve ending in my entire body. She releases with me, crying out the nickname over and over as she spasms under me, rocking her hips and milking every last drop from my tip.

Pulling out of her, I sit back on the bed and watch my semen leak down the crack of her ass; my fingers drift lazily to the sight, spreading it around her lips and stuffing it back inside. Where it belongs.

"Feel better?" I ask, raising an eyebrow as she jerks away, covering herself.

She rolls onto her side and curls her legs into her chest, smiling sloppily up at me as I stand and yank my boxers back up. "Peachy. You can go now."

Chuckling, hating myself for being so fucking weak when it comes to her, I bend and press a kiss to her forehead, pulling the comforter to her shoulders as her eyes loll closed. I sigh and get dressed in my jeans and hoodie from the night before, then push open her window and climb down the trellis, trying to ignore the protest from every part of my body.

Scanning the yard to make sure the coast is clear, I field texts from my family asking why I'm late to my father's latest checkup, as if my presence really holds any weight, and a few from Boyd with details on some security footage from The Bar. I make my way down the street the Montaltos live on, admiring the sun peeking out over Lake Koselomal, and how, if you didn't know any better, you'd never guess there's a murderer in those woods across from this row of elite homes.

You'd never guess the ghosts hidden among those trees, caught on the limbs like spiderwebs.

My Volvo sits at the very end of the street, tucked back against a wall of shrubbery on a strip of gravel typically reserved for police officers trying to hit their quota. As I approach, a dark figure I'm not at all surprised to see rounds the side; his arms cross over his chest, an expensive watch glittering in the sunlight, and I know what he's going to say before I even fully register that he's here.

"We need to talk."

"Montalto. I was seriously hoping not to see you again so soon."

Elia rolls his rain cloud eyes. "Spend less time sneaking into my house and violating my sister-in-law, and you probably wouldn't."

My tongue clicks, my arrogance as I lean against the car at his side making him stiffen. He steps away, eyeing me with a hard glare. "I'm afraid I can't do that."

"She's not some prostitute you can just use and discard, you know." He frowns. "The Harrison sisters are... in a fucking league of their own."

"Jesus, I'm not proposing to her. Just getting my dick wet and trying to keep her from spying on me." It's not the *full* truth, but with the faraway look in his eyes, I don't think he's paying me much attention, anyway. "Also, I don't fuck prostitutes. That's a Montalto staple."

His jaw tics as he snaps back and shoves his hands in his coat pockets. "You need to leave her alone."

"That sounds like a threat, Elia. I thought we'd called a truce?"

"Truces don't cover when one party fucks another's family member, dickbag. Besides, you working for me is not the same as a cease-and-desist order, which we never formalized anyway."

"Right." I rock back on my heels, nodding. "So I'm good enough to get my hands bloody for you, to save your precious Juliet from assault, but not enough for you to be civil with. Makes perfect sense. I can see why you're the unofficial king of this town. Totally diplomatic."

Taking several steps forward, he stops just a breath away; we're nearly the same height, but where I'm lean and stealthy, Elia's bulky and toned, able to throw his body weight around in more meaningful ways. Plus, I know there's a .22 strapped around his waist right now. I can see the outline of it through his dress shirt, and I don't bring weapons to sleepovers.

A stupid tactic, really, considering how easy it'd be for Juliet to kill me in my sleep. But she'd be doing the world a favor, anyway.

"Your family might have that little tech empire, but make no mistake about who you live for inside these city limits. Who cuts your checks when you bring bodies to my doorstep. Who gives you an outlet for the sick little fantasies that manifest in your twisted mind."

I smile, unable to stop it. "Are you jealous that I'm not testing those fantasies out on you? I mean, jeez, Elia, as a dad and husband now, I thought your days of experimenting would be over. But I remember the rumors about your right-hand man, Gia? Maybe—"

His hands come up, fisting my hoodie and yanking me close. "I will kill you, *cazzo*. Don't mistake my domesticity for softness. If I didn't need your help right now, I'd put a bullet through the back of your skull and gift Juliet your dick on a silver platter."

Reaching up, I grab the wrist with the expensive watch and latch my fingers around it; taking my opposite hand, I press against the thumb curled at my chest and shove him back, feeling the slightest pop at the pressure. It catches him off guard, and he drops the hold on my hoodie, staggering back a half step and swearing under his breath.

"Don't fucking touch me," I growl, brushing my chest off and straightening against the car. "Worst thing about provoking the devil is that he doesn't have anything to lose, *capo*."

He exhales harshly, his hand itching toward the gun beneath his dress shirt. I smirk, knowing the feeling.

"Do it. You know she won't forgive you."

A tic flares under his stormy eyes, the pulse of it making my skin crawl. His hand falls to his side. "You can't tell me she actually sees something in you."

I shrug. "Maybe it's more about what *I* see."

Several beats of silence pass between us, two of the most depraved men in our tiny little town. The only two with the power to make it bend to our will and bow down in our wake.

The debauched royals of King's Trace.

After a heavy sigh, Elia scrubs a hand through his black hair, adjusting his suit jacket on his shoulders. "Look, I didn't come out here to get into some sort of pissing match. I'm not interested in that shit. I want to offer my help since you're fucking around with someone important to me."

"Are you trying to make a deal with me, Elia? You know how that usually goes."

"You talk too goddamn much." He rolls his eyes and crosses his arms over his chest. "Yeah, a deal of sorts. Although you certainly stand to gain a lot more from it than I do."

I stare, waiting, on guard and untrusting.

"But I need your word. Your obedience to secrecy. *Omertà.*"

"Bless you."

He makes a face, glaring at me. "*Gesù Cristo.* No. *Omertà* —your fucking silence, asshole. We all know you went to the feds about your brother and the shit he was mixed up in. I can't risk them coming around and poking their heads in my business. I have enough on my plate trying to track shit as it is."

My palms grow slick, and I wipe them on my pant leg, ignoring the beads of sweat cropping up on my forehead. We don't *all* know that, but I suppose he's been doing his research. "I went to the feds because Murphy was in too deep, and there was no way to shut down that operation without their help."

"I don't care about the *why*. I get it. But I still need your word."

"And the fact that I kill and clean up for you on a semi-regular basis? That's not enough for you?"

"No."

Mind racing, trying to catch up with the turn this conversation has taken, I try to block out the images of the half-naked girls in dirty cages, try to stomp out the sounds of their cries and whimpers as I stalked past them looking for my brother, wondering how the fuck he'd gotten mixed up in something so evil.

Try to force away the memory of him violating their corpses, of Mel—bloodied and broken, sobbing in a heap on the concrete floor—after she'd told him no and he hadn't listened.

He became unhinged, they all said. That's what happened to Murphy. His neuro-receptors got crossed somewhere with each day he spent as a low-level crime boss, and the deviance took its toll on him.

He became chaotic. Volatile. A steaming concoction of depravity, violence, and misery wrapped in an unrelenting body—I don't think he even recognized me as the final light dimmed from his cold, green eyes.

And because he went so quietly, so quickly, all the shame and fear he'd wrought on King's Trace and Stonemore shifted to me. The real devil, the only one capable of ending his reign of terror. Of inciting another.

Years later, I'm still trying to eliminate the others. The aggressors, the colleagues, the evidence. Still trying not to wind up dead myself for sticking my nose in.

Not for Murphy's sake, but our mother's. She doesn't deserve to live with the threat of being shunned if anyone ever finds out how he hurt others. Doesn't deserve to have more than one evil spawn.

Inhaling a long breath, I nod to Elia and hold out my hand. He grasps it after a slight hesitation, giving it two solid pumps before dropping it. "All right, Montalto. You have my word. Let's go for a drive."

18

JULIET

My knee bounces, making the legs of the chair I'm seated in scrape across the floor. Caroline reaches over and puts her palm on my thigh, squeezing softly.

"It's okay to be nervous, you know."

I turn my head to look out the window, rolling my eyes. Of course, she'd think that—she's never been nervous about anything her whole life. Our father prepared her for a life of scrutiny, taught her how to handle the perception of her life under the scope of the public eye.

Although, it's possible she was nervous during the litany of abuse she endured at his hands; grooming, auctioneering, being forced to network for his political gain. Maybe the nervousness manifested itself differently in her.

A pang splinters in my chest, jagged pieces seeking my heart as the thoughts worm their way inside my brain. Almost as if they've been planted there by my father's ghost as another way to make me feel guilty when it comes to my sister.

The Stonemore County Counseling Center is a tiny white brick building that sits on the city line, half in King's Trace and half in Stonemore. Inside it's designed to make you feel cozy and comfortable, with its earth-toned walls and its slightly dated shag carpet, the abstract oil paintings on the wall, and the bookshelves lined with mental health periodicals and journals, in case you forget what you're doing here.

Clinics have always made me uneasy, but something about this one in particular has my nerves etching themselves into the fabric of my soul. My hands are clammy, balled into fists at my sides, and I can feel that familiar dread throb inside me in time to the beat of my heart.

As I stare at the iron analog clock on the wall behind the reception desk, watching each second tick by, that feeling only intensifies, and the pounding in my ears becomes all I can hear as we continue to wait.

"Shouldn't I have been seen by now?" My voice is choked, my throat tight as my words wrangle themselves free. "How long can it take to process an intake packet?"

Caroline turns the page of the *Highlights* booklet in her hands, shrugging. "We're a walk-in; those always take longer. They have to see what kind of services you're seeking, make sure you're able to pay, and find a provider who best suits your needs and personality."

The only reason I was able to be seen as a walk-in was because Caroline and Elia are already patients, and no one says no to the amount of money he shoved toward them. I suppose I should be grateful, but it's hard to ignore the butterflies in my stomach.

I don't know what I'm afraid of, exactly—that I'll be

forced to admit my inner most thoughts and bare my guilty conscience, or that I won't have to at all.

"They can't know my personality just from a piece of paper," I say. Most times, *I'm* not even sure I know myself.

"Obviously, but they can weed out the counselors who wouldn't benefit you."

My phone vibrates in my pocket, a text flashing on the screen.

Kieran: Late lunch?

I frown, my thumbs swiping over the message, debating a response. It's been over a week since he fucked me into a coma, and he's only returned once since. And when he showed up, he was back to his old self, holding me and getting me off before we fell asleep, but not letting me return the favor. Not giving me what I *really* want.

His dominance. That streak that simmers beneath the violence and the fear, the one that puts me in my place when I need it and has me begging him to own me—to push me until I break apart.

The one that makes me forget everything haunting me, if only for a moment in time.

He's walking on eggshells around me again instead, treating me like a delicate flower that'll wilt away if he plucks it and not like he's replanting me somewhere with better access to sunshine and rain. Sustenance.

And if that's the way he wants to act, putting distance between us, I'm not going to stop him.

I *can't* stop him, not when I know it's probably for the best.

Me: Can't. Doctor appt.

Kieran: Everything ok?

No, everything is most decidedly not okay. But I'm not going to tell him that. I don't even want to tell this therapist.

Me: Peachy.

Someone at reception calls my name, and I startle hearing it combined with my surname for the first time in forever. Caroline smiles up at me, encouraging, and I swallow down the knot in my throat as I get to my feet, forcing the wobble from my knees.

Kieran: Dinner then?

Making my way to where a petite woman with black hair and almond eyes stands at a white door with a keypad, I pull up my phone's keyboard as I walk, typing out my final response.

Me: I don't think that's a good idea.

Holding the button down on the side of my phone, I wait for the screen to fade and slip it inside my pocket, following the woman through the door and down a softly lit hall. She stops in front of an open door at the very end, using her elbow to erase the writing on a marker board tacked to the wall. She writes JULIET: IN PROGRESS in big block letters, recaps the marker, and gestures for me to enter.

The tiny office smells like Caroline's bakery. A large cherry wood desk sits catty-cornered on one side, an over-stuffed armchair rests on an angle in front, and a dying plant is beneath the windowsill.

"Have a seat," the woman says as she settles in behind the desk, pulling a pen and paper to the forefront of the disorganized mess of folders and papers scattered about. I flop into the armchair, feeling small inside its embrace. "What brings you to my office today, Juliet?"

WE HEAD to Care's Crazy Cakes after the appointment and I help Caroline make three different batches of scones, recounting the bare bones of the session with Dr. Zhang—who insists I call her Hana. Caroline tells me about the progress she's made at the clinic, happiness pouring from her as she mixes the batter.

Evidently, she's been seeing Hana since Poppy's birth, although back then, she was attending far more frequently than she is now. Their early meetings involved breaking down Caroline's deep-seated repressive nature, chipping away slowly at the hard exterior she'd erected as a defense mechanism against the abuse she suffered at the hands of our father.

I don't tell her that I didn't talk much today or that I don't plan on talking much at all in the future. After getting tongue-tied more than once, I'd buckled and clammed up, only offering one-word answers to each follow-up question.

What Caroline doesn't know won't hurt her, and I don't want to disappoint her more than I already have. She clearly believes in therapy, but I just don't think it's for me.

Elia meets us at the bakery not long after we've finished the scones and arranged them for display, with a large manila envelope tucked under his arm. He ducks in the kitchen as my sister pulls a three-tiered cake from an oven in the back, then returns to the storefront and settles onto the stool beside me. He slides the envelope across the counter.

I quirk an eyebrow, swiping a peach scone from the glass display case and pinching a bite off, stuffing it into my mouth. "What's that?"

"What do you think?" Without waiting for me to open it, he slides his finger beneath the seal, tearing it in one fell swoop, and shakes out the papers inside. Flyers and pamphlets fall to the counter, the UNE logo stamped on the front making my heart rate skyrocket.

The last sheet, a plain piece of printer paper with an official-looking seal, lands on top. I lean to inspect it, noting that familiar letterhead at the top. *Congratulations! On behalf of the University of New England, I am pleased to announce your admission into our summer program.*

My mouth drops, crumbs tumbling over my lips. "What the fuck?"

He pulls another smaller envelope from inside his suit jacket and hands it over, a smile splitting his face. It grows so wide that I think it might crack. "Tuition."

"Elia—"

"You held up your end of the deal, so I'm holding up mine. The semester starts in six weeks."

Opening the second envelope, I pull out the receipt, my breath catching in my throat. "This is just for one semester, though?"

One strong shoulder lifts, and he stacks the papers on the counter into a neat pile, smoothing his fingers over the edges. He slips them back into the manila envelope, then squares it in front of me. "Stick with Dr. Zhang, and I'll keep paying for school. You can't have that much left, anyway."

My heart swells as it reaches for the pride emanating from his body. I smother a grin, the weight of his words taking a moment to register. "You're bribing me?"

"I'm ensuring your future is bright. Free and uncomplicated."

"And you're just trusting me to continue with therapy? What happens if I quit?"

He squints, his gray eyes questioning, probing, trying to see through me as usual. I don't know what it is with him and my sister thinking they have x-ray vision into my soul, but I'm surprised at this point they haven't discovered I'm not as transparent as we'd all like me to be.

"I guess we'll cross that bridge if we come to it." Glancing over his shoulder to see my sister through the kitchen window, he turns back, hooking his thumb in her direction. "Register for classes tonight, and as long as you're officially enrolled somewhere in the morning, I won't tell her you flunked out of Farmington."

My hands roam the paper envelope, disbelief scattering my thoughts. "Okay." He turns to head back into the kitchen, probably to fuck his wife in the utility closet—like he thinks the people in the storefront can't hear them—but I reach out, grasping the sleeve of his Armani suit. "Thank you."

He smiles softly, and his terrifyingly handsome face transforms into something otherworldly. "You're worth it, kid. I don't take bets I can't win."

I can't stop the smile from spreading across my face, stretching my cheeks painfully as I stare at the plain envelopes in front of me. Pulling out my phone, I inform my group chat with Selma, Avery, and Carter about the new development—leaving out the therapy contingency—and pull up another number, requesting a midnight rendezvous in the spirit of forgiveness and celebration.

He shows up on time in gray sweats and a navy Yale pullover, looking ridiculously gorgeous and *normal*.

My brows hitch, and I give the sweater a pointed look. "Did you even go to college?"

Hoisting himself off the trellis, Kieran hooks a leg over the windowsill. "I did not. But my mother likes to pretend I did, and I'd do anything to make her happy, so..."

He trails off, and the dedication he has to his family makes my heart ache.

I have to remind myself as he climbs into my room, making my heart squeeze and my pulse kick up, that I need pacing when it comes to him. That the feelings blossoming inside me need time to sort themselves out and determine if they're ready for the maelstrom that is Kieran Ivers.

But it's so hard to focus on that as he stands in front of me, takeout from the only Chinese restaurant in King's Trace dangling from one hand. "I know you said dinner wasn't a good idea, but I figured if I brought takeout to you, it didn't count."

"You might be right," I breathe, trying to ignore the annoying pitter-patter of my heart, the shock against my skin as our fingers brush while trading Styrofoam containers.

We settle on top of my bedspread. He flips on the television mounted on the wall above my dresser, queuing up some nature documentary I left on pause, and settles back against my headboard.

As he tears into his egg drop soup, I push my broccoli and chicken around in my container, watching him for a few moments. I try to commit the angular planes of his face to memory, unsure of how much longer these nighttime trysts can last. It's liable to cause Elia an embolism if he ever finds out, and I don't want anyone else's suffering on my hands.

Kieran frowns, his gaze flitting to mine. "You okay?"

Nodding, I stab a piece of broccoli with my plastic fork. "Peachy."

He presses his lips together, setting his bowl on the nightstand and crossing his legs. "Do you want to talk about it?"

I shake my head, not wanting to share that I'm all talked out for the day.

His index finger taps on the bed, close to my thigh, and he exhales as it inches closer. "Everything go okay at your doctor appointment?"

"Mm-hmm," I say around a mouthful of food, my cheeks about to burst with the amount I've stuffed in them. And even though I really, truly *don't* want to talk about it, something about him seems to draw the truth from me, like a fish caught on a hook. "It, ah... it was a therapy appointment, actually."

"Therapy?"

Nodding, I drop my gaze to my tray. "Yeah, it's a stipulation from Elia. He pays for my schooling as long as I attend therapy."

"You're in school?"

"Just going back." My cheeks heat, embarrassment scorching through me for some stupid reason. "Marine biology major. I started right out of high school but withdrew because of some... personal stuff. Now, Elia says he'll pay for my return if I see a shrink."

A thoughtful look softens Kieran's features, and he nods once, pointing at me with his fork. "I think that's a good idea."

"You do?"

"Sure. Who couldn't use a little therapy?"

It's pretty much what Elia said the day he blackmailed me into going, but I can't deny it hits differently coming from someone without a forced vested interest in me. Not that Elia doesn't care about my mental well-being, but the attachment of an investment to it makes it a little more important.

With Kieran, we aren't anything official. Nothing permanent at this point. He doesn't have to accept my issues unless he wants to.

"You don't think it's weird? Telling a stranger your secrets?" I tilt my head, studying him.

"You've told me some secrets."

I haven't. Not really. But maybe, with him, I don't have to —maybe he's capable of finding them out all on his own. "Have you ever been?"

He shovels in more food, chewing for a long time. "No," he says on a swallow, "but to be fair, they'd have me committed for my secrets. Or imprisoned. And where would that leave us?"

Pushing my food away to the corner of the bed, I stretch out beside him and settle my head on a pillow. "I'd come visit you."

"Oh? Conjugal visits, eh?"

"Or the normal kind."

He watches me while he finishes his food, an unfamiliar glint flaring in his gaze that has my core tightening with need. When his plate is clean, he scoops our trays up and tosses them in the garbage, then climbs in bed with me, switching off the bedside lamp.

I can almost feel the smile crinkling the corners of his mouth as he tugs me into him and buries his face in my neck. "There's nothing wrong with it, you know," he murmurs, the sound making my skin vibrate.

"Yeah, I know. It's just... weird. A lifetime of no one wanting to listen to me, and suddenly that's all Dr. Zha—*Hana* wants. My pain, my sorrow, my joy. All of it. It's just strange."

Pulling back, he threads his fingers through my hair, lining our faces so our noses brush in the dark. "Practice on me."

My eyebrows shoot up. "What?"

"If it feels weird to tell that stuff to a stranger, practice with me first. Give me your sorrow and joy, and maybe it'll make it easier to tell her next time."

"Why..." I trail off, considering how his offer makes this thing between us feel more solid. Like an actual relationship, and I can't quite tell if the sudden spasm in my heart is a good thing or an omen. A warning of heartbreak to come.

"Because I want it," he whispers, dragging his tongue along my jaw, making me shiver. "I want everything from you."

A part of me wants to shatter the moment and ask why—what his interest in me is. We barely know each other, and this is all moving so quickly that I'm struggling to keep up.

But I don't say anything because in the next second, Kieran shifts, spreading my thighs and settling between them, beginning a trail down my throat with his mouth that has me agreeing to whatever.

If he wants everything, fine. He can have it.

I'll give myself to the devil if it means getting to feel like this.

Cherished and liquified in his arms.

It's a long time before I realize I don't even mind the compliance.

19

KIERAN

"So," Fiona says around bites of burrito, juice dripping between her fingers and down her wrist, "is no one gonna address the fact that Kieran has a girlfriend?"

Forks and mouths freeze in midair; my jaw clenches as I swallow my food, glaring at her from across the dining table. If she were closer, I'd kick her, but her decision to sit at the end opposite me, beside Boyd, now seems strategic.

My mother's eyes light up as they snap to mine, questions dancing in her gaze. "A girlfriend?"

"You're not keeping things from us again, are ya, boy?" My father chuckles, sitting back in his chair and adjusting the strap on his shoulder sling.

Setting my fork on my plate, I fold my hands together and brace them on the table, focusing on a piece of warped wood beneath the crocheted runner lining the middle. "There's nothing to address because there's no girlfriend. Fiona is terribly mistaken, I'm afraid."

Fiona clicks her tongue. "So Juliet Harrison's a free agent, then? I can tell the TA in my Intro to Psych class that he can ask her out?"

A knot forms in my throat, and my knuckles tighten around themselves; the corners of her bright-red lips twitch, the light from the chandelier making her brown eyes twinkle with deviance.

"You can tell your TA to eat a dick."

Boyd coughs into his wineglass, and my mother gasps, a tremor starting in her hands as she tries to cut the bigger leaves of lettuce in her salad bowl. It starts in her thumb as it rolls against her index finger, dislodging the utensils.

Lately, stress has been a major trigger for her spasms, and with my father's bullet wound and the hushed, general concern for our family's safety, she's been under more than usual. She doesn't even retain what exactly is stressing her out most of the time, but the agitation remains like a tumor, growing and crippling her further.

My gaze latches on to her hand, the tic in my jaw intensifying as she points a wobbly finger in my direction. "Kieran Ivers. If you've not laid a claim to this girl, you have no right going around telling anyone not to ask her out. I raised you better than that."

"To be fair," my father says, slinging his good arm over the back of her chair. "The story of how we got together isn't exactly the best model for the kids to use. Remember? You were dating that quarterback from UNC, and I was just some ex-convict with a bad reputation?"

"That's different." She glances up at him, stars in her eyes —as if she's actually recalling the time he's referencing. "You didn't tell me to stop dating him."

"No, I just befriended you and hung around until you realized he wasn't the one for you." He slides his hand down and interlocks their fingers, halting the shaking by pressing hers into her shoulder. Leaning over, he places a kiss on her temple and fixes me with a pointed look. "I have to say, though, I'm surprised Elia Montalto's even letting you *near* someone he cares about."

"She's an adult. It's not like he can just lock her in the house and throw away the key." Although, I wouldn't mind locking her in my house and never letting her leave.

"You should bring her by for dinner one night," Fiona says, cocking an eyebrow. She elbows Boyd, who sits up straighter and nods his agreement, his gaze cast down and unfocused—like it's been for weeks now. Like he's got one foot in reality, and the other is missing or severed entirely.

"Why would I ever subject a girl I like to this family circus?"

"Aha!" My father's fist comes down on the table, rattling the silverware. "So you *do* like her."

"*Hypothetically.*" I send him a dirty look, irritation at his excitement lacing my veins. As if he doesn't know better than anyone why I keep people at bay.

"Sweetie." My mother smiles with the working side of her mouth, a broken gesture that looks so at home next to the shell of my father and the eerie mansion behind them. Like a Victorian painting, a ghost in the making. "If you like this girl, you need to tell her. She could be your *person.*"

I groan. "Mom, please don't start in with that soul mate bullshit."

"Why not?" She shrugs her bony shoulders, dropping her hand from my father's. "You can't honestly believe that the universe drops people on this planet and leaves them to lead their lives *alone*, do you? That it doesn't want you to be happy?"

I sincerely doubt the universe thinks I even deserve to be happy at this point, but I don't mention that. Fiona glances at Boyd from the corner of her eye, but he doesn't seem to notice, doesn't seem able to pull himself from whatever miserable vortex he's been sucked into. But *I* see it and make a mental note to ask her about it later.

She's always been infatuated with my friend, although before the gala a few weeks ago, Boyd never even acknowledged that she existed. I'd been hoping that between school and taking care of our ill mother, maybe her crush would dissipate, but now I'm concerned something's come of it instead.

But I don't mention it now. I take a sip of my wine and look at my mother. "It's awfully hokey."

"Newton's Third Law states that for every action, there is an equal and opposite reaction." My father joins in, somehow trying to combine logic with his wife's superstitions.

"Living is the action, Kieran." She raises her eyebrows, sweeping her hand around in a circle. "For those whose very existence revolves around simply *being*, there is another out there doing that same thing. Filling in the gaps and empty spaces with the bits you didn't think you needed. It's up to *us* to find them, to want them in our lives. Maybe this girl is *it*. Maybe she's exactly what you're missing."

Tears well in Fiona's eyes, but she blinks them away and buries her face in her burrito, the air settling around us heavier than it's ever been. Guilt rains down on me for ruining a perfectly cozy evening as an awkward silence descends upon us, a thick blanket stalling any further conversation.

My mother sighs, dropping her head to my father's

shoulder and abandoning her food. This is about the time she usually quits, unable to finish more than a fourth of her food since starting a new round of Parkinson's medication. Her cheeks have hollowed out, a yellow tinge staining her pearly skin, and her collarbones seem to jut out obscenely.

Still, she continues as if nothing has changed over the past few weeks. As if she's not slowly deteriorating in front of us, threatening to join a son in the afterlife she doesn't even know is waiting for her.

A son she's expected me to visit daily since his death, but that I haven't been back to in weeks.

And I can feel a difference, can feel his weight crushing the air around me, penetrating the pinnacle of my being and shaming me for not apologizing. For doing what I needed to.

For keeping his skeleton as a reminder of my guilt, of the souls I couldn't steal back and return. The lives he ruined.

For not protecting *him*. Then or now.

For making my mother believe I'm at all worthy of someone's love, much less her own, when nothing but violence and retribution have a home in my heart.

I clear my throat, shifting in my chair as my phone vibrates in my pocket. Slipping it out but keeping it tucked beneath the table, I scan the message lighting up the screen and smother the grin tugging at my lips.

As if on cue, a full-body reflection of Juliet's perfect naked body fills my vision, sending a naughty jolt of electricity straight to my cock. An ellipsis pops up, indicating her incoming message.

> Juliet: Changing out my piercings. What do you think?

Zooming in on the picture, I squint at her perky tits, a

groan catching in my throat as I study the jewels; tiny, bedazzled hearts with devil's horns sit square in the middle of both nipples, making her look even more sinfully delicious than usual. The ruby-red stones shine against her skin, highlighting the soft swell of her breasts and making my dick pulse the longer I stare.

> Me: I think u should've asked before changing them.

> Juliet: You don't like?

I run my teeth over my bottom lip as conversation resumes around me, Boyd asking my father about physical therapy and my mother asking Boyd how he's settling in at Ivers International as if he hasn't been there for years already.

> Me: I love them. Maybe 2 much.

> Me: Any significance in the pendants?

> Juliet: Just that I have a thing for the devil.

My fingers flex over the touch keyboard, considering my next words carefully.

> Me: Be naked and ready for me tonight.

She sends another winking emoji, and it's what I focus on the rest of the evening, letting her flirtiness ground me even as I meet Elia at the cemetery later and prepare myself for a long-ass night.

His bald henchman pulls a bound, hooded figure from

the back seat of his Town Car and drags him over to Murphy's grave. Somehow, despite the fact that I've not been back since the night I discovered the vandalism, it seems to have remained otherwise untouched. But I don't assume my brother's men have forgotten about me. Just that they're lying in the shadows, biding their time, waiting for a chance to pounce and destroy me.

As if burning a house down makes up for a forest fire, like man is the sole source of blame and not the general state of the world. As if anything they do to me matters.

I light a bundle of sage and toss it on Murphy's grave, letting it singe the grass it lands on and stomping it out before it has the chance to fully ignite. Sprinkling a handful of salt over the carcinogenic earth, I recite the quick Irish mantra to appease my mother's spirit, and straighten to my feet as Elia approaches with his victim in tow.

The man struggles against his hold, his muffled grunts making me think he's gagged beneath the hood; he's a large man, muscular and tall, with that fucking Stonemore Volunteer Fire Department T-shirt on. I'm not sure what's in the pipes at that station, but it seems the majority of the men there had their hands in at least *one* aspect of the trafficking Murphy was in charge of.

At this point, I've probably buried half the squad for their involvement. Men who knew about my role in the organization's dismantling, and who wanted things Murphy promised—women and money he never provided. Things I was expected to deliver when I took over for my brother, but am unwilling to divulge.

Not because I necessarily have a conscience when it comes to these people, but I think the entire scheme is unfair. If you're going to involve people in the criminal world, they should get a say in their participation.

The way I never did. Evil was baked right into my soul upon birth, and I have spent my life living up to that expectation.

Elia cocks an eyebrow as his guard shoves the man to his knees on the ground. He glances at Murphy's grave, then back at me. "Warding off the evil spirits?"

I shrug, not really wanting to get into my family's dumb beliefs with him. "This is my brother's gravesite, after all."

He nods, like it makes perfect sense, and then kicks at the captive's shin. A guttural sound comes from beneath the hood—music to my ears. Bracing one hand on the man's shoulder, Elia jerks the black fabric off, revealing a puffy, tear-stained face with a sock shoved in the man's mouth. My eyes rove over familiar blond hair on the handsome stranger I've definitely seen before.

Gritting my teeth, I recall the night I watched Juliet fuck another man. Watched him leave her in a huff of displeasure out in an alleyway by herself at night. Watched her cry and silently ask the sky to end her suffering.

Then subconsciously swore to end it for her myself.

"Jace Allen?" I look up at Elia, my brows furrowing, angry that I even know the piece of shit's name. "What the hell is this?"

"I had your guy Boyd track some of the users on that kiddie porn site to their IP addresses, and his was the first that came up. A frequent flyer, actually. We cross-referenced it with the metadata in the flash drive files to confirm involvement."

I try not to bristle at the thought of Boyd doing work made for me, but it's been a busy week. Since Elia offered to help me with the Murphy shit, I've been able to focus more on tracking down the bastards who shot my father and touched my girl.

Besides, I gave up hacking when I chose not to continue working at Ivers International. Despite being *really* good at it and actually enjoying that aspect of cybersecurity shit, I chose solitude.

Chose murder.

Elia stares at Jace for a few beats, then slides his gaze up. "Why, you know him?"

"No." We're veering into dangerous territory, if this man's involved in the kind of shit Murphy was. Especially considering where his dick has been since and whose skin his hands have grazed and burned. "But I mean... your sister-in-law might?"

A look of pure ferocity bleeds from his eyes down his chin, sharpening every feature on the *capo's* face. His eyes darken like two turbulent seas, and his hand fists at the nape of Jace's neck, ripping it back and pulling the man's throat tight. "You get Juliet mixed up in something, fucker?"

His muffled protests send a flicker of irritation down my spine, and I reach into my coat pocket, pulling out an heirloom obsidian blade engraved with our family crest. My preferred weapon of choice.

I unsheathe it from its leather holster and point it in his direction. "I don't suggest you lie to us again. If you know something about the operation my brother was running a couple of years ago, you need to speak the fuck up now, or I'll gut you right here. And if you've somehow dragged Juliet Harrison into the crosshairs, I'll make sure your body is so disfigured when I finish gutting you that no one will ever be able to identify it."

I take a step closer and tear the gag from his mouth; he gasps, choking slightly as he draws in a deep, staggered breath, and I press the tip of my knife into his chin. He glares up at me, still bound at the wrists and ankles, and snarls. "I don't have to explain *shit* to you, dirtbag. I don't have a fucking clue what you're talking about, and I haven't seen Juliet in weeks."

"Yeah? Did you know you were fucking someone else's property that night you took her outside The Bar?" Elia curses under his breath, crossing his arms over his chest, but I don't care. Fury courses red in my vision, blindingly hot, and as I jut my hand forward slightly, just enough to break his first layer of skin, my dick throbs behind my jeans at his soft whimper of pain. "A history of stealing doesn't exactly give you an airtight alibi."

His eyes widen, frantic in the moonlight. "Dude, I didn't know. Juliet's always been down to fuck at random times, and she's never had anyone serious. I didn't know, I swear."

"Maybe she's never had anyone serious because no one's ever looked at her as more than a good fucking time." My grip on the blade tightens, heat surging through my body as I remember him rutting into her and the absolute desolation surrounding her in the aftermath.

Everything with Murphy be damned. I want to slaughter this motherfucker for that alone.

"Is that what she's telling you? That everyone else before you left her unsatisfied?" Jace chuckles, starting to shake his head but wincing when he remembers the knife breaching his skin. "Man, she's a good actress. I honestly wouldn't think she'd be able to fool a sick fuck like you, but maybe living with a criminal has taught her a few things."

The knife cuts a sliver deeper, and Elia slides in closer to me; my body feels like it's on fire, the blood boiling beneath my skin and blurring my vision. "Kieran," Elia warns, perhaps sensing my downward spiral, but his voice calls out to me in a vacuum as my ears home in on Jace.

"What do you know about Murphy's organization?"

"The Stonemore gang?" Jace shrugs, still ridiculously cocky for someone bound and at my mercy. A concept very few live to experience. "I know they deal in flesh auctions, and that creep Finn Hanson deals specifically in kids. A few of my guys have been tied up in it on account of needing extra cash. But I swear to you, that's it."

"Why should I believe you?"

"What the fuck would I lie for? You'll probably kill me regardless—if I had anything to say, now would be the time."

My stomach lurches and my throat constricts; the air compresses around me in waves, the images of that warehouse years ago flooding my brain and making me nauseous. Unease rips through me like a furious tide, and I sway on my feet, releasing Jace with a harsh shove and a kick to the groin for good measure.

He grunts, toppling over onto the grass, and Elia turns to look at me. "Finn Hanson? Don't you work for him?"

"I take jobs for him, same as I do you." I shake my head, re-sheathing my blade and stuffing it into my pocket. "That doesn't make any sense, though. Finn *can't* be the organizer of this whole thing. It's been going on a fuck of a lot longer than he's even been around. And it was one of his men who attacked Juliet, yes, but he wouldn't have any reason to believe she was involved with me, anyway. So why target her?"

Elia runs a hand through his hair, gesturing for his goon

to come over and collect the groaning mass of muscle on the ground. "Could be a subordinate, framing the boss."

My mind rattles with a million different thoughts, but I nod anyway, distant as I begin to lose myself in them. I glance at Jace as the bodyguard drags him back to their vehicle. "You bringing him to Crimson?"

"Yeah. I'll leave him in the basement, see if Kal wants a crack at him until you do whatever it is you're salivating to do. Don't leave him for too long, though; I don't want a rotting body stinking up my club. Bad for business."

Bad for business. I study Murphy's monument as the two Italians leave me in the dark, making my way around to the back and hating that the blood from before seems to have been replaced with an ink more permanent. The cross screams at me, mocking my last name, and my hands itch to destroy the slab of stone entirely.

Erase the evidence of Murphy Ivers altogether and make the town forget there was ever someone there to despise. To fear.

Other than me.

That fear is what's kept me going the past few years, kept me seeking out the others involved in the sins of my brother. It's what brought me to my knees, and what I sold my soul to uncover.

It started before Murphy's death and was exacerbated by it, the darkness within me finally having a way to manifest outward. A purpose I could funnel it into. Yet here I sit, presumably no closer to slaying King's Trace's demons than I am to exorcising them from myself.

My pulse picks up as the wind moves through the air, the slightest hint of vanilla perfume assaulting my nostrils. It picks me up, and I scramble to my feet, my hand reaching for the locket still clasped around my neck as I peer out across the cemetery at Dominic Harrison's headstone.

I expect my petite kitten, the only thing occupying my thoughts outside of the ghost of my brother and the sins of his past, but that's not what waits for me. Instead, when I step out from Murphy's site, I'm met with the short, sleek barrel of a gun, blinking into a masked silhouette of familiarity I can't quite place.

"Kieran, Kieran, Kieran. I hate that it has to end this way."

20

JULIET

LEAVING THE COUNSELING CENTER, I sling my purse over my shoulder and head to Benito's car, sliding in the back seat and buckling in without a word.

This has become our routine at this point; he's always waiting for me when I leave Dr. Zhang's—Hana's office, idling at the curb, ready to take me wherever I want to go. Usually, we go to the bakery or the house, anywhere I can give my sister false accounts of the progress I'm making at therapy.

Not that I'm not putting a little effort into it, although instead of opening up about myself, I've been hounding Hana with questions about her personal life, latching on to any crumb of information she's willing to drop me. She indulges most of the time, perhaps on the belief that it'll initiate reciprocity, but I have no intention of baring my soul to her.

Don't want to see the judgment in her eyes when she learns the truth about where my shame comes from.

Sliding my phone from my pocket, I unlock the screen

and clear the texts from Caroline saying she's going in for her last checkup before baby Noah's due, searching for a message from the one person I actually want to hear from. The one who's been ghosting me for days now.

I'd done as he asked the other night and stripped bare, unlocked my window, and lounged in my bed waiting for him. It had begun to feel like clockwork; as soon as the night shifted into day, when midnight rolled around these past few weeks, Kieran's steady, unyielding presence in my life was something I'd come to count on.

A constant I found myself clinging to as the rest of my life tried to sort itself out in an ever-changing fashion.

Someone who made me feel visible.

Whole.

Yet he never showed up that night, or the next, and he hasn't returned any of my calls or texts. If I didn't know better, I'd think something bad had happened to him. But in this town, nothing happens to the elite without the media sinking their claws into it and making it front page news.

Which is why, as Benito drives through downtown, my sister's face is plastered on every storefront newsstand, counting down the days until Noah's leaked due date.

Leaked, accidentally, by me—apparently, your body becomes accustomed to sleeping next to someone when you do it often enough, and not having Kieran around the past few days has taken a serious toll on my nocturnal habits. I'd let it slip in a sleep-deprived, politically charged rant about the state of our dwindling oceans in the age of global warming, noting that I wanted Noah to one day know what the ocean looks like, and it'd been headline news that afternoon.

She forgave me, because that's the kind of person my sister is, but it didn't stop the guilt from gnawing away at my soul. And once that started, the guilt about everything else—missing our shitty parents and wishing things were different—returned as well.

I've been miserable since, and Kieran's absence hasn't helped.

We pass the decrepit law offices and the ancient courthouse downtown, then the novelty boutiques and diners doubling as functional services like laundromats just to keep their doors open. A sea of poverty we pass through in an expensive haze, untouched by the calamity of crime in our town.

But not fully untouched—I may not share the financial hardships of my peers, but crime bleeds into every other facet of my life, a stronghold I can't seem to break out of. Since my days of sex tapes and underage drinking are behind me, I would've thought I'd be an upstanding citizen by now.

Not leeching off the comfort of known killers. Living in their house, inviting them into my bed. Missing them when they're not around.

I guess when you descend from a criminal upbringing, even unknowingly, you can never quite escape the thorns brought on by another's actions. Their influence.

That thick, deep-rooted misery inside me exists as a constant reminder, a barrier that keeps me from opening up. Keeps my soul from blossoming into something solid.

When Benito turns down the street we live on, the single strip of immaculate houses overlooking our uninhabited little lake, I clear my throat and ask him to take me to the cemetery. He looks at me in the rearview, raising an eyebrow.

"The cemetery?"

I nod, and he shrugs, pulling into a vacant driveway,

shifting gears as he makes a three-point turn and heads in the opposite direction.

He stops just outside the wrought-iron fence that surrounds the property, and I climb out on shaky legs, struggling to catch my breath as it leaves my body in quick, quiet huffs. I hold up my hand, letting him know I don't need a guard inside, and make my way to the corner of the grounds where my father's headstone sits.

I haven't been back in weeks. Haven't seen the point since my necklace is elsewhere and my shame centers more on the monster taking over my life instead of the one who already left it.

Still, standing in front of the slab of granite, the wind whispers through the strands of my hair and kisses my skin. I can't stop the usual wave of guilt from crashing over me, threatening to drag me beneath its surface and hold me there until I can't think or breathe or save myself.

But instead of allowing panic to seize the chambers of my heart with its claws at the incoming storm of sadness, instead of giving in and seeing it as an immediate loss, I drop to the ground, crisscross my legs, and let the storm roll through me. Bracing my hands on my knees, I inhale deeply and close my eyes, absorbing the serenity, that stillness in the air that only a graveyard possesses.

As if the very earth itself is aware of what lies beneath its surface and is unwilling to disturb the peace.

Something crackles, leaves crunching under pressure, drawing me from the attempt at an exercise—not that I think Hana's cognitive techniques will work on me, anyway, but I'm willing to try anything at least once.

My body stiffens as the presence closes in behind me, a different kind of storm I find myself unprepared for. With an insult poised on my tongue, an admonishment for ignoring me for days after making me start to care about him, I turn my head and start to speak.

But it's not Kieran I see.

"*Mom*?"

The thin dye-job blonde in front of me just barely resembles the woman who ditched her children two years ago—her eyes are puffy and her cheekbones sullen, as if they've not been injected with collagen recently. She has on a soft lavender pantsuit, but the blazer hangs off her chest, showcasing the weight she's lost and the gaunt appearance that makes her look like she belongs in the ground like everyone else around us.

"Juliet." Her head tilts, gaze raking over my body. "You look... different. When's the last time you had a haircut?"

She brushes a bony hand over her own hair, and I can't help but notice the chipped nail polish on her fingertips and the slight tremble in her chin, as if she might be nervous right now. As if she has reason to be anything but sorry.

We stare at each other for several moments in complete silence, the air no longer peaceful; an angry funnel cloud swirls in its place, trying to decide which of us to suck in and spit out.

My heart clenches in my chest, confusion and resentment battling inside me. Why is she here all of a sudden, and why can't I stop my stupid brain from hoping she's back for good?

Nearly two years of radio silence, and here she is. Exactly what I've been waiting for all this time, yet something tells me there's nothing good about her return.

My parents never cared for me, despite my various attempts at forcing their hands. They didn't care when I scraped my knees raw after a nasty fall from an oak tree in our back yard, or when I begged them to pay off the frat guys who'd taken advantage of me and posted explicit videos of our time together online.

They'd just shake their heads—if that—and tell me whatever happened was my penance for being a disaster. There was no love, no affection, and yet it was the one thing I craved most from both of them.

Especially after spending my life watching them shower Caroline with it, even if it was a malicious affection they'd wield as a weapon against her. When I was younger, I didn't understand that. All I knew was my parents couldn't have cared less about me.

My father died not loving me. He died angry with me, and that was that. I don't get another chance to change his mind. There won't be any redemption for him—and hell, he doesn't even deserve it.

But I wanted the opportunity to tell him that. To see his face crumple when he realized it was my love he wasn't worthy of, not the other way around.

Maybe that's what it boils down to—not me missing him as a father, but missing what could have been. I'm mourning people who never existed, and I don't know what to do with the sorrow.

I don't know how to stop, and something tells me nothing will be different with my mother. Maybe it'll even be worse.

The quiet between us stretches on too long, and my need for answers propels me forward. I take the bait. "What are you doing here?"

Scoffing, she adjusts the underside of her shoulder-length hair, sweeping it back. "I could ask you the same thing, dear. Shouldn't you be in school or... working? Keeping out of trouble?"

"What kind of trouble are you expecting me to get into at a cemetery?"

"Oh, come on, darling." My body coils against the nickname, hating the condescending venom dripping from her tone. "You can't think I haven't heard the rumors about you and the boys you like to bring here."

"Well, Mother, considering you've been MIA for almost two whole years now, I do find it a little suspect that you'd claim to know anything about me at all."

"Word travels when you're a Harrison."

"You say that like that name holds any kind of meaning anymore." I roll my eyes, brushing dirt from my palms as I climb to my feet. Beyond the fence surrounding us, I see Benito exit his car, watching me with an intensity that makes me feel braver than ever before. "What are you *really* doing here?"

"Is it a crime to want to come visit my husband's grave?"

My heart twists behind my ribs, a stabbing sensation throbbing through the meat of it, sending a sharp wave of agony down my spine and across my skin. Of course, she's not here for me.

I've been here all along. She just doesn't give a shit.

Shrugging, she reaches out and grabs a lock of my hair, twisting it around her finger. She tilts her head, watching the movement, before I swat her away. Her icy eyes harden as they meet mine, her chin dipping as she makes it a point to look down at me. "I can't even imagine what you're doing hanging around that Ivers boy, but Jesus Christ, Juliet. I thought I'd taught you better than to let men like that defile you."

I glare at her. "The only person I ever let *defile* me is you. How fucking dare you come here and try to judge me for my choices when you disappeared out of my life for years without a single explanation?"

"Well, good Lord, dear." Her bright pink lips quiver, signaling an onslaught of crocodile tears, and I roll my eyes, rage coursing through every fiber of my being. "It's not like you ever needed me around before."

A sob lodges in my throat, cutting off my air supply as I gape at her, sure I'm digging open my wounds for her to see and not caring if I bleed out in front of her. "You didn't think I'd care that you ditched me right after my father's suicide? That being left without a penny to my name in a house that felt more like a fucking prison for the majority of my life— you didn't think leaving me there to *rot* would matter?"

My chest feels tight and tears sting behind my eyes, a cold front shifting in my brain and pushing everything else out of the way. It creates a spiraling vortex of complication and sorrow—of shame and the defeat of never feeling good enough. It culminates at the foot of my soul, trying to find a way inside, but I ignore it.

She squints, haughty confusion coloring her painted face. "What do you mean I left you? Your sister took you in, took care of you, just like I knew she would. I didn't leave a defenseless child alone in the woods; if you were unprepared for the sudden thrust into adulthood, maybe you should've spent less time starring in X-rated films and more time finishing your degree."

"*I needed you.*" The sob escapes, cutting itself through my vocal cords and ripping from my mouth before I have a chance to stop it. Tears blur my vision as they slide down my cheeks, making her a watercolor blob against a smoky, springtime backdrop, and I drag my wrist over my eyes to clear it.

She looks startled, eyes wide, arms tucked at her sides. Distant, as if she can't stand the emotion she's seeing right now.

Every piece of emotion from a lifetime of not being able to rely on my parents to *be* parents floods me at that moment, frustration with the sadness in my life spewing like a volcano and pouring out of me.

"I didn't want Caroline to have to take me in, or to intrude on her new life. I didn't want to be left alone to navigate troubled waters on my own. I needed a *mother,* and you fucking left. It would have been nice if, for once, you'd thought about me instead of yourself. My whole life, that's all I wanted from you, and you couldn't even stick around after Dad's suicide to see if I was okay. You never asked how Caroline was after you found out what he did to her all those years, and you never cared to find out if he'd done it to me. You just left. Do you know what that does to someone?"

"Juliet, I—"

"Do you know how it feels to become an orphan as an adult? To lose the two people whose affection and approval you've been dying for your whole life, despite the fact that they never really deserved to give it in the first place?" I scrub furiously at my face, trying to get the tears to stop falling, but like a torrential downpour, like the words spewing from my mouth, they're endless.

"There is a hole in my *soul* because of you, Mother. This emptiness I try to fill with distraction after distraction. A tumor that grows larger every single day, that makes me feel like *I* did something wrong."

She shifts her weight from one leg to the other, lifting a

shoulder. Tears would affect a normal person, but she just seems to stare right through me, uncaring in the slightest that her own flesh and blood is crumbling in front of her.

Finally, she just shrugs. "I don't know what you want me to say."

Frustration fills me, clotting my senses, and I throw my hands in the air in an offering to the gods. For her to fucking *get it* without me needing to spell it out for her. "It can't be that difficult to figure out what I might want, Mother. When you took off with the nest egg Daddy left behind, before life insurance could touch it when he breaches his non-suicide clause, it was pretty easy to figure out what *you* wanted."

Yet she *still* doesn't see me. Her eyes are vacant, unseeing except for the dollar signs reflecting in her blue irises. All she ever truly cared about. And here I am, deteriorating in her midst while she just watches. Maybe she even enjoys it.

It makes sense, I suppose. I broke in front of her the most, allowed myself to be the most vulnerable in her presence, and she never returned the gesture. *She just left.*

An ache spreads behind my breastbone, wrapping around to my spine and fitting itself in the ridges between the vertebrae, as if trying to fill me with its toxicity. Trying to ruin me as I stare into her eyes, silently pleading with her to give me *something*. After all this time, I have to beg for even a modicum of sympathy or understanding.

A slight acknowledgment to let me know that she feels even a fucking twinge of remorse for destroying me. For destroying us.

But she doesn't speak. Doesn't give me anything. No bones are thrown, no life preservers tossed. I'm going to drown in my grief while she watches, the look of satisfaction etched into her brow something I'll never be able to forget.

Turning on my heel, I start around her, done with the attempt at conversation if she's not going to reciprocate. As I walk past her, she reaches out and grabs ahold of my bicep, pulling me in close; she may look weak, but the grip on my skin has me wincing in pain as I try to wrangle out of her grasp. My skin welts beneath her fingers and I whimper, considering the best place on her body to land some kind of hit. Something that'd allow me to get away.

"You said your father committed suicide," she says, an edge to her voice I don't quite understand. What the fuck does she have to be angry about? "What did you mean by that?"

I blink, shoving her away from me. "Suicide seems pretty self-explanatory."

Her hands fall to her sides, fingers pulling at the fabric of her pants. "Oh, Jesus. You think he *killed* himself?"

My jaw clenches, my heart speeding up as it tries to prepare for whatever bombshell she's about to deliver. Deep down, I think there's always been a part of me that found the timing of his death rather suspect—and with Elia being who he is, having the connection to Caroline that he does, it's crossed my mind once or twice that maybe he had something to do with it.

Men like him have warped ideas of what safety might encumber, and maybe getting rid of my father was his only way to ensure he'd never hurt my sister again. Still, I'd figured at this point maybe one of them would've hinted to it or let me in on their dirty little secret, considering the spiral his death sent me down that they claim to be aware of.

Kieran.

I blink, coming back to reality as my mother's lips part around his name, implicating my lover. I realize she's blaming him, saying he's behind my father's death, and it makes me wonder if maybe every inch of awareness Elia and Caroline claimed to have when it comes to me was fabricated, like some tool of manipulation to make me do whatever they wanted.

Nausea bubbles up in my stomach, launching into my throat as I stare at my mother, absorbing her words into my skin and hating what the truth does to me. Hating how it sends a wave of warmth through me, how the name that falls from her mouth makes my blood sing.

I don't know how to feel about the new development. My body reacts one way, but my brain feels conflicted.

When my mother spits his name again, like he's the dirt beneath her feet, I know I need to go find him. Sort out the kaleidoscope of emotion inside me.

Yanking myself from the toxic bubble my mother exists in, getting mental whiplash, I jog back to where Benito stands at the gates. He walks backward, keeping an eye on her, and beats me to the car, pulling the door open for me and getting in behind the wheel.

Peeling out of the cemetery parking lot, I watch out the back window until my mother's still, dazed form becomes little more than a blip on the horizon. I dial Caroline when we've turned onto a different road, and she answers on the second ring.

"Mom's in town," I breathe in lieu of a greeting.

I'm met with a long pause and then a deep exhale. "Did you talk to her?"

"Unfortunately. She accosted me at Dad's grave."

"*Dad's* grave? What were you doing *there*?"

I clear my throat, dread flooding through me as my brain

scrambles to change the subject. "Does it matter? The point is, Mom's here, and I have no idea why."

"There has to be a reason. Something she came back for. No way would she come all the way back here just to see you." A sharp gasp fills the receiver at the same time my heart plummets into my stomach, and I close my eyes, steeling myself against the truth. "Jules, that's not what I meant. I'm—"

"It's fine. You're right, anyway. Nothing we can do about that." Clearing my throat a second time, I turn and look out the window as the tree line blurs past. "I just wanted to warn you."

"Thanks," she mutters, and I hear a dull female voice call out over an intercom. "Jules, they're calling me back to this appointment, and you know how they are about cell phones in waiting rooms. If Mom happens to show up at the house, don't let her in. We don't need her negativity tainting our air supply. I wish she'd kept her shady ass in Texas."

Nodding even though she can't see me, I start my good-bye, but she stops me. "Uh, one thing before I go. I think I saw Kieran Ivers being discharged from here earlier."

"Discharged? What was wrong with him?"

"Well, Jesus, Jules. I don't know. I didn't ask him; I'm kind of busy carrying around a small horse and peeing every ten seconds. I don't even know for sure if it was him, but I know your room's been suspiciously quiet lately."

My face scrunches up. "Uh, gross. Are you *listening* to us?"

"Not on purpose! The walls aren't *that* thick, you know. Only our room is soundproofed. When I'm in Poppy's room or the office, I can hear every—"

"Christ, okay, I get it. Thanks, pervert." I click the end call button as she bursts into a fit of giggles, the events of my afternoon dissipating as I consider the fact that Kieran was *discharged from the hospital.*

As in, he was hurt enough to have been admitted at some point.

My stomach aches with the weight of the unknown, and I wonder if something happened, and that's why he's stayed away.

I lean forward, asking Benito to reroute us one more time. He looks like he *really* doesn't want to go where I've instructed him, but he starts toward the outskirts of town anyway, like an ever-obedient guard dog.

Chewing on my lip as the Gothic mansion comes into view, I lock my phone and sit back in my seat, my breathing chaotic. My throat feels tight, restricted, as Benito pulls in front of the concrete stairs leading to the front door of the Ivers's home, and I'm pushing the door open and rushing to the entrance before he's come to a full stop.

Fisting one of the bronze lion knockers, I bang against the door with every ounce of strength in my body, until my bicep tingles and the pounding resonates between my ears. It opens slowly, revealing Fiona in a denim skirt, a slight smirk stretching her red lips.

"About time." Her fingers tap three times on the edge of the door before she steps back and gestures for me to come inside. "Up the stairs, last door on your right."

I don't say a word as I book it up the grand staircase, my hand brushing against the solid railing, nerves eating at my insides. The hallway feels endless as I tread down it, one step at a time, and my palm connects with the closed wooden door at the end of the hall. It's not shut all the way, so I push it gently, the sight inside stealing the air from my lungs and putting it back all at once.

Kieran's jade eyes meet mine, a passionate fury in their depths; they burn me as I cross the room to where he lounges in bed, his back propped against the headboard, shoulder wrapped in gauze and plastic while the skin around the bandages is inflamed. Bright red proof that this devil is still very much human.

"Kitten," he breathes as my knees graze the edge of the mattress; his arm comes out, beckoning me, but I don't move.

I can't. Not yet.

"Did you kill him?"

I don't know why that's the first question I ask.

Don't know why I need to know. Just that I do.

His eyes narrow, questioning, and his head tilts, searching. Recognition flickers in his pupils, but he doesn't budge. Doesn't offer me a way out this time. "Did I kill who? You need to be more specific, sweetheart."

Because he's killed so many people.

I take a deep, cleansing breath, pressing my knees into the bed and climbing closer. My hand swipes along the wound on his shoulder, a question for later, and a slight tremor wracks through me when I make contact with him. He hisses, maybe in pain or maybe in pleasure, I can't tell. But I don't pull back.

I can't.

A part of me wants to question the wound and the rumored hospitalization, but shock overwhelms my senses and keeps me from acknowledging anything else.

"Did you kill my father?"

His chest rises and falls with labored breaths, and there's

only a slight nod as his jaw hardens. He averts his gaze, recoiling from my touch, but I press in deeper, not wanting to sever whatever the fuck this is right now. The electricity pulsing between us, the inherent desire I feel despite the confirmation of my greatest fears.

So instead of running or retreating like I should, I push forward and connect our mouths. "Thank you," I whisper against his lips, feeling as though he's slayed a demon of mine. There's a peace that washes over me in realizing my father didn't escape his crimes.

When he kisses me back, I know that this changes things. Changes me.

And I'm okay with it.

LATER, I lie naked against his chest, straddling his waist with my knees bracketing his hips, and my head brushes the bandage covering his shoulder. I sit up, toying with the edge of the material, and cock my head at him. "You were in the hospital?"

His eyes are closed, his face turned toward the ceiling. He looks more relaxed than I've ever seen him, and I can't help wondering if he feels it, too. The calmness in my presence, like the ocean settling after a rugged storm. Like I could sit with him forever and not worry about anything else.

"It's just a flesh wound. Nothing to fret over."

I dig the tip of my finger into the exposed skin that stretches beyond the width of the gauze; the hot reddish-pink area pales under my touch, and he hisses through his teeth, jerking away. "Is this why you were ignoring me?"

He sighs, peeking at me through slits in his eyelids. As if

sensing I'm not going to let up, he sighs again, deeper, the sound reverberating in my chest. "Yes. Although, clearly, I wasn't just ignoring you. I couldn't—didn't want to come to you yet."

I try not to take offense. "What happened?"

"Nothing."

"Kieran."

"I'm serious. It was nothing. And my hospital stay was a stupid precaution that Kal suggested. I'm *fine*."

Crossing my arms over my chest, barring his view of my breasts, I raise an eyebrow and just stare.

"Oh my fucking *God*. You are such a goddamn brat." He groans into the air, reaching over and pulling a pillow over his face. After another loud, animalistic roar pours out of him, he tosses the cushion aside and hauls me close, gripping my chin with his fingers. His eyes are hard, green vials mixed with lust and irritation, and it makes my stomach cramp imagining what's to come.

The surrender followed by the sweet symphony of admonition.

"What do you want me to say, Juliet? That I was careless and let someone ambush me? That I was so consumed with thoughts of revenge and atonement, not to mention your delectable little ass, that I didn't hear someone approach and see them pull a gun on me?" His lips whisper against mine as he speaks, and it makes my toes curl. "Do you need me to say that, for the first time ever, I've not been wholly focused on my surroundings or my work, caught up in the threat of danger that follows me, and that I paid for it?"

I swallow, my tongue sweeping out and brushing across our nearly connected mouths. "You were shot?"

"Not the first time. A lot of people want me dead."

"Why?"

He pulls my head back a few inches, giving me a funny look. "Do you not know who I am? I *just* told you I killed your father. You think he was my first?"

Pushing off his chest with my hands, I sit up straight, my fingers idly tracing the contours of his abdomen. "I mean, I know the rumors. But we've never really talked about that..."

His jaw clenches. "Does the truth change things?"

"It should." Drawing circles on his skin, I hook my index finger around one puckered nipple, considering the life my sister lives. How she fell in love with a man whose soul is stained with the blood and suffering of others. How he'd do damn near anything to please her, keep her safe and loved.

Sitting here, naked on top of this dangerous man I've run to for comfort, I realize I already have my answer to his question.

Because no, the truth doesn't *change* anything. Not when your perceptions are already set and your mind is made up. Not when the truth can be buried in lies and manufactured to fit an agenda.

The truth becomes little more than a telescope through which you can judge people and situations, but its lens is still foggy and subject to distortion. It's the lies you have to pay attention to. The secrets that reveal the most.

Pressing my palm into his cheek, I shake my head, reveling in the way my gesture has him brightening, as if a simple acceptance is all it took to revive his soul.

21

KIERAN

Juliet's lips form a tight seal around the crown of my dick, sucking hard with a quiet little hum that has my spine vibrating. Her fingers caress my balls, massaging with just the right amount of pressure, and I grip the back of her head, pushing her down farther on my shaft.

"Goddamn, kitten," I grunt, gritting my teeth around my supernova vision; she takes me to the back of her throat, my tip slipping just past the point of resistance at the base.

She gurgles, struggling to breathe as I fit her nose flush with my pelvis, her cheeks pinkening as she continues her ministrations. Drool pools out of the sides of her mouth, dribbling down her face to her hair and mattress, and fuck if it's not the most beautiful thing I've ever seen.

She's a fucking masterpiece, dirtied up just for me; a work of art that deserves to be hung up in my own private Louvre. A mess of pastels and mixed paints designed as if the universe had me in mind at her creation.

Propping my foot up on the edge of the bed, I bend my knee and shove deeper into her, loving the bulge against the delicate column of her neck. I stroke it with one hand, tapping lightly with my palm, reveling in how she squirms. How she moans, taking her punishment like the good little girl she is; rough and without complaint, getting off on my dominance just as much as I do.

It's been a few days since she burst into my bedroom unbidden, and in that time, something between us has split wide open. A canyon of bottled emotions and unfathomable darkness, a crack in my armor and a cut in her heart, left to bleed without a tourniquet.

The memories leading up to that moment are hazy; flashes of striking white and unbearable pain. Me crawling from the cemetery to my car, leaving a trail of fresh blood in my wake. Kal Anderson being at the emergency room when I showed up because he was volunteering, and him treating me before anyone else could ask questions.

Being told by my parents that I needed to recover and was of no use to Juliet injured.

I don't know what exactly drove her to me that day, who told her the truth about what happened to her father, but I'm fast discovering that I don't really give two shits if it means I get to have her in my bed at night. If it means knowing she's safe here with me while lunatics ravage our small town.

Elia and I have been slowly working our way through a list of men Jace Allen could recall seeing interact with my brother and Finn, but add in the hooded figure that shot me in the cemetery to the mix, and our time spent scouring the dark web and the seediest joints in all of King's Trace feels futile at best.

With both my father and I recovering from bullet wounds, my mother's ever-worsening health, and the fact that Fiona is entirely oblivious to everything, I feel more tightly wound than ever. Boyd's working behind the scenes at Ivers International, trying to keep the place afloat in my father's absence while he fields searches for me, but it doesn't quite feel like enough.

The weight of Murphy's sins, his ghost taunting me in whatever hellscape the afterlife takes on, threatens to crush me and leave me irreparably broken, unable to heal. The collection of bones in my closet serves as a reminder that maybe I don't deserve to.

My shoulder aches as I stretch down Juliet's body, tasting her sweet cunt while my hips piston into her. Swiping my tongue along her hot slit, I taste the mix of arousal and my cum that I've started to crave since this dance between us began. I moan against her skin, nuzzling her entrance with my nose.

When I'm with her, though, all the other shit disappears. All I see is her.

"I could fucking eat this pussy for the rest of my life and never get tired of it," I groan, suckling at her clit, spreading her wide for better access. The sloppy, wet sounds coming from my dick lodged in her throat make me dizzy, and I slide my tongue inside her as my thumb finds her asshole, pushing just the tip in.

She tenses, her cheeks tightening as I inch inward, gliding in and out in time with the way I fuck her throat—long, languid strokes that have her moaning my name.

"Ah, ah, ah," I tsk, pulling away from her cunt and blowing a short breath over her swollen lips. My palm comes down hard on the fatty flesh above her clit, and she lets out a wail, my dick popping out of her when she throws her head back. I slap her again, then run my tongue over the abused skin, cooling it. "What did you call me?"

Harsh breaths spill from her nose as she moves to take me back into her mouth; I shift my hips up, pinning her beneath my knees. My shoulder screams in protest, but I tamp it down, letting the fiery lust for this woman consume me.

Maybe it's wrong. I don't care.

"Kie*ran*," she groans, her voice hoarse and sultry, making my dick jump. She notices the movement, blue eyes curving upward. But still, I don't move, and she rolls her eyes, brat in full force as she mocks me. "I'm sorry, *daddy*. Please let me make it up to you."

"Oh, you're fucking going to, kitten. Put my dick in your mouth and suck it all the way down. I want to feel your snot on my skin."

She obeys, engulfing me fully in a way that makes my body ignite. Gagging only once, she bobs up and down my length, propelling her neck off the bed with ease spurred by adrenaline. Juliet's an athletic fuck, always willing to do whatever it takes, for however long it takes, to get us both where we want to be.

I try not to think about how many other dicks she's had in her mouth or how many times she's practiced this. Not that I have room to be jealous, but still—an animalistic, primal part of me hates that anyone ever touched her before me, hates that she didn't know to save herself for me.

It's unrealistic, but it's how I feel. And each night that I fuck her damn near into a coma, I make sure she knows those days of others getting a taste of her body are over.

Digging her nails into my ass as I fuck her face harder, I feel her fingers scratch toward the crack. Her teeth scrape the sensitive skin of my shaft, nicking a vein as she swallows and sucks around me, and I feel my balls draw up almost back inside my body, pleasure blinding me as release pounds through me.

I take her clit between my teeth, biting until she convulses, and slide my thumb back into her asshole, loving that she seems to relax into me this time around.

She isn't new to anal, but we've been working up to it, anyway.

A grunt falls from my lips into her cunt as I feel the tip of her finger press against *my* ass, probing an area no one else has ever touched. It's a foreign sensation, one that draws the muscles in my body tight, but isn't unpleasant at all.

She breaches the tight ring of muscle with a pinkie, and the sudden intrusion makes me come in seconds, as if on some kind of timer that detonates at her curiosity.

As she spasms through her own orgasm, I shunt myself as far into her throat as I can go; she chokes as I spill into her, licking from tip to thumb as she gets even slicker beneath my chin. She coaxes out the last drops of my cum, making me shudder, and we disentangle, flopping back on the bed without a word.

Our chests rise and fall as I wipe the back of my hand over my mouth, wishing I could keep her taste and scent on me for eternity. That I could pump it into my bloodstream and keep her with me forever.

"Are we ever gonna talk about the whole *daddy* thing?"

I roll to my side, propping my head in my hand. Her face is a sloppy red mess, and she leans over to my nightstand for a tissue, cleaning up. When she settles back down, her hair fans out beneath her head and she practically glows. A halo of light I wish I could steal for myself.

"What about it?"

"I mean," she says, turning to face me and chewing on the corner of her lip, "it's weird, right? You don't even have any kids." She pauses, her eyes wide as they flicker to me. "You *don't* have kids, right?"

"Nope. Never met anyone I wanted to be inside of without a condom, anyway." Neither of us mentions the implication of the fact that I've never used one with her. Instead, I scrunch my nose at the thought of anyone but *her* calling me daddy in a sexual scenario, and shrug my good shoulder. "Does it make you feel weird to say it?"

"Well, that's what I called my father." Her mouth purses as she looks up at the ceiling fan, eyes distant.

We don't talk about him usually, but for me, he feels like a never-ending presence in the room, a wall between us we haven't fully torn down. Despite her supposed acceptance of me being his cause of death, there's still some kind of horror living there in his memory, a ghost she doesn't seem to want to discuss.

"You know just calling me that doesn't make me your biological father, right?"

She laughs, and I think it might be the first time I've ever heard the melodious sound come from her lips. It makes my chest compress, my throat tight, and I tear my gaze from her pink cheeks before I fall into a hole I can't crawl out of.

"Obviously." Brushing her hair from her face, she snuggles closer to her pillow, blinking up at me with her baby blues. They're wide and vulnerable, an offering I want to take but know I shouldn't. "Do you want kids, Kieran?"

Acid burns hot in my chest. I peel my tongue from the roof of my mouth and swallow. "I want your kids."

Another laugh. "Be serious."

My eyebrows arch, and she just blinks at me with her glassy gaze. Disbelieving, I'm sure, because she still thinks this is temporary. Thinks I'm temporary—that she'll one day be rid of me.

I know I'm no good for her, but the problem is that I don't seem to care.

I'm not good for anyone, but that doesn't stop me from hoping to one day be.

Because a little known caveat about an angel fallen from grace is that he never stops wanting it to be recaptured. Even at his darkest, that desire ebbs at his very core, a secret prayer that maybe his soul can be restored.

And I'm wondering if Juliet isn't my shot at redemption.

"Has anyone else ever called you daddy in bed?" she whispers, dipping her chin toward the mattress and dropping her eyes.

"Have you ever called anyone else that? You *did* initiate it, if I recall correctly."

"To annoy you! I didn't think you'd be into it."

"A dominant guy like me, enjoying a nickname that gives me power over you? What a crazy concept."

A smirk tugs at my lips, and I roll over again, flattening myself on top of her. She squeals, squirming and trying to push me off as I let my weight settle, pressing my face into the crook of her neck. Her giggles fill the room, and I want to keep her here, trapped against my satin sheets and happy, for as long as possible.

"Kieran, stop! You're smothering me!" She coughs around her laughter, and I burrow deeper into her warmth, wishing I could siphon some for myself. Wishing I could crawl inside her skin and sew myself into the chambers of her heart. "God, why are you so heavy? Do you eat lead or something?"

"No, baby, but I'm carrying a sizable package. Sometimes it weighs me down."

Her mouth falls open to retort; I can feel her hot breath against my ear, but a knock on the door makes us pause. Reaching behind me, I yank the comforter up and over our bodies, not bothering to move from my spot atop her as it swings open, my entire family standing at the threshold.

"If you're gonna sneak girls in, you should probably at least be quiet about it," Fiona says.

I turn my head toward them, rolling my eyes. "I'm a full-grown adult living with his parents. Maybe I'm not sneaking her in so much as I'm trying to avoid that particular conversation."

Footsteps thud against the hardwood floor as they approach, and when I glance to my right, my mother stands at the edge of the bed, a wide smile aimed right at us. "You must be Juliet! We've heard so much about you, dear."

Juliet's jaw drops, a soft whimper escaping as she buries her face behind her hands. "Um, hi there."

"*Mom*," I snap, embarrassment spreading through me, heating my cheeks.

"Are you fucking blushing right now?" Boyd's voice joins the foray, a tickle audible in his throat, and irritation flickers low in my belly, a flame I can't extinguish.

Murder. I want to slaughter every one of them right now.

"Christ, son, don't be stingy. We want to get to know her if she's gonna be spending her nights here, using our electricity. Our son." My father comes over to stand behind my mother, placing his hands on her tired shoulders. At least he has the decency not to look directly at us.

"Can we do it when I'm not butt-ass naked?" I tuck the comforter tighter around us, making sure no inch beneath Juliet's neck is exposed. Her shoulders shake, making something in me deflate at the thought of her being so humiliated she bursts into tears. "Seriously, fucking leave. Now."

My father rolls his eyes but seems to catch on to my tone. He steers my mother's wobbly form away toward the door. "Don't forget, we need to talk this afternoon."

"Juliet, sweetheart, you're invited to family dinner! It's Fridays at six, and everyone brings a dish."

"We're just gonna leave them in here? Come *on*, if this were me, you guys would be video chatting Grandma or live-streaming it like some Olympic event." Fiona waves her arms in our direction, glaring at me.

My father grips her bicep, tugging her along as he directs everyone from the room. "Should I remind you of the compromising position I found you and Boyd in last weekend?"

Boyd freezes, hands in his jean pockets, and my head whips around to him, eyes wide. "What the fuck?"

"It's not—"

"Yes, it is!" my mother sings, disappearing through the door.

Sliding off Juliet and letting the comforter drape over her, I scrub a hand through my hair and try to make sense of what my father just said. I blink once. Twice. Three times.

And it still doesn't compute. There's a nine-year age gap between them, and I've never seen them say more than a few words to each other without getting pissed off. Which, I suppose, is how the men in our world flirt, but still.

Boyd doesn't do relationships, and he certainly wouldn't be able to put up with Fiona's dramatics.

I shake my head, and he shifts uncomfortably. "Out."

He exhales. "Kieran, I swear—"

"Get. *Out.*"

Without a second glance, he hurries from the room, a cloud of chaos suffocating the room in his wake. I drop my face into my hands, rubbing at the headache forming behind my brow bone.

"Well, that was... a lot." Juliet's fingers snake up my bicep, squeezing my shoulder. She leans into my side, slipping her head under my armpit and peeking up at me. "You okay?"

"Peachy." I toss her famous response back at her, loving the smile that lights her face. It's almost enough to ward off the wave of mortification at my family's insanity. "Sorry about that."

She shrugs. "It's cool. I like how close you guys seem."

"Aren't you close with your sister?"

"Yeah, but she's always been more like a mom than your average sister. Our parents sucked. Or suck, I guess, since my real mom seems to be trying to wedge herself back into my life."

Pain pricks at my heart, and I try to swallow over the knot that forms in my throat. I think that darkness within her, that sadness that seems to be etched in her very essence, stems from being raised by people who shouldn't have had kids in the first place. Where her sister channeled the mistreatment into something useful, into vengeance, Juliet stuffed it down so deep that even she can't find the root anymore.

And I've been here, keeping her locket out of pure spite, trying to lure her to me. To entice her, use her body and steal her secrets.

I pull away from her and slip out of the bed, walking to

the wardrobe against one side of the room. Throwing the top drawer open, I rifle around for a moment, searching for the little velvet box that holds her most prized possession. When I was shot by the masked figure, the bullet caught on the chain, lodging the jewelry into the wound, and it was removed by Kal and cleaned by Boyd, who met me at the hospital after getting my 911 text.

Parting with it makes me physically nauseous for some reason, as if I'm giving Juliet the key to her freedom. But it doesn't matter. Keeping leverage over her doesn't matter anymore.

I don't fucking want it.

Closing the drawer and kneeling on the bed, I hold out the box. She cocks an eyebrow, pushing up on her elbow, and pries it apart. "My locket?"

"Yeah. I should've given it back a long time ago."

She squeals, dropping down to the flat of her back and cradling the box against her breasts, and I swear on everything I hold close that I've never seen anything more perfect than she is at that exact moment.

BOYD SHOWS me the computer screen, a monitor centered on the back alley behind The Bar. A clip of me approaching Juliet plays on a loop, the time and date stamp permanently marking itself behind my eyelids.

"This is Finn's feed, right? I mean, a little weird that it's just constantly playing, but not weird considering it's outside *his* bar."

My father rolls his eyes, stretching his arms carefully above his head, mindful of his shoulder injury. More or less identical to mine. "That's his feed, but not his *camera*. Meaning, this is playing somewhere else. Somewhere that's not Finn's office."

"There's a warehouse in Augusta we traced the IP address to, but the city clerk's office swears the building's been abandoned for years." Boyd pulls up a map, pointing at a blurry splotch circled in red. "Last known business listed to that physical address was the New Hope Assistance Project; an advocacy group for international refugees."

Ice grips my heart, shattering my bones. I pinch my eyes closed, an ache flaring up in my shoulder as I cross my arms. "The easiest people to make disappear."

"Exactly." My father points with his index finger, leaning back in his office chair. Per the physical therapist's instructions, he's allowed back at the office so long as he adheres to their exercises and limits his mobility, and I can already tell he's relieved to be back in control.

And frankly, I'm glad he's here too; after the abrupt meeting and revelation from the other day in my bedroom, I've been avoiding my best friend like the fucking plague, and without our barrier here, things would be ten thousand times more awkward.

For now, they're just mildly awkward. A slight tinge in the air that keeps us from relaxing fully.

Boyd clicks out of the window, pulling up the security footage again. "Point being, if someone from an organization like that—*especially* one lacking federal backing, which, according to their most recent tax filings from almost a decade ago, they were—had access to this feed on this night, it's not totally far-fetched to think that whoever attacked Juliet knew you guys had some sort of connection. And considering you've both been attacked and we've received threatening mail, my first assumption would be they're the same person. And they're probably an associate of Murphy's."

Nodding as he and my father begin reviewing logistics of continued investigation, considering how deep to bring in the Montaltos, my eyes zero in on the shadowy background of the tape, sure that I can see something shift. But it's on the outskirts, almost imperceptible, a ghost in our midst.

But I see it.

22

JULIET

THE HOUSE IS EERILY quiet when I drag myself out of bed. There's no toddler babble downstairs, no cartoon jingles or timers going off. Gripping the wrought-iron railing as I creep down to the main level of the house, I peer around the corner, scanning the open concept living area and kitchen for signs of life.

Nothing.

Dread swims in my veins, goose bumps popping up on my skin as I move toward the home gym and front room, keeping my back against the wall in case an intruder has come and slaughtered my entire family, and they're still lurking somewhere in the house.

After the altercation at The Bar, I refuse to be caught off guard ever again.

My assault is the one thing I've been able to open up to Hana about, but only in brief descriptions during our sessions. Since Kieran can't sleep with me *every* night, and the paralysis caused by that feeling of always being watched, always at risk, is starting to take its toll, I figure maybe telling her about some of it might keep me from spiraling completely.

Hana thinks my insomnia might be spurred on by a loss of control. She recommended meditation exercises that could help me relax, but each night I spend staring at a faceless ceiling, feeling like the world could swallow me whole if I stopped paying attention for even a second, renews my body's dedication to staying on high alert.

Instead, I'm trying to take my safety into my own hands. Luca volunteered to teach me basic self-defense, and Caroline gave me a pocketknife she used to carry. *Just in case.*

Because when you live with and love criminals, danger is ever present. A constant possibility.

I kick open the door to the gym, noting the unused equipment and emptiness, then turn and make my way back around to the kitchen, scoping the laundry and storage closets along the way. Getting to the front door, I crouch down and look out the window. Elia's SUV is gone, but these days it always is, anyway. Benito's Town Car sits in front of the garage, and Caroline's Camry is parked behind it.

My stomach plummets even further, lurching like a roller coaster making that first drop, when it's all you can do to keep your eyes closed as you crest the hill, imminent descent the only thing visible.

Pulling my phone from my pajama shorts pocket, I send both Caroline and Elia separate messages, put out feelers to Benito and Leo and Giacomo—Elia's right hand, who hasn't been around a lot lately for some reason, but would still know his boss's whereabouts—and wait, backing into the front door.

The pool off the back patio glimmers in the sunlight across the room, sprinkling in through the large single-pane windows lining the living area. My shallow breaths fill the air, bouncing off the intricate wall decor my sister changes out every few months. Right now, it's a rustic *home sweet home* theme, although the situation makes it feel anything but.

Movement outside draws my attention, and I see a shadow dance along the concrete just beyond the sheer navy curtains. I leave the door and walk over to the kitchen island slowly, unclasping the child lock on the drawer and retrieving a bread knife; not the best option, but it's the first thing my hand comes into contact with.

Creeping over to the glass back doors, that hurricane of anticipation swirls around my stomach, destroying everything in its wake, and I hold my breath as I throw the door open, whirling on the would-be attacker before he has a chance to catch his bearings.

I'm not expecting to aim a bread knife at a retired crime boss-turned-grandfather, but that's exactly what happens when he spins on me, catching my wrist and keeping the knife from harming him.

He swears in Italian, something I can't translate because Elia doesn't really speak it, so I haven't had to learn many words. Pointing with his thumb over his shoulder, the older man directs my attention to Poppy's blonde head of curls; she's asleep in a motorized swing, tucked beneath the shade off the patio.

Gesturing for me to follow him farther away from her, Orlando Montalto yanks the knife from my hand and slips it into the interior pocket of his suit jacket. More than half of it juts out, barely contained, but he closes the flap and crosses his arms over it. "A *bread* knife, *topolina?* Were you planning on serving me with garlic?"

I glare at him; although he looks like a much older version of his son with his salt-and-pepper pompadour and dark, unwavering gaze, he lacks a certain seriousness, as if becoming a grandfather was all it took for the former crime lord to relax into suburbia.

Technically, given how much time he's spent around the house at holidays and popping in on random afternoons—or late mornings, apparently—he should feel like a grandfather to me. He complains about property taxes, loves gardening, and shows people pictures of his entire family, mobsters included, any chance he gets.

But retirement doesn't make him less dangerous or important, and I think it's the stringent air of command that follows him that keeps me from connecting fully on that level.

Besides, I have a grandfather in a home in Augusta. I'm not really looking for a replacement.

Orlando's been in Boston catching up with the Riccis, an Italian family running underground life there that serves as the muscle and financial backing for the Montaltos here.

But that doesn't explain his current presence.

"What are you doing here? Where is everyone?" The thought that maybe he snapped and killed his family crosses my mind for a split second, and I take a step back, gaze flickering to Poppy, trying to determine the best course of action for rescuing a baby from harm and escaping it myself.

His gaze narrows, seeming to catch on to where my thoughts have wandered, and he snorts, rubbing his large nose with the base of his palm. "Calm down, Juliet. If I wanted to kill you, I'd surely have done it by now. I'm old, not stupid."

Crossing my arms over my chest, I cock a hip and wait,

unwilling to give him anything else before he offers me something.

"*Gesù Cristo*," he mutters, sounding just like his son. "Did no one tell you?"

"Tell me *what*?"

"Your sister's in labor. For fuck's sake, I *told* Benny to leave you a note. They asked me to come watch Poppy until you woke up."

I blink, trying to process his words. "I'm sorry, she's in *labor*? And no one thought to tell me?"

He shrugs, tossing Poppy a quick glance as my tone climbs higher, becoming almost inaudible. "I guess they didn't want to wake you."

"I'm gonna kill her."

Heading back to the glass door, I pull it open and slip inside, letting it fall closed behind me. It opens a second later, and Orlando follows me into the kitchen, a sleeping Poppy in one arm and my weapon of choice in the other. "Want your bread knife back?"

Resisting the urge to flip him off, I take my phone from my pocket and check for messages. There are two from Selma and Avery in the group chat and one from Luca, assuring me he hasn't heard from Elia today.

Orlando walks to one of the *Viscaya* couches, laying Poppy down on her back and tucking a maroon throw around her. He slips a pillow on one side, preventing her from rolling off, and then comes back over and starts rifling around in the kitchen cabinets, pulling out various cookware and ingredients.

I press send on a scathing message to my sister, one she won't even get for a while, depending on how far along she is. Scooping the spare keys from the ceramic bowl at the center of the quartz island, I slip on a pair of flip-flops by the stairs and start toward the front door.

"Where are you going?"

Pausing, I glance at Orlando over my shoulder. "Where do you *think*? I'm not gonna let Caroline go through labor alone."

"She's not alone," he notes, cracking an egg into a skillet, whisking milk in. "In fact, she's probably being better taken care of at this very moment than you can even imagine. You know *figlio mio* won't let any harm come to her."

"Right, but it's not like he *gets* it. He's never had a baby before."

"And you have?" He cocks an eyebrow, turning up the heat on the stove. "She's fine, *carina*. Come, sit and eat a frittata. I want to chat, anyway." My foot itches to move, my fingers curling around the keys until the jagged edges dig into my palms, indenting the skin like an engraving. "If you leave, I'll have the cops throw you in jail for grand theft auto, since I know your name isn't on the title of any vehicles in that driveway. Are you ready to be charged with a Class B felony at age twenty-two, Juliet?"

Groaning, I kick off my shoes; they thud against the wall and drop to the floor as I stomp back to the island and slide onto a barstool. "You're kind of a dick."

Chuckling, he moves from the stove to the counter and starts dicing red and green peppers. I watch silently as he transfers them from the cutting board to the skillet, then switches to an onion and jalapeño pepper and repeats the motions. "You don't rise up in the criminal underworld without being one."

This is the kind of relationship I yearned for with my father, the kind of easy give-and-take that didn't leave you feeling like you'd lost a piece of yourself in the exchange. But instead, all I ever got from him was a cold shoulder, a long list of insults that branded themselves into my skin, and a massive guilt-slash-abandonment complex.

"Elia says you don't cook."

"I don't."

"What are you doing right now?"

"Making you breakfast."

My face scrunches up as he flips the coagulated egg mixture, lightly browning both sides. "What'd you want to talk about?"

Picking a plate up and transferring the food onto it, he ignores my question. Turning from the stove, he sets the dish in front of me, sliding a fork beside it, and leaning against the countertop, eyebrows raised expectantly.

Mine lift as well.

Again, he swears in Italian. "It's rude not to eat something that's been specially prepared for you."

"How do I know you didn't poison it or something?" My eyes narrow at the yellow blob, raking over the red and green spots poking through. Though my stomach growls in anticipation, I cross my hands over it and push the desire down.

"Juliet, I'm not gonna kill you. Good Lord, you'd think I'm still in the fucking business or something."

"Sorry for being cautious."

He sighs, nodding as if he understands. As if he knows more about me than he should. "I heard about what happened at The Bar. Your boy caused quite a ripple in the underground defending your honor."

I scoff, picking up the fork and poking around at the frittata, wishing he'd just go away. If Caroline doesn't want me at the birth of her child, fine, but did she need to get me a babysitter?

Okay, so she got Poppy one. Same difference, when the man won't leave me the fuck alone.

"He's not my boy," I say, avoiding the rest of his sentence. "He's not *my* anything."

Propping his elbow on the counter, Orlando leans down, resting his chin in his hand. "That's not what he's telling people."

My stomach does a little flop at that, the blood in my veins singing at the idea of Kieran Ivers considering me something more than a piece of ass that lets him use me however he pleases.

While I don't need the title, now weeks after our little fling first began that afternoon at his cottage, it's nice to pretend I matter. Nice to feel like more than just a warm body, especially when he's become such an integral part of my daily life—we text through the day and spend most nights together.

I know what he looks and sounds like first thing in the morning—groggy and hoarse, with a soft twinkle in his emerald gaze that doesn't disappear until after he's sated and seated inside me—and that his brother was his hero when he was a kid.

I know he was never really into hacking like the whole of King's Trace believes. He says he did it out of boredom at first and happened to be decent at it when he worked briefly at his father's company, but that his reputation with it had been blown out of proportion.

I know his mom has Lewy Body Dementia and is slowly deteriorating before their eyes, and it makes the entire family feel helpless. He started playing chess a few years ago when her tremors got so bad, she couldn't really go out in public. It was something the two of them could do together, although she would beat him every time and he still doesn't fully understand the game.

He occupies my free thoughts, and I occupy his free time.

By most counts, that would constitute a relationship. At the *very* least, a friends-with-benefits type deal. And sometimes, when he tucks me into his side as we drift off to our dreamscape, after he's fucked me until I can't see straight, it's easy to make believe that there's more to us. Layers we've yet to discover.

But I know that's not what this is. Sexual compatibility does not necessarily a relationship make.

Absently, I finger my locket at the base of my collarbone; the cold metal is a stark reminder that there's a countdown on our time together, an end looming closer and closer with each passing day.

I got what I wanted, and vice versa. Soon, there won't be a reason for either of us to justify being together.

Why does that make me feel so empty?

Orlando shifts, drawing my attention from the impending spiral of despair I can feel myself slipping into; tentatively, I take a bite of the frittata, savoring the explosive flavors as they hit my tongue but trying to stifle my reaction to keep him at bay.

It doesn't work. A grin curves over his lips, making the slight cleft in his chin disappear. "You love it!"

I dive in for another bite, chewing carefully. "It's not horrible."

He guffaws, tipping his head back and then snapping forward, leaning to inspect Poppy; she shifts, moving her chubby arms as she stretches, but then she stills, unperturbed by his sudden outburst. "I'll be sure to tell my ninety-year-old mother her traditional, authentic Italian recipe is 'not horrible.'"

Devouring the rest of the plate as my hunger kicks in, I finish in a few bites and push the dish back, patting my stomach. "See, I knew it wasn't you cooking. You were channeling her."

Nodding, he takes the plate and sets it in the sink, folding his arms across his chest and pressing his backside into the counter. "You're probably right. She and my late wife."

A knot forms in my chest, pushing my organs aside. "Did she cook a lot?"

From what I've gathered from my sister's occasional stories—usually initiated by too much wine or when she cooks something with a Danish origin—Elia's mom died when he was young, and it's not something either Montalto ever really talks about.

Yet here Orlando is, nodding his assent, opening his mouth like he's ready. "That she did. Was fantastic, too. Could make even stale food taste fresh. That's where Elia gets it from, his mother and grandmother. I never had that gene. Too impatient for cooking."

Silence settles between us, a ping from my phone the first to break it. It's Elia, letting me know mom and baby are doing great, and an emergency C-section was performed. That's why he hasn't been able to contact me yet.

"Noah Montalto has arrived," I say as a second text comes in, this one a picture; I turn the screen to face my nephew's grandfather, noting the rare genuine smile that lights his entire face. The baby's got big blue eyes like me, Caroline, and Poppy, and a dark head of hair tucked under his little knit cap, and it makes my stomach clench.

"A made man in the making." Orlando beams, a ray of sunshine starting to burn my skin.

It's way too fucking early for all of this.

Pursing his lips, he studies me quietly as I pull back, sending my congratulations and a promise to kill the happy couple as soon as my warden lets me visit. "Can I go now?"

"Made men are a different breed of people, you know," he says.

Furrowing my brow, I squint at him. "What?"

His fingers tap on the countertop, the massive signet rings on them glittering beneath the kitchen lights. Fingers that have inflicted pain and also warmth, a contradiction I find it hard to keep up with. "We love different. Quicker. Fiercer. *Violently.* Because we know how easily everything can be taken away. We protect, even if it means death. Even if it means *murder.*"

"What's your point?" My tongue feels thick as I swallow, nerves bouncing around in my stomach like butterflies caught in a cage.

"My *point* is, even if you don't think Kieran Ivers is dedicated to you after what he did, after the target it put on him to do it, you're not familiar with the brand. Men like us don't avenge just anyone."

It dawns on me then that Orlando's putting Kieran in the same category as his own men—*made men.* Something Kieran was long before he ever even met me, maybe long before King's Trace even knew about it.

Unease settles in the pit of my stomach, a concrete block I can't chisel away at. Not even with the meditative techniques Hana is attempting to teach me. It builds and builds, a slow-burning wildfire on a path of destruction, incinerating everything in its wake until all that's left is a shell of debris.

Orlando finally lets me leave, having said his two cents I suppose—interesting that he didn't say *more*, considering the long-standing rivalry between the Ivers and the Montaltos. It wasn't quite a blessing, not quite a curse, so I find myself drifting through a sort of limbo, confused about everything.

The sort of limbo I've spent my entire life existing in, unsure of everyone's feelings toward me. Unsure of how I feel about *myself*. Wracked with guilt and shame brought on primarily by the actions of others. Actions I had no hand in.

Like my father, a man who couldn't commit to loving me.

Yet I've spent nearly every day since his death wondering *why*, wishing he'd given me even a kernel of affection. Wishing the yearning in my heart was valid.

Then with my mother, a woman who always valued reputation and money over her daughters—a woman who disappeared during the most tumultuous time in my life and returned out of nowhere after two years of radio silence.

A woman who, against all rationale, I still wish would change and want to be my mother. Be proud of me for pursuing life even when I didn't want to.

Panic blurs the corners of my vision, clogging my veins and seizing my muscles as I think about being stuck in this same place with Kieran, a man whose sins far outweigh what most can even imagine, if the skeletons in his closet are any indication.

Like a fool, I've fallen for the glitz of a handsome face and nixed the need for sincere promises. For concrete evidence of real affection. I've never even really asked about the rumors or the darkness surrounding him.

Luca comes and picks me up a little while later, and I

spend the rest of the afternoon doting on my nephew while my sister sleeps, and Elia slips out to make a few phone calls. Caroline apologizes as she drifts off, saying there wasn't time to wake me, but I wave her off, no longer caring the second I have Noah in my arms.

There's an air about newborns. Something redemptive in their existence. I finger the paper bracelet on his tiny wrist as he blinks up at me, stirring from a fitful slumber.

My phone buzzes in my pocket, but I ignore it; Kieran's been texting all afternoon, but I'm not in the mood to chat. Not in the mood for disappointment.

As I stare into the incredibly clear eyes of this new slate, a pang shatters my insides, brokenness sloshing around like a cyclone. I hug Noah a little tighter, sending a quick message to the universe. A promise not to let the world destroy him.

He clucks and wiggles, those soft baby noises I didn't realize I'd been missing since Poppy started forming words. They warm my heart, a balm to the emptiness wreaking havoc in my heart, and it's that warmth, that innocence, I focus on later when I make my way back to the cemetery for the first time since my run-in with my mother.

Pulling a bottle of Wild Turkey from my messenger bag, I set it up beside my father's headstone. The temptation to uncap it and backslide is heavy, but I resist. The longer I stare at it, the more I connect it to his drunken rages when I was a kid. The nights he'd disappear into Caroline's room and leave her a sobbing mess.

The nights I'd spend pressed up against her bedroom door, turning the knob against its lock, begging her to let me in after he left. All the nights I went unheard, thinking she just didn't want to see me—when really, she was protecting me.

Like she's always done.

And as I try to reconcile that, try to understand why she kept me in the dark and didn't let me shoulder any of her pain, I realize I'm doing the same thing now. Getting bogged down by invisible sadness and resentment and not letting her help. Not letting anyone in.

Seeing ghosts where they don't deserve to exist.

Dawn falls over the graveyard, and I wrap my arms around my knees, barring myself against the chill as the wind sweeps through the trees, guiding the spirits home. I can almost taste them and feel death as it creeps along my skin, goose bumps preening like ripened fruit.

Although, it's not the dead I'm afraid of.

"Juliet." I'm not at all surprised when I hear him. He sounds out of breath, as if he walked all the way here from his cottage in the woods. Or maybe from the mansion on the hill, where he lives a falsely normal life, hidden away from his sins behind those walls.

I stare harder at my father's name, feeling Kieran settle on the ground beside me; I try not to lean into his side, to soak up the warmth he provides. I'm not sure how to take his comfort without feeling like I'm selling a piece of my heart in return.

We sit in silence, and eventually he reaches over, gripping my knee in his large palm. "You've been ignoring me."

I shrug, noting the way his jaw clenches. The harshness of his stance, the rigidity in his spine.

"Want to tell me what the fuck's going on here? Why I had to scour the entire fucking town, drawing attention to myself and the fact that I'm a fucking target?"

My eyes find his, the push and pull in my brain making my head throb. Of course, he's a target in part because of me, but also because that's the name of the game in King's Trace. You can't be a part of the crime without your own fair share of enemies. "Are you telling people we're dating?"

He blinks, dragging his free hand through his dark brown locks; they tumble over his forehead, curling slightly from the thick humidity in the air. My fingers itch to bury themselves in his soft tresses, to get lost in him, but I shove them beneath my butt and refrain.

"No," he draws out slowly, studying me with an unreadable expression. Blinking hard a few times, he shakes his head, turning to face me more. "Would that trouble you, if I were, though? I'm not gonna share you, Juliet, so if whatever we're doing isn't enough, then yeah. You can be my girlfriend."

A humorless laugh falls from my lips. "Oh, great. I love the lukewarm sentiment."

His lips flatten into a thin line, and his hand moves from my knee up to my arm, wrapping around my bicep and tugging me toward him. *Into him.* I press my hands into his taut chest, keeping us apart enough that I can watch him.

"Baby, nothing about us has been *lukewarm* from the get-go. It went from a tiny spark, that flare of hatred mixing with desire that neither of us could really pin down, to me murdering someone in your defense. Risking everything for you. To you consuming my every waking thought, making my dick hard and my heart ache when I'm not around you. I can't sleep without you lying next to me, can't relax unless I know you're safe. What's lukewarm about that?"

"Nothing," I whisper, bringing my thumb up and

pushing it into the crease just beneath his plump lower lip. "That's what scares me."

"Kitten, I'm gonna need some clarification."

Pulling away, I sit up straight and focus on the slab of granite in front of us. My chest feels tight, the tendons stretching against the pain bracketing them inside. "All I ever wanted was for my father to *be* a father. A normal one without any qualifying adverbs attached to the pronoun. I spent my whole life wondering why he couldn't love me the way he did Caroline, only to find out a couple of years ago that the whole time, he wasn't *loving* her either. He didn't love us at all, just saw her as a means to an end and me as a mistake."

Kieran tenses beside me, his muscles tightening, expanding against the fabric of the black hoodie he has on. But he stays quiet, waiting. Giving me room.

I swallow a breath of air and press on, despite the ache in my bones begging me not to. Despite the distant warning from my mother, a woman who doesn't deserve the space she rents in my brain.

Because even if Kieran Ivers is the devil himself, I find myself wanting to burn right alongside him.

"Every day since his death, I've wrestled with the guilt that comes along with missing someone who never treated me right in the first place. Someone who doesn't deserve my love, even in the afterlife."

Tears well in my eyes, and I glance up at him, unable to stop them from spilling over. They streak down my cheeks, and I hate the way his face softens, hate how he makes me break as much as I love the freedom that comes from fragmentation.

"He *hurt* Caroline, neglected me, and was a piece of shit

in general. What does that say about me for being sorry that he's gone? For *still* wishing he'd been better?"

Kieran's hands slip under my thighs, pulling me up and onto his lap. His palm comes to the back of my head, cradling it carefully. I wallow in the silence, soaking his shirt, the tide inside me being pushed and pulled against the shore; it crashes in sudden spurts, waning outward with each breath I take, confusing me.

But the warmth in this man's arms is constant—the only thing keeping me afloat, even as I sit and struggle with my feelings for him.

"It says you're human, Juliet. That pain in your heart? That shattering feeling that makes it hard for you to breathe? It's there because you're full of forgiveness and love." His voice rumbles in his chest. "Not because there's anything wrong with you. It is *not* your fault someone abused the love you tried to give them."

All of that only makes my chest hurt more. "What if the only people I'm capable of loving are the broken ones?"

"Then you love their shattered pieces and do your best not to get cut on the edges."

"What if they don't mean to cut me?" I hiccup, swiveling my gaze to his. "What if they can't help it?"

I can't tell if he understands what I'm saying—that I'm terrified of inadvertently getting hurt by him, when I've come to rely on his warmth for so much. I'm afraid of his broken pieces no longer wanting to shatter next to mine.

Pushing the hair from my face, he swipes his thumbs over my cheeks, drying the skin and pressing a kiss to my forehead. "I will dull my edges to keep you safe," he murmurs, moving to brush his lips against mine. "I'd much rather you cut me than the other way around."

It's the gentlest he's ever been, my breakdown seeming to shift something in him. Something between us. I can feel it, like a cosmic imbalance in the universe working itself out through us.

He dips down again, kissing me fully and stealing the doubt from my body; he lays me down on the ground, the heaviness of the conversation forgotten as things heat up between us, and he's stripping me bare and mounting me before I get a chance to really ask about *his* broken pieces.

We don't mention how what we're doing is the ultimate desecration of this once holy place, or how it feels so fucking right to come together here, suddenly.

How right it feels to defy a spirituality that only brings us sadness, how his body inside mine drives out all the evil harbored in my heart, like a sponge absorbing it and adding to his own.

Neither of us happens to notice the figure lurking in the shadows, watching. Waiting to siphon our happiness and destroy it.

23

KIERAN

THE SOUND of bone crunching beneath the weight of your shoe isn't something you ever really get used to. No matter how many dozens of hands you've broken with the same tactic, the dull crack, sometimes clean and sometimes rattling, followed by mangled screams of agony—that sticks with you forever.

For a long time, it was the screaming that kept me up at night—the look in a person's eyes as the crunching morphed into fracturing and kept going, sometimes pushing them to their utmost limits, because I knew they wouldn't be around much longer, anyway. So what was the point of holding back?

This isn't the life I asked for, but when you're born into a world where violence bleeds from every corner, tainting the innocence you were supposed to keep a lot longer than you did, eventually you sink into your role. Accept the burden and the power that comes with it.

Two of Elia's men grab the fragile-looking junkie and haul him up by his feet, securing his ankles to the hooks in the concrete wall. Crimson's basement looks exactly like a dungeon of unspeakable horrors, with a mix of Kal's medieval tools and their various weapons of torture strewn about the damp, dark backdrop.

Very faintly, the bass from the speakers on the club floor above us filter in through the copper piping, but other than that, it's completely silent down here. Almost another world entirely.

Marco Alessi is the softest of the Montalto outfit, and he steps back and lets Elia's second-in-command, Giacomo Marelli, take over the bindings. Marco runs a hand over his brown hair, studying the junkie's mangled fingers and the way his crumpled bones jut against thin, translucent skin. The Italian's face pales the longer he stares, and I clamp a hand down on his shoulder, jarring him from the sight.

"Not quite a Renaissance painting, is it?"

He scrubs at his jaw, the tattoos lining his arms dancing with the movement. We're all dressed in PPE, plastic scrubs and hairnets, except for him in his T-shirt and cargo shorts, as if he came knowing he wouldn't take part in the more gruesome acts of the evening.

"Fuck off, prick," he snaps, jerking away from me.

I smirk, letting my arm fall to my side. If it makes him feel better to lash out, fine.

He can call me whatever the fuck he wants; at least I don't have a weak-ass stomach.

The metal door to the basement swings open, Elia and his bald goon stepping inside just as it slams shut. Coming to stand on one side of me, opposite of Boyd on my left, Elia adjusts his cuff links and gestures toward the victim. "We wrapping up here any time soon? I have people waiting for me at home."

Giacomo's dark eyes swivel toward his boss for a moment, then he steps forward. He slides the metal strap in place against the junkie's ankle, placing another strap of leather between the man's incomplete set of teeth, giving his *capo* an indecipherable look as he straightens and walks over. He holds out a dermatome with one gloved hand, and I take it, approaching the bound man slowly as he hangs upside down, watching me with barely focused eyes.

I don't get to do a ton of torture; I'm mostly disposing, doing what the regular fixers can't—and most fixers like to get their hands dirty. I got lucky with Kal's weird moral compass, which sometimes lures him into the darkness and other times convinces him it's a bad place to be.

I don't need to be convinced, though. I'm right where I'm meant to be.

Setting the dermatome on the wooden table near the body, I reach for a larger instrument. One that's been rigged to act like a dermal punch, with a metal head the size of my palm. The junkie whimpers as I loom closer, running the tip of my index finger along the sharp, circular edge of the tool, his body stiffening as it prepares for what's to come.

Despite the abuse he's already taken at my hands, the purpled skin and broken bones, he still tries to fight me off. I watch him squeeze his eyes shut and press his lips together, watch his hamstrings clench when I'm only a whisper away.

None of it deters me, just like the fear of the girls he helped kidnap didn't stop him from violating them. Selling them.

Killing them.

Rage makes my hands shake as I glare down at his naked form, his flaccid dick a deformed lump barely attached to his body. His dick was the first thing to go—when Boyd tracked him down on the outskirts of Portland, living under a different name and trying to pass himself off as a veteran before we hauled him back here for questioning.

Unfortunately, Murphy's organization must have been pretty tight-lipped, because when we started breaking his fingers and toes, he still didn't have anything to offer. All he could tell us was that he'd been paid a hefty lump sum to grab girls off the streets during their regular routines. They typically hit neighborhoods on the Maine-Canada border, aiming for younger teens, and then would drop them at a hidden location in Augusta and pass them off as refugees, hoping no one ever came looking for them.

But they caught Mel instead, a fuckup that'd cost my brother everything. They'd been dating at the time, and after learning what the men did to her at the warehouse, how they stole from her in front of the other girls and the men beneath his command, Murphy went off the deep end.

He lost what little splintered pieces of his mind existed and launched himself off the cliff of depravity, sinking into the caricature of the psychopath that King's Trace had already painted him as. I found him fucking corpses at his cottage, having taken his girlfriend so aggressively she lay passed out, bleeding below the waist on his bed.

And so I, then only a monster by association, did what needed to be done. I carved the evil from his body, dissolved his flesh in my bathtub, and dumped his sloshy remains into Lake Koselomal, praying no one ever entered it and came into contact with him.

Later, I cleaned his bones, loving the way it made me feel renewed—as if taking justice into my own hands was the only way to cleanse the darkness from my soul. A darkness I wasn't entirely aware of how it originated.

When Mel asked me to help her forget the horrors she'd experienced, when she turned to drugs as an escape and spurred my dominant fantasies by letting me abuse her as a way to take back control of her body—I didn't think anything of it. I just took over as my brother, taking his place so seamlessly, it was as if we'd been the same all along.

His boss came for me, demanding payments I didn't have any knowledge of and accusing me of getting the feds involved. They burned down the operation and seemed to cut ties, but paranoia, once branded into your skin, doesn't heal very easily.

I pulled out of Ivers International and holed up in the mansion with my deteriorating mother, who most of the time pretended I was the only son she'd ever had. Or forgot, more likely. She prayed hard for my soul, but I sold it the first time I agreed to do exactly what Ivers men have been doing for decades.

But it was never the killing that bothered me, never the destruction of men who deserved it that kept me awake at night. It was the knowledge that, unless I killed everyone on the face of the planet, I'd never be safe.

So I keep doing my job—if I can't be safe, these men can't either.

Gripping the sharp instrument in my palm, I poise it over the skin above the man's knee and cock an eyebrow, pulling the leather strip from his mouth. Sweat drips off his face, his tears staining his hollowed cheeks, and the sight warms my insides. "You're sure you don't know *anything* else? No locations, no names, no timelines?"

He shakes his head, thrashing, trying to dislodge himself. "Man, I fucking told you everything I could. You said you'd let me go—"

"Oh, you poor soul." I pat his cheek, my voice saturated in condescension. He jerks back, nipping at my fingers. Chuckling, I shove the leather back between his lips, irritation flaring in my gut at yet another dead end.

Emphasis on dead.

"All deals with the devil are double-edged swords; you die on either side."

Shifting my weight, I grind the metal tool into the meaty flesh of his thigh; he's thin, so it pops through the membrane without much force, and I pull back on the handle, carving out a large chunk of skin and muscle. It falls through the head of the instrument and onto the floor, and as blood streams from the wound down the length of the man's shin, I position myself at his other leg, his gurgled wails of agony like a goddamn symphony I want to play as the soundtrack of my life until I die.

"*Wait,*" he sobs, the word barely coherent through his gag. I glance back at Elia, wondering if he's willing to stick around a while longer or if he wants me to speed things up. He shrugs, pulling his sleeve up to check his watch, and then gives me a curt nod. Giacomo scratches absently at his short, dark buzzcut, watching my every move, as if he's afraid I might snap and kill any one of them for no reason.

Like I have any interest in hurting the brother-in-law of the girl I'm falling in love with.

The realization hits me like a sucker punch to the gut, knocking the wind from my lungs at once; I stumble forward, catching myself on the wall, trying to suppress the voracious shake in my bones. The one that calls out for someone I'm not worthy of.

Someone already so broken, I'm afraid all I'll do is make her worse.

But I can't think about that now. I don't want to imagine her while finishing this guy off.

I rip the leather from his mouth, his teeth rattling as they come back together. "Speak," I bark, reveling in how he winces. Like he's aware of just what I might do to him if he pisses me off any further.

His face screws up, an expression of pure suffering twisting his mouth and making his eyes pinch closed. I tap the toe of my boot, pushing the cool metal tool against his thigh impatiently. Inhaling a deep, ragged breath, his blood-shot eyes pop back open, seeking mine.

"The woman you're looking for, the lady behind the existence of the trade in this part of the state. You kill me, that doesn't stop her from coming for you."

"What woman?"

"The *boss*."

Elia steps up, crossing his arms over his chest. "You're telling us a woman's behind the missing people and them being sold. All of that?"

"I mean, I only know the rumors we heard between transports. We never saw her or anything."

Boyd clears his throat, having tagged along because he didn't have anything better to do. Although a part of me wonders if he isn't here to prove his loyalty to me, since we've scarcely spoken over the last couple of weeks. "There's a woman on our surveillance tapes from The Bar. She's always hooded, standing just off to the side like she knows she's being recorded. Only ever watches, doesn't move to come inside the club or anything."

My head whips around, my eyes narrowing at my best friend. "Why the fuck is this the first I'm hearing about it?"

"I didn't realize it was a woman until now." He shrugs,

leaning against a crate full of assault rifles. "I *thought* the person was on the smaller side, but them being a woman didn't cross my mind. It makes the most sense, though. None of us would ever go out of our way to look for someone like that, especially as the head of a fucking sex trafficking ring."

Fuck. "Then we've been investigating the wrong fucking people."

The junkie's face pales beneath the sheen of his blood, still steadily dripping from his thigh. "Can I go now?"

Elia grumbles something unintelligible under his breath, moving back to discuss logistics with Giacomo over where to head next. How to shut this whole thing down, how to find the elusive woman. My gaze homes in on the gap in the junkie's skin, and instead of continuing on with the other, scraping out pieces of his flesh until he resembles swiss cheese, I yank the .22 from the holster at my waist and fit the barrel against his temple.

"You ever show any of those girls mercy?" I ask. He swallows, his cries starting up again, hiccups speeding up the flow of his blood with each intake of breath. "Ever let any of them go, let them leave with their innocence intact?"

Without giving him a chance to answer, as if he could alter this outcome anyway, I cock the gun and let my finger brush against the trigger.

No one says anything as a hole suddenly appears in the man's skull, blood painting the wall behind him and pouring out of his nose. It coats my skin as I step back, wiping my face with my sleeve.

I've never shown mercy myself. I don't particularly care for it.

And even though it's possible we could've gotten more out of the man, it wouldn't have changed anything. So why show mercy when you no longer have anything to prove or lose?

WHEN I CRAWL through Juliet's window later that night, I find her asleep at her desk, drooling on top of an open textbook. Her summer semester doesn't start for another couple of weeks, but she's been trying to catch up on readings so that she doesn't fall too far behind the other students.

I don't really understand her apprehension, given that she spends most of her free time living and breathing the subject, but what do I know? I'm just the person keeping her warm at night.

Scooping her into my arms, I bring her limp body to the bed and settle her in the middle, pulling off her socks and tossing them on the floor. She stirs, blinking up at me with sleepy eyes I want to drown in, then tucks her hands beneath her cheek.

"Did I fall asleep during sex again?"

"Again?" I frown, shucking my jacket and jeans off and climbing in beside her, pulling the covers up over us.

"Yeah." She yawns, scooting over and fitting herself into my side. My arms encircle her tiny, pliant body, heating from our connection as my pulse kicks up a notch. "Sometimes I do that."

My fingers flex against her bare shoulder. "Kitten, I promise that if you ever fall asleep while I'm inside you, I'll fuck you so hard you won't ever sleep again. And if you don't stop remembering the men before me, I'm gonna strap you down and fuck your ass until you bleed."

Nuzzling into me, I feel her grin against my neck, her hand splaying out on my chest. "Promise?"

"Yeah, baby, I do."

"Good."

"How's studying going?" I whisper against her hairline, flipping off the lamp on her nightstand.

She huffs. "Boring. I feel like a freshman plopped down in a five-hundred level class. My brain doesn't even know what to do with the lecture materials at this point."

I shift, pulling her higher up on my pec. "Why marine biology? You don't even seem to like it that much."

In fact, the only things she seems to have an interest in are playing with her niece and nephew and spending her nights with me. Occasionally, I'll catch her scrolling through her phone, reading local news articles or academic blogs, but any time I ask about her interest in journalism or politics, she clams up.

"I love science," she says after a beat of silence, swirling her index finger around my nipple. It puckers, and she giggles, sucking in a deep breath. "Caroline had her thing growing up, and I had mine. Only Daddy—ahem, *my father* —insisted that it was a man's world. He always used to say any company that hired a brain-dead bimbo like me would just toss me out and feed me to the sharks. If they weren't hiring me to be the company slut, that is."

There's a twinkle in her eyes as she drifts backward in time, her gaze distancing from me. I cup her chin to draw her back; she blinks, a soft smile tugging at her lips. "I guess when I applied for college, I subconsciously chose marine biology to fuck with him."

The smug glint in her irises has a confession dripping from the edge of my tongue, but I bite the tip, keeping myself in check. Now is *not* the time, but fuck if the spiteful vixen inside my little bird, my kitten, doesn't make my dick throb and my chest tight with need. With *feelings.*

"What would he think of this?" I swipe my thumb over her cheekbone, mesmerized by the smoothness of her skin, the flawlessness of her existence. She's a pure flower, sprung from the earth to bring color and joy, and I can't help feeling like I've plucked her too soon. Clipped her petals and pulled them from the stem. "Of you and me?"

"Oh, he'd loathe it. Especially since he wanted to give Caroline to you." Her smirk slips, and she leans into my touch, shaking her head. "But the only opinions on us that matter are our own."

"Oh?" I raise an eyebrow. "And how do you feel about us, kitten?"

"I feel like..." she trails off, staring up at the ceiling as she loses herself in thought. I inhale that rich vanilla scent that seeps from her pores, trying to commit every inch of her to memory in case any of this turns south. "Like you and I are gonna be okay."

I laugh. "Beautiful lukewarm sentiment."

She pushes up on an elbow, running a hand along my chest. "You'd be scared if I gave you the unabridged version."

The breath whooshes from my lungs as our eyes lock, trapping us in a chokehold we don't struggle against. There's no point—we're too far gone.

"I'm not really sure how to reconcile what you do for a living," she admits, moving to lay her head in the crook of my neck. "But I think I'm starting to accept some evils in this world exist to protect the good. Some sights are so ghastly, and some buildings are so haunted, but it's like they're trying to preserve what's left inside. And sometimes, what's left is worth the bad shit."

I gaze out the window past her, counting the stars dotting the night sky and feeling infinitesimal in comparison. I'm not sure how I can feel like the weight of the world rests on my shoulders when it's clear the stars carry most of the load. That's why they're scattered, displacing our troubles in the dark so we don't have to face them in the light.

"I think you're only evil because you choose to be," she whispers, the sound so soft I have to strain to hear it. I roll toward her, twisting my legs with hers. "I think you're scared."

"Baby, sometimes people are just bad. There's no rhyme or reason. They just *are*."

"Maybe. But you're not one of them."

"Are we just conveniently forgetting all the horrible things I've done to you?"

"I'm not forgetting them. I'm choosing to forgive you because the good you've done for me matters more." She presses a kiss to the column of my throat. "And before you say it, no, I'm not giving you an upper hand by letting those things go. Forgiveness is for *me*, not you. It's my peace of mind and my sanity on the line. If it helps you sleep at night, that's just a bonus."

Heaving a sigh, I trail my fingers through her hair, my heart beating so hard I'm sure she can feel it shake the bed. "You talking to your therapist more these days?"

"Maybe." She snuggles into my side, trying to burrow into me. "I'm working on it. But mostly, it's a battle with *me*. It's like... playing a game of chess with yourself, right? You've got all the pieces for a good game, but your opponent knows all your moves and tricks."

Her breathing evens out, the soft rise and fall of her chest causing a canyon to split wide open inside me. The feel of having her here against me, despite everything I've ever done, makes me ache.

"Maybe one day I'll teach you how to play," she murmurs, her last words before she falls back asleep.

My heart pounds so hard I'm afraid it might crack a rib and burst straight from my chest.

I don't deserve her. She's springtime, rebirth and resurrection, a field flowering after months of endless slumber. The darkness I thought stains her soul is nothing more than a blanket that's slowly being ripped away with each passing day. It's not permanent or set in stone.

Not yet, anyway.

And I fear the longer I keep her with me, the harder I fall, the more irreparable she becomes.

But now I have no intentions of letting her go.

24

KIERAN

"I can't DO it anymore, Daddy. I just can't. She absolutely refuses to let anyone but me help her, and I'm drowning in schoolwork trying to take care of her. I'm a kid. I'm not equipped to handle this shit."

Shifting my weight onto the balls of my feet, I lean against my father's closed office door as Fiona's voice bleeds past the heavy wood. His seventy-year-old, gray-haired assistant, Valerie, let me in without asking, which is why I'm still standing in the top floor lobby at Ivers International, eavesdropping.

"Sweetheart, I know it's hard." My dad's voice is slow, exhausted, and I can practically imagine him swiping a hand down his haggard face, trying to get her to listen.

There's no mystery revolving who they're talking about, and the fact that my mother has become such a point of tension between the two pierces my heart with remorse. I've barely been around lately, and Fiona's the one taking the brunt of our mother's condition.

"It's not hard, it's *impossible*. She loses more and more

control over her body every single day and refuses to acknowledge it. Half the time, she can't even remember her own name, or she's off in dreamland with Murphy, acting like he wasn't practically burned at Kieran's stake."

"Stress can have a great toll on our memories—"

Something slams down, maybe her palms hitting the surface of his desk. "Mom needs *help*. And not the kind I can give her. Not anymore."

"What're you doing?"

I startle, knocking my browbone on the door as Boyd's voice fills the air. He approaches slowly, smoothing a hand over the black suspenders attached to his gray slacks. We haven't spoken much, still, because he's not really the confrontational type and I don't normally hold grudges. Not with him, anyway.

My mother always used to call him a lover, not a fighter. The calm, quiet sort—exactly why I need him in my corner to offset the asshole vibes I toss at everyone.

We've never really had relationship issues, and I suppose I don't know how to navigate our situation.

Inside the office, Fiona's voice pitches an octave, and I slide my gaze to my best friend, taking him in. Maybe the fact that he deals with my shit so well means he'd be the perfect match for her.

All the talking I've been doing over the past few weeks with Juliet has me feeling like I need to throw him a bone and fix the rift between us. It's a rift I can't quite afford—the devil needs as many allies as he can get.

Still.

"Are you fucking my sister?" I ask in lieu of an answer, snapping up straight. Valerie glances through the glass divider at us, her fingers pausing over her keyboard, but I ignore her and lower my voice. Everyone in this town likes to sell stories to the tabloids, and I don't want this one front and center. "She's practically a kid, asshole."

His jaw tenses, eyes darkening. "She's *not* a kid, but that's beside the point, because I'm not fucking her."

"Then why did my dad—"

"He walked in on me helping her with homework in her room, and he just assumed, I guess."

No part of me can envision that. "That's a pretty large assumption."

"She's into me." He shrugs, leaning against the door. "Always has been, I think. I don't see her like that."

I squint at him, remembering how he stopped her from leaving with a frat guy at the gala all those weeks ago. Crossing my arms over my chest, I study him for a few beats of silence. His forehead creases and the corded muscles in his neck strain against his skin.

"You know I don't give a shit if you like her, right? I'm not that kind of brother. I mean, I'll cut out your heart if you hurt her, but—"

He rolls his eyes. "Thanks for the permission, but she's way too young for me."

"Nine years." I shrug. "That really matter in the grand scheme of things?"

"Look, it's great you've found your happily ever after and shit, but that's not in the cards for me, all right? I'm not the guy for Fiona." He straightens, yanking on a suspender, and I can't deny the quiver in my chest when he mentions my happiness. Because fuck if I don't hope he's right, and that the darkness in my heart isn't enough to keep out Juliet's light. "I have too much shit on my plate as it is, and I don't want to talk about it."

Cocking my head, I start to ask what's going on with him but am cut off when the door swings wide open, Fiona's red hair flying back with the force. She meets Boyd's hazel gaze for half a second, and I see a flare of hurt behind her big brown eyes, but she tamps it down within seconds, turning to look at me instead.

"Mom's moving into a home, and we're selling the house."

I blink, my brain struggling to wrap around her words. "Excuse me?"

"You heard me. All of us need out of that haunted mansion, and she needs twenty-four-hour care that I can't give her. Talk to Dad about the specifics, I'm going to drama club." Tossing her hair over her shoulder, she whips the ends against Boyd's chest as she pushes past us. She saunters out of the office lobby to the elevators, the click from the needle-thin heels of the thigh-high boots she has on reverberating in the air.

I don't miss the way Boyd stares after her, even once she's disappeared into the elevator.

With no fucking clue what just happened and no time to address it, I shake my head and enter the office. My father sits behind his desk, his legs propped up on the wooden tabletop and holding a glass of scotch in his hand. "Your sister is something else."

"You guys raised her that way." Boyd and I settle into the plastic seats across from him, and I toss a yellow folder onto the desk. "Selling the house?"

My father scoffs, taking a swig of his drink and dropping his feet to the floor. "Yeah, right. And have the spirits of everyone who's ever died there follow me elsewhere? No, thanks. They need to stay contained."

The Ivers and their fucking superstitions. I'm starting to wonder if I'd be a different man without them.

"What's this?" he asks, flipping the file open. The photographs sit in front, on top of various financial documents, shipping details, and businesses involved in the underground sex trade our little town's fully entrenched in. "You have a lead?"

"The associate we pulled from Augusta had ties to the old warehouse there, the one Murphy was in charge of. We've eliminated Finn Hanson as a suspect because the timeline doesn't add up to when he moved to King's Trace; this shit was going on long before he showed up, and the Stonemore gang doesn't have the financial backing or political reach to pull off something this large. They also don't have the interest, according to Finn. He'd rather they deal in less severe forms of sex work and laundering."

Boyd moves forward, pulling sheets from the folder and spreading them on the desk. He points at a grainy picture, one from the night I cornered Juliet in the alleyway outside The Bar, tapping on the figure lurking in the shadows.

"This person," he says, fishing out a still pulled from the parking garage security footage the day my father was shot, "is present in nearly all the frames we have of you from around town. Both of you. The associate from Augusta seems to believe the person behind the whole trade is a woman, and *I* think this shadow's stature and lithe movements point to them being a woman, as well."

"What, you're saying a woman *shot* me?" My father's eyebrow quirks, disbelief coloring his weathered gaze. "Come on, boys. I can accept female leadership, but to assault a grown man—"

Boyd clenches his fists. "She didn't fight you bare-handed. She caught you off guard with a weapon. A six-year-old could do that, so there's no reason an adult woman wouldn't be able to."

"Hey, let's not—"

"Now's not the time to lean into your sexist prejudices," I add, pulling a cloth bag from my hoodie pocket and sliding it across the table to him. "Someone's watching us, and it's awfully convenient that all this shit started happening around the same time we started being followed. And who else would know about *this* except the head of the whole operation, who Murphy tried to start his shakedown with?"

My father unties the sack, pulling out a single black flash drive. *The* flash drive, the one that holds the secret of every soul in King's Trace. Even our own.

I developed it as collateral, a way to convince Murphy to help me take down the sex trafficking ring and destroy the world of flesh sales as we knew it. I killed for the content on that drive, sold my soul to get it, and then buried it in an empty casket and spent the past two years digging up the gravesite ritualistically, obsessively, making sure no one had found it.

Not a lot of people know about its existence; Murphy didn't get very far with his blackmail before succumbing to his deteriorating mental health. I wanted to destroy and prevent it from falling into worse hands than my own, but my father convinced me to keep it. To rule the underground and keep them in line with their own secrets.

Instead, I dumped it. Tried to keep it safe.

But the vandalism, the assault in the cemetery, tells me *someone* knows what I did.

And they're trying to collect.

Lucky for them, debts with the devil are *always* paid in full.

My father sighs, long and slow, narrowing his gaze at the drive. "Okay, so it's a woman. So what?"

"How many women do you think there are involved in this? I mean, realistically," Boyd says.

"You think you can find her?" my father asks, cocking a brow.

"Better." Boyd cracks a smile, the first I've seen in weeks, and my lips tug up, mirroring his. "I think she'll come to us."

I DON'T INVITE Juliet to dinner until after her first week of classes is over; I want to give her space to settle into the routine, and I'm knee-fucking-deep in my plan with Boyd, my father, the Montaltos, and the trusted portion of Finn's unit trying to figure out a way to indulge our little stalker. Make her come out to play.

Plus, since that day in the office, I've been on high alert around Fiona, sensing a storm brewing beneath her skin, and Juliet's been busy with therapy and her growing family.

Her month-old nephew had been asleep on her chest when I climbed through her bedroom window last night; they were splayed out in the middle of the mattress, drooling, and although I've never in my life even considered kids before I met Juliet, I couldn't help but sit for a moment and imagine a version of myself where it'd be plausible.

The idea of Juliet's strong, supple body blossoming with my seed was enough to crack something inside me, make me ache with a need I've never known, and instead of depositing Noah somewhere safe, I'd snuggled in beside them, pretending it was something I did every night. Something we shared together.

It's a nice dream, anyway. I know good and well the likelihood of me being able to keep my little bird isn't great, especially considering I don't have a clue where she stands in her feelings for me. Or if she even has them at all.

Or if she'll stay with me despite every reason she shouldn't.

Today, though, she stopped by after her therapy session, and I left her in the kitchen to take a quick shower—the smell of death isn't one I can permanently wash from my skin, but I'd be sick not to even try to mask it.

When I return, she's standing at the sink separating broccoli florets from their stems and placing them into two different bowls. Sheer black tights disappear beneath her dress, drawing me into the room. Fiona sits on the edge of the counter, switching between shoveling celery in her mouth and dropping pieces into a glass baking dish filled with butter and uncooked chicken breasts.

Sidling up to Juliet, I wrap my arms around her waist and tug her tight, plump little ass into my dick. She tenses for the briefest moment until I bury my face in her neck, then relaxes against my hold.

Fiona boos. "Jesus, we're in the *kitchen*, Kieran."

"So get the fuck out." My teeth graze Juliet's delicate throat, itching to sink down until she moans.

"Absolutely not. We were just talking about what kind of flowers you might have at your wedding."

I freeze, pulling my head back to look at my sister, a cement weight settling in my chest. "Excuse me?"

A light pink blush stains Juliet's cheeks. "We weren't, really."

"She's just being modest." Fiona smirks, tilting her head as she watches us. "You'll probably have to wear a color that isn't white, though, considering who you're marrying. No one's gonna believe you're innocent or pure with him at the altar."

"If he makes it there." Juliet giggles, pushing her ass into my crotch and making me suck in a breath of air. "Can you even step foot on holy ground?"

"You want to get married in a church?"

She tips one shoulder up, continuing to shred the broccoli. "My parents weren't religious, but I always thought it'd be nice."

"The St. Killian Monastery on Third Street is *gorgeous* and totally haunted." Fiona points a finger at me. "That's perfect for you!"

Rolling my eyes, I dig my fingers into Juliet's hips, trying to bite back any scathing remarks. Dinner's bound to be awkward enough without me indulging my sister's antics and adding to it.

Unfortunately, she speaks before I have a chance to form a response. "Of course, we don't know it'll even be you she ends up marrying. So maybe a different venue would work, after all."

I don't know what her problem is, but I freeze, pulling my head back to glare at her. Fiona's eyes stay on mine, taunting, blazing like she has something to prove. My world feels like it shifts on its axis the longer she stares, and I feel my eyes hardening, turning to stone right there.

One of my hands leaves Juliet's side and reaches up, palming her jaw. I tilt her head back and my patience reaches its breaking point. I open my mouth to tell her that if she marries anyone other than me, I'll murder everyone she's ever met, but something in her face stops me.

Her gaze softens just slightly, letting me in on a little-known secret. One she's not ready to admit, but I see all the same.

Juliet snorts at the same time Fiona's face breaks out in a wide smile. The two burst into a fit of giggles, and the hot air deflates from my lungs.

Fiona pops another bite of celery into her mouth and slides down from the counter, winking at Juliet. "Told you he's easy to rile up."

My skin burns, the blood boiling beneath it. "Har-har. Stop being a fucking pain and let me spend time with my girlfriend before dinner."

She flounces from the room, and I exhale a sharp breath, pressing my forehead into Juliet's shoulder and skimming my hands down the length of the short black dress she has on. Relief floods through me like a river let free from a levy, my heart beating so hard against my ribs I can taste it in my throat.

I'm fucking gone for this woman. Trapped in a warm cocoon of love, feeling transformed just by being on her radar.

I know she doesn't hold the answered prayers to the darkness inside me, but she's a light shed in a hollowed unknown. A salve to a wound I didn't think would ever heal. Her darkness, her sadness, mixes with mine as though it understands me and wants to watch me be made whole without trying to *fix* me.

Which is kind of the point, right? Love isn't supposed to fix everything; hell, most of the time it seems to do a great job of fucking things up. It's there as a comfort—a cushion to soften our ugly realities. It's sustenance, but it's not growth.

We achieve that on our own.

Sighing, Juliet turns in my arms, wrapping hers around my neck. Her beautiful blue eyes stare up at me, two seas of unspoken emotion glittering in the overhead light. "Girl-friend, huh?"

My fingers toy with the hem of her dress, slipping beneath a fraction, and her breath catches. "Kitten, that better be a sarcastic question. You're *mine*, and you know it." She rolls her eyes, and one of my hands leaves her leg to wrap around her blonde hair, fisting a handful. I bring my lips close so they ghost against hers as I speak. "Something to say, baby?"

Her mouth parts, and my cock stiffens at the movement, remembering how fucking good it feels to have her wrapped around me. "What will you do to me if I say yes?"

I force a swallow, desire constricting my lungs, and press into her even more. "What do you want me to do to you?"

"*Everything.*"

Without another word, I shove her hips into the counter and claim her mouth with my own, devouring her like she's the last delicacy in the fucking world and I'm a man who's lived his whole life without a single luxury.

And Christ, just kissing her does feel like a goddamn gift.

Pushing my tongue past her lips, I flick in and out, my hands tangling in her hair. Hers slip from my neck, scraping down my back, and then cup my ass, grinding me into her even more. A soft moan escapes, though I'm not exactly sure who it belongs to; it sets off fireworks behind my vision, and they explode with the light of a thousand bursting suns, blinding and incapacitating all at once.

Her teeth catch my bottom lip, biting hard enough to draw blood, and I grunt against the pressure; it's a shock straight to my dick, making it jerk behind the zipper of my jeans. I grip the backs of her thighs and haul her up onto the counter, forcing myself between her legs and deepening the kiss. Nimble fingers tug at my hair, and I push up the hem of her dress, exposing more of her creamy thighs and the garter attached to the tops of her stockings.

"Christ," I breathe, yanking my face from hers and leaning back to get a good look. Shoving the dress to her waist, I admire the lacy, crotchless pair of panties she wears, and how the lingerie accentuates the soft curve of her hips and highlights her bare pussy. "Are you trying to kill me?"

She grins, dropping a hand to her sex and swiping a finger over her slit; she pushes between her swollen lips, the lewd sound turning my knees to jelly—so wet I can see her arousal coating the tip of her finger. With a jerk of her hips, she pulls away, bringing the digit up and slipping it into her mouth. She pushes to the back of her tongue as she clamps her jaw down, sucking so hard her cheeks hollow out, and I almost come in my jeans before I've even gotten inside her.

"You okay?" she asks, dragging her finger out, then tracing the seam of my mouth with the residue from hers. "You look awfully pale."

Yanking her down off the counter, I spin her around, knock her elbows out so her chest presses against the cool granite, and shove her dress the rest of the way up. Her ass looks delicious in the lingerie set, and I can't stop myself from dipping down and biting one fleshy cheek, landing a rough smack on the opposite.

She jerks forward, a guttural grunt tearing from her throat. "Kieran..."

"Shut up, brat. You want to tease me, play with me before an important dinner where I introduce you formally to my family?"

She nods, face flush with the counter, and I chuckle at the sight, spitting on her asshole.

The tight ring of muscle doesn't ease open much at first, even when I've worked two fingers inside. I scissor slowly and spit again, watching every muscle in her body tense and listening for the little sounds of excitement that bubble from deep within her. It's not the first time we've done it this way, but it certainly doesn't get old.

Her hands white-knuckle the edge of the granite, her breaths coming out in short little pants, as I use my free hand to work my cock from my pants, stroking it through her sopping folds.

Writhing beneath me, she shifts, trying to get more friction on her clit like the dirty little slut she is. "Kieran, we're in your parents' kitchen—"

I pry her ass farther apart, spitting once more and slipping a third finger inside; she moans, loud enough that anyone on the first floor can probably hear, but I'm too far fucking gone to give a shit.

She relaxes her muscles, her ass finally stretching easily around me, and I quickly replace my hand with the head of my cock; her juices drench me, making the entrance smoother. I sink in an inch, then another, the muscles in my body drawing so taut it feels like it they might snap at any given second.

Tight. So goddamn tight I'm seeing stars—no, not stars. Heaven, maybe. I think I've died and gone straight there, somehow.

Pleasure ricochets up my spine, and I huff a low breath to

steady myself. Her hips move backward, coaxing me in, and I slide into the hilt as she lets out a low groan, the sound entirely animalistic and hot as hell.

"Oh my *God*."

"Nope, not God. *Never* God. You know good and well who's fucking you right now, kitten, so you'd better address me appropriately."

"Yes, yes, daddy, fuck me. *Please*."

Clawing at the counter as I fuck her into oblivion, she comes around me when I stuff four fingers in her cunt, her body folding and molding for mine like she was made for me. "Ah, fuck, kitten. Your ass is too perfect. I'm not gonna last."

"I don't want you to. Fill me till there's no room for anyone *but* you."

"I haven't done that yet?" My hips piston faster into her, my balls slapping against her backside. I curl my fingers up, stroking her inner muscles, and feel her flutter around me again. "I swear to God, Juliet, if you're even thinking of another man at this point, I'll knock you up right now. Tie you to me *forever*."

Dragging myself out of her tight hole, I rip my fingers from her at the same time her orgasm crests, then stuff my dick into her cunt as my own rounds that same peak. I shouldn't, knowing she'll want to clean herself now before dinner, but I can't help myself.

White-hot electricity zings up my spine, setting my skin on fire as it shoots through me, and I thrust as deep as I can get, my cum painting her cervix as she spasms around me.

Sweat gleams on her shoulders, and I use the flat of my tongue to lap it up. She shivers, moving her head to the side. "You're crazy. You know that?"

"I've come to terms with it, yes."

"Would you really knock me up?"

There's an unfamiliar thread of uncertainty in her voice, something timid I've never heard from her before. Even at her lowest, this is a girl who knows herself, even if she doesn't always like what she sees or who she is. She's always confident in that regard, never letting fear get in the way of what she wants.

I just can't tell what she wants my response to be.

So instead of answering honestly and saying fuck yes, I'd knock her up if given the chance—because she's just called me crazy, and having those thoughts after knowing her such a short time, regardless of my budding feelings toward her, certainly feels crazy—I just pull out and mention we should get ready for dinner.

She berates me for taking her cunt after fucking her ass, and her ire makes me so hard that I fuck her again in my shower.

It's not until way, way later, after my parents walk in on us rearranging our clothes and drag us to dinner to pepper her with millions of questions about her life, when we're lying in my bed drifting off to sleep, that I start to worry about what happens to the earth without sunshine.

When the sun dies, the earth goes with it.

For the first time in my life, with the embodiment of the lifeblood to our universe cradled in my arms, I find myself praying the sun sticks around.

25

JULIET

CARTER PULLS a mini flask from the breast pocket of her navy pencil dress, offering it to me as we move through the reception line.

I hiss under my breath, shoving her hand flush against her chest. "Have you completely lost it? Put that away before Father O'Leary sees you. Or worse, someone from *The Gazette*."

The whole of King's Trace is out in full force for month-old Noah Montalto's christening; cars are parked on the usually tailored lawn of the St. Francis Cathedral, one of about a dozen Catholic churches strewn about within the county lines.

Considering what he does for a living, it's hard to imagine my brother-in-law has much attachment to the institution itself. But men in the Mafia are bound by a code of ethics we mere mortals can't quite comprehend. Slaves to their blood loyalty, monsters by design and forced submission.

Pouting her pillowy lips, Carter stuffs the flask back

inside her dress and pokes at my chest. "Why'd you wear such a slutty dress to your nephew's church service?"

An elderly couple a few steps ahead of us pauses, the wrinkled old woman turning her turkey neck to shoot us a dirty look. *God, this town is the worst.* I elbow Carter in the side, and she winces, her breath wafting over my face. My nose scrunches up, the scent of alcohol far too pungent for the little sips she claims she's been slipping since Benito dropped us off.

"My dress isn't slutty," I say, running my palm down the white lace; it's an old number I dug out of Caroline's closet and made her cry when she realized she couldn't fit into it any longer. The neckline plunges between my breasts, emphasizing the golden locket against my chest, and flares out around mid-thigh, too short for church but long enough that Elia didn't mention it.

Of course, maybe he didn't even notice. He's been away a lot more often and falls asleep in his coffee sometimes at breakfast, apparently taking on a huge workload in preparation for a "long-ass family vacation," as my sister put it. Who knew ripping the underworld's king from its meaty claws would be such hard work?

Not that it'd have mattered if he *did* mention it, because my father he is not. I can only deal with one controlling asshole at a time, and the sex god that occupies my bed and my thoughts almost every night is more than enough for me right now.

Maybe even forever. That familiar twinge pinches my stomach, and I try to focus on regulating my breathing.

In love with a murderer. How does that make me any better than my father?

Shaking off the thought, I move forward in line, looping

my arm through Carter's. "And I thought I asked you to go easy on drinking today."

She shrugs. "Jesus, Jules. It's a fucking *baptism*, not Judgment Day."

"Actually, it's a christening."

"Who cares? The point is, it's fucking boring. If everyone here isn't plastered by the time they serve cake, it'll be a miracle."

"The only way they'll be plastered is if they've snuck in miniature flasks like you."

Snorting, she nods, taking the flask back out; she unscrews the cap and tips it up to her lips, downing a large gulp. "And we all know the citizens of King's Trace are such paragons of virtue."

Something breaks in her voice, a thread tearing that I can't find the end to, and I can't help wondering if the stress of being poor and practically excommunicated from her family is starting to take its toll.

There's no chance to ask, though, because in the next second, she scrubs a hand over her face, plasters on a wide smile and squares her shoulders as we approach the ornate metal doors at the front of the building. They're pushed in, the happy little family poised at the entrance; after the ceremony, we all left the nave where the congregation has service to allow cleanup and for Elia's men to set up banquet tables, and this is the first I'm seeing them since.

As I move forward, a hand wraps around my bicep, holding me in place. I jerk against Carter, the unyielding grip making me stumble.

"Juliet."

I cringe at that voice, hating the way it makes me shrivel inside despite all the progress I think I've made.

Whirling around, I come face-to-face with the sorry sack of bones that is my mother. Anger simmers low in my veins, heat just waiting to boil over as I take in the age spots and wrinkles, the yellow glint of her updated dye-job, the puffiness of her lips that tells me she very recently had work done.

All my mother ever cared about was her looks, after all.

According to Luca, she's been in town since she approached me that day in the cemetery, and this is the first I'm seeing of her. Clearly, she's been too busy to attempt amends. Makes perfect sense. It's not like she came back for me in the first place.

"Mother," I say, scanning her from tip to toe. "What are you doing here?"

She rolls her eyes, clear blue pools mirroring mine and Caroline's. Except there's something hidden in their depths, something I can't quite place, a distant secrecy buried so deep it's become a part of her. "You didn't honestly think I'd miss my grandchild's *christening*, did you?"

"Well, you missed the first one," Carter says under her breath.

"*And* you weren't invited," I add.

Smiling down at me, she reaches out and grips my shoulder, patting it with a calloused palm. I can't remember her hands *ever* feeling worn, and I shake her off. Shake off the tiny seed of thought that accompanies her presence and threatens the loose knot holding together my sanity; the idea that she's changed.

Because even though I *know* she's not here for me, and I *know* she hasn't, I can't stop the flutter in my heart from attempting to morph into a full-blown earthquake. Can't stop thinking about how much easier everything would be if she would just *grow*, if my father was still alive to atone for his sins and she wanted to make actual amends.

Then I wouldn't have to deal with all the guilt and shame of holding out hope to be loved by people wholly incapable of returning the favor. Maybe it'd be easier to give out in return if I wasn't in constant fear of being taken advantage of.

Maybe that's what drew me to Kieran in the first place; morbid fascination with being the object of someone's all-consuming affection. How he takes what he wants, no questions asked, and doesn't apologize. Doesn't retract his feelings or attach conditions.

The devil might not have a soul, might be criminally dangerous and dipped in sin, but he makes up for it with a bleeding heart.

My mother has no redeeming qualities. She's a succubus, taking without thought and never giving anything back. Never caring about the lives she destroys in the process.

I used to wonder how she managed to stay with my father, even at a point when it became obvious the only thing he cared about was his political career. Turns out, they had more in common than any of us ever knew.

Her mouth presses into a thin line when I step away from her, fingernails scraping my skin as her hand drops to her side. Clearing her throat, she brushes a strand of hair back from her face, eyes darting to the front of the line as we advance on it. "Good thing St. Francis is a public church, then, isn't it? And that I've got an in with Father O'Leary."

"Elia's not gonna let you in," I say.

"Oh yeah? What's he going to do, kick out a defenseless, middle-aged woman? Shoot me in front of the whole town?" She laughs, the sound crude and short. "Face it, darling, but your knight in shining armor doesn't hold as much weight here as you all seem to think. Money does a lot for people in King's Trace, but so does reputation."

"After what Daddy did, and how you left with no word about anything that went down, do you honestly think anyone in this congregation would defend you?" I gesture toward the nosy couple in front of us as the woman glances back from the corner of her eye. As if I can't see that movement. "You're crazier than I remember."

"Ah, but the apple doesn't fall far from the tree, does it?" Her eyes harden, hatred swirling in her irises and making my chest feel tight. "I heard you started therapy. Good for you, darling, considering how your mental health has stupendously stunted your growth."

"That's fucking rude," a lilted voice comes from behind me, and I turn to see Fiona standing there, arms crossed tightly across her chest. She glares at my mother so hard I start to wonder if she's trying to make her combust.

Boyd's at her side, and his jaw works as her shoulders square, prepping for a fight. "Fiona..."

"What?" she snaps, not even sparing him a glance. "You want me to sit and be quiet while an old hag insults my friend? I think the fuck not." She steps forward, and he reaches out, snatching her palm in his hand.

I watch them curiously; he levels her with a stern look, one that'd heat my blood if it were turned on me. It's the kind of look Kieran gives me when I'm being a brat, the kind that threatens a very good punishment.

She jerks away. "Let me *go*."

"Stop trying to make a fucking scene."

"You're not allowed to tell me what to do, dick. You're not my father, my brother, *or* my boyfriend. *Remember*?" As her voice climbs in pitch, the crowd around us starts to pay attention, but that doesn't deter Fiona.

Boyd notices, though, and drops her hand like she's burned him, adjusting the collar of his suit with one tattooed hand.

He takes a step back, shrugging his broad shoulders. "Have it your way, *princess.*" Shooting her one last patronizing glance, he turns on his heels and stalks off, leaving my head spinning with everything that's just happened.

Fiona stares at his retreating form for a long, long time before offering me an apologetic smile. She takes off after him, her heels sinking into the soft earth with each step. I don't see them meet back up, don't get to witness the clusterfuck of a fight that's sure to be, and can't mask the disappointment and intrigue. *What the hell was that?*

My mother seems momentarily stunned, as well, studying Fiona's retreating form as several beats of silence settle in around us. She comes to after a while, blinking and offering us a wide, fake smile, glancing out over the crowd. "In any case, Juliet, I need to speak with you."

"I'm not interested in whatever it is you're selling."

She frowns, hard. "I think you might change your tune if you knew it's a matter of life or death."

My eyes narrow, and I pull away from Carter, shuffling her figure behind me. I know the couple ahead of us is listening in, but right now, I don't care. "What are you talking about?"

"Not here." Because she knows about the eavesdroppers too and can feel the dozens of eyes locked on us, interested in figuring out why *the* Lynn Harrison returned to town out of nowhere.

I feel Caroline's gaze on me, and sure enough, when I

glance up, she's watching us with alarm. Her hand reaches out for Elia's, tugging hard as he talks to Benito behind him.

Not wanting to cause a scene on my nephew's big day, I try to communicate silently as I follow my mother away from the crowd that everything's okay. That she wouldn't hurt me, at least not physically.

Because that was never her MO. She liked psychological abuse, neglect that makes you wonder if anyone can ever love you. Surely, two years in hiding hasn't changed my mother that much.

Fear etches into Caroline's features, worry making her bottom lip tremble. I turn from it as we round the gray stone corner of the cathedral, disappearing from her line of sight, but not before Elia's focus snaps on us, his body immediately flickering to high alert.

"You'd better talk fast," I say, leaning against the wall. "Elia will be here in seconds."

She scoffs. "I'm not afraid of that brute."

"Your funeral," I mutter.

"No, darling."

She brandishes a handgun from the main pocket of her black leather purse, aiming the barrel directly at my face. A somewhat sad, sinister smile spreads across her lips as my lungs deflate, the air leaving my body at once. As far as I know, my mother's never held a gun in her life, and the sight stuns me into a place of complete disbelief. One where I don't react at all, even as she fingers the trigger.

"Actually, it's yours."

Kieran

"Where the absolute fuck could she have gone?"

My father scrubs a hand over his face, fingers tapping idly against his keyboard. The surveillance in front of us shows only the curb outside of the St. Francis cathedral, where we've tracked our mystery financier to. It appears she's attempting to use the large crowd as a cover, although we haven't quite figured out what she's doing there.

Leaning back in my desk chair, I glance around Boyd's office, a slight twinge of nostalgia hitting at how I left it so prematurely. But I refuse to dwell on it, or to live in the shadow of my regrets. My mother taught me to keep looking forward, and it'd be a disservice to her ever-worsening memory if I started focusing too heavily on my past.

It's not like I can change how everything turned out, anyway. Not like I'd give any of it up.

I wouldn't bring my brother back, even if I had the option. And if I kill him every time, in every possible alternate version of my past, what *really* changes?

Nothing.

No use in stewing in that filth.

"We've been tailing her for days," Finn says, clasping his hands behind his head. "And she hasn't done anything that even remotely suggests involvement in this whole ordeal."

"She's a fucking con artist," I say, scanning the monitor again for any signs of her blond hair and pressed pantsuit. It's obvious she comes from wealth, most of which she probably accumulated from the trafficking ring itself, but we've not been able to get a good look at her face. It's almost as if she knows she's being watched, knows how many cameras are stuck in the corners of every building in King's Trace.

"Kieran's right," Giacomo, who's been helping out with the investigation when Elia can't or just plain doesn't want to, says, sitting forward with his hands on his knees. "We shouldn't be looking for signs directly tying her to the long list of crimes. We should be looking for details that might make her stand out among civilians. Think of her like a crime boss, expect that air of arrogance and pride and the belief that she's untouchable. Look at her gait and the people she interacts with. Count how many times you see her glance up at corners and around at others, ensuring she's not ever caught off guard."

"You hear that, Boyd?" I speak into my comms unit as he comes into view on the screen, Fiona tagging along because she was bored and didn't have anything better to do. She begged me to let her join, to let her "be a real Ivers," and I figured an intelligence mission at a fucking christening was probably the safest thing she could do for us.

I hate that I'm not the one there right now, especially considering I'm the only one who got an actual invite; Juliet had asked me before I left this morning, a slight quiver in her voice that I've come to recognize as her demons manifesting themselves.

She was nervous. Afraid I wouldn't want to go.

And Christ, I fucking hate that she has demons other than me.

So I pushed her to her knees and made her suck my cock, apologizing for thinking I might not *want* to do something with her. And when I came down her glorious throat, I hauled her up and lapped at her little pink cunt until she cried from the pleasure, drenching my chin like a goddamn waterfall.

It's the kind of give-and-take I know she's most comfortable with; physical pleasure is so much easier to explain away than emotional attachment. And even though I can tell therapy is changing her, alleviating some of that darkness, I can also tell the self-doubt from years of abuse and shame hasn't disappeared completely.

Which is why it damn near broke me when I told her I couldn't attend, but that I'd send my sister in to at least say hi.

Boyd sighs into his mic, the sound crackling in my ear. "Your sister is a fucking nightmare."

"So ignore her. You're there for a job. Don't make me send in a replacement."

"I'm not a fucking kid, Kieran. I can do this. I just thought you should know that I might end up binding and gagging your sister and tossing her into my trunk before all of this is over."

I don't comment on the threat because I know he doesn't mean it, and also because I spot the figure as they crest the small, grassy hill and approach the grand church. Its stone walls are dull in the sunlight, but the stained glass windows glitter on screen, a prism of color you can almost get lost in.

The woman has her back to us, naturally, as my father switches to the security camera mounted above the front doors of the church. My heart plummets into my stomach when I see who the woman approaches, and fury laces my veins as I watch her grab her arm.

Juliet doesn't look scared, though, or even slightly alarmed at the contact, which makes me bristle. Discomfort settles in the chambers of my heart, pumping blood furiously through my body in an attempt to calm me.

It doesn't work. The hairs on the back of my neck stand up straight, and I lean forward, glaring at the screen. "Boyd, who the fuck is touching my girl?"

His head tilts as he and Fiona get closer, shaking almost imperceptibly. "No clue. Let me get closer and—"

On the screen, Fiona says something snarky; I can tell by the way her lips curl over her teeth, a snarl marring her face. The group stills, Juliet cocking her head at my sister, and I watch Boyd reach for his ear. A soft click cuts off our communication, and I see blood red as the white noise between my ears amplifies, a raging rapid come to life.

"What. The fuck. Just happened?" I bite out, slamming my fist on the table.

"Christ, boy, don't get your panties in a twist," my father says, pointing at Boyd as he grabs my sister's arm, holding her back. "Looks like the ginger trait is in full effect. You know your sister is a hothead."

Clenching my teeth until my jaw starts to ache, I watch as Boyd's hand falls away, a nasty look etching into the lines on his face. His mouth turns down, his eyebrows draw in, and he steps back, shoving his hands into his suit pockets. He says something, then turns and walks off, leaving my sister there with a woman who wants the entire Ivers clan dead.

When his unit comes back to life, I hiss, "You got a death wish, Kelly? Because I'm about three seconds from hopping in my car and driving over to mow you the fuck down for leaving them alone like that, and for cutting off the conversation. I don't fucking tolerate insubordination, and right now, your ass works for *me*."

"Goddamn." I can practically hear him roll his eyes. "She was about to blow our fucking cover. I had to intervene, had to walk off before she caused trouble."

Fiona turns after a brief pause and chases after him; I can hear her calling his name in the distance even as he reaches the parking lot. My father zooms in on them as they meet up, her arms gesturing wildly, words inaudible through the unit.

"Did you see who she was?"

"No, I didn't stick around long enough. Didn't want her to recognize me in case she can make a connection."

"*I* saw her." Fiona yanks out Boyd's earpiece and disposes of her own on the ground; hers is the only one without a microphone. "That's their mom. Lynn Harrison, or something? Don't you remember she fled town right after all that stuff with the senator went down?"

Time seems to stop for an eternity at her words, the reality of my situation settling in like a flood around me. A flood I'm ill-equipped for and can't escape.

Of fucking course.

Who else would know I'd killed Dominic and be eager to tell Juliet in an attempt to turn her against me?

Who else but a social parasite—concerned only with her self-image and never the well-being of her kids—to throw money at an organization in an attempt to gain power and notoriety among the inner circles of the underground?

And because trafficking is almost always inexplicably tied to politics, who fucking else but a senator's wife to fund the racket?

It makes sense that she disappeared, the fear of being found out driving her away. Murphy was dead, and then her husband, and I never stopped ticking off the boxes. Never stopped hunting her inferiors, grinding information from their bones and stringing them up at my cottage like Christmas lights.

A nice little show for the lives lost due to the trade. Something for them to enjoy in the afterlife, if it exists.

My gift to them.

My apology.

Giacomo swears under his breath as Lynn says something to Juliet; the two pull away from the crowd, starting around the side of the building, even as Caroline alerts her husband and he follows belatedly.

The strain in Juliet's eyes, the slope of her shoulders, tells me everything I need to know.

This woman has hurt countless others, ruined lives, and destroyed futures, but *this* one was the first. Juliet was her initial victim; she must've loved how it tasted. The bittersweet victory that comes from stealing someone's soul and trying to break them beyond repair.

Heat flares in my cheeks as I shove back from the desk, nearly toppling the monitor as I jump to my feet, swiping the flash drive from the wood. My father swallows, gesturing to his shoulder, which is *still* healing. "Son, I—"

I hold my hand up, cutting him off. The screen switches to the side of the building, where Juliet stands with her mother. It only takes a second for me to recognize the way her mother reaches into her purse, pulling out a gun that was in my face just weeks ago, before I'm turning on my heel and bolting out the door.

26

JULIET

"WELL, Mom, I have to say. This is a first for me."

She shuffles me down the concrete steps to the church basement, the mouth of her gun digging into my lower back; when she heard footsteps and Elia's familiar growl, she'd dragged me even farther around the building, shoving me along quickly. Dropping a key into my palm, she gestures toward the large metal door. "Open it."

"Are we allowed to be down here?" I ask, my normal defense mechanisms struggling to take root. Despite my reckless behavior over the years, I've never actually *faced* death, and doing so now at the hands of the woman who brought me into this world feels too surreal to even deal with.

"Shut up, Juliet."

I slide the key into the lock—a large, gaudy hunk of metal that I'm pretty sure most places don't even use anymore—and turn it hard. It unlatches, and my mother reaches over me to push the door open and shove me inside.

We're thrust into a damp darkness when she slams the door closed and refastens the lock. My hands shake, and for a moment, I'm grateful for the invisibility I've spent my whole life lamenting. At least she can't see how she's affecting me.

My relief is short-lived, however, when she flips on an overhead switch, revealing the disgusting dungeon she's led me into. Plastered on the far wall are hundreds—maybe even thousands—of photographs and news article clippings; some have my face, my body at various venues around town. My own bedroom.

Other pictures are of Caroline and Elia, the kids, Kieran, and his entire family. His cottage on Lake Koselomal and inside The Bar where I was assaulted.

My gaze flickers over each one, and I get to the end of the familiar scope of King's Trace and the devils I know, coming face-to-face with ones that have gone undiscovered. Malnourished bodies trapped in metal cages, girls of varying ages and sizes dressed in burlap sacks or nothing at all, and pressed into each cell like sardines.

Dead bodies in various stages of decomposition.

They stare back at the camera, alive and not, cheeks gaunt and eyes haunted—an image I'm not sure I'll ever be able to erase.

My stomach twists, bile rising in my throat as I look at the mass burials; mounds of abused flesh set on fire and photographed in their last moments of existence. I cross my hands over my abdomen and press my sweaty, shaky palms inward, trying to keep the vomit at bay.

"What the hell is this?"

Chuckling, my mother makes her way over to a

makeshift table; a large slab of wood straddling two sawhorses, with sheets of paper and coffee mugs and flash drives strewn about. She keeps the pistol pointed at me even as she moves items around with her free hand, as if this isn't the first time she's ever waved a gun around.

Which is news to me, because growing up, my mother loathed anything that even resembled a weapon. We weren't permitted to have foam swords or water guns, crossbows or darts. Nothing with the potential for harm.

Interesting that she never considered the mind to be the most deadly asset, given how hers nearly ruined Caroline and me.

"What's it look like, darling? Come on, you got into college just fine. I know you're not as dumb as your father always claimed you were." She flops into a black chair with rollers on the bottom, clutching a USB drive in her free hand and gesturing around the basement with the other. "I told you I had an in with Father O'Leary."

I tear myself from the pictures posted on the wall and glance around further; behind her are empty cages built into the cellar walls. Some are familiar, appearing in the photographs, but there's one in the corner that seems untouched.

The cell door is locked, though I can see through the iron bars. Plastic-wrapped bricks of what I can only assume to be cocaine—given I've never seen any packaged like this —stacked in tight columns around the cell.

Am I in a church basement, or is this hell?

"What's going on, Mom?" A chill grips my skin, goose bumps popping up in the waves, and I back away until my spine presses into the cool, wet concrete wall. Beside the collage of horrors.

My pulse skyrockets because up until this point, I didn't think she'd actually hurt me. Not physically, at least. Mothers are supposed to be your champions, the ones least likely to cause you harm. But the scar tissue in my heart says otherwise, and I'm beginning to realize how naïve I was in thinking she brought me down here for any other reason.

She could've broken my spirit more among the crowd, could've humiliated me beyond belief in front of the whole town. Yet she brought me down here.

Where we'd be alone, and I'd be afraid.

Her favorite color on me.

Holding up a little black Tracfone in one hand, she angles the camera toward my face and holds still for a beat. "Just a little temptation to get your lover down here as quick as possible."

"My *lover*?" I blink, unease sloshing around in my stomach. "What do you want with Kieran?"

Setting the phone down, she fixes me with cold, unfeeling eyes. They remind me so much of my father—of how he held a knife to me while Caroline had him at gunpoint, the blatant disregard for something he helped create entirely too evident.

How I'd begged her to shoot him at that gala two years ago, even if it meant taking me out in the process.

This situation is so similar and I feel dizzy, whiplash an invisible force that whisks the air from my lungs and blurs my vision. My hands press into the wall as if trying to dissolve into it, wishing for that cloak that I always seemed to don in my parents' presence.

The one that made me so insignificant, they never paid me any mind.

Somehow, I've ended up on the receiving end of death threats from both of them.

Shrugging one shoulder, my mother places the gun gently on the wood, keeping her fingers on top of the handle in case I make a sudden move. "What don't I want with him? He's only wrecked my entire life's work and destroyed any claim to wealth I've accumulated over the years. I want him to pay for it in blood."

My chest heaves with each breath as they become labored, the deep pre-hyperventilation gasps I'm all too familiar with. Terror pumps through my bloodstream, edging out the oxygen, and I try to focus on keeping her talking while I silently look for a way out of this.

"What do you mean, your life's work? I didn't think you'd ever had a job." My eyes dart around the room, over a plethora of guns stored in containers, scrap metal pieces, and junk from the church attic. An old nativity scene sits beside the main door, the face of Jesus completely worn off and molded.

"You never were very observant. Always so wrapped up in your little personal bubble. Oblivious to the things going on right around you." She tilts her head to the side, blue eyes boring into my soul, and it makes me shrink slightly.

Bravado is much harder to keep up in the face of the person who destroyed it in the first place.

I swallow over the knot in my throat, wishing I had the pocket knife that Caroline had given me. *'Keep it tucked in your underwear,'* she'd told me, but I didn't think I'd need it at a fucking christening.

"Do you honestly have no idea what's going on here?"

"No, but I'm starting to worry you think you're a real-life movie villain."

Getting to her feet, she keeps her gun trained on my forehead, and after a few silent minutes where she paces back and forth in front of the cages, I can start to feel the threat of a bullet burn a hole in my skin.

"You're just collateral damage, darling. It's nothing personal."

"Holding someone at gunpoint certainly *feels* personal." I clench my jaw against the fear pulsing through me, trying to remain calm. "Jesus, Mom, whatever personal vendetta you have, I could've been left out of this."

She shakes her head, coming closer to me. Pausing at my side, she stares up at the wall of gore, the hint of a smile pulling at the corners of her lips. I inch away, putting distance between us while she's distracted and inch toward the door.

"Unfortunately, I can't seem to kill the Ivers boys, though not for lack of trying. Your Kieran certainly did me a favor when he got rid of his brother all those years ago. I had been starting to think he was gonna blow my operation."

"Operation?"

One long, manicured fingernail taps against a picture of a group of girls, standing outside of what looks like an abandoned warehouse with its silver garage entrance and ancient beige siding. There's no business marker on the building, no way for it to be identified, and I can't quite wrap my brain around what she's suggesting.

"What do you think a flesh sale is, Juliet?" When I don't answer, my mind blanking, she rolls her eyes and lets the gun fall to her hip. "Christ, you've lived with your sister all this time, and you two never talked about what happened to her?"

I glance up at the pictures, then back at her, confusion

causing a deep throb in my head. Nausea rips through me as I process, recalling how my father used Caroline, how he was trying to *sell her to Kieran* before Elia proposed to her.

But then, what she's insinuating is *trafficking*. Girls being kidnapped and sold to the highest bidder, then forced to commercialize their innocence for someone else's monetary gain.

Tears sting my eyes as the realization sinks in, weighing me down like a concrete block tied to my ankle. My hands curl into fists, my guilt amplifying tenfold when I remember how badly I missed my father, how I ignored Caroline's pain and experiences in light of the loss I had endured.

How, up until this moment, the blackest, most evil part of my soul was still hoping my mother would change.

"I tried to get your father to involve you as well, said you'd be worth twice as much as Caroline based on age alone. But he swore his men didn't want damaged goods." Her lips press into a thin line, and she shrugs as though she doesn't know how her words cut me.

Or doesn't care.

A piece of my soul breaks off and shatters, dissolving into my veins. It drags my sadness along with it, coating my insides like a Picasso, making my body wobble even as I prop myself against the wall for support.

"We thought we could buy Kieran off, keep him from siccing the FBI on us after he took down his brother, Murphy. So your father offered Caroline in exchange for his silence, money he owed, and a flash drive that would damn the entire town if it got into the wrong hands."

Distance grows in her irises, memories stealing her attention; I scoot the soles of my feet across the floor, edging farther away as she continues.

"Of course, we didn't know he'd already ratted us out. They shut down our whole operation and forced your father to rely on the connections he'd made. They *gutted* us, Juliet. Took the majority of our girls, our resources, and seized a huge portion of *my* finances. And they didn't even know who they were dealing with."

She points the barrel of her gun up at a picture of Elia, then another of the Ivers posing in front of Ivers International. "It was easy to redirect attention from an esteemed senator to the crime lords running this shitty little town while I spread business around and took it elsewhere. Churches like this one, factories, and businesses already delving into criminal territory that had less to lose. I tried to locate the flash drive Kieran has, but I know he buried it in that tomb instead of his brother. You ever ask what he did with his body? I bet that's a fun story."

Blinking, I force away the haze forming behind my eyes and the knowledge that one of our town's revered priests is involved in criminal activity. The bones I found in Kieran's closet all those weeks ago now have a likely ID, and I wring my hands together just for something to do. I can't focus on the latter half of that statement, not considering I knew about it—knew what I was getting into when I chose to sleep with Kieran.

And every subsequent time, I knew. He never tried to hide himself or make excuses. The only apologies I get from him revolve around my pain. Hurt he's never inflicted, at least not on purpose or without reason.

Skeletons in my closet he's not responsible for.

Even with the knowledge of what he does for a living, the unconventionality of the Mafia and its contrast with ambiguous codes and breaking the law, *this* still seems worse.

Maybe that's how Caroline justifies Elia's trade.

Goodness outweighing the evil inside, like a reverse preservation.

Because even industry criminals have rules. Limits. My parents, Father O'Leary, Murphy—they aren't the same.

They're depraved in a way that makes even the devil's skin crawl.

I finally find my voice. "Are you... are you telling me you've been running a sex trafficking ring?"

"You didn't think your father would be the brains behind it, did you? That man was about as bright as a bag of rocks. Where would he have gotten the money to fund something like that, anyway?" Laughing to herself, she swipes hair back from her face, returning her attention to me. "What do you think you're doing?"

I freeze in place, my heart stuttering. I'm closer to the door at this point than I am to her, but she still has that damn gun. My odds aren't great.

But after a lifetime of being her emotional punching bag, of trying to navigate the rift she caused between Caroline and me, I'll be damned if I let her keep me here without a fight.

There's no point in acknowledging any growth in myself if I can't make use of it. Put it into action, Hana says. *Manifest it.*

Even if it hurts.

Even if it kills you.

My hand flies to the locket around my neck, and I channel some of my sister's strength, some of Kieran's determination, and Elia's protection. It warps inside me, a hurricane building until I feel it implode, an explosion lighting up every inch of my being.

When I launch myself at my mother, throwing as much of my weight into the jump as possible to carry me to her, I concentrate on the euphoria that speeds through me like a drug now that I'm finally confronting my demons.

And now, this isn't a fight I intend to lose. Not when I've already squandered so much.

The attack throws her off, and she startles, stumbling as my fist connects with her jaw, my fingers scraping for traction in her scalp; I grip at the roots of her hair, yanking back and shoving her into the wall.

Her arm jerks into me, a defensive move, knocking the gun into my ribs and stealing the air from my lungs. It stuns me for a split second, pain radiating through my body like a bomb detonating inside, pushing a paralyzing tingle down my limbs.

Regaining my momentum as she tries to shift her fingers back over the trigger, I land a fist into her stomach, reveling in the whoosh of breath that escapes her, then slam the side of her skull into the concrete wall, the soft thud of bone splitting beneath the force not one I think I'll ever forget.

She crumples into herself, cradling her head in her hands as an ear-piercing shriek emits from her lips; the gun falls to the floor, and I scramble away, sprinting for the door before she has a chance to recover.

I reach the door and glance over my shoulder, watching her writhe and cry out in agony; blood mats the back of her hair and stains her hands as she yanks them away. I know there's no time to do what I'm about to, but I can't tear my thoughts from the flash drives on her table, the incriminating files. All that evidence.

Even if I make it out of here, what're the chances of her still being around, of this being here once I find Elia or a cop? She's injured, but that doesn't necessarily mean she's incapacitated, and the doors against the far wall likely lead down halls I'm unfamiliar with.

Halls she probably knows like the back of her hand, if everything she's said tonight is true.

Rushing over to the makeshift table, I scoop as much material into my arms as possible, keeping an eye on my mother's bloody form. I stuff multiple flash drives down the front of my dress, catching them in the cups of my strapless bra, then shove papers into a green folder and tuck it under my arm, racing back to the door as she stirs.

My nails scrape against the metal door as my fingers fumble with the lock, unlatching it at the same time I'm grabbed from behind, and a blunt object connects with my skull, making me see stars.

Kieran

Elia stares at two of his goons, barking orders to secure the premises as he attempts to console his sobbing wife. She fists his suit jacket in her hands, drenching his button-down with tears. Panic ebbs inside me as I approach the church, the fear of being too late rising up like a tidal wave and pushing me ahead of Giacomo and Boyd.

"Where is she?" I snap, the snarl in my voice seeming to surprise the small, dainty Caroline. It hits me that this is the first time we're actually seeing each other in person, and the features she shares with her sister catch me off guard. That same golden hair rains from her head, and she has the same cerulean eyes, though hers lack the twinkle Juliet gets when she looks at me.

There's no sharp intake of breath, no pupil dilation, no smattering of soft freckles across her nose or tiny half-crescent-shaped scar beneath her left eyelid from when she got into a bar fight on graduation night, and the other contender nearly stabbed her eye out with a straw.

None of that's present here as I stare down at her sister, wishing selfishly that they could trade places. That Elia could fill my shoes and feel the desperation that accompanies helplessness and the fear of the unknown.

"I don't know, but they couldn't have just disappeared," Elia says, his forearm flexing as he pulls his wife closer.

I wonder where their kids are for a moment before spotting Elia's father off to the side with a brunette I recognize from The Bar—one of Juliet's friends. She holds the newborn while Orlando Montalto holds the toddler, distracting them from the fact that their parents aren't accessible.

A pang tears through my abdomen, and I clench my jaw until my head starts to throb. Pointing at Boyd, I tell him to head inside and scour every square inch of this godforsaken building; if what my father updated Giacomo and me on while we made our way over is true, the Catholic order in this town is about to have one hell of a reckoning.

One the various crime organizations they've stolen from and framed is gonna have a fantastic time fulfilling.

But none of that matters while Juliet's in danger.

Turning from the little group we've gathered at the corner of the cathedral, I start toward the side, aiming to run the length of the perimeter. A small hand grips my bicep, halting me. Caroline peers up, worrying the light pink lipstick off her bottom lip with her teeth. "She's with our mother."

"I know. She's in serious trouble. I'm not sure if you know what your mother's been doing, but if you thought your father was a piece of shit, your mom takes the fucking cake."

She pinches her eyes closed, sucking in a deep breath, and then pops them back open. "I didn't want to say she couldn't contact her, but something about her coming back all of a sudden was off. Something didn't feel right in my gut. I told her to stay away, but..."

The Queen of King's Trace breaks off on a sob, fat tears streaming down her face. Elia's hand slides up from around her waist and over her shoulders, tugging her into him. "She's gonna be okay, *amore mio.*"

My head tilts, a bit jealous of their open affection, but there's no time to linger. "I have to find her."

"Last I saw, they turned right here, and I was right on their trail." Elia shakes his head, fingers white-knuckling the fabric of his wife's dress. "There's no way they could have gotten far."

Nodding, I start toward the back of the church again, this time flanked by Elia as he hands his wife off to a woman with brown skin, big black eyes, and tightly coiled black hair. She wraps her arms around the blonde, ushering her over to comfort the wailing toddler calling for her mother.

Caroline clears her throat, pausing before she reaches her kids. "You love her, don't you?"

I can practically feel Elia's eyebrows shoot up, can sense the tension settling thickly in the air, but none of that matters right now. Meeting Caroline's stoic, determined gaze, I give her a curt nod, not sure I should be telling anyone before I've even told *her*, but unable to keep it a secret.

Because Christ, I fucking do. And I'll burn the entire goddamn world to a crisp if I don't get the chance to say it to her face.

A slow grin spreads along Caroline's lips, and she points over my shoulder. "Then go fucking get her."

27

___

KIERAN

WE ROUND the back corner of the church just as a muffled scream pierces the air, drawing our attention to the far end of the wall. Elia reaches under his suit jacket, producing his ever-present .22, and I slip one of mine out from my coat pocket, leaving the second pistol tucked into the waistband of my slacks.

A wide, thin metal door sits at the bottom of a concrete set of stairs, presumably the basement of St. Francis; we share a glance as we descend, and unease floods through me like a fucking avalanche, nearly stunting my progression.

I don't get nervous, especially not during shit like this. Usually, I'm the most prepared man in the entire fucking room, but right now I don't have a clue what we're about to walk in on, and the fact that there's so much at stake makes my chest tight with anxiety. I'm paranoid about what might go wrong.

What I stand to lose.

Rearing his calf back so it bends at the knee, Elia shoves his leg into the door on the inside of the lock, kicking so hard it nearly flies off its hinges. He steps inside quickly, gun in hand and held away from his body, turning in circles to assess the threat.

Moving in once he gives me the okay, I peer around the dark, damp cellar, using the sliver of light from the door to make things out. A slab of wood on top of a couple of sawhorses sits at one end in front of a few cells with iron bars as doors. Weapons and papers are scattered all over the place, and there's a wall filled from top to bottom with pictures of *everything*.

Every crime committed in the last century in King's Trace and every person tied to it.

The evidence on my flash drive.

My stomach heaves as I reach up and start tearing the photos down, anger swirling through me at having been duped.

Exposed.

"There's no time," Elia hisses, coming up behind me and bumping my shoulder with his. He nods toward a pool of thick, bright-red blood—fresh, the metallic scent still pungent in the air. With the amount puddled on the floor, there's no way the victim could have gotten very far, and the fact that I can't immediately identify the owner makes my nerve endings stretch and groan, terror taking root in my heart.

Making our way around the basement with cautious, calculated steps, we move in separate directions—him to the right and me to the left. Backs against the wall, just in case.

"Goddamnit," he grits out, doubling back by the door and peering around the makeshift desk. "More blood."

The blood coursing through my veins turns icy as I continue, spotting a familiar pair of feet, attached to a pair of calves I know better than my own, calves I've had wrapped around my head and waist more times than I can count.

Only now, they're scuffed and muddied, ankles bound together and tucked into a corner of one of the cells. She's gagged, with a thick fabric tied around her mouth, and her blonde hair is coated in sweat and blood. The little white dress she has on is stained beyond repair, and I can practically smell her fear.

Can feel it in every erratic beat of my heart as our eyes connect.

Hers widen, something caught between relief and horror pooling there, and the closer I get to the door barring her to me, the more I see. The reasoning behind why she's so silent, why not even a whimper escapes her—a man holding the sharp edge of a hunting knife at the base of her throat.

"*Father?*" Elia's voice echoes off the walls, drawing near.

The old man's white hair sticks out at odd angles, a large purple bruise forming just above his left cheekbone. There's a slight tremor in his grip that reminds me of my mother, causing a waver in my step.

He's still dressed in his robes from the christening ceremony, a stark contrast to the scene around him.

Rage blinds me for a moment, splashing crimson against my vision as my entire body heats. I'm pulled by some invisible force against the metal bars, watching as the priest pushes the tip of his knife harder into Juliet's skin. A thick bead of blood leaks out and drips down the blade, just barely visible in the thin streams of light provided by the open doorway.

My free hand wraps around one metal bar, gripping it so tight it starts to cramp. "Get the fuck off her."

"You're hardly in a position to be making demands, dear."

A female voice assaults my ears, loud in this dark chamber, the lack of light and furniture providing little to be soaked up by. Elia and I whirl on our heels, guns trained at the shadows until Lynn steps forward, holding a scarf against the back of her head and a gun in the opposite hand.

Trained right at my chest.

It's not the first time I've stared down a barrel, and while I doubt it'll be my last, it's the first time I'm concerned for anyone else's safety in the mix. Normally, I'd charge her, take the bullet, and let it cure the world of the monster and violence inside me.

A part of me still wants to, even knowing Juliet sits behind me, petrified and helpless. Elia could certainly save her, especially if her mother was no longer a problem.

But that doesn't do *her* any good. Not really. It would just be another issue to work through, another light snuffed out in her life.

So I stay still, even as my legs itch to carry me to the middle-aged bitch. Even as my finger twitches against the trigger of my gun, the vision of her blood spraying the walls and coating my shirt is all I can see as she moves toward us, her steps unsteady.

"What the fuck is going on right now?" Elia barks, anxiety stretching his voice so it comes out thin and scratchy.

My nerves wring tight in my chest.

Lynn's mouth opens, her blue eyes curving up as she watches me like a predator with its prey in sight. "Put your guns down, and we can have a little chat."

"I'm not going to *negotiate* with you when you've got your

daughter tied up and held at knife-point by a fucking priest." Elia cocks his gun, clenching his jaw. "Let her the fuck go or I'm just gonna blow your brains out."

She shrugs one shoulder, pulling the scarf away. It falls to the floor as she grips her gun in both hands, turning it from me to Elia. "God, I never did like you. Maybe I'll just do away with you first. Serve you right for stealing my good daughter and making her your whore."

"The only whore here is you, *stronza*. Orchestrating an entire sex trafficking ring is a pretty low way to sell out," Elia says, not backing down.

Turning my head ever so slightly, I glance at Juliet from the corner of my eye, needing her form to remind me not to act on the violent urge coursing through me. The low heat simmering in my bloodstream and the ire prickling in my stomach, making my fist clench and unclench at my side.

She watches me, seemingly unperturbed by the knife prodding her skin; her back is ramrod straight, her head leaned forward slightly as if to get the best angle possible. When her eyebrows knit together, confusion marring her beautiful features, I damn near lose every ounce of self-control I possess.

The demon inside me is fast losing its cool, shaking with untethered wrath, but if I make a sudden move, I can't trust we'll all get out of here alive.

I told her weeks ago that if she stopped running, I could keep her safe. It's one promise I intend to keep.

My fingernails dig into my palm as I tear my gaze away.

"...do what we have to in order to keep our control in this world," Lynn's saying, stumbling slightly as she takes another step. "Don't act so high and mighty, Montalto. As if you have any less blood on your hands than me. Dominic and I got into this racket to pay off his debts and advance his political career. A career we used to try to better King's Trace. Small price to pay for a lot of good, no? What's *your* excuse?"

"I'm not out here hurting *innocent* people. Everyone I encounter is a willing part of this world, and you know as well as I do that blood is a part of the game."

Glancing at me, perhaps to make sure I've not made any sudden moves, she shrugs again, then looks back at Elia. "And what about the people who buy your drugs, hmm? Or does it not bother you to feed their addictions?"

Elia swallows, eyes hardening. "It's not my job to care about the vices of other adults."

"Well, what about the families you destroy by enabling them? How do you sleep at night knowing the inordinate amount of cash tied to your name is hurting *them*?" She cocks her head. "What about the loved ones of the made men you torture and kill? Aren't they innocent?"

"If you're trying to paint yourself in a better light," I say, finally peeling my dry tongue from the roof of my mouth, "reminding us of our crimes really isn't the way to do it. Ours still pale in comparison."

Glaring daggers through my forehead, she redirects her aim and attention my way. *Perfect.* I share a quick look with Elia, gesturing with my eyes to Juliet, and he nods almost imperceptibly.

"*Do* they?" she asks, a wicked smile stretching her thick lips, evil emanating from every pore of her body. "I have to say, Kieran, I didn't think anyone's record could even touch yours. How many real-life skeletons do you have hidden in your closet? Can you even keep track anymore?"

She tosses it in for shock value, I know, but I still bristle, because *how the fuck does she know there's anything in my closet at all?* Sliding my gaze back to Juliet, I cock an eyebrow in question, and she blinks rapidly, as if trying to communicate through Morse code.

I can't imagine she'd divulge that information to someone she hates, though, so I ignore the comment and brush over it. "Just admit it, Lynn. You're mad I fucked up your organization, and you want me to repent for my sins."

"Repent?" She laughs, the sound maniacal and unhinged. "No, sweetie, I won't even give you the chance. I want that flash drive, and then I want to see a bullet pop through the other side of your head."

"You think Juliet will forgive you if you kill me?"

Scoffing, she tosses a flippant look over my shoulder. "What do I care if she forgives me? Her opinions on things never mattered much, anyway. She'd just do or think whatever we told her." She tilts her head to the side, disgust pulling her features taut as if she's just remembered a bad scent. "But I'm sure you don't need me to tell you that, Kieran. She *listens* to you, right? A good little slut, just like we always told her she needed to be if she wanted any kind of decent life. Never was good at much, but word around town is she can suck a cock like no other."

My nostrils flare. I want to melt the skin from this woman's body. "How can you—"

"You Ivers boys are so *weak*. A pretty face just does you right in, huh?" Lynn laughs, her chest wracking with the force of it. "It was so easy to convince your brother he'd hurt that girl he was dating, so easy for him to just lose it and throw himself to the wolves. Made for a perfect scapegoat."

"What are you talking about?" I ask. "Murphy didn't hurt Mel?"

"Oh, he did eventually. You saw that. But she wasn't the reason he got picked up. Dominic planted her at the transport site on purpose because we needed an older girl for a particular bidder. Murphy's reaction just played right into our hands."

Her speech is slurred a bit, trailing off at the ends of her words. I wonder how badly she's injured.

Rage slithers down my spine, urging me to end this conversation. To rush forward, jam the barrel of my gun down this woman's throat, and keep it there until she chokes on her own vomit. The image is so pristine in my mind, so daunting for the briefest moment, that when I snap back and hear Elia's low growl, I'm surprised to find I've remained still.

"That's quite enough." My voice is harsh, almost inaudible, as I fight to remain in control. Pulling the flash drive from my pocket, I hold it up in the air between us, noting the wobble in her stance and the blood dripping onto the concrete floor beneath her. A head wound, most likely, and probably draining fast.

Pride at the probable origin of the injury makes my chest swell, knowing Juliet fought back. That my girl held her own as long as she could, despite the fear and sadness that probably flooded inside her when she was brought to this place, thrust into this life by parents who never deserved her.

That she chose to fight, to *live*, in the face of her demons.

Bending down, I drop my gun to the floor and kick it behind me, heart pounding in my ears. The one in my waistband digs into my skin—a constant reminder.

I inch forward, holding the USB drive in my palm. "You want it, Lynn, take it. If you need to kill me, fine. I deserve it. You're probably right. But Juliet has no part in this. You'll let her leave here with Elia, or I'll shoot out those gas pipes hanging on the walls and kill us both right here, right now."

"Shoot them out with what? You've just ditched your weapon."

I smirk. "You really think you can overpower me, Lynn? Try it."

Elia pulls out a Zippo, weirdly in sync with my plan, and tosses it over; I catch it and raise an eyebrow at her, watching carefully as she weighs her options.

"This isn't an ongoing offer. Make a decision, *now*, or I'll blow all of us up." I can practically feel Murphy's presence at that moment, the ghost of him less haunting and more encouraging. A sort of acquiescence in my solutions, as if he's finally accepting me in the afterlife.

Forgiving me for not being faster. Better.

But only at the expense of destroying the one who broke him in the first place.

It lifts a lead weight from my shoulders, chipping away at the burden his death has kept on me for so long.

"Fine." Lynn nods at Father O'Leary, who pulls the knife back from Juliet's throat a fraction, allowing her to stand and move away from him. He gets up with her, sawing through the binds on her ankles and wrists, then unties the gag from around her mouth. Elia rushes over to the cage and yanks the cell door open, doing a double take when he notices something in the adjoining cell.

Juliet's head swings back, knocking into the priest's chin; it catches him off guard, kicks him off balance, and he stumbles into the wall, hitting his head on the concrete and falling to the ground. I smirk at her vengeance, returning my attention to Lynn.

"*Kieran.*" My little kitten's voice rings through the air, the sweetest of symphonies, warming my blood in a way that doesn't leave me ill or weak. She's the best thing in this darkness, the light I wasn't expecting in the slightest but feel immensely grateful to have experienced.

Lynn rolls her eyes, and I try not to make a snarky retort. "Can I have a minute?"

She looks annoyed, her lips pressing into a thin line, but nods anyway.

"Stay back, kitten. I want you to go with Elia." I don't turn my head, afraid that one look at Juliet's baby blues will have me caving, running to her and endangering her out of selfishness. Out of the prospect of holding her for even one more second. And I can't let her get hurt.

"Don't do this. Not for me." There's a tremble in her voice, and it wafts closer, like she's coming to me. Disobeying me, even when her life is being threatened. Her fingers graze mine, uncurling them from the fist they make. "Getting yourself killed isn't as valiant as they make it seem in the movies."

"Not even when it's for love?"

Growing impatient with my conversation with her daughter, Lynn cocks her gun at my words, prepping to kill me before she's even gotten the flash drive back. Smart move, since I'm planning on shooting out the pipes before she grabs it.

Juliet's fingers slide between mine, and I can't stop myself from looking down at her. Towering over her, I can see the tears pooling in her eyes, the misery I'm causing. And fuck if it doesn't make my throat burn, my chest tight, and my brain fight against what I'm doing.

"If you loved me, you wouldn't leave me," she whispers, a

tear spilling over and down her cheek. "You wouldn't put yourself in this situation."

I squeeze her hand, shuffling her back behind me as her mother edges closer. Agony claws its way through my heart, tearing it to shreds with each passing second. "I'd do anything for you, baby."

"Then don't do *this*." She drops her voice, so low only I can hear. "Let me talk to her. Maybe I can convince her to let us go. Maybe we can fight back, ask her—"

Unlinking our fingers, I reach up and cup her cheek, reveling in the feel of her soft skin and hating that this is the last time I'll ever feel it. The last time I'll ever see her blush, feel the heat of her flesh against my own.

My throat constricts, a knot making me stumble over my words. "No, baby. That's not how this is gonna go. I need you to leave with your brother-in-law and go on with your life. Finish that degree, keep on with therapy, get a sweet-ass job and forget about all of this. You deserve so much more than this life. You are so much more than the sadness inside you. So much stronger than you even realize."

"Don't I get a say in what I deserve? Don't I get to choose?"

"I wish you did. But some things are just out of our control." Lynn taps her foot, and I sneak a glance at her from the corner of my eye as she moves even closer, her gun practically brushing my skin at this point. "It was always gonna end like this, kitten. We were never permanent. Just one lonely night sky lucky enough to have your light in his orbit."

Her tears fall freely now, and Elia steps up behind her, gripping her biceps. She tries to shake him off, but his hold is too strong. She sniffles, blinking rapidly. "But I—"

"*Go*, now," I snap.

Elia begins dragging her away toward the light pooling in through the door, and she digs her heels into the floor in an effort to slow him down.

"I love you," I whisper, hating the way it seems to catch in the air and drift to her. She chokes on a sob, and just when I think she's about to break out from Elia's grasp, he hoists her over his shoulder and exits the same way we came in.

It's the sound of her screams that haunts me when the bullet hits my shoulder; they keep me company as I drift off, aiming for the piping and tossing the lighter to the ground, engulfing the entirety of this nightmare in flames before I have a chance to remember that she didn't say it back.

Juliet

Caroline tries to comfort me as we sit in the back seat of Elia's parked SUV; she wraps her arm around my shoulders and lets me cry into her dress, soaking it with my tears and staining it with our mother's blood, still not fully dry from before.

Carter left with Liv and Orlando after checking to make sure I was okay. I'm not, but there wasn't anything her presence would have added for me. Nothing she could do to change matters.

"She was trafficking people," I murmur into my sister, unable to focus on anything else at the moment. I can't think about what *just* happened—don't want to focus on the ache in my heart just yet.

My body is numb, my heart splintering with every passing second. Like someone's reached in and injected it with a slow-acting poison, leaving me here on this planet to suffer. A thick blackness ebbs through me, tainting my insides with its vileness and making me shake.

I feel catatonic, my mind disconnecting from my body as it tries to cope with such monumental loss.

Caroline smooths her hand over my hair, keeping my forehead in the crook of her neck. "We really got a raw deal in the parent department, huh?"

"Yeah." My eyes burn, my brain struggling to catch up. I pull back to look at her, gripping my locket between my fingers. "But I got you from it. I wouldn't change that for anything, and I'm—" A bubble in my throat cuts off the sentence, fire spreading through my esophagus as I consider how fucking lucky I've been all along. "I'm sorry you didn't get quite as good of a bargain."

She smiles, a tear rolling down her cheek, and cups my jaw between her hands. "You're right, I got a *steal*."

Fiona makes her way to our vehicle, nodding solemnly at Benito; Boyd went back with Elia to check out the damage after we heard an explosion in the basement, indicating Kieran had rescinded his deal with my mother. Ensuring my safety and preserving our town's legacy.

Leaving me empty.

Twirling a lock of hair around her finger, Fiona shifts on her feet. "I was hoping I'd be a lot older before I'd have to bury another sibling."

Sparks ignite in my chest, setting my soul on fire at her words, and all I want now is for the earth to swallow me whole in a completely different way than I used to.

"I told you not to believe every rumor you heard about him," she says through a watery smile, her nose reddening with the effort it takes to suppress her own tears. "Kieran is

—was, I guess—the most selfless guy on the planet. Cared too much about his loved ones, if you ask me. Loved too hard, burned too bright, and didn't even realize it. A star like him, filled with perceived darkness and haunted by his demons, was bound to die out before his time, anyway."

"Fiona, I'm so—"

Holding her hand up, she shakes her head softly. "Don't apologize for his choices. He'd have done the same for me." She shrugs, taking a step back, rapping her knuckles against the door of the vehicle. "That's how you know it was real."

Turning on her heel, she walks off, the sway of her hips lacking sorely as she makes her way back to the parking lot.

Another sob rips through me, and Caroline hugs me tighter.

It's an impossible feeling, losing someone who became threaded into the very fabric of your being. Who stole your soul, repaired it, and made sure it was returned before you even realized what he'd done.

A rock in a sea of loneliness, the first seedling of growth and understanding that spurred the beginning of your healing.

Who saw you when you needed to be seen.

How do you go back to being invisible once you know the warmth of detection?

I cry on Caroline's shoulder until my throat is raw and scratchy and the tears dry up, spent. We sit in silence, and I appreciate that she doesn't try to offer condolences or false security. She just holds me, lets me wallow, and it makes me wonder for the first time if maybe she gets me, too.

If maybe she has all along, and if that's not part of what Kieran tried to show me.

And while it causes a slight stutter in my heart, an

attempt at resuscitation, it's not quite enough to bring back the dead.

Elia returns after a long, long while, hopping into the driver's seat and rushing Benito in, his movements frantic, words foreign, as if he can't contain his emotions and therefore can't control what language he uses to express them.

Caroline sits forward as we peel out of the church drive, falling in behind a Jeep I don't recognize. He floors the gas, weaving in and out of traffic, beeping at anyone that gets in his way.

"What's going on?" Caroline asks Benito, who shrugs for a moment, staring at his crazy-eyed boss.

"That bastard's not dead."

28

KIERAN

THERE'S nothing quite like waking up in a King's Trace Medical recovery room.

I'm trapped behind a cubicle of curtains, able to hear the murmurs of doctors and patients, the beeping of machines doing their best to keep people alive post-op, still slightly drugged and unsure if anything I'm experiencing is reality or dream.

Like the blonde occupying the chair beside my bed with her head in my lap, sleeping more peacefully than I've ever seen her. I reach down and thread my fingers through her tresses with my left arm, the other seeming to be numb and immobile, though I can't quite remember why.

The last thing I recall is Lynn snatching the USB from my hand and pulling her trigger at the same time I pulled mine, the force of the blast knocking me on my ass and out cold.

Juliet stirs, swiping the back of her hand across her mouth and startling out of my grasp, blinking around the room. Her gaze connects with mine, deep oceans of every emotion staring straight through me, making my heart stutter in my chest.

"Kitten—"

"You're an unbelievable ass, you know that?"

I blink, the biting tone throwing me off. "I'm sorry?"

"Yeah, you fucking should be, you asshole." She hoists herself up on the edge of the bed, and for the first time, I notice she's changed from the dress she had on at the christening into a pair of black yoga pants and a black oversized Ivers International sweatshirt. I realize I have no idea what day it is, or how much time has passed since all of that went down at the church.

No idea what happened to Lynn or Father O'Leary, or any of the evidence.

Pausing, Juliet leans over and pulls back the thin paper gown I'm wearing, exposing my gauze-wrapped shoulder and sucking on her teeth. Her fingers spread over the site, grazing almost reverently. "Do you remember what happened?"

I shrug the shoulder I can move. "Your mom shot me, didn't she? Although, I have to say, the pain is much less excruciating than what I would have expected. Last time, it hurt a hell of a lot more."

Heated anger flares in her eyes as her hand retreats. "Yeah? Let me see if I can help."

"What are you—"

Her elbow rears back past her shoulder, her arm whipping forward so fast I don't have a chance to react or defend myself before her palm connects with my cheek. A stinging sensation ripples along the skin, blacking out my vision for a split second. I shake my head when she settles back on the mattress, glaring at me, and blink away the purple splotches from my eyes.

"What the hell was that for?"

"Did it hurt?"

I sputter, my mind bouncing around in my skull like it's got whiplash. "Yes, but why—"

She slaps me a second time on the opposite cheek, so hard I bite my tongue and taste blood. Hissing at her as she brings her hand back for a third hit, I lash out with my arm and catch her wrist before she makes contact, yanking her to me and trapping her other hand between us.

"Okay, kitten, I probably deserved those two, but if you do it again, I'm gonna get turned on and fuck you right here where everyone else can hear. They'll hear you mewl as you milk my cock and hate themselves because you're all *mine*."

Jerking against me, she tries to pull back, but my grip is too tight. "How can you joke right now?"

Tears well up in her eyes, and she tries to blink them away, but one slips out and drops onto the base of my throat. It feels like an ice pick to the chest, knowing where the tears are coming from. Knowing I caused them.

"Are you really mad at me?"

"*Yes.* How could you put yourself in danger like that?"

"Baby." I release her wrist and tangle my fingers in her hair, gently fisting at the back of her neck and pulling her close, careful to avoid irritating any injuries. Our noses brush, our lips a whisper away, and my heart's never felt so fucking full. So absent of darkness, so unburdened by my namesake and the ghosts following me around.

"When given the option between you and me, I'm never gonna bet on myself. I gambled on a necklace months ago, gambled on a girl and her dark little soul, and I'll double down and bet on you every single day for the rest of my life.

You're rain and sunshine wrapped in an unbelievable package. I *choose* you."

Letting out a soft whimper, she drops her forehead to my chin, her weight crushing me on the hospital bed. But it's a weight I welcome, letting go of her hair and wrapping my arm around her waist.

"You're an insane person," she mutters, her lips against my skin, sending a tingle down my spine that I'm not sure is appropriate given the setting, but that I lean into, anyway. Shifting my hips up, I fit myself more snugly into her pelvis, wishing I could stitch us together and keep her close to me forever.

"You love me," I say into her hair, softening the blow, noting the way her shoulders stiffen.

When she sits up, as much as she can with my arm attached to her waist, she grins. "Do I?"

My pulse kicks up, and I shrug the good shoulder. "Well, I guess I don't actually know if you do or not."

"A shame, really, given your keen aptitude for reading me." Rolling her hips into mine, she arches her back and sits straight up, dislodging my arm to place my hand on her heart, just over her breast. I don't know if she can feel me growing hard under her, but fuck if I'm not ready to make good on my threat to take her right here. "You feel that?"

My fingers flex around her tit, her nipple piercing hard against my palm, and I jerk my hips up into her. "Do *you* feel *that*?"

She rolls her eyes. "Focus, *daddy*, and maybe I'll let you punish me later for slapping you."

I groan, my cock twitching. "Like you have a choice, kitten."

"*Anyway*, you fucking caveman," she snaps, her attitude

making my chest swell, "if you could stop being a pervert for two seconds, you'd feel the way my heart speeds up at your touch. And maybe then I'd be able to tell you that yeah, I do."

"Do what?"

"Love you!" she whisper-shouts, the sound seeming to quiet the rest of the area for a moment. A deep blush pinkens her cheeks, and we both freeze, waiting to see if anyone comes and peeks in. When they don't, she smacks my pec, sending a wave of pain through me.

"*Christ.*" My head swims as the burning sensation swirls inside my chest. "What the fuck was in that bullet?"

"Normal bullet, but it nicked your brachial plexus, and we had to extract the bullet from your shoulder through surgery."

We both jump at the added voice, Juliet scrambling off my lap and nearly toppling over in the process. She settles into her chair as Kal Anderson yanks back the curtain, a wide and rare smile plastered on his chiseled face. He scrubs a hand through his dark hair, adjusting the lapels of his white lab coat, and steps inside quickly.

I've never seen him in a clinical setting, and the juxtaposition of him having a decent bedside manner versus his normal standoffish, self-righteous nature is jarring. Still, I'm surprised to see him here, given that I hadn't known he was in town, anyway. I can't help wondering why he's stopped by.

"So what? Am I okay?" I point at my injured arm with my good hand. "Why can't I feel anything?"

He inhales deeply, letting it whoosh from him slowly. "To be honest, we can't be sure at this point. It looked as if the nerves were only stretched, but given this is the first you've been awake post-op and the blocker we gave you pre-op, it's difficult to tell the full extent of the damage. Sometimes these injuries can take months to show up and years to heal fully."

"But I *might* have nerve damage? In my good arm?"

"*Might* being the operative word, Ivers. If it's just a good stretch, you'll heal up without further treatment. If it's more severe, or if the injury gets embedded in scar tissue over time, there are avenues we can take to restore function. We'll know more when your block wears off, and we can run some tests." He tilts his head, studying me. "So maybe you won't be able to pursue the same career path. Is that really such a bad thing?"

Crossing my other arm over my chest, I remain silent, glowering.

He shrugs, moving on. Like it's so easy to take a man out of the grasp of the Mafia. I'll never get out from under Finn and Elia, and frankly, after experiencing the loyalty I thought only myself capable of during the whole investigation, I'm not sure I'll ever want to.

"Most people only take a few hours to recover from the kind of anesthetic we gave you, but given the amount of trauma your body suffered, we were all hopeful it'd take a natural course and let you rest a while longer."

I slide my gaze between the two of them. "How long have I been asleep?"

"Approximately fifteen hours."

Juliet cringes as my head whips to her. "Were you gonna mention that? Jesus Christ, what have I missed out on? Where's your mom and Father O'Leary? How bad was the damage to St. Francis's basement?"

"We had other things to discuss." She shrugs, unbothered by my outburst. "You didn't actually blow anything up;

apparently the pipes you shot at were just regular old sewage, so all it did was make them burst and flood the cellar some. Mom made the mistake of sticking around to collect all her files, so when Boyd and Elia went back to check on you, there she was. It didn't help that she was practically bleeding out from when I bashed her head in the wall."

Kal smirks, pulling the clipboard from the end of my hospital bed and scanning it. "You Harrison sisters aren't to be trifled with."

She shrugs. "I guess. Only took my whole life to stand up to her, but whatever." She picks at the corner of the white knit blanket draped over me, but I don't miss the small smile playing at her lips. "Elia hauled her ass off to the detention center, where she's awaiting arraignment for a myriad of crimes, including, but not limited to, aggravated sex trafficking, deceptive business practices, fraud, bribery, and trafficking contraband. Mom's got a very colorful rap sheet."

"Does that... bother you?"

She glances at Kal, swallowing. He gets the hint, slipping the clipboard back in its holster and nodding at me. "Right. Well, since you're up, I'll send in a nurse to do a full panel on your post-op condition, and they'll probably want you to eat, walk, and be merry. Depending on what the tests show once you're able to move from recovery, I may be ordering you physical therapy, as well, to keep your joints from getting stiff or locking up." He gives Juliet a warm smile, then juts his chin in my direction. "Glad you're not dead, kid."

I nod back, focusing on my girl as he slips out. "So?"

Blowing out a long breath, she rests her head against my thigh. "I guess you're not really asking if my mom's criminal charges bother me?"

"Nope."

Chewing on her bottom lip, her face softens as she seems to drift off in thought. "You know, I was a soft shell of a person before I met you. Sad and lonely, letting guilt consume me. Being abused by the people who claimed to care about me and who were supposed to love me. If that's what I get from living a normal life, and the emptiness that comes from being without you, I don't want any part of it. And if my sister can come to terms with being married to a Mafia boss, I can get down with a little torture in my lover."

"I'm not a good guy, Juliet."

"You never claimed to be. But I still think you're wrong." Her eyes shimmer up at me, a smile spreading across her plump lips. "I can only think of one other person on this planet who would've done for me what you did, and she's the best person I know."

I exhale softly, the vise grip around my heart lessening at her wholehearted acceptance. The violence in me isn't something that can be extinguished; you have to learn how to fan the flames and keep them contained except when needed. "Maybe I'm just good for you."

Hauling herself up and snuggling into my side, she nods, wrapping one arm around me. "Maybe you're right."

Later, when I'm wheeled to a private room and undergo a series of EMG tests and x-rays, our families finally pile in. My mother practically smothers me with her trembling arms, mascara streaking her cheeks and making guilt flood my chest.

She pulls back, smoothing her hands down over my face, and gives me a sloppy forehead kiss. "I *told* you she was the one."

Clasping her hand in mine, I squeeze carefully. "You're always right, aren't you?"

"About most things." She beams, pulling Fiona and my father down for a massive group hug.

And for a moment, it's almost possible to imagine Murphy's presence, a thorn in my side I don't think I'll ever rid myself of. But the pain from the pricking dims each day, as the darkness inside me begins to swallow it whole, giving me hope that maybe one day his ghost will actually forgive me.

EPILOGUE

JULIET

A WARM, wet sensation between my thighs pulls me from the deep slumber I've fallen into. My eyelids peel open, meeting the electric green gaze of the man I love as his mouth devours me, coaxing pleasure from my soul with each swipe of his tongue against my pussy.

My back arches, my head twisting to the side as he spears into me, and I notice the curtains in our bedroom are pulled aside, allowing the shaded midmorning sun to trickle through. The soft, gray October sky is the perfect weather to drive people into a fundraiser being held by Elia tonight.

Well, sort of. He's sponsoring the charity drive for the proposal to create *A Free Hand*, a legitimate advocacy group for victims of human trafficking. Not long after Lynn Harrison's arraignment, girls who'd managed to escape the horrors in the aftermath of the federal shutdown began crawling out of the woodwork of King's Trace and surrounding areas, offering witness accounts sure to put my mother away for a long time.

If her trial ever stops being delayed, that is.

What can I say, the criminal justice system in this country is slow and often yields infinitesimal results.

Still, as long as she rots in the Stonemore County Prison, I don't really give a shit.

Caroline and I don't ever visit. Sometimes I think she gets the urge to, maybe to give our mother a piece of her mind or try to understand why she did what she did, and I recognize that flicker of guilt in her gaze. Recognize the shame that slumps her shoulders, the nervous twitch that accompanies resistance.

I never mention it.

What could I even say?

I've been there, and we're both still healing. Still coming to terms with the course our lives took.

My grief over our father is still tucked deep inside me, but I don't go to the cemetery anymore. I've stopped giving myself to ghosts that don't deserve it.

We have group sessions with Hana scheduled every three months, although we've only been to one thus far; I didn't say much, wary of opening up around my sister when we've spent our whole lives repressing ourselves, but seeing how she came undone in that room, as if those four walls held some key to her frustrations and soaked up every ounce she vented, then locked them up for safekeeping, makes me hopeful for the next round.

Because a part of what once made me so broken was feeling disconnected from Caroline; as close as we always seemed to be, with both of us holding back most of our lives and trying to shield each other from our pain, our bond never really rooted.

But we're working on it, and I help out around Care's Crazy Cakes twice a week, getting to know Caroline as my sister and not my white knight. I'm set to graduate at the end of this semester, and she's been helping me get applications together for internships at different labs across the state.

'Healing is an ongoing process,' Hana keeps telling me. *'It's not an overnight destination, and sometimes wounds never fully recover. Sometimes they scab and scar, leaving behind visible, painful residue we can only work to soothe but never rid ourselves of entirely. And that's okay, because those imperfections remind us of our humanity.'*

I'm not totally sure about her or her insistence on practicing meditation when I wake up and before I go to bed, but I can't deny that I've been sleeping better in the months since I started seeing her.

At least, according to Kieran, who still wrestles with his own demons from time to time. But I think he's got a better grip on his darkness, like he's using a bit of my light for himself without trying to squander it.

It turns out he had some minor nerve damage in his brachial plexus as a result of the gunshot wound; although he still had primary use of his arm and hand, there was numbness, tingling, and weakness that bothered him, so he underwent a nerve graft a month and a half ago. Since then, he's been rigorous with his physical therapy, determined to regain full, unencumbered use of his hand again so he can go back to work.

I try not to think about his career. Like Caroline and the other significant others of the underground, it's something we compartmentalize and separate from our realities. Pretend we don't know why they occasionally come home with blood on their hands or wearing non-tracking army boots.

The skeletons in his closet are none of my business. He

gutted his brother's cabin last month and has been working on renovating the entire thing, top to bottom, erasing the evidence of any and all evil from the dwelling. His mother even gave it the seal of approval, although with her rapidly declining memory and health, I'm not entirely convinced she knew what she was talking about.

We've been renting an apartment downtown while the house is being done, having decided on moving in together when he started the renovations. I wasn't entirely sure about the decision, especially so early on in our relationship, but Kieran is not deterred by time. And I'm sick of letting fear rule me.

A selfish approach to criminals and life, maybe, but I'm starting to not care.

"*Fuck*, kitten," Kieran growls into my skin, biting down on my throbbing clit. I cry out, both in pain and rapture, my fingers twisting in his dark hair and holding him against me. He sucks me into his mouth, flicking me with his tongue. "You're close, aren't you?"

I nod vehemently, squeezing my eyes shut as his hands pry my thighs farther apart, one slipping beneath and cupping the curve of my ass. His pinky dives in, teasing the tight ring of muscle and making my body clench with anticipation.

From the moment we met, he's known me without my needing to spell things out for him. Saw me when it felt like no one else did and made me feel worthy of existing.

He didn't heal me, but made me feel like maybe I don't deserve to hurt anymore.

"Don't come yet," he commands, and I squeal as he laps at my skin, his finger pushing deeper inside me, electricity zinging through my body like a supernova.

Gritting my teeth, I try to stave off the release swarming in my belly. "I want to come. *Please.*"

"You'll hold it until I say so." He releases my thigh, landing a harsh slap above my pussy, sending my eyes to the back of my head. "Or I'll pull out of you right now and leave you with nothing."

I groan, my head thrashing on the pillow. *God, I will never get tired of this game.*

"Now," he says, rearing back and stuffing his thumb in my pussy, sliding in and out of both my holes with a devious glint in his eyes. Hovering over me, he watches where he disappears inside me, lust coloring his cheeks. "I have a question for you, and depending on how you answer, maybe I'll let you come."

"Oh, *fuck.* Ask me, ask me."

"You don't make the demands here, kitten." His fingers retreat, leaving just the tips in, and I practically weep at the loss, shifting my hips down in an effort to get him deeper. Pinching one of my nipple piercings with his free hand, he grins, rolling it between his thumb and forefinger until I'm shaking. "Can you be a good girl and let daddy ask his question, or do I need to gag my little brat?"

I shake my head, growing even wetter at the thought of him stuffing my face too full to speak, knowing I'll come immediately if he does. "No, please. Just ask me. I'll be good, I promise."

"I'm not so sure..."

"Daddy, *please.* I need it. I need you."

"Well, since you begged so nicely."

My body heats as he slips his fingers in another inch, my inner walls trying to suck him in and force the pleasure from him. I press my lips together as his head dips and he pulls a nipple into his mouth, sucking so hard it feels like he might tear it off. My clit throbs, my pussy leaking as he begins fucking me with his hand, and my hips ride the wave of his movements, euphoria spiking down my spine as he lets me have it.

"What's your question?" I gasp, my vision blurring at the corners as my orgasm nears, the muscles in my thighs drawing tight together as I try to hold off. I don't know if I can handle my punishment right now—not this early in the morning.

"So impatient." He chuckles, shoving and twisting until it feels like his whole hand is inside me, and he bites down on my nipple until it aches. Pulling back, he presses a hard kiss to my lips and rests his forehead against mine as I convulse beneath him. "I want you to marry me."

Tingles shoot through me at his words, the notion completely foreign. Not something we've ever really talked about. I always assumed he wasn't the conventional type, and that'd be just fine with me.

"Is that even a question?"

"Just pretend for a second you have a choice."

My breathing is labored, my chest heaving as I stare up at him. "Are you sure you want to marry me?"

He grins, his hand moving quicker, fingers curling against my inner muscles. I squirm, stars dancing in my eyes, and buck against him. "I've never been more sure of anything. You are the greatest gift this life could've ever given me, and every day that passes by where you don't have my last name makes me more miserable than the last. I know it seems sudden and too soon, but fuck it, baby. *Life* is short, and it's up to us to make it fucking memorable."

Yanking his hand from me, creating an absence that I

feel in my soul, he shifts, stroking his cock and pushing inside me before I have a chance to answer. I cry out at the fullness, my hands wrapping around his neck as he thrusts, bending my thigh so he hits as deep as possible.

"*Say yes.*"

"I—"

His hand comes up, gripping the column of my throat, robbing me of the slightest bite of air. I clench around him, feeling the strain of his muscles as he holds his own release back, and moan so loud I think our downstairs neighbors might hear. But I don't care.

"*Say it.*"

"Oh my God, *yes!*"

"Yes, *what?*"

"Yes, daddy! I'll marry you!"

He thrusts faster, his hips slapping against my pelvis so hard I'm sure he'll leave bruises, squeezing my throat and making me hoarse. My orgasm barrels through me, dousing me in liquid fire and making my toes curl as it burns my insides. I pulse around him, feeling the exact moment he spills inside me, my pussy milking out every last drop of his warm cum.

Sagging into my body, he doesn't bother separating us, drawing out the flutter in my inner walls. I thread my fingers through his hair, my heart so ridiculously full as he strokes the locket around my neck with a faraway look in his eyes.

"You didn't have to fuck me into submission, you know." I lick the seam of his lips. "I would've said yes if you'd asked me at dinner."

Smirking, he releases the locket and buries his head into the crook of my neck. "Maybe. But this was way more fun."

When he leaves me to pull a black velvet box from his

pants pocket and slides a solitaire diamond onto my finger, I burst into tears, unable to keep the happiness inside me at bay.

Unwilling to, after a lifetime of bottling up all the sadness. These days, I'm trying to learn to live with both sides of the coin.

Things aren't perfect, but they never will be. They're muddy and unclear, sometimes truly dark in manifestation. But the absence of light doesn't always mean an absence of *goodness*—just that, like some flowers, some souls learn to bloom at night.

For now, I choose to embrace the darkness.

THE END

DID you love Kieran and Juliet's story and want more? Subscribe to my mailing list by tapping this link to get their BONUS epilogue and see what they're up to in the future.

Keep reading for a sneak peek at the next couple in the King's Trace Antiheroes series. Boyd Kelly is in for a rude awakening in Sweet Sacrifice, available now!

FIONA IVERS HAS BEEN **in love with her brother's best friend since she was a kid.** He's older and oblivious to her existence—which only makes her want him more. She's always believed he was disinterested, until a charity gala pushes them together. There, she realizes maybe he pays more attention than he's ever let on.

Broody, tattooed loner Boyd Kelly has a low tolerance for distractions, and has no issues letting those around him know. **His best friend's younger sister doesn't seem to care, though.**

Each time the high-strung redhead bats her doe eyes in his direction, Boyd gives in a little, secretly desperate for the affection she so clearly wishes to give him.

But opening up to love might be more dangerous than either of them knows.

KEEP READING for a sneak peek at Boyd and Fiona!

EPILOGUE
FIONA

FIREWORKS ERUPT in the night sky like kaleidoscopes of color and noise. An explosion of celebration, but all it does now is drown out the sound of a gunshot as it reverberates through the air.

My palm burns, heat searing me where the cold metal presses into my skin. Beads of sweat pop up despite the cool fall temperature, and I swipe the back of my free arm across my forehead, sucking in a deep breath.

I'm a murderer.

I suppose I should've seen this coming; it's practically in my blood, after all. When you come from a long line of Mafia associates, the only real choices you have in life are to fall in line with the family business or die trying to escape it.

But I thought I'd found a third option. Crime completely unaffiliated with anyone but me.

Retaliation.

Self-preservation.

Something tells me a court of law won't see it that way.

Prying the pistol from my grip, I throw open the dumpster lid and drop the weapon inside. A throb flares in my temple like a hammer beating against my skull, telling me I'm in trouble.

I spot a dirty, discarded plastic tarp buried beneath various pieces of trash and use both hands to extract it from the metal container. Draping it over the body, I dig my palms under his back, shift all my weight into my biceps, and roll him against the brick wall of the restaurant he'd taken me to.

To be fair, I was warned against him. Told that he didn't have a decent bone in his body—and coming from my brother, whose own fiancée sometimes still refers to him as the devil, that said a lot.

But I didn't listen, too wrapped up in being vindictive and the Italian that rolled off this man's tongue. My mother called it a flowery, romantic language—something we've grown up with, living in King's Trace, that sometimes blocks out the ugly reality of the words.

And because I'm an Ivers and we've made a legacy of evasion, I run.

My sneakers beat a dull thud against the pavement as I sprint from the alley, my lungs struggling to catch up with the surge of adrenaline.

I run until it feels like I might burst or pass out, until that familiar ache threads through the side of my abdomen, and my vision blurs, exertion clogging my body.

I run until I collapse to my knees in a yard I've not seen in months. The memory of the house's owner kicking me out and telling me not to come back plays on repeat behind my eyes as I stare up at the dilapidated craftsman-style bungalow. The glowing night sky illuminates its algae-ridden white siding and the screen door hanging off the frame on the covered porch.

A familiar retro motorcycle with forest-green paint sits before the front steps, indicating its owner's presence.

Miles away from the Ivers mansion, from the parts of King's Trace I frequent, this home looks nothing like you'd expect. It's practically falling apart at the seams, and it's impossible to think he spends any time here.

But he grew up in the majority as far as wealth in this town goes—or, rather, lack thereof—and even his cushy job at my dad's company can't take the boy out of squalor completely.

Sucking in a breath, I try to calm the rapid pace of my heartbeat as I push forward, making myself reach the lopsided porch. The fireworks overhead only serve to set my nerves on edge, goose bumps rising on my skin as labored breaths wrench themselves from deep in my chest.

Technically, I should be at Kieran's. But ever since he moved in with Juliet and began renovating the cottage he has in the middle of the woods, exorcising his demons, I don't want to rain on his parade. He's in a state of euphoria I've never seen him in before, despite the black cloud that hangs over him as an associate of two different organized crime units, and it's not something I'm keen on ruining.

My dad would also be more than willing to help out, given his own ties to the Stonemore unit, an Irish crime family in the next town over, but he's been dealing with his own problems, and I don't want to detract from that.

This bungalow is my only real option, even if its inhabitant loathes my entire existence. He's still my brother's best friend, and in a town where sworn loyalties prevail over everything, I'm hoping he'll extend assistance to me.

I'm not naïve. I know he helps Kieran occasionally. I

know that, despite his morals and the tight-lipped air about him, he's not as innocent and clean as he appears.

A monster lurks just beneath the surface of his inked golden skin, searching for an outlet. And maybe I'm about to give him one.

My foot presses into the bottom step just as someone's arms wrap around my waist from behind, pushing me up on the porch fully and shoving me against the wall. A tattooed hand wraps around my mouth, the entire length of his tall, muscular body holding mine in place, and I can't stop the wave of desire from washing over me at the position.

One we've been in before, under very different circumstances.

His breath is harsh and hot against the shell of my ear, making my skin tingle. "I fucking told you not to come here anymore."

I mumble against his hand, hating how my body betrays my mind, craving his violent nature and salivating over the way he dominates. How he takes without asking and devours without formality or control. It's the one area he seems to allow himself to be free in.

My thighs clench of their own accord, the memory of his head between them all I can recall with him restraining me.

He shifts his hips, trying to relocate his growing erection from where it's lodged between my ass cheeks, and clears his throat. In one fluid movement, he yanks his hand from my face and spins me around, pressing my back into the siding, gripping my wrists in one hand, and pushing them up above my head.

Biting the inside of my cheek is the only way I can suppress the moan collecting at the base of my throat; I stare up at those warm, hazel eyes, hating the rage I see vibrating within them. Hating that I'm about to make it so, so much worse.

Swallowing over the lump in my throat as he glares down at me, I take a shuddering breath and release it slowly, the fireworks doing very little to calm me, though I can't tell if it's from being in Boyd Kelly's presence or the blood on my hands.

"I need your help."

SWEET SACRIFICE IS AVAILABLE NOW!

BONUS EPILOGUE
KIERAN

"You are *so* late."

I plant my shovel in the ground next to my feet and level my best friend with an unimpressed look. Boyd stands across from me with his hands in the pockets of his black tuxedo, a half-smoked blunt hanging from his lips as he surveys the scene before us.

"*We* are so late." My hand slides up to my neck, confirming that my unfastened gold bow tie remains draped beneath my collar. "You realize you're supposed to be there at a certain time, too, right?"

He sucks on the joint, inhaling and exhaling slowly, smirking around a plume of gray smoke. "Yeah, but it's not my wedding."

A jolt of excitement zips up the length of my spine. To be fair, at this point I'm not exactly sure I can still call it *my* wedding, given how thoroughly my sister has taken over bridesmaid duties and beyond. I'd been sure Juliet would want nothing more than a small, simple ceremony with only her closest friends and family in attendance, but Fiona insisted on a whole ordeal.

I could have killed her with my bare hands the second she started mentioning a string quartet and ice sculptures to my beautiful—but easily influenced—fiancée, aware that no matter what, I'd be jumping through too many fucking hoops before I'd be able to call Juliet mine.

Legally, anyway. She's mine in every other way that counts, and I remind her multiple times a day—when I wake up with her in my arms, when I bury myself between her luscious thighs, or when she goes out with her friends for drinks and I tag along in the shadows, waiting for an opportunity to steal her away and shove my tongue into her perfect little cunt.

Just in case. Wouldn't want her to forget who owns her body and soul.

I push the sleeve of my own tux back, checking the time on the sleek black Rolex on my wrist. My stomach drops, and my eyes fall to the two-feet deep hole in the ground in front of me.

Boyd's right—I'm fucking late.

At this rate, with the sun already hanging low in the orange sherbet sky, I'm not sure I'll be able to make it there in time for even the reception.

But in my defense, he asked me to come. Said the matter was urgent, and when I arrived at the desolate clearing just outside the King's Trace city limits, I'd found him digging this grave. In the backseat of his ruby red Audi was a man with long blond hair, bound at the ankles and wrists with zip ties.

His eyes and teeth had already been removed, though he was still very much alive.

I'm not sure which part disturbed me more—the fact that Boyd knew I wouldn't want to see the creep's gaze, or that he'd known just how to sever the oscillatory nerves and staunch the flow of blood so he didn't immediately die.

Maybe Boyd's been spending more time with Kal Anderson than I realized. Then again, I suppose he has his reasons.

"What are the chances of me escaping this ceremony with my balls still attached to my body?" I ask him.

"Fiona wants to be an aunt, so I'd say pretty good. The odds of her bitching about you being late for the next fifty years, though? Not in your favor."

If my sister can do anything, it's bitch. She's still holding a grudge against our father for some infidelity issues she discovered a couple of years ago, even though she swears she's over it.

Still, she doesn't look at him the way she once did; like he was a king who'd put the stars in the sky just for his princess. Though maybe that has more to do with how quickly she had to grow up and the burden of responsibility that was placed on her than anything else.

Maybe it's a result of everything. The latter half of the past decade was hard on us Ivers, and it only recently started feeling like we could claw our way out of the hole of despair the universe had tossed us into.

I no longer visit the cemetery for my brother. A few months after the whole incident at St. Francis, my father decided to have Murphy's grave exhumed and relocated to my mother's family mausoleum three hours away. It's where the rest of the Ivers bloodline will be buried, unless we choose differently.

Of course, Murphy's casket is empty, so the relocation

was more symbolic than anything else. I still have his skeleton in my possession, although now it's buried deep in the attic of my home–an ornate cabin on Lake Koselomal, close to where my brother's cottage once stood–so that Juliet can never stumble upon it again.

Especially considering his bones aren't the only ones in there.

The collection has grown over the years.

Boyd crouches low to the ground, where the corpse-to-be lies prone at our feet. He's still bound and gagged, just conscious enough to know he's in deep shit.

Or is about to be.

Pathetic whimpers puff out from around the rag taped inside of the man's mouth, and bloody, gaping holes exist where his eyes used to be. They're sloppy and jagged, and I know Boyd used a dull knife and took his time.

For these men, he refuses to do anything less. The slow, agonizing torture sends a message to the people haunting him, and while I'm not sure if it helps him sleep at night, I do know I'm not willing to deny him.

Not when I have done the same for far less.

Worse for less.

Boyd removes his joint from his mouth as he rolls the man onto his back, then takes the lit end and presses it into the base of the man's throat. His groan reverberates through him—I can almost feel it in the ground, and the sound is music to my ears.

But still, I'm late. I can't exactly take my time on this the way I wanted to.

Unsheathing a Bowie knife from the pouch I brought with me, I reach down and slice through the zip tie around the man's wrists. A strangled breath of relief rattles his chest, and I snort.

"Wouldn't get my hopes up if I were you. Does this feel like it's going well?" I ask, tearing at his shirt so I can drag the tip of the blade in an x-shape over his heart. He writhes against the pressure, moaning brokenly, and I use my free hand to hold his shoulder down as blood pumps quickly from the cuts.

"Can you not talk to him?" Boyd snaps, his hazel gaze hardening.

"You sound like my sister." I roll my eyes, ignoring the mental image that gives me, and pat the man's mud-stained cheek. "Anyway, no can do, Kelly. Part of my process."

"Your process is annoying."

"You want my help or not?" I sit back on my heels, aware of why he's taking his frustrations out on me but also unwilling to weather it fully when none of this is my fault.

When he doesn't say anything more and just glares down at the man as he groans in pain, I give a short nod. "That's what I thought. Now, be a good boy and roll him into that grave, will you?"

"Fucking bossy," he mutters, though he does what I ask, anyway. Hooking his palms beneath the man's side, he starts rolling, until he lands on his back in the shallow hole.

I toss him a couple of box nails and a bronze mallet from my toolbox, then reach for the long, steel fence post that I brought with me—a six-foot-long steel pole with a razor sharp, blunt-edged tip. Boyd secures the man in the grave by hammering the nails through the middle of his hands.

He doesn't make any noise when he's pinned to the ground. His chest rises slowly, but I think he may have passed out, which is a pity, but unfortunately I don't have the time to wake him back up and drag all of this out.

Boyd straightens, sliding another pre-rolled blunt from the inside of his jacket and slipping it into his mouth. He lights up with a silver Zippo, then grabs my shovel from where it juts out from the ground and begins throwing dirt back into the hole.

Right on top of the man's lower half.

Walking around to our victim's head, I pick up the discarded mallet and lean against the steel post, a bit disappointed that there won't be any fanfare with this hit. He'll die unconscious, quickly and silently, and then will be buried in this grave for a few days before Boyd digs him back up and we dispose of the body properly.

But as I glance at Boyd's frustrated face, I know this won't be the last opportunity. His ghosts stretch far and wide across the state, so many names still left to uncover. He won't stop until they've all paid for their transgressions against his family, and I can't say I blame him.

I can't even begrudge him the secrecy surrounding exactly what happened this year to trigger the hunt of people more deeply involved in sex trafficking than even Lynn Harrison.

The man in the grave was a low level runner for some ring out of Portland, with connections to Boyd's past in some way he refuses to elaborate on. All I know is that things aren't safe for him, or for his family—and that's not acceptable.

So when our victim stirs, attempting to suck in air through his gag and starting to thrash when he realizes he's been nailed into the ground, I take the tip of the pole and position it right over the X I left on his chest.

As Boyd continues filling the hole, covering the man's legs, I raise my hand and beat the curved end of the post with the long edge of my mallet.

The spear-shaped end pushes in, resisting against bone for a moment. I retract it, stepping inside the grave and using my boot to stomp on his chest until I feel the plate shatter beneath the force.

He screams, and it fills me with a perverse thrill. Waves of excitement rain down over me the same way they do every time I participate in this kind of thing–the main reason I keep doing it.

I like holding life in my bare hands and being able to squash it out if I choose. Perhaps that's a curse of my family name, or something far worse, but it's a trait I've simply learned to deal with in the years since murdering my brother.

But it's why I still work for Elia and Finn, and why I never went back to Ivers International, even after being shot. Eventually, you have to stop fighting who you are and learn to embrace it–otherwise it might kill you.

And I have too much to live for these days.

Situating the post back in place over the man's heart, I resume hammering, driving it home until his wails of horror morph into broken gags of wet air and hollow noises.

His heart is a thick cushion that the post impales slowly, and though I don't like eyes in my victims, a part of me wishes his were still intact so I could watch the life drain from them. Feel his fear the way the people he hurt certainly felt it.

I blow out a long breath once the screaming and writhing cease. Blood spurts from the wound for a moment after, and then stops altogether–and suddenly, Boyd and I are blanketed in complete and utter silence.

It's eerie. A shiver skates across my skin like a soul traveling from this world to the next, and when I glance at him to see if he felt it too, Boyd's face is just an impassive mask.

These days, it takes a lot to get anything more out of him.

I walk around the grave as he blows out a cloud of smoke and clap my palm over his shoulder. "She's all right, you know?"

He doesn't look at me, and I know my words ring hollow given the reality of his situation, but still. It's all the comfort I've got to offer.

"You better get to your wedding," he says after a moment, pointing his blunt at me. "Before your sister comes looking for us."

Nodding, I shuck off my latex gloves and drop them on top of the rest of our belongings. "You coming?"

He shakes his head, scratching at his inked neck with those tattooed fingers. "Nah. Not yet. I'll be there soon... gonna clean up here first."

So I leave him there, because who am I to come between a man and his demons?

Besides, I have better things to do.

Like my fiancée.

Soon to be wife, if she doesn't murder me when I finally get to the venue.

BEFORE I'VE EVEN PARKED my Mercedes in the designated lot, my father's standing there with a beer in hand, his own gold bow tie dangling from the pocket of his matching gold vest.

Behind him, sprawling meadows with gorgeous yellow wild-flowers stretch beneath a few big, white tents and a wooden deck with a stone altar that overlooks one end of Lake Koselomal.

The pure, non-residential end.

This blueberry farm was a special find of Fiona's, and when we came to tour the place, I watched Juliet fall in love with the acreage. It was the main reason I let my sister stay on to help plan the event, knowing that she'd turn it into a ridiculous ordeal.

But Juliet was happy, and I would suffer through just about anything to see her smile.

"Your mom always said you'd be late to your own wedding," my father notes as I climb out from behind the wheel. He places his beer on the roof of the black vehicle and reaches out, adjusting my bow tie.

I don't miss the faraway look in his cloudy eyes while he holds my gaze—the last two years have been the least kind to him, and it shows in the deep creasing of his forehead and the frown lines around his mouth. He's weathered like an ancient tree, now the single thread holding the fabric of our family together.

No part of me envies his position.

"Are you all right?" I ask, though we don't talk like this. Not about our feelings or personal lives. Never have.

He gives me a crooked smile, then drops his bad arm slowly, mindful of that shoulder injury that never healed properly. "I'm all right, boy. And damn proud of you. Your mother—" Cutting himself off with a sudden clearing of his throat, he sidesteps me and grabs his beer again. "She's proud, too."

Emotion burns in my chest, but luckily I'm saved from a

reply as a frantic, high-pitched voice joins the foray. Fiona stomps her way from one of the white tents in a shimmering crimson cocktail dress, her dark red hair pinned high on her head and an irritated look painting her freckled face.

As she approaches, she glances behind me, searching for someone else. I pretend not to notice the way she partially deflates when she realizes I'm alone.

"You're fucking *late*," she complains when she's within earshot, waving a clipboard in my direction.

"Fiona," my father chides, pressing his lips together to hide his smirk.

Her eyebrows draw inward. "Is he not two hours late, Daddy?"

"Well, yes, but this is Kieran we're talking about. Don't pretend you didn't bake in a little extra time with his knack for tardiness in mind."

"Everyone wants to talk shit until they need something from me," I grumble, growing irritated. The longer I stand here, the longer I go without demolishing the final barrier separating Juliet and me as a couple.

I've had her in nearly every conceivable way at this point. Legalese is the last battle, and one I've been waiting to conquer since the moment I laid eyes on her.

"Don't be such a baby," Fiona says, looking down at her clipboard. She scans the page, then looks up and across the venue at the deck.

A minister stands in front of the stone altar, speaking with Caroline and her brood of children while Elia grabs a drink from the bar.

It suddenly hits me in the stomach what I'm about to do.

Stake my claim on my woman in front of all these people.

My throat constricts, though I don't really know why, and my palms suddenly grow clammy. Heat floods my face, and as Fiona drones on about nothing important, I find myself shoved back in time to the first night in the cemetery—the night I heard Juliet there with another man.

The despair I felt then rears its massive, unyielding head as if Murphy's decided to make himself present on this day after all. I suppose it's only fair, since I was a witness at his ex's wedding to some movie producer last year.

It takes several long, erratic breaths before I realize Fiona's fingers are snapping directly in front of my face.

I blink, swallowing over the gravel in my throat. "What?"

"Where's Boyd?"

"Ah..." I pause, scratching the back of my neck, unsure of how much information to divulge. My father's eyebrow arches, and Fiona taps the toe of one strappy black heel. "He's on his way."

Her frown deepens. "Which means he's a half hour out, at least."

Tilting her head back toward the sky, Fiona sighs. Her shoulders are tense, and when she turns to survey the venue again, I notice the peach-colored nicotine patch stuck to the back of her arm and wonder how many she's gone through today.

"Okay, okay. It's fine. We can still make this work." She gives our father a look when she sees his bow tie hanging from his jacket pocket, then turns her attention to me. I can barely even pay her any mind, though, as my brain tries to swim against an onslaught of misery.

Most days, I keep my guilt at bay. There are too many ways I've fucked up, too many things I've done wrong, that if I wallowed in my past, I'd never be able to function. Yet now, it's as if all the mistakes I've made—every horror wrought at my fingertips—has come back to haunt me all at once.

Nausea rises in my stomach, sloshing around like a turbulent sea.

Fiona continues, "If we get you into a change of clothes right now, we should still have time to send you through a quick rundown of the reception lineup, and then—"

"I need a minute."

"A minute?" Fiona's jaw drops as I push past her, my legs carrying me toward the first tent in my path. "You're late and asking for a minute? You can't—hey! You can't go in there! *Kieran*, she's—"

Somehow, her words are drowned out by the thick canvas walls as I step inside the massive tent. It looks like a dressing room exploded, with two huge floor fans angled toward the center of the room where a red velvet sofa and three white arm chairs sit around a lighted mirror and circular platform.

Clothes are everywhere—hanging from ornate, antique-style trunks and metal racks on wheels, while makeup and hair products litter several pop-up vanities around the tent. I pass through a haze of hairspray and eye a drink cart near the sofa, the breath forcibly escaping my lungs when I see the woman sitting on the sofa arm, two crystal tumblers in hand.

Outstretched, like she's been waiting for me.

Relief flushes my system, though my feet feel rooted in the ground as I blink, trying to decide if I'm seeing things. My vision corrects itself, and she's still there, her golden hair twisted into a long braid that spills over one bare shoulder.

And the dress—

Jesus fucking *Christ.*

"Jesus fucking Christ," I repeat out loud, my dick hardening the second a blush starts creeping up her porcelain cheeks. "You look..."

I trail off, unsure of how to even put my awe into words. The strapless, off-white gown clings to her chest and tapers at her waist, flaring slightly over her hips as the lace-covered material runs to the ground. She's strong and elegant, her breasts obscene as they cradle her locket between them, and I stumble forward a step, unable to do anything aside from drool.

Mine.

This incredible, beautiful human is all mine.

Lucky doesn't even begin to cover how I feel.

"You found me," she says, pushing up from the sofa and crossing the tent to me in a few strides. The dress swishes with each step she takes, though I don't move my eyes from her face.

As she shoves one of the tumblers into my hand, I raise a brow. "Were you hiding, kitten?"

"No," she says, her blush deepening, reminding me of the furious pink I painted her ass last night. She swallows, and I wonder if she knows why my gaze has grown heavy–if she remembers, too. "I was just wondering if Fiona would keep you from me before the ceremony."

"She tried." I shrug, stepping closer. Needing to be closer. My knees brush hers. "Not very hard though, might I add. She's liable to come in here and interrupt."

Juliet shakes her head. "I told her that we weren't to be bothered if you came before."

That makes my heart hum. "Technically, I'm late."

"Technically?" She snorts, raising her tumbler to her lips. "Sure, let's go with that."

I love that she doesn't ask where I've been. Doesn't care, really. Over the last couple of years, she's really grown into herself, and the amount of strength she possesses and the trust she has in me makes my soul feel raw as hell with emotion I'll never be able to put into words.

My hand lashes out, stopping her before she can take a drink. I'm mesmerized by the shape of her red-painted lips, like two lush pieces of candy I want to devour.

I set my glass down on a nearby end table, wrap an arm around her waist, and bring the tumbler to her mouth. Her hand is trapped beneath mine as it wraps around her, pressing the lip of the glass to her plump flesh.

Her blue eyes shimmer like fucking starlight, crinkling at the corners as she opens her mouth for a sip. The amber liquid trickles in quickly, and her skin seems to heat against mine despite the ice in the glass, making me dizzy.

When she swallows, I feel it in my dick.

"Cat got your tongue?" she quips, that sweet gaze of hers turning positively feline.

"If she wants my tongue, she can have it," I breathe, taking a drink of the alcohol myself and letting it calm my racing nerves.

"Just your tongue?"

"Well, I'd hate to deprive you."

She takes the tumbler from me and downs the rest, then places it beside the full one on the end table. Slowly, she lets her gaze fall down the length of me, snagging when she gets to my pants. I squeeze her against me, letting her feel the torture she's putting me through.

"Oh," she gasps—the fucking brat. Acting like she doesn't know exactly what she does to me. "That might be a problem for you, huh?"

"I doubt our guests would appreciate my erection, no."

"Hmm." She clicks her tongue in disapproval, then slides her palm between us, cupping me through my slacks. I jolt forward into the gesture, a low grunt falling from my lips. "Since I invited them, it's kind of my responsibility to make sure this whole thing goes smoothly, right? So... I should really help you with that."

Goddamn. When she licks her lips, my blood boils. "I agree."

Her brows furrow, and her teeth sink into her bottom lip, worrying it. "We really shouldn't. Everyone's waiting–"

"And they'll keep waiting."

My free hand slides up her side, over the buttons clasping the corset bodice of her dress together, and tangles in the underside of her braid. I give a rough tug and shove my hips into hers, backing her against the sofa.

"*Hey*," she whines, glaring. "You can't mess up my hair."

"I can mess up any part of you I damn well please, kitten." I pull harder, digging my fingers into her skull and reveling in the small breath of air she greedily gulps in. "If I want to take this braid down so I can ride you properly on this couch, I will. If I want to smear that lipstick of yours with my cock, I'll do it, and then paint you with my cum just because I can. And you know what *you'll* do?"

Her tiny pink tongue darts out, slowly laving over her lips. She shakes her head.

"You'll be a good little slut and *take it*." I bend her back over the sofa and then climb with her, lowering us so we're horizontal on the seat.

"Oh *God*," she whimpers, lifting her hips as my hands disappear under her skirt. "Fiona will kill me if I wrinkle this dress."

"We're gonna do more than wrinkle it, baby."

All my earlier anxiety and despair dissolves the second my hands are on her, brushing over her buttery smooth skin and absorbing all of her warmth. God, she's so fucking perfect I can hardly breathe in her presence.

I'm mindful of the dress as I peel it up, cursing when I see the sheer panties and garter set she has on beneath. A growl escapes me as I reach to rip them off, but her hands come to mine, halting me.

"Don't tear them," she pleads, shifting and parting her thighs to give me a better look. When she does, a sliver of pink flesh appears in the center of the white lace, and my fingers curl into themselves, desperately clinging to my last shred of self-control. "Just fuck me with them on."

"*Christ*, Juliet." Dropping to my elbows, I use two fingers to hold the panties open, and then lick right up her wet center. "You have a lot of nerve telling me how to fuck you, brat."

"Just didn't want you ruining the set," she says, breathless, threading her fingers through my hair as I lower my mouth to her cunt.

I start slow, almost lazily, knowing that it drives her fucking crazy. She pulses under my touch, and she's wet–so fucking wet that I can't stand it, can't hold back when she begins writhing against me. Drawing my thumb over her clit, I rub in smooth circles, then shove her thighs wider apart and spear into her with my tongue.

When she cries out, I almost send a solitary prayer up–to God, the universe, whoever will listen. I almost pray to stay like this forever, my head between Juliet's legs while I drown in the perfect taste of her.

But instead of voicing that plea, I make Juliet my altar. Her whimpers my gospel and her cum my religion.

Removing my tongue from her, I bring my lips down around her clit and suck, pushing three fingers into her.

"So tight, baby," I grunt, barely able to speak with the desire coursing through my bloodstream. My dick is rock solid, weeping with the need to sink into her, but I hold off.

"Kieran, *please*," she moans, tightening her grip on my hair.

My eyes narrow at her, and I pause my ministrations. "What was that?"

She lifts her head, defiance gracing her flushed features. Her hips buck, searching for friction, and I pull back a bit more. "You heard me."

Oh.

A slow smirk spreads across my face. My free hand retreats, and I rear back, bringing my palm down in a fierce arc against the top of her cunt.

Her blue eyes flare, heating with liquid arousal. If possible, she clenches even tighter around my fingers, and I throb behind the zipper of my pants.

"Address me properly, *slut*."

"Or what?" she challenges.

My fingers curl against that sweet spot deep in her cunt, and her mouth goes slack for a moment. I pinch her clit in my other hand, then smack her a second time, dipping to soothe the inflamed skin with my tongue.

"Or you'll fucking regret it." I withdraw from her completely, earning a look of pure rage as I sit back on my haunches. Undoing my belt quickly, I shove my pants and boxers down my hips, and my angry red cock springs free, hard as hell and desperate for her.

Giving a rough stroke up the shaft, I cock an eyebrow at her, waiting. A pearly bead of arousal bubbles from my tip, and I use my thumb to smear it around the head, grinning when her throat bobs on a swallow.

"I'll send you out there without letting you come," I tell her, my voice dark with its warning. I won't, of course, and we both know the words are hollow–there's no way I'll let her leave this tent without getting her off first.

But the threat still seems to do the trick.

"Daddy," she whispers, clearly too far gone to go into full brat mode today. She normally doesn't give in this easily, but maybe the excitement of the wedding is getting to her.

Maybe she just wants me to fuck her.

I won't deny the love of my life anything she wants.

Stretching out over her, I grab her behind the knees and push them to her chest; she grunts with the pressure, and tries to shift so she's more comfortable, but I weigh too much for her to really move. Her tits are almost spilling from her dress, and I reach down and pull one out, bending to scrape my teeth against a ripe nipple.

My cock nudges against her, and I grab her knee again, spreading her wide.

"Put me in, baby."

Swallowing audibly, she reaches down and wraps her fingers around me, dragging the tip through her soaked flesh. I curse as she readies us, her pretty blue eyes hooded, and she gives me a devious smile before pushing the head inside.

Her body tenses. "God," she gasps, pinching her eyes shut. "You're too–too big."

"I am a perfect goddamn fit for this sweet cunt." Chuckling darkly, I squeeze her thighs so hard, I'm sure she'll have bruises. "You'll take it all, kitten. *Every. Last. Inch.*"

I don't give her time to adjust before shunting my hips forward and burying myself all the way. The veins in my neck bulge and my breathing scatters as her wet heat envelopes me, soft as fucking velvet and tight as a glove.

My release already pools at the base of my spine, ready to explode the second I start fucking her. The sofa scoots loudly across the cement ground as my hips piston into hers, and I'm certain her little groans of delight can be heard outside the tent, but I don't give a shit.

This is all I wanted on our wedding day.

All I want for the rest of my fucking life.

Sawing in and out of her, I watch as her face morphs from erotic awe to intense pleasure–her orgasm crests quickly, her mouth falling open as her cunt closes in around me, trying to sever my dick from my body.

She comes on a strangled noise, something half-joy and half-inhuman, and the sound of her arousal flooding me is like a symphony to my veins. I move harder, thrusting in quick, brutal strokes that have our pelvises cracking together.

I'm on the edge, toeing the line of euphoric relief when she takes my hand and brings it to her throat, curling my fingers around the delicate column. I apply the slightest bits of pressure on the sides, gritting my teeth when she smiles seductively.

"Oh, by the way," she whispers, lifting her hips and meeting me thrust for thrust, "I forgot to take my birth control today."

My eyebrows shoot up, and it takes a second for me to

understand through the haze of lust clouding my judgment and logic.

She scrapes her nails up my ass, then clutches and drags me closer, almost guiding my movements. "Consider it my wedding gift to you," she says, and that, combined with her confession, sends me over a fucking cliff, spiraling toward a violent release that rattles my goddamn bones.

I shove myself all the way in and come, spilling and spilling inside her until I feel it leak down the crack of her ass. She spasms around me, finding a second climax on the tail-end of mine, and we spin out together, a heavy mess of limbs and sweat and happiness.

Happiness. Yeah.

It's that emotion I focus on as I collapse on top of her, despite her vehement insistence I not ruin her dress even more.

"Shh," I say, burying my face in her neck. My body feels heavy, and I no longer want to move from this spot, or this moment.

"Kieran, there are a hundred people outside waiting for us."

"You said they could keep waiting."

She pauses, then snorts. "No, *you* said that."

"Oh, yeah." My brain is barely functioning, too high on the last few minutes. Eventually, I lift my head and brush some sweaty hair from her face. "So... your gift..."

We've not really discussed the possibility much–not since before we were dating, and even then, I'm not sure she knew I was serious about her. Not enough to marry and have kids with, anyway. And since she just got hired as an ecology instructor at the community college in Stonemore, I was certain any permanent plans like those would be pushed to the future.

Which I would be fine with. I would take anything at all if it meant having this woman by my side and in my bed every night.

Pink stains her cheeks. "I mean, obviously it takes more than a day for it to leave my system. But, if you want..."

I grin, leaning in to press a harsh kiss against her mouth. "I want."

After a few more minutes, I finally catch my breath and drag myself away from her. She goes to one of the vanities and fixes her hair and makeup. I come up behind her and just stare at our reflections in the mirror.

The homicidal maniac and the sad party girl.

A beautiful siren and her deranged devil.

"I love you," I say into her hair, my arm coming around her neck. I toy with her locket, suppressing a smirk when I recall how a seemingly insignificant piece of jewelry altered the entire course of our lives. "More than anything in this world, you know? You're my life, Juliet."

Her hand comes over mine, and she tilts her head up, beckoning me close. I kiss her slowly, sensually, cupping her jaw with my free hand.

"I love you too," she says, her smile widening until it's basically all teeth. "Now, let's go make me your *wife*."

BECOME A SUCKER!

Want to be the first to get important announcements,
exclusive access to bonus material, and find a place where
like-minded readers can share the love of all things Sav?
Visit savrmiller.com for more information!

ALSO BY SAV R. MILLER

ACKNOWLEDGMENTS

When I was finishing my last semester of college two years ago, the indie publishing world was completely unknown to me. Even a year ago, I had no clue that there are hordes of amazing authors out there taking their dreams and success into their own hands and creating incredible art. I'm honored to now be a part of this industry and can't imagine my life any other way.

I'm sure you're all are tired of hearing me sing her praises, but since I can't simply dedicate every book to her, I have to stick my love in the acknowledgements. Emily McIntire, you're the very best friend I could ever ask for. I'm so glad we met by swapping beta reads, and I'm so thankful for our constant simultaneous stream of messages across various platforms, your support, and the dog gifs you send when I need them most. You are the greatest person I've ever met, and my life would not be the same without you in it. I love you the most and can't wait to look back at this in five years when we're bathing in money in the Smokies for writing retreats.

To Bee: thank you for the incredible new covers for this series. I adore them and you, and can't wait to make more magic.

To my fabulous editors and proofreader at Editing 4

Indies and My Brother's Editor: thank you for making my words beautiful. You've got me on the hook forever.

To the bloggers and bookstagrammers: your support means more than you will probably ever know. Seriously, I love each and every one of you and your talent at creating and reviewing and reading is unmatched. Thank you for your love of books.

To my family: you guys keep me grounded and I can't wait to write a book one day you're comfortable reading. It'll probably be awhile before I do, but I promise I will. Probably.

To my betas and ARC team: I love you guys more than I can express. Thank you for reading my words.

To LB, Poe, and Arrow: I love you. Thank you for being the best companions and for literally keeping me sane.

And lastly, but certainly not least, to the readers. You, looking at this page right now. None of this means anything without you. Thank you for reading Kieran and Juliet's story, and I hope you enjoyed it as much as I enjoyed writing it.

ABOUT THE AUTHOR

Sav R. Miller is a USA Today bestselling author of adult romance with varying levels of darkness and steam.

In 2018, Sav put her lifelong love of reading and writing to use and graduated with a B.A. in Creative Writing and a minor in Cultural Anthropology. Nowadays, she spends her time giving morally gray characters their happily-ever-afters.

Currently, Sav lives in Kentucky with her dogs Lord Byron, Poe, and Arrow. She loves sitcoms, silence, and sardonic humor.

For more information on announcements, bonus material, and Sav's other books, visit savrmiller.com

Made in the USA
Las Vegas, NV
22 December 2023

83435405R00256